George Valentine's Retirement Plan

George Valentine's Retirement Plan

Laurence Cooper

★

This is a work of fiction. All names and characters are either invented or used
fictitiously. Places may be invented or real but none of the events central to the narrative
has yet taken place.

Strathmere Press
55 Marmora Road
London SE22 0RY
www.strathmerepress.com
e-mail: strathmerepress@outlook.com

ISBN 978 0957662 100

British Library Cataloguing in Publication Data.
A catalogue record for this book is available from the British Library.

Typeset in 11pt Minion Pro by Troubador Publishing Ltd
Printed and bound in the UK by TJ International, Padstow, Cornwall

MIX
Paper from
responsible sources
FSC
www.fsc.org   FSC® C013056

For Priscilla
Always there, through thick and thin
And Elizabeth and Katie
Team Laurence

'I have lost the immortal part of myself, and what remains is bestial. My reputation, Iago, my reputation!' – **Cassio.**

Othello Act 2, Scene 3.

London, September

Westminster Inside Track

https://www.witreport.co.uk

Number 10   Whitehall   Around Westminster   @witreport

Back Door Man

Westminster Inside Track

Your eyes and ears on Westminster and Whitehall; exposing the rumours, conspiracies and whitewash at the heart of government; a virtual voice in a new age of accountability.

TODAY: 11 a.m. No sooner is the Prime Minister back from his summer break than a top Harley Street man slips into Number 10 by the rear entrance and stays for two hours. The Number 10 Press Office seems confused. First they said he wasn't there, then it was to see someone else, now it's to treat a toe injury from a coastal bike ride. Two hours to prescribe an aspirin at Harley Street rates? If the PM has a health problem shouldn't the nation know about it? And if it is a stubbed toe could someone tell us who's footing the bill?

Style Upgrade at DEFRA

Blair had his babes, Sarkozy and Berlusconi theirs, now DEFRA has ex-supermodel Eleanor Porter, the planet's most glamorous politician. Evidently the new Parliamentary Under Secretary is having an effect on officials at the Department for Environment, Food and Rural Affairs. Designer labels abound, there's no sign of dandruff and a source tells us, at a recent retreat, two director generals and a scientific adviser were wearing *The Lady Eleanor*, the fragrance launched in La Porter's modelling heyday. We know the department is responsible for air quality, but maybe they're taking it a bit far?

Chamberlain Challenge?

Meanwhile the Home Secretary would like to bring back hanging. And so would most of us it seems. A YouGov poll following Ken Chamberlain's off the cuff remark on Gloucester radio last week places the Home Secretary ahead of the Prime Minister as the person who most would like to lead the country. The gaffe set Marsham Street civil servants scurrying and has widened the rift between the PM and his former ally. And just what is Robert White up to? The Cities Minister and Chamberlain yes-man has been popping up everywhere playing down the prospect of a leadership challenge. WIT thinks the minister doth protest too much. Our money is on the Home Secretary raising the standard for a battle royal.

WITLINKS: <u>PM's summer poll disaster/Exposed – ministers on the beach/World's Top Ten Capital Punishments/Tea Room Talk</u>

1

Being at the bottom of London's social ladder, the man on the bench might have woken to all kinds of interference – a fellow vagrant stealing the bottle hidden in his coat, a paramedic restarting his heart, or a young policeman perhaps, keen to exercise his stop and search powers. Instead he discovered an old motorbike coasting towards him in the moonlight. A Triumph Tiger Cub. It rattled past and on to the edge of the square where it stopped under a tree. The man watched as the rider dismounted, kicked the bike onto its stand, shrugged a rucksack from narrow shoulders onto the seat and produced a camera from a side pocket. The figure jogged to the perimeter and crouched, visor raised, looking through a hedge and railings at a Georgian mansion opposite.

A dark blue limousine was parked out front and its driver was opening a rear door. The shutter clicked as the biker-turned-photographer captured a man in late middle age and a blonde in pink as they emerged from the car, walked up the steps to the house and were greeted by two doormen in black livery.

The biker returned to the Triumph, replaced the camera, took off the sleek helmet and smoothed down her spiky hair. The man on the bench sat up, his interest deepening as the woman unzipped and peeled off her leathers to stand almost naked under the tree, her skin mosaicked in pale light that filtered through the canopy. He reached for his bottle. She was slim, early twenties as far as he could guess, with a tattoo across her lower back. A tramp-stamp. As she moved the light flickered across her body, dappling her breasts and legs as if she were showering in silver. Secure in the gloom of a denser tree, the man took a slug from the bottle and settled down to watch the scene unfold.

The young woman plucked a black cocktail dress from the rucksack, then a matching clutch bag, pearl string and sling-back shoes together with a make-up case. She worked quickly, slipping on the dress, removing nose- and ear-rings, juggling a mirror, brushes and make-up, all the time moving to catch the light, until at last, satisfied, she repacked the rucksack and fastened it to the bike with a padlock. She attached a new pair of ear-rings, smoothed her dress and walked out of the square, a cautious catlike padding that unfolded into a confident stride as she approached the doormen.

She could see they were in two minds. Woman alone. No car. Piercings.

'Good evening, Miss,' said one. 'Are you a member?'

'I'm with Mr White,' she said.

'Mr White?'

'Robert White. The Cities Minister. You just let him in.' She read indecision in both faces. 'Don't panic. I'm not another girlfriend. I'm his assistant.'

The two men looked doubtful. She assumed she wasn't their idea of a civil servant, but who was these days? She certainly wasn't paparazzi. Or a terrorist. Nothing could be concealed under this dress.

'I'll be on a list, I expect,' she said. 'Inside?'

The doormen hesitated, then nodded her through.

★

Inside, the young woman found herself in the anteroom of a magnificent town house, where visitors once warmed themselves in front of a great fire while awaiting entry to the grander parts. The fire no longer burned but guests were still drawn to its hearth. Portraits stared down from yellow ochre walls above a chequered marble floor and white busts flanked the windows on plinths, looking inwards, as if reflecting on the class of visitor the house received these days. Designed by Robert Adam, the building had served as a residence and embassy and was now a private members' club and casino. The receptionist rose from behind an antique desk.

'Hi. I'm with Robert White. Mr Ledakov's party,' said the visitor.

'Your name, please?'

'Norah Jones.' The young woman smiled. 'Not *the* Norah Jones of course.'

The receptionist checked a list, then placed a form and a pen on the desk.

'Name, address and date of birth, please.'

The young woman sat and filled out the form and the receptionist asked for identification.

'I didn't think you needed it these days,' said the visitor.

'You might win.'

'Oh, I won't win. I don't play.'

'You could be under-age.'

Apparently it wasn't negotiable. The young woman shuffled through her bag and produced a plastic identity card. The receptionist examined both sides and handed it back.

'This is a 'novelty item',' she said. They regarded each other with icy smiles.

'I shouldn't keep them waiting,' said the young woman.

The receptionist held her gaze. If she was nervous about keeping Mr Ledakov and a government minister waiting she didn't show it. The young woman went back to her purse and handed over a driving licence.

'This one says Laura Valentine,' said the receptionist.

'Norah's my stage name,' said Laura Valentine, unmasked. She made a note to upgrade her fake ID if she was to make a habit of this. They must have improved since she was under-age.

'You're an artiste of some kind?' asked the receptionist.

That was definitely a sneer, thought Laura.

'I like to think so,' she said. 'But mostly I use it for first dates. Sometimes it's easier, don't you think? When they won't back off? Men. Do you know what I mean? Maybe you don't?'

The receptionist amended the form and angled the camera on her desk. Laura guessed she'd overlooked bigger things for Mr Ledakov.

'Look this way, please.'

The older woman logged Laura's details and printed a temporary membership card, which she handed over with a complimentary £5 chip.

'Don't worry, I'll find my own way,' said Laura, rising from her chair.

'I'm sure you will,' said the receptionist.

Laura slipped from the anteroom into the grand hall and passed an iron staircase curving within a dome of pastel green panels and gilt borders, inlaid with paintings and classical motifs. Revellers and gamblers passed each other on their way to the tables while music played quietly through hidden speakers. It was cool, air-conditioned by architecture.

She walked briskly along a corridor, counting doors. At the third she turned an ornate handle. Inside was the ladies' room, hung with prints of eighteenth-century women of fashion and empty apart from the woman in pink from the car. She was touching up her make-up in front of a mirror. Laura took the washbasin beside her. They produced lipsticks and weighed each other up.

'You must be Ruby,' Laura said. The woman smiled. Tall and slim with platinum blonde hair, she was dressed entirely in pink and gold. Laura guessed she was forty. She carried off casino glamour as if born to it. Maybe she was.

'And you must be George and Dot's daughter,' she said. 'I hope you are half so smart. You need more make-up.'

'Why?'

'Not so smart,' said Ruby, puckering in the mirror. 'They are Russians, darling. They like their women to look like prostitutes. Here, try this. And be bold.' She tossed Laura a red lipstick, while applying another pink flourish. 'You know what you are doing?' she asked. Laura cast a glance at the cubicles, which were open and unoccupied.

'I need to get a shot of the Cities Minister, Robert White, with you and a Mr Ledakov. And I need to get out of here by midnight.'

'Like Cinderella.' Ruby inspected her. 'That is better. Where is your camera?' Laura opened her bag and held out a pack of spearmint gum.

4

'Cigarette lighters went out with the smoking ban,' Laura explained. The older woman seemed impressed.

'Just be careful,' Ruby warned. 'Most of them will be ex-KGB. They know this game.'

'Are you Russian?' Laura asked.

'I am from Estonia.'

'"Ruby" isn't Estonian.'

'No. It is temporary name,' said Ruby. 'I change it every three years. One day I will go to America. There I will be Alice or Rosalie and live in Sacramento. Ruby is Barbara Stanwyck, Hollywood star. Her real name was Ruby Stevens. My grandfather loved her.' She snapped her bag shut and started towards the door. 'He saw *The Lady Eve* in London during Second World War.'

I bet *her* ID works, thought Laura. She could learn from this woman. Ruby paused at the door.

'Just one more thing. Bobby thinks you are friend and we are going to have threesome at hotel. They…the Russians…they think you are 'colleague'.

'An escort, you mean?'

'Yes.'

'Fuck.'

'They may want to,' said Ruby. 'This is normal with Russians. You play along, please. This is also dangerous game for me. We must go.'

'Dangerous? What do you mean dangerous?' Laura asked, but Ruby was gone. Laura followed her back to the staircase, up to a balcony beneath the dome and into another anteroom. There were a number of questions she wanted to ask Ruby of the many aliases, things her dad had forgotten to mention as usual, key elements of the job. She knew she was to get a shot of a minister doing things he shouldn't in a casino. But what was with the KGB thing? And in what way exactly might this be dangerous? And while she was at it, what was Ruby's grandfather, an Estonian, doing in London, watching *The Lady Eve*, during the Second World War?

They passed through a frame of fluted columns into the gaming room. Laura was distracted for a moment by the glittering world in front of her, captured in a vast gilt mirror above another Adam fireplace: sparkling chandeliers and paintings of aristocrats in rural settings amid walls adorned with urns, scrolls and garlands; above, a pastel green ceiling inlaid with cherubim and Wedgwood blue. Below, punters clustered around gaming tables scattered across the room while waiters hovered with drinks.

Laura raced to catch Ruby, who was threading quickly through the room. She disappeared via a doorway into a succession of smaller chambers, each hosting a game; blackjack in a blue room, backgammon in a music room and poker in a Chinese room. They came to another doorway set within a classical frame. This time the doors were closed and in front of each column stood a thickset man in a blue suit. Ruby smiled at the older of the two.

'Welcome back, Miss Ruby,' he said, and opened the doors. The younger man cast an eye over Laura, lingering longer than was necessary for security purposes.

'Nice ass,' he said, as she passed into the salon. Russians.

Laura followed Ruby as she made for the roulette table in the centre of the room. It was crowded and noisy and seemed to be the only game running; the half dozen card tables surrounding it were closed. Ruby took a glass of champagne from a waiter, sidled into the crush and slipped an arm around a man who looked about sixty. Laura recognised him as the man from the limousine, Robert White, Minister for Cities. Next to him was another woman, also a busty blonde, and next to her an overweight man about the same age as White, who was placing a large bet amid sighs of approval. Several beautiful women pressed around him to his evident delight. This must be Ledakov, Laura concluded; billionaire mining baron, chess grandmaster, occasional actor in Russian politics and owner of the top ice hockey team in Canada.

The croupier spun the wheel and moments later the Russian won to a round of applause. He counted his chips with a gold-toothed smile, the other winners irrelevant. Laura realised this was the shot and that she might not get another chance. She rummaged in her bag for the pack of gum as a waiter offered her a drink, which she declined.

Almost immediately another Russian dressed in a dark suit was at her side.

'Good evening,' he said, holding her arm tightly above the elbow. She had both camera and a real stick of gum in her hand. 'So unusual for a lady to refuse Krug. Particularly a friend of Ruby's.' Laura struggled to free her arm and tore open the wrapper of the real stick. She popped the gum into her mouth.

'Fresh breath first,' she said and winked at him. 'Then champagne.' She snaked a crystal glass from a passing tray. 'A girl should always be prepared.'

'An admirable sentiment,' said the man. He was short yet attractive and expensively dressed. Mid-forties she guessed. 'You are here for Mr White?' he asked.

'He's a dear friend,' Laura said, 'of a friend.'

'Quite so.' Laura felt the hand that had squeezed her arm slide down her back to another part of her anatomy. 'Perhaps when you have finished with Mr White, you will visit me?' asked the Russian.

'Perhaps,' said Laura, trying not to flinch at the appendage now clamped to her bottom. 'But I understand Mr White is quite demanding.'

'He is old man. I am demanding,' promised the Russian, a bony finger probing her left buttock. She struggled with the urge to punch him in the face.

'I'm glad to hear it. And who, may I ask, are you?'

'Anton Zakharovich Ledakov, at your service.' He bowed slightly and produced a business card. 'Call me. We will have dinner.'

'I thought...'

'The man at the table?' He smiled. 'That is cousin. He likes to gamble with my money. I don't gamble. I bet on certainties. Like you. Excuse me, please.' Ledakov smiled and turned away from the table. The composition was getting stretched. Laura grabbed his wrist.

'Won't you introduce me to Mr White?' she asked. 'I haven't met him yet.'

The Russian laughed.

'What is your name?' he asked.

'Norah,' she said and remembered the fiasco downstairs.

'Pretty name,' said Ledakov. He offered Laura his arm and escorted her to the table, the perfumed crush parting before them. Ruby reached out as they approached, her arms stretched wide.

'Bobby, darling, this is the friend I was telling you about. You will love her.' She beckoned Laura with bejewelled hands.

'I'm sure I will,' said the Minister for Cities. He was grey and unkempt, his suit made to last but faded, and he greeted Laura with an intimacy out of proportion to a first meeting. She noticed Ledakov turning away.

'Anton Zakharovich,' Ruby called. 'You must stay. You will bring us luck.' Ledakov smiled once more and folded into the group around the head of the table, a benign monarch tonight. The croupier requested bets.

Laura drained her glass and, pretending to be eager for another, pushed along the table until she was at the end, behind the wheel. The players placed their chips and the croupier spun the wheel, then whisked the ball in the other direction with a white-gloved flourish. Laughter and chatter continued until the ball's momentum drained and it made its inevitable drop into the wheel, to begin its random clicking, jumping progress into one of the coloured pockets. The group hushed as the ball settled and the wheel slowed to reveal the lucky number.

Laura raised the pack of gum to her mouth, holding a real stick behind it. She slid the stick into her mouth and held the pack steady for a second. And that was the shot. Robert White, with a scotch in one hand and a fist clenched in victory, Ruby on one side of him kissing his cheek, Ledakov on the other clapping him on the back, and a bevy of attractive women looking on with glee, while the fat cousin stood behind, glum at the loss of attention. Tight in the centre would be the government minister, the oligarch and the escort.

Laura was lightheaded, caught in the euphoria that followed the adrenalin rush. It happened every time. She knew the power of a photograph. It could change things. A single image could make or break a reputation: Marilyn's dress fluttering over a Manhattan air vent, Gandhi at a spinning wheel, Che Guevara defining revolution in an instant. OK, this wasn't big league. It might break White. It might embarrass the government but it wouldn't bring it down. It wouldn't change the world, like Kim Phuc, the napalm girl or Mohamed Bouazizi. It was a picture that would flit across the news, have its moment and be forgotten along with its subject, joining last week's cross-dressing mayor or swastika-wearing aristocrat. It wasn't art and it wasn't a force for change, but it was the picture she'd set out to get. And for Laura, there was a kick in getting the shot. Making a difference could come later.

She dropped the gum into her bag and moved to the back of the group, while the people closest to White congratulated him. She crossed the space to the door and slipped out, mouthing 'bathroom' to the security men, then walked quickly through the gaming rooms. She realised the younger of the two guards was following her when she was on the stairs, so headed for the ladies' room. He caught up with her at the door.

'You're leaving casino?' he asked.

'I'm going to the bathroom.'

'There is bathroom upstairs.'

'Are all Russians like this?' she asked.

'Like what?'

'Suspicious brutes with roaming hands. And no definite article.' He placed a hand on the door above her head and leaned into her. He smelt of aftershave and cigarettes.

'Don't pretend. You are no innocent,' he said. 'We go inside now and fuck.'

'It's a toilet.'

'Yes.'

'There will be people in there.'

'We will be silent,' he said, pushing her against the door.

'Listen, Rimsky-Korsakov, it's not going to happen,' she said. 'You *don't* want to do this.' Before he could assure her that he very much wanted to do this, she slipped a hand into her bag and pulled out Ledakov's card.

'I'm taken,' she said, showing him the embossed script. It had the desired effect. He stepped back.

'My apologies. I will wait outside and escort you back to game,' he said.

Inside, the bathroom was empty. Laura looked at her watch. She could go back and brazen it out, but she had promised to send the shot before midnight. She looked around the room. The main window was barred and there was only one exit. She pushed open the doors to each cubicle. In the last there was a small window above head height behind the cistern.

★

The man on the bench had considered the motorcycle for some time. He was comfortable with his arrangements and the prospect of finding another bed for the night did not appeal. He was also keen to see the woman again and watch her change back into leather. On the other hand the rucksack and its contents would convert into ready cash. Then there was the bike itself, a Tiger Cub, similar to one he had owned in another life, one with winding country lanes and trees that passed in a blur. Before he had wandered. He would like a closer look, for old time's sake.

When he felt sure all would remain quiet in the square, he shuffled over to the bike and ran his gnarled hands over the handlebars. He twisted the throttle and squeezed the clutch and brake. For a moment the hundred facts he had known about two and four stroke engines promised to surface, then faded again as he examined the rucksack. It was attached to the bike by a padlock and chain, each pocket fastened with a smaller lock and the helmet secured in its own locking device. It was good protection against an opportunist but wouldn't stand up to perseverance. What he needed was leverage. He went to the edge of the square and was testing for a loose railing when the young woman appeared from the side of the building. She was limping, one of her heels was broken, her dress was torn at the shoulder, and she was soaking wet with black material clinging to her skin. The man retreated to his lair.

When Laura reached the bike she unfastened the rucksack and pulled out a laptop, which she rested on the seat. Leaning back to avoid dripping on it she booted up the computer, pulled the pack of chewing gum from her bag and connected it, all the while watching the house opposite. A picture appeared on the screen, which she studied, cropped and emailed. She repeated the operation with her original camera, then packed everything away, slung the rucksack over her shoulders and, grabbing the handlebars, rocked the bike off its stand. She climbed astride the machine and kicked it into life, breaking her other shoe heel, then jammed on her helmet, rode around the square and out by the entrance furthest from the house, the bike sputtering smoke and dripping oil and her wet dress rippling in the breeze.

The man on the bench sat for a minute or two after she was gone, studying the square's four gates to see if there would be further interruptions. The silver light that had illuminated the night's events faded as a cloud passed in front of the moon. He lay down on the bench, pulled his bedding around him and tried in vain to find the position that had been so comfortable an hour ago.

2

George Valentine looked up from the armchair at his wife Dorothy, who was standing by the window peering through the curtains. He considered her a fine figure of a woman, even if that figure had spread as the years advanced, and the sight of her broad bottom rarely failed to provoke his admiration. He wondered if it was too late to nip to the garage for some flowers, open a bottle of wine and attempt a night of romance. Perhaps he should change the music, after all Vivaldi could get a little strident. *Phantom of the Opera* always put her in a good mood.

'She'll be fine, Dot,' he said. 'She knows how to ride that bike, even if it's not been out of the shed in years.'

'I'm not looking for Laura,' Dot said. 'I'm waiting for that musician to sneak in. The little tyke owes two months' rent.' George winced. Very little got past Dot when it came to money. 'He paid us once when he arrived and we haven't seen a penny since. He pays up this week or he's out on the street, with all his paraphernalia.' She turned towards her husband. 'And I don't care if his dad was a mate of yours. *He* was a sponger. You just couldn't see it. It took us years to get rid of him.' George knew better than to stop his wife when she was on a roll, raking over the past, drawing eternal truths from isolated incidents and invariably highlighting some failing on his part.

'And it's the last time we have a musician as a lodger,' she said. 'They stay in bed all day, make a racket all night, his rooms are a tip and God knows what he's smoking up there. We'll have the neighbours complaining.'

'Look well if he becomes famous,' said George.

'We'll put up a plaque,' she said, one eyebrow arching. There was a ping as an email arrived on the laptop perched on George's knees.

'I think I'm what they call a digital snail,' he said as he pounded the keyboard. The screen filled with images: Robert White and Ruby Stevens climbing out of a government car; White with his arm around her stepping into the casino; White, Ruby and Russian friends celebrating victory at the tables. George whistled.

'Sen–sa–tion–al. The girl's done good, Dot,' he said.

Dot left her station and crossed the sitting room to view the screen.

'She's got talent, that girl,' she cooed, looking over his shoulder. George could feel her bosom swelling with pride; her perfume enveloped him and he inhaled dreamily, then swore as he punched the wrong key.

'Oh, move over and let me do it,' said his wife. George vacated his seat and Dot shuffled into position, put on her glasses and peered into the screen, a pianist poised at the keyboard, checking her music, her fingers exercising in the air, the moment before the first magnificent chord.

'Where do you want it to go?' she asked.

'That blogger, WIT. Westminster Inside Track.' A flurry of fingers across the keyboard and it was done. George smiled. 'That'll set the cat among the pigeons.' That and the other items he had gathered.

Dot was about to hand him the laptop and return to the window when George picked up a well-thumbed brochure and sat heavily on the sofa. He reached out to the side table for his glasses.

'Not long now, my love,' he said, and flicked through glossy images of a pearl-white villa with a turquoise pool, perched above a cove and baking in the Spanish sun. He lifted his feet onto the footstool in front of him and leaned back in his chair. Vivaldi's *Mandolin Concerto in C* became the soundtrack for dreams of lazy, wine sodden lunches, warm sea breezes and dark starry nights.

Dot took the opportunity to check her email.

'The lawyers are on the ball,' she said. 'They've prepared the deed of purchase already.' George nodded, not hearing, he was lost in a Mediterranean scene, ordering sardines on a quayside while considering which boat to charter for the afternoon.

Dot didn't complain. She was in charge of the retirement plan. George took care of business. The next step was to have the purchase notarised, then pay the balance and the taxes. With a following wind they would be in possession within the month.

With an arpeggio of keys Dot opened a document. She congratulated herself as she ran over the seven items listed within.

1. Passports
2. Bank accounts & credit cards
3. Lawyers & accountants
4. Purchase of Spanish property
5. Sale of businesses
6. Old identities
7. Sale of 54 Mersley Road

There were ticks against the first four, which was no mean feat. The retirement of George and Dorothy Valentine was not a simple matter. In fact, such was the irregularity of their affairs it required the creation of new identities and the elimination of any trace of their former selves. Consequently, Passports, the first item on the list, was not simply a case of ensuring theirs were valid for travel, but had involved brief encounters at remote underground stations, where documents including false passports, NI numbers, birth certificates and even a degree in forensic anthropology were exchanged for envelopes full of cash. New bank accounts had required the new passports, the credit cards had followed and all had needed an address; a rental property which they held for the briefest period. To be untraceable their money had to leave their old accounts and journey via various locations to new homes. Half a million of it presently sat in cash in new names in a safety deposit box. The lawyers and accountants had been easy to find once the other documentation was in place.

She scrolled down to item 5, Sale of businesses, which listed the various enterprises owned and managed by the couple as well as their status. They were in fair shape, she thought, having completed on most. The cheque had cleared for the digital business, Babes in the

Woods, a chat site dedicated to those seeking intimate encounters in the open air, bought by a dogger from Kent called Kieran. The escort business, Babes Anywhere, had also gone. That left the corporate hospitality business, Valentine's Perfect Parties, which was under offer, and the investigations business, Valentine Competitive Insight, which was yet to find a buyer.

Dot sighed and looked at George, whose eyes were now closed as he conducted the Leningrad Chamber Orchestra. She doubted they would find a buyer for the investigations business. Realistically, it was nothing without George and his view was that it needed a younger person to bring it into the twenty-first century. As he said, 'it's all phone hacking and spyware these days'. So far no one had shown any interest and business didn't seem to be Laura's thing even though she was working for them. Still, it had served them well.

Eliminating their past lives was impossible but Dot had done all she could, destroying documents and photographs, deleting web references and images, even changing their polling declaration. There was a police record or two they would never eradicate, but both the police and the taxman were several addresses behind them.

'Getting shot of this place is what's going to hold us back,' said George. He had finished conducting and was now browsing through their CD collection. Dot looked down. The last item on the list was the sale of their home, 54 Mersley Road. George was right. It had been on the market for months without a glimmer of interest, not even a nosy neighbour turning up to compare values. Maybe they should have renewed the kitchen or repainted the exterior. It was a bit run-down, she had to admit. The trouble was they didn't invest in their homes because they never knew when they'd have to move on.

'I was thinking of trying another agent,' she said. She made a note to order packing crates. If they got rid of some things the place would look tidier. And they should be ready. Knowing them, when the time came they would have to leave quickly.

'We could do a couple more jobs before we go,' said George, selecting a CD. Dot's mouth tightened.

'George. We've had this discussion.'

'Another half million and we'd be in clover.'

'We're fine, George.' She logged out and looked at him sternly. 'We said sixty. And we're sixty. You promised.'

'I know,' he said. He slipped on the CD. The opening bars of 'All I Ask of You' from *Phantom* filled the room. 'I promise. The next job that comes in, whatever it is, is the last.' Dot looked up as George moved to the edge of the sofa and leaned over to kiss her. Six seconds was their rule. A kiss wasn't a kiss unless it lasted six seconds. They made it to four before Dot broke off, leaving George puckered in mid-air.

'He's back,' she said and headed for the door.

*

Will Sharp and Laura reached the front gate of 54 Mersley Road at the same time, one dragging a Vox AC30 amplifier, the other pushing a motorbike that was trailing oil; both items were vintage and heavy, their custodians breathless.

'You,' they wheezed as they recognised each other. Will was the first to get his breath back.

'I didn't know you were a biker,' he said. He placed the amplifier on the pavement and stretched his back. 'Cool.'

It was Laura's least favourite word. The generic adjective, the one you used when you didn't know what else to say or couldn't be bothered. It was the equivalent of saying 'insert what you like that's positive: great, excellent, awesome, sweet, sick, boss, dandy.' There was only one possible reply.

'Whatever.' Laura looked at him blankly. He never had a follow-up line. They'd passed a dozen times on the stairs but he'd always botched it. It was a shame. He was good-looking in a bohemian way with a boyish face, slim-hipped with blue smiling eyes and dark hair that struggled to escape a pork-pie hat. But no lines. Was it too much to expect wit in a man? Then again, maybe it was a good thing. The last one had a line for every occasion and look where that had ended up. And anyway, she reminded herself, wasn't she avoiding men in general and the music business in particular?

'Would you mind moving that thing?' she asked, nodding towards the amplifier, which was blocking the gate.

'Sure,' he said and heaved the box into the front garden. He turned and smiled, a big, open, beaming grin. I bet he thinks it's a breakthrough, she thought. It was the most they'd said to each other since he'd moved in. To be fair he'd tried to start a conversation a couple of times but she'd closed him down. He probably thought she didn't like lodgers. Since then they'd passed on the stairs with minimal recognition of the other's existence, raising the bar each time on a line that could break the ice. She looked at the amplifier.

'Rehearsal,' he said, she guessed by way of explanation, and then added, 'You're wet.'

'I am not wet,' she replied, a hand straying to feel her dress, which she had hoped would be dry after the ride across town. 'I'm damp.'

If he had any inspiration for a smart reply it dissolved as they became aware of a sheet of light spreading up the path towards them and two faces peering out from a ground floor window. The light shrivelled as the faces disappeared and the curtains shivered back into place.

'You've had it now,' said Laura. 'That's Mum and she wants the rent.'

'Shit,' said Will. He looked for an escape route but the bike was blocking the gate. Laura sat on the seat, amused, unfastening her helmet.

'Shit, bugger, bollocks,' he cursed as he spun in a circle looking for other avenues of retreat. Finding none he begged her to let him through.

'No way,' she said. 'You're a musician. Face the music.' The front door flew open and Dot, triumphant, filled the doorway. She bustled down the path with George attached to her hip. Will gave Laura a last hopeful look then turned to face his landlady.

'Mrs Valentine. Hi.' Laura shook her head as he tried a smile that conveyed genial helplessness. If he was hoping it would bring out Dot's maternal instinct he was going to be disappointed. Dot strode towards him.

'Don't try that struggling artist routine, it'll cut no ice with me,' she said. 'And it sounds like a struggle half the time, I can tell you. What I want to talk about is the rent. Have you got it?'

'Dot...'

'Do not Dot me. I do not want a sob story. I do not want a song, a serenade,' she said. 'I want cash, I want it all and I want it now. Have you got it?'

'Yes.'

'Yes?'

'Yes,' said Will. 'In the sense that I'll have it *very* soon. Almost immediately. But if the question is do I have it physically on my person, at this precise moment in time, no.' Dot looked at George.

'What did I tell you? Just like his father.'

'Maybe we could think of it less as rent and more as an investment?' Will suggested. 'Like a derivative?'

Dot backed him up the path towards the house, her finger poking at his chest, while she told him the only thing he was derivative of was his father. Meanwhile George had noticed the trail of oil beneath the Tiger Cub.

'What have you done to my bike?' he groaned. Laura looked at the puddle of oil by her feet.

'Me? Dad, it's got no oil,' she said. 'I had to push it half a mile. I thought you said it was re-conditioned.' George dropped to his knees.

'It is,' he said. 'But you still have to check the oil.' George lay on the pavement to inspect the gearbox. Laura decided to go on the offensive.

'Look at these shoes, Dad,' she said, dangling a broken heel above his forehead. 'And this dress. They're ruined.'

George mumbled from beneath the bike, something about sensational photographs and miraculous talent.

'And I need an ID that works,' she continued. 'You might have told me I was doing a photo shoot with the Russian mafia. They thought I was a prostitute. Dad, I was nearly impaled in the Ladies.'

Dot called from the doorway before George could answer.

'What have you done, George?'

That's Mum, thought Laura. She was by the front door, holding Will in an iron grip and telling him to get a job or a suitcase, yet able to keep tabs on everything within a fifty foot radius. George was saved from further interrogation when one of three green dustbins, packed into a covered shelter by the wall, toppled over, spilling bags of rubbish across the path. All eyes turned towards the noise. Behind the dustbins a figure crouched in the darkness. Blackened with bitumen and smelling of refuse a man emerged from the recess. He was young, in his twenties and slim with long, light brown hair, a goatee and piercing green eyes. Even covered in crud Laura could see there was something about him.

'Luka,' Will shouted. He rushed to the grimy figure, hugged him then turned to face the Valentines, his arm around the young man, as if displaying a prize. The young man stepped forward and held out a hand to the matriarch.

'Good evening, I am Luka. I am from Croatia,' he said, adding, 'I am singer,' as if it explained everything. Dot turned to Will, her eyes narrowing.

'Is there something you'd like to share with us?' she asked.

'Luka is the singer in my new band,' said Will.

'And what's he doing behind my bins?'

'Waiting for me, I think,' Will replied. 'I said he could stay for a few days, until he finds his own place.'

'You're assuming *you* have somewhere to stay,' said Laura, laughing.

'Is *he* paying the rent, then?' George asked.

'I doubt he has any money, Dad, he's a singer,' Laura said.

Will looked at Dot this time with a confident smile.

'We just need a few days, Dot. This band is going to be hot. We're already rehearsing and now we've got Luka we can get some dates. And then I can pay.' Dot's hands were on her hips.

'George. Are you going to stand for this?' she demanded.

'Sing us a song, then,' said George.

Dot looked at her husband as if he'd gone mad. Laura laughed again.

'Let's see if he sounds like he can make any money,' George said with a chuckle. 'He can sing for his supper.' Dot looked skywards.

'That's a great idea,' said Laura. 'Sing us a song, Luka.'

Luka shrugged. He gazed at them for a moment, deep in thought, then stood in the middle of the path of number 54 Mersley Road, Forest Hill, London and sang 'My Country 'Tis of Thee'. Laura recognised the English national anthem wrapped in the American flag. She knew the tune from before she had memories, and remembered the words from when Aretha sang it for the President. Maybe it was Luka's gift to his hosts, summing up dreams of liberty, a free land and music. She guessed he sang himself into and out of trouble at the drop of a hat. As she listened she realised his voice was special. The song soared rich and free, all soul and blues and jazz, yet classical and religious at the same time. At the end there was silence.

Will looked smug. A few doors away hands clapped and across the street a man leaned out of an upper storey window and called for more. Further down, a woman bellowed for them to shut the fuck up and go to bed.

'Very nice,' Dot said. 'But you won't make a penny working with him.' She pointed at Will. 'George, will you do something, please?'

'All right, you can stay the night,' he said. 'Tomorrow, the pair of you start working for me.' The two men smiled. 'And you stay working for me until you can pay the rent some other way. Eight o' clock sharp.'

'That's not what I had in mind,' said Dot. George put an arm around his wife and squeezed.

'Come on, sweetie, let's open a bottle of wine and watch some telly,' he said.

Laura rolled the bike around the side of the house and threw a cover over it. She returned to find Luka foraging in the darkness behind the bins. He fished out a backpack then followed Will to the front door. He seemed to like this England, sweet land of liberty, where people argued with each other one minute then formed an orderly queue. As he reached the doorway he glanced up at the night sky and the porch light caught his face. Laura looked at him. If anyone were to pass by at this moment and look up the path, no matter their religion or lack of it, she knew they would think of Jesus.

Westminster Inside Track

https://www.witreport.co.uk

White's Winning Ways

Maybe Robert White the Cities Minister feels his job entitles him to a night on the town. Pictured at Bentley's Casino last night (see **_Rogues Gallery_**) the night owl raked in £5,000 on a single spin of the wheel.

Westminster Inside Track

Your eyes and ears on Westminster and Whitehall; exposing the rumours, conspiracies and whitewash at the heart of government; a virtual voice in a new age of accountability.

White was accompanied to the private club by blonde bombshell Ruby Stevens, whose website describes her as an 'up for anything gentleman's escort from Estonia'. The gentleman in question spent the evening as guest of Russian billionaire Anton Ledakov. This is the same Ledakov whose controversial plan to revamp his Mayfair mansion received surprise approval last month.

Not Quite White

WIT has it on authority the approval was the result of a direct intervention by the Cities Minister, and was followed by a substantial donation to the Minister's constituency funds by the same Anton Ledakov. We wonder what odds we'd get on it being a coincidence.

We're also wondering what Mr White plans to do with his latest winnings. Blow it on another number or set it against his departmental overspend? If he has found a new way to boost the public purse, his next stop could be the Treasury where they need all the help they can get.

WITLINKS: Rogues Gallery – Exclusive pictures of White's Night On The Town / The bank statement – Russian cash boosts constituency funds/Ruby Stevens' wicked website / Canoodling in Cannes – White with Ruby on Ledakov yacht

ELSEWHERE IN WESTMINSTER...
Chamberlain denies rift with Prime Minister / Supermodel MP turns author – Eleanor Porter's publishing debut will be 'out of this world' / PM signs up for 10k charity fun run

3

'White wine is good for the heart,' said Charles Franklin. The chairman of The Reputation Works smiled at the prettiest of the fifteen graduates gathered round the boardroom table. What was her name? 'In fact, it's good for a *woman's* heart. Do you believe that?' he asked, gently shooting the cuffs of his crisp white shirt, which he knew offset his holiday tan and matched his perfect teeth.

Shuffling. A cough. Clearly beliefs about the efficacy of white wine were mixed, but no one was going to risk looking foolish in front of the chairman of the most powerful public relations agency in London, not on their first day.

Franklin's iPhone vibrated in his trouser pocket. It would be another text from Robert White, he was sure, the fifth that morning. The man was drowning. Charles picked up a copy of the *Daily Mail* and read from it.

"New medical research suggests white wine, taken in moderate amounts, is as effective as red in protecting against heart disease, particularly in women." He looked up from the paper and offered another smile. 'It goes on to cite new research into antioxidants and quotes a leading cardiologist who supports the findings. It was on breakfast TV this morning, wine buffs and health nuts will blog about it for the next week, then health authorities will issue statements playing it down. Now do you believe it?' He tossed the paper aside, threw yet another smile at the pretty graduate with the red hair and produced a bottle the colour of the Caribbean with a pastel pink label.

'Women will want to,' he said. 'And into this world will come Clos d'Amonceler, a stylish white wine, calorie reduced and chemically modified to increase its health properties. Wine buffs will endorse it,

23

A, B and C-listers will be drinking it. It will be the wine of choice for the next wedding in *Hello* magazine. It will be everywhere. From next week sales will rocket and the rest of the wine industry will be scrambling to catch up. It tastes good too.' Charles set the bottle aside. 'The Amonceler family is our client. What we have done so far is condition the market. This weekend we launch the product. We sponsored the research, found the cardiologist, hired the celebrities, did the deal with *Hello*, we courted the wine writers, we blogged. We sent the client a large bill. That's PR.' The graduates were impressed.

His eye caught the pretty redhead's for the third time. This time she held his gaze. Excellent, thought Charles. She was hooked. And why not? He may be a little distinguished around the temples, but he was still magnificent. A lion among men. And she was obviously keen to get on. It could be a perfect match, to be made in a luxury boutique hotel, if not heaven.

Charles looked round the other eager faces. Now he would make it about them. Make people feel special and they will follow you. It was a simple lesson learned years ago and now he was applying it to this year's intake of bright young things. 'You are fifteen from five hundred applicants,' he said. 'And you are here, not just on your academic merit, but because you, of all the people we met, get it. You have a feel for The Reputation Works and what it takes to be an image-maker.' He paused for a moment to allow his audience to bask in their rising confidence. After all, confidence was the single most important attribute he wanted to foster in his protégés. The more they had, the more work they could take on, the higher they could rise in client organisations and the more money he could make out of them. 'This is a factory and in this factory we make reputations. We sell products, move share prices, win investment, we even change law. We breathe life into brands: products, companies, even countries.'

The group's concentration broke and heads turned as a lean figure with an explosion of grey hair walked past the glass wall that ran the length of the board room. Two of the boys lost their studied looks of detachment and gaped as they recognised Hammond Marshall, better known as The Marshall, one of the biggest rock stars of the 1970s. He had a scowl on his craggy face. Charles effortlessly drew the distraction into his script.

'Celebrity brands too,' he said. He waved at The Marshall who gave him the finger. Charles wrapped up his talk, told the group to forget everything they'd learned at university and when their chance came, do whatever it took to impress.

With a last wink at the pretty redhead he left the room and walked briskly along the corridor, reaching for his iPhone. He turned into an open space that ran the width of the building and sank into a leather sofa, his back to the panorama of spires, blocks, domes and the wheel that make up London's skyline. He scanned his mail, deleting politicking internal memos, arse-covering updates and bulletins of who was following whom on which social media. In the end he was left with confirmation of lunch that day and the five terse messages from the Cities Minister.

Charles glanced up at the meeting rooms ranged along the ninth floor. This was the public face of The Reputation Works, the place where consultants met their clients in ultramodern glass cubicles, within a 1920s mansion block, behind a faux Georgian façade. The idea of the building having one image layered upon another appealed to him. It was busy this morning. In one room the information minister of an African government wanted help convincing the world of his country's good record on human rights; next door anxious executives from a pharmaceutical company considered the laxative side-effects of their new drug; and next to them the agency creative director was holding a 'thought shower' for ideas to launch the latest online retail experience. And, in the cubicle behind him, there was Hammond Marshall. Charles cleared his mind, took a deep breath and entered the room.

'Charles, you've got to do something about this fucking woman,' Hammond Marshall growled. He was standing at one end of a table, a wizened pirate king with a black bandana, reading *The Sun*. Tabloid papers were strewn in front of him. A young account executive, one of the most attractive women in the agency and purposely chosen for this assignment, was pouring coffee. Charles remembered flirting with her in the agency bar but couldn't recall her name.

'She's fired,' he said.

'Not her, you dickhead,' Marshall snapped, looking up from the paper over a set of gold pince-nez. 'I'm talking about my fucking hopefully soon to be ex-wife.' He pulled an e-cigarette from a waistcoat pocket and sucked desperately. 'Listen to this,' the old rocker intoned, holding his breath as if smoking a joint. He held open a double page spread of a sequinned beauty stepping out at a red carpet premier. Arranged around her were photographs of an overweight man in his sixties: unloading groceries from the back of a 4x4; trimming the lawn with a Black & Decker strimmer; and fast asleep in front of the television, pince-nez on his chest, his belly stretching an AC/DC T-shirt. The headline ran 'Is The Marshall Firing Blanks?' The guitarist exhaled, took another hit from the e-cigarette and read aloud.

'"Two months before a nationwide reunion tour, seventies guitar hero Hammond Marshall looks old and bloated. 'And he hasn't been effective in the sex department for a long time,' says German wife Karoline von Gunderrode (28)."' The rock star looked over his glasses. 'What the fuck?' He continued reading. '"Can the aging musician, famous for his excesses and once voted Star Most Likely To Expire, get it up in time?" I mean sweet Jesus, Charles. Aren't I paying you to stop this kind of thing? I've lost two stone since those were taken. I'm fitter than I've been in thirty years and I'm having a facelift next week. I'll look younger than when I started. And AC/DC for fuck's sake! That was a private moment.'

Charles reached for one of the papers as Marshall sank into a chair. The account executive brought the guitar hero a cup of coffee to which he added liquor from a brandy miniature.

'At least it's publicity,' said Charles. 'You've been out of circulation a long time, Marshall.'

'Do you have any idea what this will do to sales?' said the guitarist. 'We're only sold out in Doncaster. We've still got half the fucking tickets and I'm guaranteeing them. And we need a sponsor.' Charles made a noise that was supposed to indicate empathy. 'Charles, my fans are fat old men who sleep in front of the TV. They don't want to see themselves on stage. I am everything they never were, for fuck's sake.

26

I have to look wasted and like I'm banging everything that moves.'

'You have young fans too,' said the account executive. 'Boys who want to play the guitar.'

'Right. And *they* want me to look wasted and like I'm banging everything that moves. I'm there to prove they don't have to end up like their dads. And they won't turn up if they think I have.'

Charles looked up from his paper.

'She says you made her take part in unnatural sex acts,' he said. 'Before you became impotent.'

'I am *not* impotent,' Marshall shouted. 'And what if I did? I'm a rock god not a vicar. And what's unnatural these days? Tantric sex – that's what I call unnatural.'

'A haddock, apparently.'

'That was Zeppelin, years ago,' said the guitarist. 'Anyway, I thought I couldn't get it up? She can't have it both ways. She's making herself out to be some kind of angel. Charles, this is the woman I caught with my guitar tech, blowing coke up her arse through a straw, after her nose went and she couldn't get it in any other way. I'm the one who's clean. Since the bypass.'

'It's not coming across.'

'I can see that. The point is she thinks I'm worth a hundred million quid, and that bouncing on my balls for eighteen months makes her worth half. Fact is I'm broke. The seventies were a long time ago, Charles. We had three platinum albums. After that I don't remember much. There was a Christmas hit in the nineties, since then nada. This reunion tour is my pension. If she wrecks it, I'm fucked.' He stared at the newspaper. 'Any more of this and the only sponsor we'll get is Saga Holidays.'

Charles poured himself a coffee and sat down.

'You could try Viagra,' the girl said. Marshall wheeled round. 'For sponsorship.'

'Where did you get this girl?' asked the guitarist.

'She's fired,' said Charles.

'No, keep her, I like her.'

'What have you got on your wife?' Charles asked.

'Nothing,' Marshall replied. 'Truth is I don't know much about her. She doesn't like to speak English. That was half the attraction. And there are memory blanks.'

'Well, don't worry. I have someone looking,' Charles said. 'We'll find something.'

'I should have stayed with Brenda. I'm too old for this,' said Marshall.

'What you need next time is a pre-nup,' Charles said. Marshall sucked the miniature of any remaining brandy as the fifteen young graduates trooped past the room.

'It's like I'm supposed to have found the secret of eternal youth,' said the guitarist. 'Look at me. I don't smoke, hardly drink, I haven't taken non-prescription drugs for two years. The only things I'm addicted to are vitamin pills. I've got a personal trainer and I'm fitter than when I was twenty. I feel like shit. What I need is a quiet life and a country wife.'

'It would bore you rigid,' said Charles. 'Believe me.'

'I suppose it could be worse. I could be Angus Young. At least I'm not poncing about in short trousers. He must feel a total prat.'

Charles' PA popped her head around the door.

'Your car is here, Mr Franklin,' she said. 'And the Cities Minister called again.'

'Marshall, I have to go,' said Charles. 'Keep calm. We will sort it.' Marshall gave a tired flick of a wave. Charles signalled the account executive to follow him. 'Look after him, cheer him up,' he said when they were outside the room. 'Whatever it takes.'

She looked at him, disgusted.

'Charles, you know I will do anything for you,' she said, 'but I am not going to shag an old homeless person.'

★

Charles called Robert White from the back of the Mercedes.

'Where the hell have you been?' shouted the Cities Minister.

'Sorry, Robert. Litigation case. Blood all over the walls.'

'Charles, I am dying here,' White bleated. 'Have you seen this story on Westminster Inside Track? The tabloids are all over it.'

'It's impressive, Robert. An oligarch, an escort *and* gambling,' said Charles. 'But it's the planning thing that will screw you. What's going on?'

Charles relaxed into the grey leather upholstery. He knew what was coming next. So far things were going exactly to plan. He tapped the iPad on his lap and BBC News Online appeared. There was nothing on White yet but there would be. As far as Charles was concerned the minister was finished as a politician and as a client. Not that he was ever much of a client. It wasn't as if money changed hands. It had been a case of advice in return for connections. Almost pro bono. And now Charles was trading up.

'Anton Ledakov bought a place in Mayfair last year,' White bleated. 'Big place. Grade II listed. He got planning permission to develop it, even though it had been denied to the previous owner.'

'So?'

'They're saying I fixed it.'

'Who is?' asked Charles.

'WIT. *The Telegraph*. And now *The Sun*.'

'Did you?'

'I may have put in a word,' said the minister. 'Nothing untoward. But they have an email from me to the Chair of the Planning Committee supporting the development and a copy of a bank statement showing a donation to my constituency funds, from a subsidiary of Ledakov's. How do they get this stuff, Charles?'

Charles could have told him it was getting easier by the day, one of the perks of the information age.

'What do I do?' asked the minister. He sounded desperate. Charles tapped the pad in front of him and opened *The Sun*'s website. Nothing there yet, either. Health was the theme of the day at the tabloid, with questions over the Prime Minister's health, a celebration of the rude health of the day's topless model, and a feature on celebrity impotence quoting a specialist in erectile dysfunction and Hammond Marshall's wife.

'And there's a picture of me on Ledakov's yacht,' White said. 'At Cannes.'

'I'd say you're fucked, Robert,' said Charles.

'But I didn't do anything!'

'It's not going to look that way.'

'I didn't know Ruby was an escort,' whined the minister. 'I thought she cared.'

'How did you meet her?'

'On the yacht.'

'There you go,' said Charles. Completely fucked. 'You've been had, Robert. All the ways you wanted and a few you didn't. Anything else?'

'No. What do I do, Charles?' Franklin paused just long enough to give the appearance of having considered the matter.

'Resign.'

'Resign? Is that the best you can do? Charles, I've had that advice from the Department. You're the private sector. I thought you could spin this?'

'Robert. Get real.' Charles shut off his iPad and pulled a tie from his jacket pocket, which he flipped around his neck. 'You're a Minister of the Crown. You're supposed to support your Secretary of State and give boring talks to women's groups and after dinner speeches to the Royal Town Planning Institute, not hang around casinos with Russian mobsters, fix their planning applications and consort with Estonian prostitutes. And you are expected to know who's making donations to your funds. You can fight it for a day or two. Then resign in the best interests of the government and swear to fight to clear your name. Will your ex-wife stand by you?'

'To put her knife in.'

'Shame. After that you keep your nose clean on the backbenches; write a bit, do some telly. Wait it out and make a comeback. It'll take a year. But for the next few days you should stay out of sight.'

The car pulled up outside Nablat's restaurant in Mayfair. 'I'll have someone draft you a denial.' He promised to call the minister back then closed off the conversation. It was lunchtime and he had bigger fish to fry.

4

Inside the restaurant Sir Frank Porter, London's highest paid banker, was deep in conversation with his beautiful wife Eleanor. They sat at a corner table that had all the appearance of discretion but was carefully positioned to be in view, though out of earshot, of all other diners. The table was held each lunchtime for the golden couple of the day and today, as was the case on most days and almost all places they visited, Sir Frank and Eleanor Porter were the golden couple.

London's richest banker possessed a narrow fame, being recognisable to almost everyone with an interest in finance and no one on the street. His wife, his second, turned more heads. A Member of Parliament and now Parliamentary Under Secretary for Environment, Food and Rural Affairs, Eleanor Porter was on the first rung of the ministerial ladder. But her move into politics had been preceded by a glittering career as a top international model, when she was known as Eleanor Barry. Together, the combination of power, glamour and politics placed the Porters high in the pecking order at Nablats. They could only be displaced from the corner table by a top A-lister, and that would require much fawning from the staff, a table close by and an introduction, though this latter courtesy was rarely necessary as the Porters knew everyone who mattered.

Charles arrived at the table, apologised for being late and slid into a third seat. A waiter appeared immediately.

'We've ordered,' said Sir Frank, glancing at his watch. 'Eleanor needs to be back at the House by two.' Parliament was back after the summer recess and Charles guessed that meant a lot of catching up. He barely glanced at the menu and ordered the special before asking the topic of the day at the House.

31

'The Home Secretary,' said the banker.

'Not Robert White?'

'Is that out already?' Eleanor asked. She seemed surprised. 'That's just come up on the radar screen. No, he's a diversion. He'll have to go of course, but it'll be seen as the Prime Minister cleaning house; and to be frank he won't be missed. No, Ken Chamberlain is the issue.'

'Ken Chamberlain has always been an issue,' said Sir Frank.

Kenneth Chamberlain, the Home Secretary, had come up the hard way. He had scraped into Parliament in a Gloucester marginal at the 1987 election, Margaret Thatcher's third and last election victory, after which he spent a dutiful period on the Conservative backbenches and in select committees, toeing the government line. A lawyer by training and sceptic by nature he proved useful, drafting legislation and neutralising opposition attacks. After a spell as a whip he was appointed Chairman of the Employment Select Committee and worked his way through junior ministerial positions before the Labour landslide of 1997.

By the time his party returned to power he had occupied Shadow Cabinet roles in Environment, Defence and Justice. Any ambitions he may have had for the top slot were shelved when a succession of brighter and younger stars came forward to shape and change the party and ultimately secure power, albeit shared.

Chamberlain continued to act the dutiful adjutant and, after the inevitable departure of a few senior ministers, the result of dispute or misconduct, he was rewarded with one of the high offices of state, Home Secretary, with responsibility for law and order, immigration and home security. However, within a year of his appointment, as the government's popularity waned and the Prime Minister faced criticism from within the party and outside, Chamberlain had become a thorn in the administration's side, arguing over policies that offended his Euro-sceptic, climate-sceptic and generally retrospective sensibilities. His personal view in favour of reinstatement of the death penalty, expressed recently on local radio, had created havoc within the party as well as the Home Office, but vastly increased his popularity in the supermarkets. At the same time, following two poor performances in the House before the summer break and the recent visit to Downing Street by a leading physician, a rumour had started that the Prime Minister was suffering from serious health issues. There was even speculation, fed by Robert White among others, that the leadership of the country might be at issue and a perfectly adequate and healthy replacement was waiting in the wings in the shape of Ken Chamberlain.

'He doesn't really think he can make a challenge, does he?' asked Charles.

'We think so,' said Eleanor. 'It's difficult to tell with Ken. He's a bit of a wild card.'

'Is the PM ill?' Charles asked.

'Of course not,' said Sir Frank.

'Robert White started that one,' said Eleanor. 'Which is another reason we won't be sorry to see him go. No, he was off colour for a week with summer flu. That's why he had a check-up. He's as fit as a fiddle. It's the silly season.' Her mobile rang from within the sleek Mulberry bag by her side and an elegant hand reached into it. She glanced at the display.

'I'm sorry,' she said. 'I have to take this. Don't wait for me.' A waiter was behind her in an instant, withdrawing her chair as she rose. Porter and Charles stood and observed the ripple of glances as she crossed the dining room as if on a catwalk, fluid and feminine, in a grey trouser suit by Stella McCartney. She almost always wore British.

'She is stunning, Frank,' Charles said, watching as she turned towards the ladies' room. 'In every way.'

'I know,' said the older man, sitting again. Porter was himself a handsome man though his hair was grey and thinning, a natural tonsure spreading from the back of his head, and the stomach he'd fought to keep trim was finally softening. He made up for it with the most expensive tailoring money could buy, a tan borne of years sailing the finest yachts into the finest ports, and exclusive accessories, such as the Rolex Oyster Perpetual Yacht-Master on his wrist.

'She's a gift for a PR man,' said Charles. 'Former supermodel, marries London's star banker, then a First in Economics, children, politics, now one of the PM's favourites. She's the most beautiful woman in politics since Cleopatra. You're a lucky man, Frank.'

'So are you, Charles,' Porter replied. 'The further she goes the further you go.' Charles picked up a glass of wine that had appeared from nowhere.

'And how far is that, Frank?'

'All the way,' said the banker. Charles wasn't sure if he was joking. The banker wasn't noted for humour. He looked into a poker player's eyes.

'You're serious?' he asked.

Porter shrugged, as if it was the most obvious thing in the world. Charles was stunned. Surely the banker didn't think he could guarantee Eleanor's rise? The career path from Member of Parliament to Prime Minister was labyrinthine, potentially involving an apprenticeship on a select committee, a period as an unsalaried Parliamentary Private Secretary (PPS) or whip (an 'enforcer' of party discipline), followed by a seemingly random zigzag across ministries; first as Parliamentary Under Secretary, then Minister of State leading to Secretary of State. Along the way the opportunities for failure were legion, from misjudged alliances and fatal flops, to misdemeanours, ambush and outright treachery. If you got past these the grail was to hold one of the great offices: Home, Foreign or Treasury and finally Prime Minister. Some managed to short-cut the process. Tony Blair had held no such positions, barely shadowing the Home Secretary in opposition before being catapulted to the leadership of his party and then the country.

With his power and connections Sir Frank Porter could simplify his wife's path. But get her to the top? Was that the plan? He was a banker and before that an economist. Maybe he saw it as a simple mathematical problem – a question of probability and taking every reasonable action to increase that probability. If that was his ambition it was breathtaking. And if he was successful and became the power behind his wife's throne, he would be one of the most influential men in the world.

'Why not?' Sir Frank asked. 'What would she need for that to happen, Charles?'

Charles thought for a moment as the Sancerre slid across his tongue.

'Brilliance. Money. Friends in high places,' he suggested. Porter nodded. These were attributes Eleanor already possessed in abundance. 'And luck,' Charles added. 'Blair got the job because John Smith died.' He felt like he'd scored a point against a superior squash partner. 'And Thatcher because no one else had the balls to run against Heath.'

'I don't believe in luck,' said Porter. 'You make it or you buy it, yours or other people's, it's a commodity.' Food arrived amid a flurry of waiters. Porter waited until they were gone and raised a glass of tap water.

'Thanks and congratulations are in order,' he said. 'That business with White was brilliantly done. You are truly a master of the dark arts.' Charles responded with a self-deprecating smile.

'You're welcome,' he said. 'He'll put up a fight but I can't see him lasting. It was easy, actually; he'd left a trail and it was just a question of ferreting it out. It will be all over the papers tomorrow and he'll be out next week, I expect.'

They selected from an array of sparkling cutlery before Porter spoke again.

'He only has himself to blame, of course. Politicians are so venal. They ride into Parliament on a high horse promising to sort out the world. Straight out of university, most of them; never had a proper job, just the conviction they have the right to run the country.' Charles slid his knife into the sea bream and lifted flesh from bone as Porter warmed to his theme. 'Most of them have no money, but they mix with those who do and get used to the life. Next thing you know their snouts are in the trough. They're easy meat for a man like Ledakov. It probably started with an invitation to dinner, innocent enough, then Formula 1, then the yacht, and then the mistress.'

'It's those Cold War skills,' said Charles. 'The art of exploiting human nature.'

Porter grunted. 'There's plenty of opportunity in the House,' he said. 'The place is awash with human nature – freeloading, philandering, incompetence and delusion. If it was a business it would have gone under years ago.' The banker sat back in his chair and regarded Charles for a moment. 'Now, what you did with White, that was impressive.' Charles basked in the compliment.

'I know a man with a peculiar gift in the information retrieval business,' he said.

'No doubt you'll send me an equally impressive invoice,' said Porter. 'The PM will be delighted to see the back of him. He was Ken Chamberlain's right-hand man.'

Charles leaned across the table, conspiratorial but deferential.

'If I may ask,' he said, 'how does this help you?'

Porter looked at Charles through steel grey eyes, over cutlery held in impeccably manicured hands.

'We're creating space, Charles. Space for Eleanor. The PM is favourably disposed towards her. In fact, he's pretty much promised her she'll get the next ministerial position that becomes vacant. Which most likely will be White's. She'll make a fine Minister for Cities. And after that, we'll find another space.'

Charles' eyes widened. He was awed by his host's ambition, his decision to hook his fortunes to those of the man before him vindicated. After all, he reasoned, if you are going to ride on someone's coat tails they might as well be Gieves & Hawkes'.

'Life is short, Charles, and I'm an impatient man,' said the banker.

When Eleanor returned she was ringed by waiters.

'I'm so sorry, but I need to go back,' she said. 'There's a meeting to discuss this issue with Ken and the PM wants me there.' Charles stood and they kissed.

'Sorry, Charles, talk next time,' she said. 'By the way, how is everything with the book launch?'

'It's going to be fabulous,' he said. 'Don't worry about a thing. Everybody will be there. It will be perfect.'

'You're brilliant. Best PR man in town.' She bent and kissed her husband on the top of his balding head and Charles was suddenly aware of the disparity in their ages. Porter was a vigorous sixty, but his wife passed for considerably fewer than her forty-five years and for a second or two the relationship seemed filial.

'The smoking has to go,' Porter said, with a trace of irritation.

'Nobody saw,' she whispered, and left with her entourage of waiting staff.

'It's a hangover from modelling,' Porter said. Charles wondered if he was referring to smoking or dieting, as he noticed her untouched salad. After she left, London's most powerful banker moved his glass to one side and leaned across the table.

'There's one more thing I wanted to talk to you about,' he said in a low voice. 'I have another assignment for your friend with the peculiar gift.'

5

George Valentine adjusted the wing mirror in time to see Will and Luka race round the corner into view. Will was clutching an immense black bag while holding his pork-pie hat in place. Luka was running beside him, juggling two bags, one of kitchen rubbish and another of recycling. Behind them bounded a snarling Doberman. George glanced up at the roof. He'd told them to be discreet. He squeezed between tired seats into the back of the ancient van.

He could hear the boys outside, intent on making the twenty paces to the van before the Doberman's teeth sank into one of their backsides.

'Is–he–gaining?' Will's voice, anxious.

'Yes.' Luka.

'How–do–you–know?' yelled Will. 'You–didn't–look–back.'

'I–smell–his–teeth,' Luka again. 'Why–we–steal–rubbish?'

'Fucked–if–I–know.'

George opened the van's rear doors and stood above the bumper, dressed in white overalls, white boots and a plastic mask, his head and hands covered by a surgical cap and gloves. His eyes bulged with encouragement and the gloves beckoned, a curious semaphore guiding the runners home.

'Christ! It's the Cybermen,' yelled Will, as he and Luka dived for the finish line and, as rubbish and runners flew into the van, George slammed the doors in the face of the slavering dog. For a while the Doberman attacked the back of the van, spurred by the muffled gasps and panting within, until gradually it realised the futility of its mission and the yelping and scratching subsided. Soon the leafy side road in Belsize Park was sunlit, silent and serene again, save for a confused hound that must have strayed its bounds and was now chasing its tail, and a white van burping black smoke as it lurched into the road.

Later, parked by the bottle bank in a Sainsbury's car park, George, Will and Luka crouched on corners of plastic sheeting spread across the floor of the van several layers thick. They were all dressed as Cybermen now, each armed with a bamboo stick. In the centre of the van was a small mountain of waste from one of the bags.

'You start by separating the solids from the organic matter,' George said. He leaned forward and stabbed the pile of sludge, loosening blackened banana skins and yoghurt pots from a thick mass of pasta, fish and lentils on a bed of potato skins. A saucepan with a broken handle grudgingly parted from the sticky mess and rolled from the pile. A beer bottle followed. The neck of a wine bottle emerged and beneath it the edge of a sodden pizza box. Each disturbance refreshed the van with the stench of rotting vegetables. Will retched.

'You'd think rock star rubbish would be cooler,' he said. 'Where's the smashed TV set?'

'Or set-list on Camel pack,' Luka suggested. 'This would fetch money in Zagreb.'

Will slid out another pizza box.

'George, what are we doing here, exactly?' he asked.

George probed deep into the mound.

'Investigating. You're working for Valentine Competitive Insight. It's a small business Mrs Valentine and I set up with a government grant,' he said. 'The Americans call it opposition research. That's when you find out stuff to embarrass a candidate during an election. They do the same thing in Hollywood with Oscar nominees, only they call it sliming. That's more a West Coast thing.'

'This feels more like sliming,' said Will, looking at the pile of congealed kitchen waste currently under investigation.

'We're entrepreneurs,' said George. 'This is just one of our little enterprises.'

'Dad said there were no flies on you,' said Will. 'Though there should be, if this is how you spend the day.'

'We dig for dirt in the dirt,' Luka said, stabbing a greasy tub that once held fried chicken.

'That's the idea,' said George.

'So why are we sliming The Marshall?' asked Will. 'I wouldn't have thought there was much left to slime. Oh, I get it...the divorce. We're sliming the wife.'

'She's got the London house,' said George with a wink, 'so this is *her* rubbish.'

'What are we looking for?' Will asked. George sat back on his heels.

'Some little secret,' he said. 'Something in her past or present; maybe a conspiracy. It's easier with men, they're so obvious. Women are more complex and better at covering their tracks. With men it's lust, gluttony or sloth; with women it's pride, envy and avarice. Either way, it ends up as money or sex.'

'Is it legal?' asked Will, nodding towards the bags lined up for inspection.

'There might be a technical issue of trespass,' said George. 'But it's not theft. I mean, you can't permanently deprive someone of something they've thrown away, can you? And we only expose what's true but hidden. This is our rule. We never distort.'

'I see. So we're the good guys,' said Will. George's face hardened.

'It pays the rent,' he said.

'This is shit,' Luka said.

'You get used to it,' said George.

'No, I mean it is *shit*.' Luka exhaled through his nose as he rolled a small black sausage from the mound.

'That'll be our four-legged friend,' Will said. Luka uncovered two more pizza boxes.

'This is lot of pizza for one lady,' he said. 'And KFC. She has many people visit.'

'Your friend has the knack,' said George. He had hoped Will would show an interest. Instead he turned to Luka. 'Well done, son. She's a vegetarian and we're seeing meat and pepperoni. That usually means men. Women have mushroom or goat's cheese.'

Luka picked a can of deodorant from the mush.

'Maybe one of them stay the night?' he suggested. George took the aerosol with a gloved hand, cleaned it, waved it under his nose and read the copy on the side.

"Scent of the Cave". Young lad, I'd say. And The Marshall's sons live in Santa Monica.' George squeezed Luka's shoulder. 'Good boy. Let's try another bag.'

'Got anything less ripe?' asked Will.

George gathered the corners of the plastic sheeting, folding the rubbish into the centre, and sealed the bundle with a plastic tie. He wrote 'H. Marshall' on the tag and lugged the sack into the corner. In its place he emptied the contents of the recycling bag. This time the mound was made up of magazines and papers, whole, torn and crumpled. Will picked up a magazine and began to leaf through it. George swiped at him with a newspaper.

'You're supposed to be searching for secrets,' he said. His phone rang, a *Ride of the Valkyries* ring tone, and he searched through his boiler suit to find it. 'OK. Take a break,' he said. Stripping off masks and gloves, Will and Luka piled out of the van. Meanwhile George climbed back into the driver's seat to take the call. It was Charles Franklin.

'Charles, hi. We're on the Hammond Marshall job…no, nothing yet.' George listened intently, his face registering concern. 'Who? Charles, you must be out of your mind. There'll be security all over the place. And we haven't finished here yet. What are you up to?' He stared through the windscreen, hardly noticing Will and Luka larking about outside. 'All right,' he said. 'But Dot won't like it. And this is the last job, Charles. After that we're heading for the beach.'

He reached into the back of the van and grabbed a sheet of paper from the new mound.

'What's the address?' he asked, rifling the glove compartment for a pen. He scribbled down the details. Turning over the paper he read the back and chuckled. 'I think we've got something here, too,' he said.

At the top of the page was a black and white image of trees in a moonlit forest and a logo, a pentangle within a circle within a square.

Beneath it was a caption in gothic script, which he read aloud over the phone:

"Sit Back and Witch;

Custom Spells Cast to Order.

Use the herbs that work the best,

Then let nature do the rest."

There was silence at the other end.

'It's a receipt from The Westbourne Wicca Emporium,' said George. 'Some pretty strange stuff too. What's mugwort? And what would she want with a werewolf's nail?' George held the paper up to the light as if that might reveal more. 'Looks like she's a witch, Charles.' He heard a cheer at the other end of the phone. 'Who'd have thought it? She may have a warlock or two in tow as well. And we've still got two bags to go.'

The conversation returned to the new job and George promised he would leave right away. As he hung up he smiled, imagining how Charles would use the receipt. The next he would know of it would be a headline in *The Sun*: 'Rock Wife in Pizza-Fuelled Occult Orgies – Marshall Fears Children Bewitched'. Of course Hammond Marshall's children from three previous relationships had seen much worse. After all, what was a witch's coven compared to thirty years of rock excess? But it would level the field in the divorce and might even improve ticket sales. He and Charles were a great team. He would miss that. He wound down the window and shouted at the boys, who were sitting on a car bonnet, singing.

'Bag it up and tag it, boys. We're moving on.' They gave him blank looks. He shook his head. 'You bag up the rubbish, label it and stick it in the corner of the van,' he explained. 'We've got another job.'

'Another rubbish job?' Will called back.

'Don't knock it, son. Where there's muck there's money.' George laughed as he turned the ignition.

6

They pulled up outside 54 Mersley Road in the evening and unloaded the van. Will and Luka carried six bundles into the house and left them, as instructed, at the door to the cellar. They returned to find George spraying the back with disinfectant and listening to Beethoven. He told them to leave their overalls in a plastic bin on the pavement. After disrobing they hung around waiting for him to take a break, realising after a while that he rarely did.

'George, I was wondering, is there any chance of an advance?' Will shouted over the music. Perspiring, George pulled his mask free of his face.

'No need to wonder. There's no chance,' he said. The mask snapped back into place and George continued cleaning, but Will was not so easily dismissed.

'You should be paying danger money for that second job,' he argued. 'The first one was just a dog. That last one had CCTV. And detectives.'

George didn't look up.

'They had headphones, George. They were professionals.'

'Nonsense.'

'One had a gun.'

George stopped spraying and took off his mask.

'Let's not over-dramatise, boys.'

'George, that was not a minimum wage assignment.'

George laid the spray down and wiped his hands on a rag. He advanced on them, all smiles and arm-spreading bonhomie.

'Boys, boys, boys,' he said. 'You did well today. I should have said. First class. It's a demanding job, competitive insight. It can be stressful, but you passed the test and I'm keeping you on.' His voice took on an edge. 'And that's going to keep you off the streets.' He looked at his watch. 'I've something completely different for you tomorrow. Tomorrow you're working for Valentine's Perfect Parties. It's a clean job, flash venue, plenty of food, celebrities; you'll be mixing with the crème de la crème. Who knows where it might lead?'

'Valentine's what?' asked Will.

'Another of our little enterprises,' George said. 'One of Mrs Valentine's in fact. It was Parker's Perfect Parties until we married. Do you have a white shirt?' Will shook his head and George shook his, as if in despair at the sartorial standards of the young. 'And we're one short. Do you have any reliable mates?'

'Maybe.'

'Bring one. Downstairs, three-thirty, tomorrow afternoon. Uniform will be deducted from your wages.'

'So, we get paid tomorrow?' asked Will.

'You get paid when you've caught up with the rent,' George growled. 'But you get fed. Now sod off, the pair of you, unless you want to clean the van.' Will swore as he and Luka trudged up the path.

'What's wrong?' Luka asked.

'We need fifty quid for the rehearsal studio on Saturday.'

Once inside Luka led the way upstairs, eager to shower. Halfway up Will noticed an open door and stopped. It was Laura's floor. He had the attic rooms, with a bedroom, a living room, a tiny bathroom where the ceiling sloped up from the taps and a minute hallway that doubled as a kitchen with a sliding door to the stairs. George and Dot lived on the ground floor and Laura had the floor in between with rooms that spread across the landing. The door to her workroom was ajar. Inside he could see a desk piled with cameras and a laptop, but it was the far wall that drew his attention. It was covered with a framed triptych, three poster-sized photographs, each of a similar patch of blue sky and cumulus clouds, one crossed by power lines, the second by telephone cable, the last by barbed wire; simple images in sharp colour and dramatic light. On another wall was a collage of sketches, studies and unframed prints, mixed with postcards and calligraphy.

Framed prints extended along the landing, which he'd noticed before but now realised were Laura's: studies of things consumed, brands as trash. He was examining one of them, an island of plastic water bottles floating in a turquoise sea, when Laura came out of the bathroom, dressed in a robe, her hair wrapped in a towel.

'What are you up to?' she asked.

'You're good,' Will said. She glanced at the pictures.

'And you smell.'

'No, you're *really* good.'

'And you *really* smell.'

'I'm working for your dad,' Will said, as if the fact excused any consequence.

'And that stinks?' she asked. He couldn't tell if she was showing sympathy or loyalty. She was toying with him.

'I mean it,' he said. 'I thought you were just a photographer. You know, weddings and babies. But this is great. Would you shoot us?'

'Someone should,' she said, pulling the robe around her.

'I mean shoot the band. With your Canon. Or whatever,' he said. 'It's a new line-up and we'll need pictures.'

'I'm fifty quid an hour.'

Everything in the world seemed to be fifty quid at the moment. It might as well be fifty thousand.

'Have you paid the rent yet?' Laura asked. Will flinched. What was it his dad used to say? If you want to know what a woman will be like when the bloom has gone, look at her mother. This one was certainly her mother's daughter.

'You don't have a band yet,' he said and waved at the pictures on the wall. 'It could be cool. Annie Leibowitz did alright from music; and they'll be worth a fortune when we're famous.'

'Yeah.'

Will pointed to the triptych.

'And *that* would make a great album cover,' he said. 'If we still had album covers.'

'It's juvenile. Art school crap,' she said. But Will knew she was flattered.

45

'We're rehearsing in St Pancras,' he said. 'Saturday. I'll get you the address.'

'What are you called?' she asked.

'Don't know yet.'

'That could work.'

'Maybe. So we'll see you there,' he said. It wasn't a request.

'Don't know yet. Will you be taking a bath before then?' she asked. He saw the suggestion of a smile and wondered if she had a boyfriend. Or maybe she'd broken up with one.

Laura went into her room and closed the door, leaving behind the smell of soap and steaming clean skin before the stink of rubbish returned. Will smiled, recognising the jolt of chemistry, then ran up the flight of stairs to the top floor, stripping off his shirt.

7

Charles Franklin was clearly in his element, the stem of a champagne glass between his fingers, leaning over a steel balcony looking into a party of his own creation.

'You've got a hit, Charles,' said George, standing beside him, dressed this evening as maître'd. 'It's sensational.' Tonight his boss was the puppet-master.

Below, to the sensuous beat of an African dance band, amid a landscape of large rectangles draped in white silk, B and C-list celebrities mixed with the same categories of politicians, looking over one another's shoulders for A-listers of either, while journalists flitted from one group to another, butterflies after nectar.

'Politics, celebrity and media, George,' Charles said with a grandiose sweep of his arm, 'the holy trinity of news.' He pointed to a small group paying court to a young woman in an emerald gown. 'And there it is in action. It has a code. A minor royal trumps a soap star, a footballer and a newspaper editor, irrespective of couture or place on the civil list.' Charles turned to a nervous young woman next to him who was holding a clipboard and unloading stress into her phone.

'We need more Africans,' he said. She muted the call.

'Charles, we've invited every embassy and consulate,' she said, checking her lists. 'Nigeria, Kenya and Ethiopia are here, the High Commissioner for Botswana is on his way and we have a dozen more coming. And that was the chief executive of the Comawi Investment Agency. He's got a flat tyre.'

'Comawi?' Charles enquired. The young woman returned to her clipboard.

'Union of Comawi, 197th member of the United Nations. Would be an island paradise if it weren't for the coups. We're trying to find him a stretch as he's bringing his family.'

Two drummers, muscular and glistening, stepped from the stage, taking the music into the crowd and causing a minor sensation.

'You'd better tell Eleanor and Sir Frank to get a move on,' Charles said. 'Things will be peaking soon.' He glanced at the crop circle that had formed around the drummers then scanned the room for imperfections.

'George, what's that waiter doing?' he asked, pointing at Luka. Dressed in a white tunic the singer was backing through the crowd, hunched over a tray of over-filled glasses, which spilled with every movement. Charles' finger found another target. 'And that one's watching the band.'

George knew 'that one' would be Will. He found him in the crowd, also in a tunic, holding an empty tray, a cloth over one arm, standing stock still, rapt in the music. At least he wasn't drinking. Unlike the other one, Johnson, the extra hand they'd brought along who seemed to be downing as much champagne as he was distributing. Fortunately Charles hadn't spotted him yet.

'I'll have a word,' said George. 'They're new.' He noticed someone else had caught the PR man's eye. Charles turned to the woman with the clipboard.

'Who's that young lady?' he asked.

'That's Laura,' she replied. 'She's taking photos for the house.'

'Laura,' Charles said, testing the name.

'That's my daughter, Charles,' said George.

'And highly accomplished, I'm sure.' Charles laughed and slapped his companion on the back. 'I must see her portfolio.' He turned to the nervous young woman. 'I'd better join the party. Keep up the good work.' Charles headed towards a circular staircase that descended into the melée.

'And I'd better check on Mrs V,' said George, thinking less of his wife, who would be in the kitchen worrying about the next tray of hors d'œuvres, and more about knocking a few heads together among the waiting staff.

Unaware of admiration above, Laura was working hard, capturing duos, trios and quartets of guests for vanity shots to be sent out after the event. The perfect combination was the minor royal, a celebrity, a politician and a rich businessman or his wife. Framed, the shot would end up in the businessman's living room, the politician's study and the celebrity's loo, a reminder of their social success and the power of Charles Franklin and The Reputation Works. The royal might have it filed somewhere.

Laura looked around, hoping to catch a moment the *Hello* photographer might miss and pick up some extra cash. Stepping back to compose a shot she bumped into Will. She turned, apologising, before realising it was the musician. He grinned.

'Hot band,' he said.

'Amazing. Everyone's here,' she replied.

'Are they?' Will asked, a blank look on his face.

'Don't you recognise anyone?'

'Should I?'

'You must live under a rock.'

'I live above you,' he said. She laughed. A line at last.

'Come on, I'll give you a tour.' Laura took shots as she talked, plying the camera in an effortless arc from left to right and working the zoom lens and focus with precision. 'See those two on the left? She's the evil lawyer in that daytime soap, the one who killed her lesbian lover's husband; and he's the marathon runner who does the ad for slippers.' She took the photograph. 'Next to them is the full back who shagged the former Miss Iceland, who was also the manager's wife. The one talking to Ken Chamberlain and his wife Mary.'

'The Home Secretary, right?' said Will. 'The one who wants to bring back hanging?' The shutter clicked.

'Well done,' said Laura. He was on the scoreboard. 'That could make a diary piece.'

'Whose party is this?' Will asked.

'Eleanor Porter's.'

'She's the model who became an MP,' he ventured. 'Went out with Brad Pitt once. She's hot.' He clicked his fingers. 'I can do this.'

'She's married now, to some big wheel in the City. Anyway, she's publishing a book, *Out of Africa*. It's a collection of images taken on mobile phones to raise money for one of her charities. That's Charles Franklin, the PR guru and Eleanor's unofficial spin doctor. He organised it all. My guess is her husband paid for it.'

'Now, that guy I know.' Will looked impressed for the first time as Hammond Marshall stumbled into the room, bangled and beaded in homage to Africa complete with voodoo bandana. Charles Franklin made his way towards him, his arms outstretched in welcome.

'He's a legend,' said Will. 'He had three of the biggest albums of the seventies and died four times during an overdose; and he has a chord named after him.' Laura photographed the greeting. Cropped, Charles Franklin and The Marshall would become the closest of friends for eternity. One for Franklin's study, thought Laura, which he would publicly disown but privately relish.

'Who's that?' Will asked, spotting a middle-aged woman standing by the entrance.

'The county type with the pearls?' said Laura. 'That's Franklin's wife, Melissa.' She clipped off three shots. 'She's the money: Northamptonshire family who made their fortune in leather, though I think they're on their uppers now. They say she funded his PR business. She doesn't usually come to these things, bit of a country bumpkin, I heard.' Laura zoomed in for a close up. 'She's lost a lot of weight.'

'You know these people,' Will said.

'It's part of the job. You have to know who's in the shot and what they're worth.' She looked up from the camera. 'Not what they're worth themselves, what the picture is worth.' She focused on another target but became aware of Will's gaze.

'Yes?' she asked.

'You smell fabulous,' he said and appeared to regret the words as they came out of his mouth. It was as if he'd missed his step on a ladder, trodden on the head of a large snake and was about to slide back to the start of the game.

'You smell better than you did,' said Laura and brought the camera level with his face, clicking the shutter to capture his embarrassment.

'That would be the annual bath,' said a voice beside them. Laura turned to see a stocky waiter with a shaven head and unshaven face. He was balancing an empty tray and swaying slightly. 'Is this a private moment?' he asked. 'Or can I force myself between you?'

'This is Johnson,' said Will. 'Our drummer.' Johnson touched an imaginary forelock by way of a greeting and smiled, a hint of lunacy in his eyes. Will joked that he was named after an alias used by John Lennon and not, as some said, for an abiding interest in his penis. Laura wasn't so sure. So far, not only had he quaffed more than any guest, she'd seen him make passes at a waitress, a TV presenter and the minor royal, the last of whom seemed to find the direct approach of 'You'll do' a refreshing change from the usual cringing servility.

'Have you seen Jesus?' Johnson asked.

'He means Luka,' said Will.

'Don't you think he looks like Jesus?' Johnson asked, with a leer. 'But does he sing like him? That's the question. And who would Jesus sing like? Michael Bublé? I'm thinking Elvis in Vegas. What about you?'

George's voice boomed over his shoulder.

'*I'm* thinking it's time to get back to work,' he barked. They turned to find their employer standing with hands on hips, his face glowering. 'When your tray is empty you take it back to the kitchen for refills, or you pick up some nibbles. Mrs V will tell you what to do.' Laura looked at the boys' platters, which were bare save for glass rings. 'And when you get back,' George continued, 'you do not consume the merchandise and you don't stand around waiting for it to fly off on its own. You circulate, you entice, you engage. 'Drink, sir? Blini, Madam? The hollandaise is sublime.'

'It's Sainsbury's, Dad,' said Laura.

'Only the finest at Valentine's Perfect Parties. Right, Jimi Hendrix, you and your friend, follow me.' George headed towards the kitchen, followed reluctantly by the two waiters. Laura brought the camera up to catch the three from behind but her view darkened.

'It's Laura, isn't it?' Charles Franklin was standing in front of her, with a smile fit for a toothpaste commercial.

'Hello, Mr Franklin.'

'Call me Charles, please.'

'Really? I see you more as a Charlie.'

'I've been watching you,' he said. 'From up there. You're very professional.' He ran a hand through his hair.

'Thank you.'

'I'd like to see your work. Maybe I can help.' Charles smiled again, an innocent boyish grin, no doubt the one that melted all hearts.

'I'm sure you could,' she said.

'We could have dinner somewhere and talk about your career.'

Laura turned the camera so Charles could see the viewfinder and flipped through the last few images.

'I'd like that,' she said. 'Now, what do you think? I'd like your opinion. I really like this one of your wife.' As if on cue, Melissa Franklin arrived in a state of agitation.

'Charles, I'm so sorry I'm late,' she gasped. 'You know what it's like getting ready for the county show.' They exchanged a perfunctory kiss. The moment of half-hearted intimacy over, Laura noticed Charles distance himself and treat his wife as he would any minor guest.

'Melissa, darling,' he said, 'this is Laura Valentine. She's a photographer.' The two women exchanged hellos then Melissa glanced self-consciously around the room.

'We were just looking at this shot of you,' said Laura. She offered the camera.

'How awful. Please get rid of it. I hate pictures of myself.' Melissa turned to her husband and whispered in an injured tone, 'You might ask how I'm feeling.'

'I'm sorry,' said Charles, reddening. 'How are you?'

'Much better, thank you.'

'I'm sorry, have you been unwell?' Laura asked, unsure whether she was supposed to have heard the exchange.

'I'm fine. I had an operation.' Melissa fiddled with the catch on her bag as Hammond Marshall joined them.

'Hey babe, you are looking fabulous,' he said, emphasising every syllable of his greeting, and to Laura's surprise, he hugged Melissa affectionately.

'Oh, Marshall, you are dreadful,' she said, smiling for the first time.

'Sweet Melissa. You've lost pounds. How did you do it?'

'Melissa's found a new regime,' said Charles.

'Hey, willpower, babe. I'm impressed,' said the guitarist.

'Liposuction,' she mouthed.

'Whatever it takes, babe,' said Marshall. 'Sure beats a laxative. Now don't you lose any more; I like my women to be women, if you know what I mean.' He turned to Charles. 'She's looking great, man. Babe, your tits are amazing.'

'Thank you for that,' said Charles. Marshall was in a fine mood this evening, influenced, Laura suspected, by a dusting of chemicals.

'No problem,' said the former rock god. 'So, Charles, the bitch is a witch? That is *so* cool. How the fuck did you find that out? Are we going to tell the media? Spread the news?'

'Let's talk about it tomorrow,' said Charles.

'Sure. Then we'll stick it to the witch bitch.' Marshall sucked his e-cigarette and smiled contentedly. They discussed the guitarist's forthcoming tour, until the nervous woman with the clipboard sidled up to Charles and whispered in his ear and he excused himself. Laura took a few shots of Marshall and Melissa. They were an unlikely pairing, but there seemed to be genuine chemistry between them as they chatted about cattle prices and show prizes. Another rock star turned country squire, she supposed.

The drummers had returned to the stage and the band was at full stretch, guests were the right side of tipsy, food and drink flowing. Laura peered across the room, looking for her next shot. She saw Charles prise the minor royal from a conversation with the full back with the reputation for shagging his manager's wife and escort her to the foot of the stage as Sir Frank and Eleanor Porter arrived in a blaze of flashing cameras. There was a ripple through the crowd as people sensed a new source of energy in the room. The golden couple, Eleanor beautiful in African chic, her husband in a tailored suit, strode through the parting crowd, pressing flesh, according time to status, until they reached Charles and the minor royal. He introduced them before running up a small flight of steps onto the stage and taking the microphone.

'Your Royal Highness, Excellencies, ladies and gentlemen, welcome. This evening is about Africa and what comes out of Africa. Tonight we launch a book and a website with a difference. We've all seen images of the agony of Africa, the charity case and victim. But there is another Africa: a place of infinite potential, where fifty-four countries are struggling to develop, each on a unique journey. Tonight we celebrate progress, we recognise the successes and the people behind those successes, we show Africa captured by Africans using the technology that is connecting the continent, the mobile phone. Tonight is an invitation to discover a new world. The profits from this project go to Entrepreneurship in Africa.'

Charles paused as a few stragglers entered the room and picked glasses of fruit juice or champagne from a tray. The house was full.

'I'd like to introduce the woman who made this happen, former supermodel, goodwill ambassador, philanthropist, Member of Parliament, a success story in her own right – Eleanor Porter.'

Eleanor arrived on stage to applause, which she acknowledged with professional grace. She spoke without notes, not as a gushing celebrity but as an articulate and practical humanitarian, and talked of the challenge of Africa, its importance in terms of policy and world order, and the need to engage beyond a donation at the sight of a red nose. She challenged the celebrities present to move on from highlighting plight and point towards progress, from identifying with suffering to recognising achievement; restoring dignity as well as revealing its denial. She acknowledged the royal presence, the representatives of the African states present, the sponsors, and the thousands who had contributed photographs. She touched every individual in the room, making each feel vital to the cause.

Laura climbed up to the balcony and tried to compress the

atmosphere into a single frame. Looking down she saw that men and women alike, Europeans and Africans, were captivated by this woman; all save Charles who was fawning over the minor royal and Luka who was whispering with the manager of the African band.

On stage the musicians began to play, a powerful tribal rhythm, as sheets of silk in yellow, orange and red, stretching the width of the stage, waved and curled and rose, symbolic of a vast sunrise, seeding the notion of a mighty civilisation rising across the continent. At the same time the white drapes slipped from the rectangles arranged around the room to reveal images of people and projects making a difference: huge dams and clean water pipelines; exports of cut flowers from Kenya and mangos from Mali; cotton production in Cameroon and gorilla tourism in Rwanda; schools overflowing with children in Guinea and Niger; and African banks and mobile phones financing and connecting the continent.

There were speeches by the minor royal as patron of Entrepreneurship In Africa, the sponsor – the CEO of a telecommunications giant – and a High Commissioner, then the band returned for a second set and drink, music and food flowed again.

Once the minor royal had departed Eleanor and her husband joined the Home Secretary and his wife along with Charles and Melissa. Laura returned from the balcony and circled the group, just within earshot, seeking a shot of the Chamberlains with the golden couple.

'Frank. So good to see you,' Ken Chamberlain said. He and Sir Frank shook hands, Chamberlain emphasising the greeting with a squeeze from his free hand behind the banker's elbow. Laura imagined this was a special salutation reserved for trusted friends, photo-calls and his most powerful enemies.

'Good of you to come, Ken,' Sir Frank replied.

'Anything for one of our rising stars,' said the Home Secretary, inclining his head towards Eleanor who smiled modestly. 'Very good effort,' he added. 'But it's a bit off your brief, isn't it? I thought your turf was coastal erosion and the finer points of EU Fisheries regulation?'

'Eleanor did the book in a private capacity,' said Charles. Chamberlain shrugged.

'Not to worry,' he said, smiling through clenched teeth. 'You might irritate a few people in International Development, but I'm sure the PM's right behind you. And it will play well in the tabloids.'

'We have the *Today* programme tomorrow,' said Charles, preening, 'and BBC *Breakfast*. More champagne?' He waved at the nearest waiter, Johnson, who made his way unsteadily towards the group.

'I hope you'll buy a copy,' Eleanor said.

'I hope you'll sign it for me,' Chamberlain smiled back. Laura's shutter clicked, and an image was forged of acquaintance and accord, if not outright friendship. Chamberlain had obviously fought enough elections to pull a face at the right moment. His wife was less accomplished and was caught looking down her nose in an off-putting sneer. Mary Chamberlain ran eyes filled with jealousy over the former supermodel.

'Lovely dress,' she gushed. 'So bold. Not everyone can wear orange. But you'd look good in a sack. I bet you can wear anything.'

'Oh, I have, believe me,' Eleanor laughed.

'Do you point-to-point?' asked Mary Chamberlain, steering the conversation towards her favourite pursuit. Eleanor didn't. The group split in two, Melissa and Mary Chamberlain discussing country matters, while the rest stayed with politics. Laura stayed with the politicians.

'Of course, Africa's all very well,' said the Home Secretary, 'but it's the home front that's the issue at the moment.'

'Do you mean the PM's health?' asked Porter.

'That's one thing, I suppose. Did you hear the rumour about the booze?' Chamberlain asked. Eleanor and Sir Frank exchanged looks. 'Some hack wanted me to confirm he drinks like a fish and that's behind the health issue. I don't know where this stuff comes from, I really don't.' Sir Frank scowled. 'No, I was thinking of the economy, immigration and, of course, crime.'

'Bring back the rope, eh?' said Johnson, who had arrived with a tray of champagne. The group froze, their heads turning slowly towards the waiter, faces blank apart from Chamberlain who gave him an icy look.

'I'm up for that,' said Johnson. 'While you're at it, let's bring back the ducking stool. I've always thought there's a lot we can learn from the Middle Ages.' Eleanor laughed, took a glass of champagne and winked at the drummer, which he took as permission to leave. Laura grinned as he stumbled back into the crowd. After all, George had told him to engage. What did he expect?

'How *are* things between you and the PM?' Porter asked. Chamberlain glanced around, probably wary of microphones.

'The man's paranoid,' he said. 'The real problem is he's in a corner on the economy and down in the polls. And he has this health issue which he should be straight about.'

'He's absolutely fine,' Eleanor insisted. 'And he doesn't drink.'

'Anyway, there is no question of me making a bid for the leadership,' Chamberlain continued. 'He's blown this out of all proportion and I wish he'd stop briefing against me. Anyway, if you want to know what he's thinking, you should ask Eleanor. She has the inside track.'

'Do you think Robert White is finished?' Porter asked, changing the subject.

'Completely, silly man,' said Chamberlain. 'He could get away with the Russian and maybe the prostitute, even the gambling, but the e-mails to the planning committee? No, it was all wrapped up too neatly. A very nice job, if anyone had a hand in it. Of course, this means a vacancy for a junior minister. I shouldn't be surprised if you're on the list, Eleanor.'

'You think so?' she asked.

'Why not? He needs something to perk up the administration. A little glamour would work wonders. And of course, you will do a fine job. And you're loyal, in fact I'd say dogged in your devotion.'

'Perhaps you'll put a word in, Ken,' said Sir Frank.

'That might not help you at the moment,' Chamberlain replied, his face betraying irritation. 'And you don't really need it, do you?' he added, sourly. The veneer of camaraderie was wearing thin. 'Everyone knows you'll get the next job that comes up.'

Attention was shifting to the stage again, as the music changed tempo and a new voice snaked through the air. Laura turned to see Luka on stage with the female vocalist in the band, singing '7 Seconds', a fusion of African and European music sung in a Senegalese language, English and French. People turned from their groups to face the stage and the party took on the air of a concert. All eyes were drawn to Luka.

'Who is he?' asked Eleanor.

'He looks like a waiter,' said Mary Chamberlain. 'Is it like those opera people who sing 'Nessun Dorma' with the coffee?'

Laura looked across the room to see George waving wildly, and Will and Johnson weaving their way through the crowd towards him. She followed and caught up with them in front of the stage.

'What's he doing?' George bellowed at the two musicians. 'He's supposed to be serving Mrs V's desserts. She'll be apoplectic.'

'He's got a pair of lungs,' said the drummer. 'I'll give him that.'

Laura photographed the singer, who looked more Christ-like than ever and in command of his congregation. Lean and lithe he began to writhe around his microphone stand. He wasn't her type but he was magnificent, a messiah in the making. Will stood beside her staring. He seemed torn, as if he wanted to listen to the voice and hear it soar yet his face was lined with worry. Laura could see he had a problem, there were powerful people here, and this exposure was premature. In a matter of seconds Luka would be discovered and Will's band consigned to history before it had formed. In another minute Will would be a footnote to music history: the man who put Luka up for a night before he hit the big time.

'You're in danger of losing your golden goose,' she said. People were turning to their neighbours, confirming a moment of mutual discovery, and The Marshall, alone in the centre of the crowd, was standing erect, on the scent, looking straight at the singer.

'She's right, mate,' said Johnson. 'We'd better do something.' Will remained paralysed for a few more seconds, as if all his energy had been drained, then he snapped out of it.

'Where's the fuse box?' he shouted and turned to Johnson, but the drummer had disappeared.

Laura scanned the crowd, peering through her viewfinder. Every face was turned to the stage, displaying looks of awe and excitement. Even the security staff were spellbound. It was all an unwanted guest would need. She felt a lurch in her stomach as she recognised Robert White slipping into the room. Dishevelled and drunk, he hooked a glass from a waitress's tray and began pushing through the crowd, the only person not caught up in the entertainment. For a moment she thought he was heading her way so retreated to the balcony to avoid an encounter. Reaching the top of the stairs she looked down to see him reach his quarry.

'Chamberlain,' he bawled.

'Robert, how nice to see you,' replied the Home Secretary, offering a hand.

'Bollocks, Ken,' White slurred. 'I've only one question for you. Are you going to back me? Or fuck me up the arse?'

'Robert. Mixed company, please,' said the Home Secretary. He looked nervously at Charles Franklin, who in turn waved in the direction of security, but the team were engrossed in the band. Shouldn't Chamberlain have a detective somewhere, Laura wondered. She zoomed in on the group of politicians below.

'Well?' asked White.

'It's difficult.'

'What's difficult, Ken? I've followed you on everything, every sordid twist and turn.' Chamberlain put his arm around White and tried to hive him off from the group, but the minister shrugged off his senior colleague.

'You're a little hot to handle at the moment, old boy,' said the Home Secretary.

'So you're throwing me to the wolves?'

'You've rather thrown yourself to them.'

'I'm going to fight,' White said, with defiance.

'And I'll back you as much as I can, from the sidelines.'

'You bastard,' said White. 'I've fucked a lot of people for you, Ken.' Charles waved frantically to his staff as White balled a fist. Eleanor, Porter and Mary Chamberlain stepped back, while Chamberlain continued to produce affectations of support, which only served to inflame the junior minister. Laura looked across the crowd. Still no sign of a detective or security guard. The fist was about to fly so Charles grabbed White from behind, pinioning both arms.

'You should leave,' he said, through gritted teeth.

'You invited me,' shouted the minister, squirming.

'That was then. You're upsetting my client.'

'I thought *I* was your client.'

'I was going to talk to you about that,' Charles panted. The minister was putting up quite a struggle.

'Are you firing me?' White shouted. 'You're my PR and you're fucking firing *me*!' White kicked out, Charles slipped, and the two tumbled to the floor with the PR man underneath, still clasping the minister's arms. White struggled, his bright red face glaring upwards. Laura thought they looked like a crab flipped on its back. Chamberlain and nearby guests stepped back from the altercation, forming a circle which spread gradually outwards as the crab spun round on its shell, its legs flailing. Cameras began to flash.

It was enough to distract the crowd from the music, and in that instant Johnson shot across the stage and bundled Luka off the other side. Laura looked up too late to capture the moment. The voice disappeared, the mic tumbled to the floor and the two waiters, white-liveried missiles, flew into a group of guests, creating a second sprawl on the floor. The band looked up from their instruments, wondering what had become of their male vocalist.

Unfortunately, Dot chose that precise moment to emerge from a door beside the stage that led from the kitchen. Dressed in carefully accessorised black she was making her entrance to the party, presumably intent on receiving plaudits for her culinary efforts during the last few hours. She had with her the last two trays of her finest miniature desserts. As the door swung shut behind her she surveyed the party for the briefest moment before being knocked off her feet by the flying waiters. Not only did the three of them floor several high-ranking diplomats and a Nobel prize-winner, but delicious titbits rained down around them. It was not turning out to be the Valentines' most perfect party.

Security staff, confused by the two altercations, were now on their way in both directions, one team moving towards the shambles by the stage, a second led by Chamberlain's detective to the centre of the room. Luka and Johnson untangled themselves and helped Dot to her feet. She was winded, speechless and pock-marked from miniature double-chocolate brownies.

'What was that for?' Luka wheezed at Johnson, just as Will arrived.

'We've got to leg it, Luka,' yelled Will. 'They're after us.' Will pointed to the security team making its way towards them, brushing guests aside with all the diplomacy of an enraged elephant. He and Johnson shoved Luka and Dot towards the kitchen, the latter still mouthing soundlessly. As they passed a serving area Johnson grabbed two bottles of champagne. They pushed through swing doors and headed for the fire exit.

The second security team reached the Chamberlain party, hoisted White to his feet and bundled him towards the exit. He screamed obscenities until someone clamped a hand over his mouth. As they reached the door the chief executive of the Comawi Investment Agency, who had in fact required two limousines, arrived with twenty-five of his closest family and friends.

High above on the balcony Laura recorded all for posterity, though probably not, she suspected, for the newspapers.

Westminster Inside Track

https://www.witreport.co.uk

Number 10   Whitehall   Around Westminster   @witreport

WIT@witreport
What's going down in Westminster and Whitehall; the rumours, conspiracies and whitewash at the heart of government.

TWEETS:

WIT@witreport Bad boy Minister @RobertWhiteMP got trashed tonight. He crashed @EleanorPorterMP's book launch and was taken out with it…#OutOfAfrica

WIT@witreport White now spotted at @StringfellowsCG with a black eye and pair of waitresses, trying to buy a six-pack, or is that an icepack? #outoforder

WIT@witreport Politicos who've written books on their way up include JFK, Disraeli and Hitler. Luckily @EleanorPorterMP's has more pictures #OutOfAfrica

WIT@witreport Hubby Sir Frank Porter dropped £150k for the launch – that include paying the guy who called to tell me to put a sock in it? #OutOfAfrica

8

George spent most of Saturday on a stool hunched over his workbench in the cellar of 54 Mersley Road. He wore a pair of heavy optician's glasses with thick interchangeable lenses, the kind used for eye tests. Holding a pair of tweezers between nimble fingers, he picked slivers of paper from a freezer bag overflowing with the tangled waste from a shredder and arranged them on a square of plexiglass in front of him.

In the background a Mozart serenade played from an old Roberts radio that sat on one of the shelves ranged against the wall in front of him. At first sight his bench, pitted and aged, looked like it belonged to a hobbyist, a DIY enthusiast with a penchant for electronics perhaps, but closer scrutiny revealed a more specialist interest. In addition to the traditional handyman's tools, worktop and shelves were hosts to an unusual array of equipment, crammed in boxes or in loose yet ordered piles: an assortment of optical lenses and magnifying glasses; sets of binoculars; a shoebox of surveillance cameras of all shapes and disguises (including Laura's spearmint camera); a broken CCTV unit; a pile of microphones; a rack of torches; and to his right within easy reach, a desktop PC and a laptop, both switched on, one set to Wikipedia, one to its screen saver; and next to them, writing pads and a jar of pens and pencils.

George pulled an angle-poise close, until the light around him was intense, a bright glow amid the darkness, all of it focused on the paper pattern he was creating. Outside it, in the shadows, were the low tech elements of his occupation: tagged and coded rubbish bags; folded plastic sheeting; shovels; car batteries and road signs. On the wall a rack was hung with overalls and coats and an assortment of headgear, including construction and firemen's helmets.

This was George's domain; a long, low workroom, where investigations were conducted, plots hatched and plans made, whether for Laura's education or his and Dot's next entrepreneurial venture. George was at home here; if the kitchen was the heart of the house, then George was happiest in its lower bowel, which was perhaps appropriate given the nature of his work.

'Do you want a glass of wine?' came a voice from above. Hesitating long enough to recognise his territory but without waiting for an answer, Dot made her way carefully down the wooden steps, a bottle of Rioja in one hand and two glasses in the other. George swivelled on his stool to see a blurred blob approaching.

'Take that contraption off,' said his wife. 'You look like a serial killer.' She poured them both a glass. George removed the optician's paraphernalia and pulled a second stool from beneath the bench. Dot perched next to him, passed him a glass and George turned the radio off; a ritual smooth from being observed a thousand times.

'You've been hiding down here all day,' said Dot. 'What are you up to?'

George had been hiding from Dot. The events of the previous evening had not left her in the best of moods and over breakfast he had received a haranguing for ruining her dress and night, hiring incompetents and giving board to feckless musicians who would ruin their reputation and quite possibly their finances. By the time he finished his scrambled eggs George felt as if he had been convicted without trial of acts of terror that would make Al-Qaeda blush, following the matrimonial equivalent of water-boarding. After breakfast he had decamped to the cellar on the pretext he was overloaded with work. He had spent the day there, happy among his things, and gradually his sense of injustice had evaporated. The best path now, he judged, was to let sleeping dogs do what they did best.

'You first,' he said. Dot had read in a women's magazine, a long time ago, that partners should take turns listening to each other for at least twenty minutes each day. Active listening, it was called, not the odd nod while one, usually the wife, nattered into thin air.

George had learned the nodding technique from his grandfather, who used to turn off his hearing aid while his wife recounted the myriad of minor crises that had befallen her through a long day. Unfortunately Dot was quicker than his Nan and after several memory failures on his part, involving dry cleaning, a dentist and the death of a distant relative, she instituted the new system. George had reluctantly taken part in the daily exchange of emotional and factual minutiae, until he realised it would work just as well in their business relationship, after which he applied it with gusto, delighted in his discovery of a new technique for better business management. When you were an entrepreneur without the benefit of a business school education, you had to use everything that came your way.

Dot had little to recount this evening. There was no movement on selling either the house or the businesses, though she had made progress with eliminating their past. She had also used the online census records to research a new family history for when they moved to Spain. They would become Mr and Mrs John and Hannah Ward, now retired, with detailed genealogies; his leading back to a sawyer in the 1850s and hers to a more genteel and well-to-do draper in south London. She had also taken delivery of a dozen crates, which she had placed about the house and begun to pack with the least used of their things.

'So, who's the mark?' she asked, after George had toasted her achievements, indicating it was his turn.

'You don't want to know,' he said. 'I think Charles has finally gone off his trolley.'

'Surprise me,' she replied, and sipped her wine. George adjusted the angle-poise so it shone on a large square of cork tiling on the wall at the far end of the bench. Pinned to it were pictures and sheets of paper covered with his precise script. He slipped off the stool and walked to the board.

'Ken Chamberlain, the Home Secretary,' he said. Dot nearly choked.

'No, George.'

'Ours is not to reason why,' said her husband, 'ours to render high and dry.'

'It's too much.'

'It's our last job. We agreed. Whatever it was, we'd take it.'

'Not this one, George. It's madness.'

'We could go down in history.'

Dot stared at him. 'We could just go down,' she said.

'It's a challenge,' he agreed. 'But what a finish. It's good money. Premium rates.'

'George. He's in charge of law and order. He runs Special Branch.'

'We'll be careful,' George insisted. Dot ran her eyes over the pinboard.

'Do you think Charles is working for the Prime Minister?' she asked. 'I mean everyone knows he hates Chamberlain.'

'I doubt it,' said George, 'he could just reshuffle him.'

'Not if he's too popular. Or if Chamberlain has something on him. I wouldn't put it past him. I always thought he was too good to be true.' Dot looked at a photograph of the Home Secretary, pinned to the board. 'He's got piggy eyes.' There was a moment of quiet as Dot ruminated over her Rioja.

'All right,' she said. 'But that's it, after this we're finished. No scope-creep. And no slip-ups.' George raised his glass, giving no sign whether he was signifying a promise or celebrating victory. 'This is it, George. The last mark.'

'This is what I've got so far,' George said. He moved to a flipchart next to the bench and peeled back the top sheet to reveal his work. 'There's Ken Chamberlain; his wife Mary; a teenage son doing A levels, Russell; and a daughter, Mariot.'

'They were at the book launch,' Dot said, 'Chamberlain and the wife.'

'That's Charles keeping his enemies close,' said George. 'Now, Chamberlain has a reputation for being pompous, and of course he's in this spat with his nibs, though he's popular with the public, probably because he's anti-everything.'

'Except hanging.'

'Anyway, he's riding high while the Prime Minister is struggling. Most of the Cabinet despise him for rocking the boat. Other than that his record is spotless. He came out of the expenses scandal pretty well, just a couple of indiscretions while he was shadowing Fisheries. He restocked his pond with koi carp which he claimed was to entertain the Japanese ambassador and there was some business about flying wild salmon down from Scotland for a dinner party. He said that was for a rivers and oceans conference. The environmentalists had a field day over the carbon cost of the flight, but it was nothing compared to what the rest were up to, so it was ignored.' George moved from the chart to the laptop and refreshed the screen.

'Their credit rating is fine,' he said, 'though his wife is a big spender. There are Visa bills you could use as a map of Knightsbridge.' He picked up a pile of credit card statements and waved them. 'They have a house in London and a pile in Gloucester. They claimed for the London house but were within the rules. The rubbish we got was from there. He inherited money from his father who was a stockbroker in the good old days and he was a solicitor before he went into politics. The London house is his old family home. Gloucester is hers.'

'Doesn't look like money, then, does it,' said Dot, topping up their glasses. 'What about sex?'

'Nothing so far.'

'Addictions?'

'I don't think so,' said George. 'There's a healthy wine bill, but nothing over the top.'

'Dodgy dealings in the constituency?' asked Dot. George shook his head. 'Or on the way up?'

'That'll take some digging,' he said. 'There was an issue during his first election in '92. Apparently he was the victim of a smear campaign, but managed to expose it.' Dot raised an eyebrow, but George shook his head. 'Something to do with a boating holiday. But he came out on the side of the angels.' He took a mouthful of the wine and savoured it for a moment or two. 'They're fairly careful, most things are shredded, others not, so not so careful they look like they're hiding anything, but you never know.'

'He's done something,' said Dot. 'They've all done something. What about the children?'

'The son could be a possibility. I mean, he's got to be up to tricks at his age, but probably not enough to do any real damage. We'll just have to keep an eye on all of them until we find something. We will find something. It's just a matter of time.'

They fell into silence as they considered the sins they had seen and sold, which were many, trying to close on the one most likely to fit this profile, but both came separately to the conclusion it could be anything and you could never judge a book by its cover, particularly a political memoir.

'Trouble is we don't have a lot of time,' said George. 'Charles is in a hurry for some reason and there's the retirement plan, of course.' He held himself back for a moment before adding, tentatively, 'If we get stuck, I suppose we could manufacture something. Just this once.'

Dot looked at him, horrified.

'I can't believe you said that,' she said. 'We don't do that. We never do that. We expose the truth that's hidden. We state we don't create.'

'Sorry, it's our last job, I –'

'No.'

'Just a thought.'

'Don't even think about it.'

George's mobile rang. Dot gave him a withering look before heading upstairs with the bottle and her glass. George settled on his stool and answered the phone, while refocusing the angle-poise on the glass square.

'Ruby,' he said. 'My little star. You sound fabulous.'

'George, I am always fabulous,' said Ruby Stevens in a husky voice. 'Now what is story?'

'Great news, babe,' he said. 'You're in the *Sunday Mirror* tomorrow. Centre page spread. Big headline: 'My White Hot Nights.' It'll be sensational.' George reached for his wine glass. 'They're using one of your old glamour shots, the one of you as a dominatrix, as well as the casino shots Laura took. And there'll be a profile of you based on your interview. Ruby, you're going to be a star.'

'That's fabulous, George,' said Ruby. 'What about the money?'

'It's already in your account.'

George sensed relief at the other end. Ruby was going to need a lot of money, he knew, to put distance between her and Anton Ledakov. It had taken him a long time to persuade her to spill the beans on Robert White. She and Dot went back a long way, to the time Ruby had first arrived in London, homeless and unemployed, and Dot had given her a start in the escort business. So when he found out White was keeping her as a mistress he knew he had cracked the assignment. Minister has a mistress who happens to be a call-girl, minister gets exposed, call-girl makes money. It should have been straightforward. However, it turned out she was working for Anton Ledakov, kept not for him – he preferred younger western girls – but for acquaintances he wanted to ensnare and ultimately control. White, like several other politicians, was such an acquaintance.

Technically, Ruby was his employee, and the oligarch was unlikely to be pleased at finding himself splashed across the Sunday papers alongside her, even if their true connection was to remain a mystery. George had to negotiate an unusually large fee for Ruby's co-operation, as well as guarantee her all the proceeds of the media coverage that would follow.

'And I've found you an agent,' said George. 'He'll be calling you tomorrow.'

'Why do I want agent, George?' Ruby asked.

'There's an opportunity,' he said. 'Now I know you want to disappear. But there's a lot of interest in you now. There's a new reality show for celebrities. It's called *Escape from Wight.*'

'No, George,' said Ruby. 'I have to lay down.'

'Lay low, I know,' said George. 'But hear me out. I think you'll like it. They've re-done an old holiday camp on the Isle of Wight as a prison, like a World War Two prisoner of war camp. It's all 1940s clothes, guards, food and so on.' There was no sign of protest so he continued. 'They put two teams of celebrities in the camp, one girls one boys, and the first person to escape to the mainland is the winner.' She was still listening. 'It starts filming next week and they want you. They love the double play on Wight. You'll be sensational. It'll make you a star, Ruby. And it's a lot of money.'

'How much?'

'A hundred thousand.' George could feel the cogs turning as the lure of fame and fortune danced before her.

'What about Ledakov? He will be looking for me.'

'I know,' said George. 'Just thought I'd run it past you. Maybe Ledakov will forgive you when you become a star. You'll be even more useful to him if you're a celebrity.'

There was silence at the other end of the phone. George guessed Ruby was coming to the same conclusion. Maybe she could take the money and not have to run.

'And you should be safe in a prison camp,' said George. 'Sometimes hiding in plain sight is the safest place to be.'

'I'll think about it,' she said.

As he hung up, George looked down at the scraps of paper on the plexiglass. He had fiddled with them throughout the call without paying much attention, adding scraps from the bag, the larger pieces, each with an unintelligible fragment of writing, and moving them around, trying to link them. He froze as he saw sense appearing in the pattern. They were all scraps of a certain size and shape. He rifled through the freezer bag for similar fragments and worked for another half-hour, selecting, arranging and discarding pieces of paper until he had a whole letter in front of him. He placed another square of plexiglass over the paper to hold it in place then clipped the two sheets together.

'Sensational,' he sighed, then emptied his glass and rushed up the cellar steps, calling for Dot.

As he strode into the hall, the front door swung open. Laura, Luka and Will stood in the entrance, their clothes and hair smeared white, dust thickening around them as they took turns to stamp their feet on the mat.

'What have you lot been up to?' George asked, temporarily forgetting his errand.

'We brought the house down,' said Laura.

'The roof fell in at the rehearsal studio,' Will explained, slapping his arms. 'Luka did a Roger Daltrey with his mike. Straight through the ceiling.' The group trooped into the house.

'Will's band has a gig,' said Laura.

'For money,' said Will with a click of his fingers. He was in high spirits. 'Blake's Ride. It's a live gig at The Rialto, King's Cross, with a simultaneous web-cast. Everyone watches it. And it's paid.'

'Is that Jack Blake?' George asked and looked at Laura. 'Did you do that?'

'I made a call,' she said with a shrug. He was surprised. The last time he'd heard the music promoter's name was when Laura had slammed into the house, shouted that she'd dumped the narcissistic, megalomaniac prick, and that if he rang would he or Dot please tell him to stab himself.

'Well, good for you,' he said. 'In the meantime I need you two for a job.' George was pointing at Laura and Will and peeled them off as Luka made his way upstairs. Dot came out of the kitchen and looked at the carpet.

'You're leaving footprints,' she shouted up the stairs. 'Take your shoes off.'

'First thing tomorrow,' said George.

'It's Sunday,' Laura protested.

'Double time,' he said. 'You're going to Gloucester. And take your camera.'

'Gloucester?' said Will.

'Gloucester. Now take your shoes off.'

'George, what have you found?' Dot asked as Laura and Will climbed the stairs, footwear in hand.

'We've had a bit of luck,' he said, trying to contain his excitement, and handed her the plexiglass plate. Dot read the letter. It was addressed to Mary Chamberlain from the secretary of the West Gloucestershire Equestrian Society, dated two weeks earlier:

Dear Mrs Chamberlain,

Regretfully, I write to inform you of the judgement of the Management Committee relating to the incident at the Under 16's Junior Show Jumper of the Year competition last month. After an exhaustive enquiry, the Committee has concluded that a serious breach of club rules occurred.

As you know, following your daughter Mariot's success in winning the Junior Show Jumper of the Year title, we received a number of complaints from parents of children who were also competing. Several claimed you were seen feeding ponies on the morning of the event. Asked at the time what you were doing you said you were giving them mints.

A number of the ponies performed well below expectations during the event and several failed to complete the course. In the case of Mrs Brereton's entry, High Jinx, the pony became unsteady very soon after you were seen in the vicinity and was judged unfit to start.

You will recall after these complaints an inspection of your horsebox and car took place, despite your resistance, where a large quantity of the veterinary sedative, acetylpromazine (ACP), was found. Tests taken at the end of the day found traces of ACP in nine ponies, all of whose riders were considered strong contenders for the Junior Show Jumper of the Year title.

The Committee felt it was unable to accept your assertion that the complaints were made by jealous and pushy parents, who could not accept their children's failures, and the complaints are upheld.

The conclusion of the Committee is that the trophy awarded to your daughter will be withdrawn forthwith, your family membership of the club is suspended until further notice and you will be fined £500 for a gross breach of the club rules. We understand the sensitivity of this matter to someone in your position, but feel we have no alternative but to refer the issue to the local police, who may wish to consider further action.

We will be grateful if you would return the rosette and trophy as soon as possible so they can be presented to the rightful winner.

Yours sincerely,

Ellen Wood (Mrs),
Club Secretary.

'She was so furious, she just tore it up,' said George. 'She didn't put it through the shredder.'

9

Holding her camera in the shade of the van, Laura replayed the shots she had taken at the Chamberlains' house. Crisp images of twelve-year-old Mariot and her pony flitted across the screen: a plump girl in pink jodhpurs and hard hat circling a paddock and jumping small fences, her mother in each picture, leaning on a rail or pacing, shouting encouragement. Laura stopped at a shot of Mariot dismounted and holding her pony by the bridle, pouting while her parent looked sternly at a stopwatch. That was the one. The girl was probably excusing herself for some mistimed manoeuvre or complaining at the hardness of the ground, but it fulfilled George's brief: a photograph that would read as spoiled child and ruthlessly competitive mother. Laura switched the camera back to shoot mode. No doubt about it, she worked miracles.

'Get what you need?' Will sang, as he prepared a joint. He was sitting cross-legged under a tree a few feet from the van, a sunburst Telecaster on his lap serving as a rolling table. He picked strands of marijuana from the smooth body of the guitar and placed them carefully in the rolling paper, then cleaned the surface by licking his fingers, dabbing them over the instrument's surface and sucking them; then he got down to the business of rolling the cigarette.

They were parked in a field near the top of a hill on the Cotswold Way, a few miles from Cheltenham, with a view across the Gloucestershire countryside. It was a clear blue morning and the sun was arching towards midday.

'Do you turn everything into a song?' Laura asked, as she looked for a vantage point, considering the light, always the light. 'Being with you must be like living in a musical.'

'*The Rocky Horror Show* would be cool,' he said.

'I was thinking more of *Shrek*.'

She climbed the last few steps to the top of the hill and looked through the viewfinder to the village below. Chocolate-box cottages lay scattered along a main street and clustered around a crossroads, with a pub and shop on one side and a Saxon church on the other, its dishevelled graveyard rising towards them. Bells were sounding the end of morning service. A riding school lay in the foreground screened from the village by trees.

She trailed the lens from Chamberlain's house outside the village to the school, tracing the route the family would take. A chain of ponies and riders trotted into the viewfinder and around a brownish paddock, while another line headed into a large field on a trek. In the stables children, parents and stable hands milled about, saddling up and chatting. Beyond, in the car park, the sun glinted on a sea of SUVs, the ponies' shiny descendants, waiting in their paddock. Laura took a couple of abstract shots to play with later, then pulled back to concentrate on equestrian life.

'Why the sudden interest in horses?' Will asked as he sealed the joint.

'Don't ask me,' replied Laura, as she scanned the school. 'I just take the pictures.'

'Your dad's a case,' said Will.

'He certainly is.' Laura focused on a family group standing in front of a stable feeding apples to a pony.

'And your mum's a force. It's a shame I owe her money. Dad warned me about that.'

'Oh yes?'

'Dot doesn't do debt,' he said. 'Otherwise she's the salt of the earth.'

'I don't think she'd like that,' said Laura. 'She sees herself more as sugar and spice.'

'I don't think she liked Dad much,' said Will. 'You're not like them.'

'We're all in the exposure business.'

'You don't sound like them. You went to a posh school.' The unlit joint was between his lips now. He hunted for a lighter. 'Bendene, I'd say,' he said, producing a Bic. Shazam.

'How do you know that?' she asked, unable to conceal her surprise.

'Perfect pitch.' He tapped his ear knowingly while he inhaled, prolonging her insecurity, then exploded into smoky laughter. 'I don't have perfect pitch. I saw it on an envelope. Bendene Alumni Appeal.' She was impressed he'd found a way into her past.

'I don't know why they send me that stuff,' she said. Will inhaled again and waved the joint at her.

'Want some?' he asked in a voice that came from his forehead. She wavered then walked over and took the cigarette.

'How much do you know about Mum and Dad?' she asked.

'Well, Dad met George in Brixton.'

Laura took a cautious drag.

'I went to a lot of schools,' she said. She returned to the van and leaned against the bonnet, lifting her face towards the sun. 'Something always happened. We ran out of money, or the business went bust. Then the cars went. They had matching Jags for a while, but they disappeared. That's when Dad bought the bike. Then I'd move schools.'

'What happened at Bendene?' Will asked. She took another toke.

'They thought George was on a scientific project in the Andes, then found out he was doing six months for breaking and entering.' She laughed. 'He was spying on a captain of industry from a roof and fell through a skylight. Unfortunately, it was above a jewellery shop. He couldn't say what he was really doing so he went to jail. I guess that's when he met your dad. What was he in for?'

'Nutting a policeman. And resisting arrest. He was on the Grunwick picket line.'

'Union man?'

'He'd say revolutionary.'

'They were good about it at school,' she said. 'It was that sort of place. Then Mum was all over the papers for running a brothel in Bromley. The one where they served tea and cakes, do you remember that?' Will didn't. 'It was popular with the judiciary,' she said. Laura returned the joint. 'Everyone said it was in my best interests to move on. I guess it didn't help that two of the governors were regulars. So, I went to Camberwell Art School, and lived happily ever after.' Laura looked out over the landscape, surprised she had told him so much. They had hardly spoken on the way.

'What about you?' she asked. Will realised it was his turn and it wasn't negotiable. He took a quick hit.

'Simple story. I hated school, found this –' he said, fingering the guitar – 'left school and went on the road.'

'And?'

'Nearly made it, five years ago,' he said. 'We had a following, a manager and a record company. We even had a single.'

'Oh yes?'

'You won't have heard of it. Then we fell apart, before we started, before we even released the song. Usual ego shit. I thought I was the magic ingredient. So did the singer, the drummer and the bass player. The manager said we were the biggest bunch of wankers in the history of the music business. He deleted the master and smashed up our flat with a hedge trimmer. Daytime he was a landscape gardener. I've spent the last five years trying to put it back together. It's not quite rock and roll. Usually you get the success first.' He offered Laura the joint, but she declined.

'I knew you had arsehole qualities,' she said.

'Flawed genius is how I like to put it. No, you're right. We were arseholes.'

'Ever thought of doing something else?'

'Nope,' he said. No trace of defensiveness. She assumed there wasn't anything else he could imagine doing.

'Where did you meet Luka?' she asked.

'Busking in Brac. I was on holiday in Croatia. The rest will be music history.'

'He's good.'

'We're all good.'

Laura looked at him. For a moment the music nerd had disappeared. He had no doubt.

'So Blake's Ride is the next big play?'

'Maybe the last one,' he said. 'Twenty-eight is old in this business.'

He stood up, leaned his guitar against the tree and brushed down his jeans. 'I owe you for that. Big time. How do you know Jack Blake?'

'Let's say I knew him.'

'Ah.'

'What's that mean?'

'Sounds like you knew him, knew him.'

'I knew him. He had arsehole qualities too. You'd better watch him.'

'Why?'

'You'll find out.'

'Seemed OK to me.'

'That's what I thought. You want to do this?'

She could hear the edge in her voice and was annoyed with herself for still feeling angry. She'd only dated the guy for a few weeks and thought she was over it. It had been a familiar story: charmer turns out to be self-obsessed with another girlfriend and maybe a third in tow. The call about the band was to show him he meant nothing to her.

'Well, big thanks with flowers, chocolates and dinner in the West End,' said Will. 'As soon as I can afford them.' He waved in the direction of the stables. 'So, what's all this about?'

'Power,' said Laura.

'Yeah?'

'Power corrupts, and those who want it get it by exposing those who have it. It's the circle of life and Dad is its middleman.' She started to pack her camera. 'Come on,' she said. 'The pub's open. We'll see what we can find out down there. I'm buying. Expenses.'

'Cool. But I still don't get it,' he said.

'Really? OK. Rewind. Remember Chamberlain? The Home Secretary?' Will nodded. 'Well, someone wants to dig up the dirt on him and George has found out his wife has been poisoning ponies so her little angel can win all the prizes at the local gymkhana. It's probably a tiny nail in a big coffin. Anyway, one of the stable-hands at the riding school just slipped off in a car and my guess is he's heading for the pub. So you and I will go down there for a drink and see what we can find out.'

'You really are part of the family business,' Will said. Laura lifted the camera strap onto her shoulder.

'Born into it,' she said. 'When I was a baby I was the beard. Who'd suspect they were being followed by a mum with a shrieking toddler?' They walked to the back of the van and Will opened the doors.

'What about the work?' he asked. 'In your bedroom.'

'What about it? That was art school. This is the real world.'

'You've got talent.'

'A million people have talent. Right now I just want to make a living.'

He left her to fetch his guitar.

'Your call. Everyone pisses away their twenties,' he said, as he returned with the Telecaster. 'It's just that now has a habit of leading to another now. Then one day you're out of nows.'

'That's deep. Is this a morality attack?' she asked. 'Are you worrying about a politician or two? Will, they're narcissistic, lying scum. We're doing the country a service.' It was the first time she'd said his name.

'My dad would like you,' he said. 'All I'm saying is you have a gift. I wouldn't leave it too long.'

He perched on the rear lip of the van and strummed a few chords. The sound was tinny but audible.

'Listen to this,' he said. Laura frowned. 'Indulge me. It's called 'Betcha'. It's for you.' She stood impatiently then awkwardly as he played. The song had a country feel and he sang in a pleasant tenor:

'You should have a song about you,
Bet you'd like a song about you,
It should be a song that's bright but blue.

How you style your hair, how you climb a stair,
How you wear with flair whatever you choose.
How you clearly see all that hides from me
So gifted and free, you're getting to me.

Bet you never lose your power to amuse,

You are a muse and you're capturing me.
You turned my head with something you said;
I can't be led but I'm following you.

Now you have a song about you,
It's a bright blue song about you,
A simple song from me for you.'

Something struck her about the way he held the guitar. It was as if he was suddenly whole, the instrument the missing part of him. His fingers fluttered over its neck, his face relaxed in his gift. He was confident and in control and suddenly athletic. He strummed on, amusing himself until he found a chord on which to end, the last piece of some puzzle.

'What do you think?' he asked.

'Betcha sing that to all the girls,' she said. They placed the guitar and camera bag in the van, shut the rear doors and climbed into the front. Will drove. They said nothing as he manoeuvred out of the field. Laura was unsettled. She found herself wondering whether there was an equation that related talent, time and meaning and if there was, where did spiking politicians' careers fit exactly? She looked at the guitarist, noticing the lightness of his touch on the wheel. How had he done that? For the first time in a long while she was thinking about what she was doing with her life. It was only with the village in sight that she spoke.

'When did you write that?'

'On the way here,' he said, 'and before we started talking.' She nodded. It was as much appreciation as she was going to show, but she saw him smile and knew that he knew he'd reached her. With the minstrel under the balcony thing. He'd won a round at last and the game had moved to another level.

'Come on, Dylan,' she said. 'Put your foot down. It's opening time.'

*

The pub was pretty much as Laura expected. Low beams, white plaster and horse brasses, half a dozen farmers gathered in the bar complaining and flirting with the barmaid while a farmhand gambled on the solitary fruit machine. A dining area was set for lunch but empty. They found a table by an inglenook, its blackened fireplace clotted with brasses, and looked across the pub. The stable-hand was at the bar, laughing with the youngest of the farmers. He was jockey-short and bowlegged, his red face pimpled. Laura guessed he was about twenty.

After a short negotiation Will went up to the bar and stood beside him, as if waiting to order. He nudged the boy and nodded towards Laura.

'That girl wants to talk to you,' he said. 'Can't see why myself.' The stable-hand looked across to Laura, who was smiling coyly.

'Oh yeah?' the boy replied. He was suspicious. 'What's her name?'

'Laura. She's from London,' Will said, emphasising the capital in a way that suggested loose morals and explained the forward approach. The jockey nodded knowingly and winked across the bar at Laura who smiled again.

'City girl, eh?' the stable-hand said and winked lewdly at his mate. There was no point getting picked up unless your mates knew about it.

'What's she want, then?' he asked, though it was obvious he was already considering all manner of delights, most of them taking place in a hayrick or the back of his ancient Fiat.

'You'd better go ask,' said Will. 'She's drinking cider. And mine's a pint of lager.'

'Where are you in all this then?' asked the stable-hand. 'You're not one of those city couples down here for the dogging?'

'I'm the gay cousin,' Will replied. 'But don't worry, you're not my type.'

The stable-hand ordered drinks and Will helped carry them to the table. The boy sat across from Laura with a leer. Will sat next to him.

'What's your name?' Laura asked.

'Billy Sinclair.'

'Well, Billy Sinclair,' she said, 'I don't remotely fancy you and if you try anything you'll find a pint of cider all over your bollocks, which will make you look a complete prat in front of your mates. This is about money. I want some information and I'll pay you for it.' Billy looked at Will.

'You said...'

'Women,' said Will, lifting his pint and angling it in a toast. 'Fickle or what?'

'How much do you make at the school, Billy?' Laura asked.

'Minimum wage.'

'That's what I thought. In this envelope is a month's pay. I want everything you know about Mrs Chamberlain and little Mariot.'

'Are you from the papers?' he asked.

'Indirectly.'

'It'll cost you a grand.'

'That's right.' Laura tapped the envelope. 'If it's worth it. Now, tell us a story.'

'Cool,' said Will, with another tip of the glass, this time in Laura's direction. 'You're good at this.' He picked up a menu and studied it while the stable-hand squirmed under Laura's interrogation.

'Do our expenses stretch to roast beef and Yorkshire pudding?' Will asked.

10

Charles Franklin chuckled as he viewed the Sunday papers arranged on the magnificent mahogany table in his equally impressive study, the Jacobean library of one of Northamptonshire's more notable houses, commandeered for his use since the death of his father-in-law.

He felt an exquisite pleasure in seeing his handiwork dominating the news. He had scanned the papers before lunch, but could not resist returning to his success, his ego fired by a Sunday roast and the best part of a St Emilion Grand Cru. Coffee in hand he wandered the length of the table soaking in the headlines and slowly turning pages. He could find it all on the web but there was no substitute for seeing a story in print, feeling it between the fingers, caressing it until the ink left smudges on his fingertips. And this was huge success. Pilloried and punned upon, Robert White was as infamous today as he was ever likely to be.

The red tops were having a field day, declaring 'A White Old Scam', 'White's Big Night' and 'White Up Against It'; the quality papers raised their eyebrows over 'City Minister's Big Gamble' and 'Minister Expected to Resign Over Russian Favours'. Best, as planned, was the *Sunday Mirror*, which promised five full pages of in-depth and exclusive exposure: 'White's Russian – Cities Minister Goes To Town'.

The five pages began with the picture of White, Ruby and Ledakov at the roulette table above an article detailing the latest in Westminster debauchery. A whole page was given to White's shady relationship with Ledakov and his intervention in the planning application for the oligarch's Mayfair mansion, complete with floor plans, security features and an artist's impression of its sumptuous interiors. The oligarch's murky rise to power was documented together with his flight from Moscow to a cushion of property in London and a place in *The Sunday Times* Rich List.

The centre pages were dedicated to Ruby, who was spread diagonally across the paper, smiling in fetish gear, under the headline, 'My White Hot Nights'. She chatted happily about her penniless beginnings in Tallinn and hopes for a showbiz future along the lines of the Cheeky Girls, and spoke affectionately of the minister, his robust performance and penchant for wearing her underwear to briefings at Number 10. At the bottom of the page, ashen-faced, White was pictured being muscled into a car amid a crowd of reporters. The success was as impressive for what was not reported. There was no mention of the unfortunate scuffle at the book launch and even WIT had been persuaded to abandon its carping. Charles Franklin was truly the master of his universe.

He picked up another red top, *The Sunday People*, which led with another expose: "Wife's A Witch' Claims Former Rock God.' Pictures of Hammond Marshall and his wife in happier days, with two Elvises at their Las Vegas wedding, were juxtaposed with images of amulets and mugwort and the receipt from the Westbourne Wicca Emporium. The proprietor of the Emporium was featured in a suitably macabre outfit, proudly confirming Marshall's wife as a regular customer and highly experienced caster of spells. Marshall was interviewed and spoke of his concern for his children's wellbeing. Beneath, a young man from Domino's Pizza was pictured ringing the doorbell at the London house above the caption, 'What a Load of Warlocks!' Charles was particularly proud of this piece as he had personally arranged the interviews, staged the pizza shot and negotiated the exclusive, knocking a transvestite rugby international off the front page. Charles' smile widened as he flicked past a picture of the Prime Minister in training for a charity triathlon to find promotions for Clos d'Amonceler and glowing reviews of Eleanor Porter's book on Africa. His mastery of the media was complete. He was a god. His staff only knew the half of it; while they sweated to pepper the papers with people and products, none were aware of just how profound and dark was his power. He caught sight of himself in the glass of a locked bookcase where the rare editions were kept.

'Handsome as David and a genius,' he sighed. He felt as potent and special as the most precious folio. He drained the last of the coffee and looked around the vast room, finding his surroundings a fitting backdrop to the scale of his achievement and certain his time was coming and coming quickly. The fact that these surroundings were not his own did not rankle as it once had. They might as well be. He looked up at the portrait of Melissa's father, stony-faced above the granite fireplace.

'See, you old buzzard? I told you I had a brilliant future.' Charles opened a cigar box at the end of the table, took out a Cohiba, clipped and lit it and blew smoke up at the old man. They'd never seen eye to eye.

Melissa's father was almost the last of a faltering line of lesser nobility stretching back to James I. His ancestor, Henry Ashbee, was an adventurer who distinguished himself in a minor war in the Low Countries, then set sail as a privateer, arriving in Northamptonshire with a modest fortune hewn from slavery and sugar; this he shrewdly invested in wool and later leather, and, sealing his success, purchased the house and a baronetcy from the king. Since then, scions of the boot and shoe industry, the family had shod the armies of England for every engagement until the industry's decline in the 1960s. Now the estate had dwindled to the house, three hundred acres and a bank balance padded by land sales, all of which Melissa had inherited on her father's demise.

Her father, the 15th baronet, also Henry Ashbee, considered himself shrewd as his forbears and judged Charles Franklin a chancer from the moment he set eyes on him. He vowed to protect his too-trusting daughter from the slick suitor with the Simon Le Bon haircut, convinced this could not be a love or even lust match. He saw an ambitious social climber, the product of a minor public school that educated the progeny of farmers, a jumped up oik whose father ran the Post Office. The idea of him as a son-in-law was unthinkable. True, the first baronet had been a slick opportunist, but the fifteenth holder of the title wasn't going to hand everything on a plate to another one.

Even when he chanced upon them in a field one night, in the back of Melissa's Metro, and it was clear that lust was playing its part in the relationship, he was not swayed; in fact his resolve deepened.

Despite protests, threats and bribes the relationship continued, but his opinion of Charles never changed and had no reason to do so, as the young man flunked his economics degree, blagged his way into, and out of, a short career in the City and finally tumbled into PR – in the baronet's mind, a flea on the back of another flea sucking the blood of real people and their endeavours. Eventually a marriage took place in the village church among Melissa's ancestors and at the reception, emboldened by a bottle of Moët, Charles asked the old man for a loan to start his own business, which the baronet provided at an extortionate rate of interest, the better to keep the chancer on a tight rein. Even the appearance of an heir did nothing to mellow the old man's opinion and before he died he set up a trust to ensure Charles could not get his hands on a penny. Everything would pass to Melissa for life and then to her eldest son, the 16th baronet. If she signed away any of her rights she would lose the lot. Charles would be limited to what he could beg or borrow from his wife's significant, but not unlimited, income. The baronet's last act was to transfer the loan to his most inflexible business associate, ensuring the chancer would remain under pressure. So the old buzzard was able to die with a smile on his face before he was loaded into the crypt of the same church alongside his forbears.

Charles looked up at the portrait. One day you'll be up in the attic, you old goat, he thought, and my portrait will be up there. Everyone will assume I own it all and that's all I need. Perception is reality.

He walked over to his desk, another vast antique that faced into the room, with a reassuring view of the door so he could never be surprised. A huge bay window behind him overlooked lawns that rolled away to a lake and folly. When he needed inspiration he could look inwards to learning or swivel round and gaze upon nature; but mostly he drew all he needed from the thought of how impressive he must seem to the guests he occasionally invited to his inner sanctum. Yes, even a Prime Minister would be at home here. And maybe that was something for the future; and later perhaps, there would be something a little more impressive than a baronetcy – after he and Sir Frank Porter had taken Eleanor to the top, having crushed all who stood in their way. For now he would celebrate the day's successes.

He popped up the email he had been working on earlier. It was a note to the pretty redhead at the graduate induction. It was only two lines, but he wanted to get it right; something simple that would convey his intent, but could be read, if forwarded to others, as innocent. He tapped the keyboard.

'Hi. Great contribution to the Clos d'Amonceler launch, I'd like a personal update on the results. Contact my PA and she'll fix a time. Best. CF.' That time would turn out to be lunch at Soho House and he'd take it from there. Excellent.

His finger hovered over the mouse and a split second before online adultery was initiated the door to the study opened. In the time it took Melissa to pop her head round and ask if he had a moment, Charles deleted the email and shut down five windows on his screen including a review of the new Maserati, a game involving a helicopter gunship and Afghan terrorist camps and three porn sites specialising in celebrity lookalikes, strangers on trains and pursuits with fruit. He put on a tired frown.

'I'm really busy, Mel. I need to watch Eleanor's piece on the Andrew Marr show,' he said, but seeing the desperate look on his wife's face he switched to an accommodating smile. 'But come on in.'

Melissa walked uncertainly towards the desk, looking from Charles to the window behind him. He turned to see their two sons playing on the lawn. Their game involved the 16th baronet staggering about like a monster while his younger brother darted, rolled and cartwheeled around him as they exchanged laser shots. With each blast the monster shuddered and approximated a piece of his body being mutilated or vaporised and then repairing itself, while his adversary seemed to skilfully avoid being hit. They'd watched *Terminator* on DVD the previous evening, a treat on the last night of their exeat. Charles judged they would be fine as long as they had weapons and kept some distance from each other. The trouble would start when they discarded the plastic guns and moved to hand-to-hand combat; this would be to the death and require Melissa's intervention. Charles judged their meeting, whatever it was about, would last no more than five minutes. He pushed his chair back and offered his wife the wide white-toothed smile that never failed to charm.

'You are looking great, Mel,' he said. 'I meant to say at lunch. How's the bruising?'

'Oh, fine, it's nearly gone,' she replied.

'That's tremendous. You must feel so much better.'

'Yes, I suppose I do,' she said, as if surprised.

'I mean better than before,' he said. 'With all that weight gone, it must be so much better on your heart. Do you have more energy? You look fabulous.' She looked at him nervously.

'I do feel better, I really do,' she said. 'And I know I look better. But Charles, that's what I wanted to talk to you about. I don't want to go back into hospital.'

Charles sighed. He was used to her lapses of faith. Counselling mode was required.

'I see,' he said. 'Why is that, darling?'

'It's too soon. And I don't think I want any more.'

'That's OK,' he said. 'Don't worry.' He glanced out of the window then turned back to his wife. 'But why, Mel? You're looking so attractive.' He resisted adding 'again'. That would be incendiary, leading to a crisis of confidence and an excruciating and emotional discussion about the nature and depth of his affection, which in turn would require painstaking reassurances over several days or even weeks. But it was the truth, as far as he could see. She'd been a good-looking girl and an attractive enough woman, sexy in a naïve and uncomplicated way, certainly possessed of boundless enthusiasm, but she'd let herself go completely after the boys were born, stuffed herself with chocolates and cakes until she had ballooned, reaching the point where she had to wear dresses like tents that could house a family of asylum seekers. Then she'd say, 'Does my bum look big in this?' and expect him to tell her she was a waif when her arse looked like the back of a tractor, whether she covered it in chiffon or a tarpaulin. He would never understand women. Did they want to be beautiful or just be told they were?

'You're nervous, darling,' he said, soothingly. 'It's only butterflies in your tummy.'

'I don't have a tummy anymore,' she said with a half-hearted smile. And this was largely true, as not only had substantial quantities of subcutaneous fat been sucked from Melissa's midriff, but her stomach had been stapled to ensure it would never expand again.

'I know. Isn't it fabulous?' Charles said, with enthusiasm he hoped would be infectious. She remained downcast.

'I feel so...poked about. And people in the village don't recognise me.'

'They will when they get used to you.'

'And men are looking at me.' She raised her eyebrows. 'Scaffolders. And the vicar.'

'Really?' It was Charles' turn to arch an eyebrow. 'He must be ninety. But that's great, isn't it?'

'I don't know,' said Melissa. 'I don't think I want all that again, Charles. I'm a mum. And I'm forty-five. And the women don't like it at all. They're calling me Mrs F behind my back. For Frankenstein.' Better than Forklift, he thought. Then again, it could be for Franklin.

'Don't worry about them,' he said with a dismissive wave. 'They're jealous. They'd all do it if they could. Mel, it's one last procedure – and then you'll be back to your old self. But even better.' And Paris would have his Helen, he thought. After all, what was the point of possessing irresistible good looks unless you were partnered with equal beauty; it let the side down. It certainly meant they would never be featured in *Hello* magazine as a golden couple. Worse, until recently he'd been at risk of being caught in the company of a farm vehicle, which was no help to the sleek public image he was creating. They could pass muster now, but they needed to be ready to stand with the A list. His time was coming and when it came, both would be noticed.

'That's the other thing, Charles,' Melissa continued. Her whining was beginning to annoy him. 'It's three procedures: eye-lift, face-lift and rhinoplasty. Multiple procedures can be risky. All sorts of things can happen, like facial paralysis.' Charles wondered how long this was going to take.

'Stephen Oliver is the finest cosmetic surgeon in the country,' he said. 'He says it's fine. Are you practising the neck elevations?'

'Yes.' Mel arched her neck, which gave her a Victorian look of disdain which Charles did not find entirely unappealing.

'And you're applying the ice?' he asked.

'Yes. The fridge is full of icepacks. But Charles, I like my nose.'

'So do I, Mel. But you can have a better one,' he said. 'Don't you like the one I picked for you?'

'It's lovely,' she said. 'But it's not mine. I have Daddy's nose.' She nodded towards the picture.

'And that was fine for Daddy,' said Charles. 'But you deserve a beautiful nose. Mel, it's just nerves.'

'Charles, I don't think I have any nerves left – they've all been trimmed, cut or numbed with something. What if I get cold on the table?' she asked, fear flashing across her face.

'I thought you wanted this,' he said, his good humour beginning to slip.

'I don't know what I want right now,' she replied, tears welling in her eyes. 'I think *you* wanted it, Charles. I am better for it, I know. But I've had breast implants, liposuction, a tummy tuck and a bottom lift. I defy gravity, but I'm beginning to feel I'm not me. All I wanted was for us to grow old together, not younger.'

Charles tensed, knowing Melissa was close to bringing up all the other things he had wanted but promised she would enjoy too – the Aston Martin, the condominium in St Bart's, the large pink vibrator; all of which had their moments, she would admit, but it was always what he wanted and her going along with it. Except the boys, of course. They were her idea. Fortunately, this line of argument was avoided when she noticed her sons were now engaged in unarmed combat on the lawn. Presently the Terminator had the upper hand over his younger brother, who was squirming in a half nelson.

'Mel, we can do both,' Charles said, frustrated that she didn't get it. 'We are the lucky ones. We can have it all.'

'Don't you love me the way I am?' she asked. 'And the way we were?'

'Of course,' he said. 'But we can be more, Mel. Don't you see? We have the power to design our lives.'

She looked at him through tears.

'Sometimes I wonder if you ever loved me, Charles,' she said. 'Was Daddy right? Was it always the money?'

Charles closed his eyes. This was the killer blow, the danger zone and he always backed off. He rose from his chair to enfold her in a hug.

'Of course I love you, Mel,' he said. 'You are always beautiful to me. And this is the last time. The cherry on top of the cake. I thought it would make you...OK, both of us...happier. But it was always about you.' His hand stroked away her tears. 'But don't do it. If you aren't sure, you shouldn't do it. I shouldn't have pushed you. I just want us to be the best we can possibly be. Together. I'm sorry. I love you, Mel.'

He felt her melt into his arms and looked into her eyes with as much devotion as he could muster.

'Remember the sun,' he whispered. Melissa looked back at him with a dreamy expression. He relaxed. He was back in control now and pretty sure he knew what was going through her mind. She would be remembering the boy she met at the Young Farmers' dance, the new romantic with the Duran Duran look and the best-looking boy there. And 'Hungry Like The Wolf'. That was the night they merged their big hair and danced to Nik Kershaw singing 'I Won't Let The Sun Go Down On Me' and they vowed they wouldn't. Later they had fumbled in his father's car while Queen played 'I Want To Break Free'.

Charles' own thoughts followed a different path. He was envying those men who traded in their wives when they got past their sell-by date. Apart from Hammond Marshall, of course, he'd made a bad call and it would cost him millions. But Charles couldn't do that. Those men had money so they called the shots even if the price was high. In his case Melissa had the cash. He had debt, thanks to her father. The only thing he could get his hands on was a portion of her income. Divorce was out of the question, he counted on her largesse, so the best he could do was arrange an overhaul.

Melissa was still warm in his arms.

'I think it's just nerves, Charles,' she said, tearfully. 'And I don't want to disappoint you. I'll do it.'

'It has to be your decision, darling, something you want. It has to be for you.'

'I want to do it,' she said, firmly.

'Are you sure?' he asked, holding her for a moment longer. 'That's great. I'll come with you. And later, when you've recovered, we can go shopping for a whole new wardrobe.' They would trawl Knightsbridge with her credit cards and create a consort fit for a media king – and a photo shoot. 'You won't regret it, Mel,' said Charles. 'We are going to be fabulous. Trust me.'

'I have to go,' said Melissa, blowing her nose. Charles followed her gaze, which had shifted to the garden. The Terminator, aka the 16th baronet, was lying vanquished and crying while his younger brother sat on his chest and punched his face. A referee was required urgently or their eldest son would also be having plastic surgery. Melissa left the room hurriedly.

Charles shook his head. Marriage was a bizarre institution. He saw things simply. In every couple one was better-looking, more loved, and the leader. And in their case it was him. He had the vision, knew where they were going and how to get there, he was the motivator and navigator. Mel's role was to support him through the journey, with love and money, an icon of wifedom and maternity. Was it wrong for him to expect the body of a model as well?

He wheeled his chair to the desk and brought up BBC iPlayer and the morning's *Andrew Marr Show*. He sat back to watch Eleanor Porter review the papers and chat through the issues of the day. Now here was an absolute beauty, with grace, symmetry and wit; the camera loved her whether she was talking about her book ('Africa is the new frontier'); climate change ('As a mother I feel a responsibility for our children's future'); her career ('It was time to change more than my clothes'); or neatly sidestepping probes into Robert White's nocturnal ramblings, Ken Chamberlain's row with the Prime Minister and rumours of her own promotion. Charles marvelled at how well she took a brief and produced soundbites that seemed spontaneous. He revelled as his words tripped from her tongue. Pushed one last time on her own prospects, she answered, 'I'd be honoured to serve in government, should I be asked.'

It was a tour de force and Andrew Marr, along with millions of viewers, was spellbound. Clearly *her* time was also coming. Charles looked up at the old man above the fireplace. He picked up the Cohiba from an ashtray and relit it.

'Well, you old buzzard,' he said. 'If I'm a parasite I'm living off something infinitely bigger than a flea.'

11

George was parked by the kerb; a thermos on the dashboard, a bacon sandwich in his hands and a copy of *The Sun* propped on the steering wheel. To a casual observer he was just another van driver, loafing at the start of the working day, part of the morning ritual that passed for rush hour in Gloucester's city centre. It would take a brush with the bonnet for someone to notice the engine was still hot from a long drive and peg him as a stranger. He bit into the sandwich, teeth sliding through crusty white bread into a fusion of butter and bacon fat, then sinking into pork and a satisfying shot of salt. He could never be Jewish, he thought. Nor Muslim. There had to be pigs in Paradise.

Unlike other white van men, who bragged about what they would do if they met a Page Three girl, George had met and made one or two in his time, though strictly in a commercial sense. He looked down at the paper. Ruby Stevens smiled back, naked apart from a pair of impossibly large red earrings, above the caption 'Rubilicious! Wot A Pair!' He read the bawling copy beneath:

Exotic beauty Ruby Stevens has dumped knicker-wearing minister Robert White to appear on Escape from Wight, *the new reality show where showbiz celebrities pit their wits to escape everyone's favourite holiday island. Ruby, who hails from Estonia, will join a group rumoured to include a comedian, a football coach, a former girl-band star and a yet to be named politician. The Sun says, Good luck Ruby, who wants to be bigger than the Cheeky Girls, we know you'll sparkle.*

George turned on the radio. A newscaster was announcing a reshuffle.

Robert White had resigned to avoid further embarrassment to the government while he cleared his name and Eleanor Porter was appointed Cities Minister in his place. Surprisingly, the ministry was transferred to the Cabinet Office due to the urgent need to revitalise urban economies across Britain. This meant Eleanor Porter reported directly to the Prime Minister.

A studio interview with the Home Secretary followed. Ken Chamberlain applauded White for doing the right thing and welcomed Eleanor enthusiastically, as a gifted and spirited politician, quite apart from, and perhaps in spite of her international celebrity. The interviewer went on the attack, asking if Westminster could ever be free of scandal and if a career in politics was simply a fast track for the greedy or hedonistic. Interviewer and interviewee jousted with animal metaphors. Chamberlain met 'pigs at the trough' with 'bleating about a few fat cats'. He countered accusations that Parliament had 'gone ape and was making a monkey out of the electorate' with recognition that Westminster was indeed 'in the doghouse', but must avoid 'scapegoats or sacrificial lambs'. The government was 'taking the bull by the horns', he promised, and would not 'weasel out of its obligations', unlike the previous administration which he sideswiped as 'riddled with vermin and dinosaurs' who had 'pulled the wool over everyone's eyes'.

Beaten and bored, the interviewer changed tack to the row between Chamberlain and the Prime Minister, asking if there was a schism within the party. They circled each other for another minute as Chamberlain claimed there was little separating him and the PM and they remained the closest of colleagues and friends. As the interview came to an end he added that he had no doubts about the Premier's health and would like to put an end to any speculation about his fondness for Lagavulin sixteen-year-old malt.

George switched off the radio. He had watched the building for fifteen minutes and judged it safe. He balled the wrapping from his sandwich and dropped it onto the passenger seat before checking his mirrors and slipping across the road, whistling, to the three-storey house opposite. With white-van swagger he collected the bins from the side, emptied them in the back of the van and drove away.

He was glad not to have the boys with him, even if it had meant an extra trip. Training was a slow process and sometimes it was easier to do the job yourself. Besides, Will was proving curious and George didn't want him joining the dots on this particular job. Instead, he and Luka were learning the intricacies of surveillance, keeping an eye on Hammond Marshall's wife, watching for warlocks and pizza deliveries. George expected little from the exercise as the house would be surrounded by paparazzi along with a handful of irritable newsmen chastised by their editors for missing the scoop and sent to capture or create its next twist. Marshall's wife would give them something, he felt sure, a dash down to the shops perhaps, though witchcraft aside he couldn't imagine how she would conjure an iconic symbol of martyrdom. George thought of the image of Princess Diana in a pale blue swimsuit, sitting on a diving board against a Mediterranean sky, head low and melancholy. Now she knew a thing or two about the image business. In any event it was good for the boys; it would keep them occupied and they might pick up a trick or two.

As he drove back to London, George returned to the notion that had come to him in the middle of the previous night. He often had his best ideas in the early hours, as he woke to exercise his bladder, or drifted back to sleep afterwards. But this was so powerful it had woken him, a dream exploding into consciousness, and after staring into the dark for a few minutes, listening to Dot snoring, he had slipped out of bed and down to the cellar to make notes. Only then did he visit the bathroom and return to bed, by which time Dot had turned on her side, her bricklayer's snore mellowed into an endearing wheeze.

Now he considered if the idea stood up in the light of day, whether the fancy could become reality, and if it could, would it work out as he imagined? It still wasn't fully formed; just a collection of images, of dramatic actions and their effects, but it was bold and promised a lucrative and spectacular end to his career. There was even an element of redemption. It would make a grand finale. And didn't he deserve as much, after twenty years of endeavour? There were no awards in his line of work. No Oscars or medals. Yet wasn't he as important a part of the image industry as anyone else? Perhaps he could leave a story of legendary achievement, one that might live on, to be whispered reverently among his peers and those who came after.

There was one fly in the ointment. Dot was not going to like it. There were risks and the legality was questionable. It also stretched their credo of providing a service that simply unveiled the hidden truth. Dot did not stand for nonsense and could smell manipulation a mile away. He decided not to tell her until he'd worked it through thoroughly, both execution and justification. But George could tell, by the knot in his stomach – this was an idea that had survived the daylight. It gave him purpose, changing a task into what his management books called a Big Hairy Audacious Goal.

As he reached London he needed a toilet and pulled into a pub car park. The pub was open but empty, offering an all-day breakfast to supplement the declining returns of roadside alcohol. He ordered a coffee and went to the Gents. When he returned he found two regulars on stools at the bar, waiting to be served, patient in the knowledge that pints bought with a pension must last. They were discussing the grainy picture flickering on the TV set above the bar.

'It's in black and white deliberately,' said the older of the two. 'That's the point. It's supposed to be like a prisoner of war camp in World War Two. Like one of those old films with Kenneth More. Now the huts,' he said pointing at the screen as a camera panned across the camp, 'that one is for the girls' team, that one's for the boys and the small one is the punishment hut.'

George took a seat at a table, intent on thinking through his idea, but he was drawn to the two men at the bar.

'They're dressed in 1940s uniforms, see,' said the old man. 'And the guards are German soldiers with splatter guns. In the German version they're using Russians.'

'So what's the point?' asked his companion.

'It's a race to see who can get to the mainland first. They've got to escape from the camp, get across the island undetected and then cross the Solent to Portsmouth. First one back gets the prize. If a group make it together they share it. Now, hidden in the camp are two tunnels that are nearly finished, a glider and a set of wire-cutters. And civilian clothes.' The old man rapped on the counter. Patience only went so far, even on a pension. 'Now the great bit,' he continued, 'is that the islanders win cash prizes if they capture the escapees before they get home. Get it?' George smiled as the scene on the television changed to the interior of one of the huts, where several women in uniform were huddled around an old stove. One of them was Ruby Stevens. 'That's the Women's Escape Committee,' said the old man. 'They've found the tunnels.'

*

George was deep in thought as he lugged two bin bags past empty packing crates in the hall and down to the cellar, where he found Dot perched at his desk. They exchanged a nod as he dragged the bags past her.

'Bins from Chamberlain's constituency office,' he said. 'We can test for misuse.' He slid the two bags into place by the bench. 'Like that woman who used her staff to run her plumbing business, then applied for government grants.' He lifted one bag onto the bench and opened it at the neck before he noticed the look on Dot's face. 'Have you found something, my love?' he asked.

'I think so. I went through the shredded stuff again, from the London house.' Dot held up a scrap of paper with a pair of tweezers. 'I found this.' George put on his glasses. It was part of an internet address: ROWMAR.NL

'I ran through a few possibilities.' She tapped the keyboard in front of her and up came a website – GROWMAR.NL. 'It's a Dutch site that specialises in growing marijuana, they sell teach-yourself books and equipment and host a forum on gardening tips.'

'Dot, you're a marvel.'

'Then I looked at their house on Google Earth,' she said. She tapped again and a satellite image popped up. She zoomed down as far as she could to a picture of the Chamberlains' house and gardens. 'See? A big attic, probably a cellar and greenhouses; plenty of places to grow it.'

'It's the son,' said George.

'We could be lucky, but you're probably right,' she said. 'That would give us a mother who dopes ponies and a son who grows dope.'

'It's not enough,' said George. He sat on a stool and they were quiet for some time, thinking through the possibilities. He enjoyed the moments when they worked together, applying their individual minds to a common challenge. George's concentration usually broke first; this time his thoughts strayed as he noticed the way his wife's bottom splayed over the stool.

'Keep your mind on the job, George,' said Dot, knowingly.

'We might as well take a closer look,' he replied, attempting to cover his lapse. 'We've got nothing else.'

'We'll have to be careful,' said Dot, stretching and massaging her back. 'They saw us at the party.'

'We'll think of something.'

'And you're right. It won't be enough,' said Dot. 'We're going to have to dig deeper, go further back. There's usually something in the early years and then they spend the rest of their careers covering it up. There will be something.' Dot climbed off the stool and George felt his sap rise again.

'Tea?' she asked.

'That'll be lovely,' he replied. 'I'll start on this bag.' He placed a large aluminium tray on the bench beside the bag from the constituency office and avoided watching Dot mount the stairs as he filled the tray. Maybe later, he thought, as he pulled on a pair of surgical gloves.

It looked like litter from wastepaper baskets: envelopes, failed drafts of a press release, a broken pen, the occasional sandwich wrapper and scrunched coffee cups. George began to sift through the rubbish but found it difficult to concentrate, as his mind wandered first to Dot's ample charms, then to his grand design and finally to an image of Dot and himself having breakfast on their terrace in Spain, looking out to sea, a smile of satisfaction on his face as he poured champagne into two flutes half filled with fresh orange juice. He imagined that at the same time, somewhere in a London suburb, an old pro would be sitting in a white van as it rained outside, saying to his young apprentice, 'Ah, my boy, but this is nothing compared to the exploits of the great George Valentine.'

12

'Breakfast,' said Laura. She held up a brown paper bag speckled with grease. 'Pain au chocolat or croissant?'

Bleary-eyed, Will slid open the door and stood aside. He was barefoot, wearing only a pair of black jeans. She hadn't expected that. She noticed his stomach was flat and tanned then walked past him, through the kitchenette into the living room and drew the curtains, flooding it with sunlight. Will flinched.

'What's the time?' he asked.

'Eight. And it's Tuesday. You're late.' She glanced around the room, taking in the tangled blanket on the sofa, the clothes and bottles strewn across the floor and the table with its ashtray and container of half-eaten chow mein, noodles spilling over its edges like miniature vines.

'Do you have coffee?' she asked. Will pointed in the direction of the kitchenette. 'Do something with that,' she added, looking at the table. She followed Will's finger towards the kettle, leaving him to scoop the rubbish into the waste paper bin.

'What's up?' Will called. She imagined him grabbing a T-shirt and smelling his armpits before putting it on, then picking up his socks from the floor and slipping them under a cushion.

'Dad wants us to post a letter,' she said. 'Deliver it, actually. I thought we'd take the bike.' She popped her head round the doorway and caught him holding a pair of grey underpants, which he hid behind his back. Why were boys orang-utans, she wondered, even the good-looking ones?

'The fridge is empty,' she said.

'Yes.'

She shrugged. 'Black is good. Is it just us?'

'Luka,' Will yelled, one hand still behind his back. There was no answer. 'Must have gone for a run.'

'Good of you to let him have the bed.' She smiled. 'Unless of course...you two?'

Will waved in the direction of the laptop.

'Oh, no. No. We were recording and he crashed before I was done. It was easier to let him have the bed.'

'This place is a tip,' she said. Aside from the bottles and bedding the room was littered with the detritus of electric music, the furnishings were moth-eaten and the desk by the window on its last legs, all of it set within faded mushroom walls that sprouted from a threadbare carpet. Laura disappeared again, leaving him folding a blanket and secreting his underpants inside.

'I didn't know you were coming,' he said.

'I blame Mum and Dad,' Laura called, 'they should have repainted years ago.'

'Waiting for me to go, I expect,' Will said.

'They're trying to sell the place. If it was me I'd paint over you.'

'Cool,' he replied. That adjective again. He lost points for that one.

Laura was soon organised. She found and wiped a tray, arranged pain au chocolat and croissants on clean plates and poured coffee into mugs. She carried the breakfast into the living room and set it on the table.

'Tra-la!' she said, with a flourish. She turned the desk chair to face the table and sat down. Will sat on the couch opposite. Each chose a flaky pastry.

'On the way back I'll take some shots of you,' she said, looking at him closely. 'Dad won't mind. He's got Luka.'

She picked at her croissant and dusted off the flakes that flecked her jeans.

'So,' she said.

'So,' he shrugged. She waited and wiped a flake from her mouth. Boys were so slow. When would he realise? She'd made the decision. It was time to try again and he was her choice. He was tall enough, good-looking and she sensed he had promise. He was also available if a little too convenient. She wondered how he would kiss. She'd known a sink plunger or two in her time, but his lips looked soft and his manner was gentle. But you could never tell. It depended on what crazy ideas had been planted in his head by early girlfriends, idiot mates, parents or porn.

'I went out last night,' she said.

'Yeah? How was it?'

'Fabulous. But that's Blake. He only does fabulous: flunkies opening doors, celebrities, TV people. We went to the Groucho. He loves famous people shaking his hand.'

'Ah-ha.'

'What's that mean?'

'What?'

'Ah-ha.' She wiped another flake of pastry from her lips and wondered how else she could flirt with a croissant.

'Nothing,' said Will. 'I stayed in. Thought I'd search the sofa for coins.'

'Any luck?' Laura blew on her coffee.

'No. You?'

'What do you mean?'

'I thought you didn't like him,' said Will.

'I don't. But there's no such thing as a free lunch. You get a gig. I had to have dinner. No big deal. It was a good dinner.'

'Good,' he said. 'Great.'

'So you wouldn't be upset if I said we went back to his place and fucked our brains out?'

'Ah-ha.'

'There you go again.'

'I'm sure that would have been invigorating,' he said. 'If you had.'

'Good.' She wiped her hands together above the plate and stood up. 'Great. Come on, let's go. I need my bag. Get yourself together and I'll meet you outside.'

*

She was waiting for him by the gate with a spare helmet. Hers was the sleek racing model while his looked like something from World War Two.

She thrust her rucksack into his hands and mounted the bike. 'Put that on,' she said. 'And be careful, my camera's inside.' She kicked the bike into life while Will struggled into the pack and straddled the seat behind her. He tapped her helmet and she cocked her head back to hear him above the engine.

'Why does George want us both to go?' he shouted.

'He doesn't. I want to try this with someone on the back.'

'Ah-ha,' Will said, this time to himself.

'Pick your feet up.' She twisted the throttle and the Triumph rolled into the street.

Laura rode well, compensating for the additional load as she threaded her way through the traffic. They took the South Circular to Clapham then on through Wandsworth. She could feel him sitting snug behind her. He was a good fit apart from the occasional panic when she crossed a red light or weaved among giant trucks. She wondered if he was jealous. He hadn't met Jack Blake yet; his band was hardly on the guy's radar screen. Laura had made a call and Blake had listened to a demo. She hoped he was a little jealous. Maybe it would spark him into action.

They reached Wimbledon with its tree-lined streets and high-walled gardens. Laura pulled up outside a large house set behind a brick wall.

'This is where we came for the bins,' Will hissed, trying to jam his helmet further down around his head. She nodded.

'It's Ken Chamberlain's place. Wait here.' She took an envelope from inside her jacket and trotted up to a tall iron gate. A man in a dark suit met her before she could ring the bell. She handed him the letter and felt him watching as she returned to the bike. Will hunched down on the seat as she re-mounted.

'They're probably filming us,' he said. 'What are we doing?'

'Posting a letter.'

'What's in it?'

'I don't want to know,' she said. 'Let's go take pictures.' The man was still watching as she kick-started the bike, then he turned and walked up the gravel drive, tapping the envelope against his thigh.

They rode into Wandsworth High Street and parked in an alley. Emerging onto the street Laura selected a shop with an invitation scrawled across its plate glass window: 'Amazing Sale – Big Deals Inside'. She pushed Will towards it and pulled her camera from the rucksack.

'Could be the title of your next album,' she suggested. She moved close to him and levelled the camera. 'So, what kind of hero are you, Will Sharp?' The shutter clicked.

'Hero?'

'Teenage girls want a hero,' she said, 'so what's it to be? Poet, pirate or prince? You can be a bad boy, so long as they feel they can change you. So?'

'Urban rebel?' he suggested. The shutter closed.

'With or without a cause?'

'Like world peace, you mean?'

'Without, then.'

'I'm against hunger.'

'Yours,' she said. 'OK. Let's try it. Sit on the kerb and look bleak.' Will squatted and did his best to look moody. Laura laughed.

'You look like you've had a night in Newcastle,' she said. 'But I like the sockless thing.'

He smiled as she moved around him, oblivious to pedestrians. She plucked a hoodie from her rucksack and ordered him to put it on but discarded it after a couple of shots. On his feet again he walked along the street as Laura danced around him, calling instructions as they went. She had him loiter on a traffic island and outside a pub. Further on she pushed him against a billboard in front of a construction site. It promised an urban Utopia, where people of all creeds and colours would live happily in a tower-block estate with grassed roofs, coffee bars and terraces, where minorities had the best flats and chatted with one another on their sundecks. She played around with settings, knowing most of the work would be done later on her Mac. Will did his best to pout and pose but after a while looked bored.

'Can we go to the pub?' he asked. 'I'm also against thirst.'

Laura laughed. 'I'm glad we've got that out of the way,' she said. 'Now I can take you to my studio.'

They packed up and rode back across Clapham Common, through Dulwich and on past Peckham Rye until they came to a quiet road with a public garden on one side and a wooded hill rising on the other. It was a stone's throw from Mersley Road. Laura chained the bike to a railing and they walked into the wood. The city was gradually blotted out, its sounds deadened by trees, the light changed and filtered through their canopy.

'This is One Tree Hill,' she said. 'Don't you love it?' She danced backwards up a winding track, taking pictures of Will as he followed. She stopped at a great gnarled tree whose jagged branches reached across the path. Light flecked its gothic boughs. Laura ran a hand over ancient bark.

'Isn't it beautiful?' she said. The shutter clicked as Will looked into its upper branches. 'How old do you think it is?' she asked.

'Definitely before Elvis.'

'I think it's the tree in all the children's stories,' she said. 'The Magic Faraway Tree and Cinderella's tree – did you know Cinderella had a tree?' Will smiled. 'And the Whomping Willow. Can't you just see it coming to life?' She told him to stay still while she photographed him against the patterned trunk. 'The light does great things here,' she said.

They walked for a while without talking, listening to birdcalls above the rumble of distant traffic. The path wound around the edge of the wood past brambles and fallen branches. Near the top they came to a clearing with a flat patch of sunlit grass and a rope swing hanging from a tree. The grass was scorched from illicit barbecues. Will took to the swing and Laura photographed him. Then they sat on the grass in the late morning sun, ringed by blackberries and a screen of trees.

'Have you always lived round here?' he asked.

'Longer than anywhere else,' Laura said as she changed lenses. 'Mum and Dad slowed down as they got older. Either that or they got smarter.' She studied him for a moment. 'We're getting closer,' she said.

'Closer to what?'

'To you.'

'What do you mean?'

'The shots in the street, the image thing, that's a game for your band,' she said. 'A deception. A portrait is a truth. I don't think your truth is urban rebel.'

'Ah-ha,' Will said.

Laura laughed. 'I've scared you now.' She sat cross-legged and added a lens hood. 'Tell me your story,' she said, as she looked at him through the lens, bringing him in and out of focus.

'What do you want to know?' he asked. Laura put the camera down and rummaged in her rucksack, pulling out a folded package that sprang into a silver disc once released.

'Here,' she said. 'Sit up and hold this in your lap. It's a reflector.' She manipulated the angle of the disc until the pockets under his eyes filled with light. 'Tell me about your parents. When they were young.' Will thought for a moment.

'They met at Greenham Common,' he said. 'Don't know what Dad was doing there. They wanted to change the world. Trouble was by the time they arrived the revolution was over. Instead of bringing down the government they got Margaret Thatcher. They made the best of it. They lived in squats and were at all the right protests. Then I came along and they had to find jobs and move out of London. Now they'd settle for bringing down Basingstoke Borough Council.'

Laura made a minute adjustment to the reflector.

'How come your dad lived with us?'

'That was before Mum. He had nowhere to go after he got out of Brixton. He couldn't find work. Mind you, work wasn't his thing in those days, unless it involved a picket line. Don't think it's ever been his thing. He stayed with them for a while, until Dot threw him out.'

'Problem with the rent?' Laura shot him a mischievous look.

'Something like that. He and George kept in touch and when I got evicted George offered to help.'

'You have great eyes,' she said. He flinched. 'And nice hands. And don't even think of saying 'ah-ha'. Laura adjusted the reflector. 'Now tell me about you. Something true.' Will frowned. 'I'm trying to decide if you're worth my time.'

She lowered the camera and waited for an answer. Did he want to be worth her time?

'OK. A truth,' he said. 'I was hopeless at school. I didn't do sports, didn't win prizes. I was not the cool guy. I was the nerd. Most people think you pick up a guitar to show off and get laid. I fell in love with it. From the age of fourteen I spent two years in my bedroom, but unlike most boys I wasn't wanking. I was practising. OK. Truth. Sometimes I was wanking. Then I found a band, left home and went on the road. I'm good at what I do. The guitar, that is. Not wanking. Though I suppose I can hold my own.'

Laura laughed.

'And I'm funniest when I don't intend to be.'

'And girls?' More truth was required.

'Not as many one-night stands as I thought there'd be. Except during the arsehole period when I thought I was a star. I've had three relationships. One when I was fourteen. She became a policewoman so that was probably not to be. Another was during the arsehole period so I completely fucked it up. And the last one finished when she told me I'd never make it.'

The shutter clicked, locking in an image of vulnerability and a streak of sunlight across his face.

'I don't like football, I read the Beano and I'm so ambitious sometimes I get a pain in my chest. The ambition comes from Mum, the hypochondria from Dad. Is that enough truth for one day?' She nodded and he looked relieved.

'Can I talk about music?' he asked.

'We can give it a try.'

'OK. So, there must be a million chords, right? But most songs have four. That's what got me started. Then it was the notes. Did you know there are twelve notes for the whole of Western music? But we never use them all. It's all about the ones you choose and the order you put them in, along with pitch and rhythm. It's amazing, like a puzzle with infinite possibilities. And that's before you start on the words.'

She watched him as he talked, fluent and passionate, his face alive and full of optimism. She realised she'd forgotten to take photographs.

'And what is it about now?' she asked.

'I want to leave a trace,' he said. 'Life is short, death is long. How do you make a mark on a short fast ride? One song might be enough. What about you?'

'I'm working. That's enough.'

'You said.'

Laura shrugged. Why did he do that? He may want to leave tracks but she was fine as she was. Wasn't that a boy thing? And anyway there was time for all that, wasn't there?

'I've one more thing to show you,' she said, packing the rucksack. 'Follow me.' She led him through a break in the bushes to a bank of stone steps, hooking her arm in his as they climbed. They emerged from the trees onto an exposed hilltop where she pointed out an oak tree Elizabeth I was said to have knighted, a gun emplacement from World War One and a rusted brazier that was lit as a beacon for a king's jubilee.

'That's three things,' said Will.

'They're not it,' she said. 'Look behind you.' Will turned to see London spread before them, a vast panorama framed by trees. 'It's my favourite view,' said Laura. 'And I still haven't caught it.'

Will sat on a bench while she photographed the vista. She knew he was watching her, and as she stretched for a shot she wondered if he was studying her tattoo, the pale blue crescent moon and stars woven into a black tribal band that extended across her lower back, giving the impression of wings.

After a while she joined him on the bench, clucking with disappointment, and showed him the images.

'It's a little bit fuzzy,' she said, looking at the view. She turned to look at him. 'What are you thinking?'

'It's a little bit fuzzy,' he sang.

'Ah-ha.'

'Don't you start,' he said. 'Laura…'

Her name. He had chosen his moment.

'Are you looking for a fairy tale?' she asked.

'Isn't everyone?'

'I'm not good at happy endings.'

'I'll take my chances.'

They said nothing for a while.

'What are you going to free me from?' she asked. He looked at her blankly. 'In a fairy tale there's a princess and a hero,' she said. 'Every girl wants to be a princess and every boy wants to be a hero. Well, sometimes he has to be a frog first, but we'll skip that bit. Anyway, the hero has to prove himself, which boys like to do. There's an impossible quest where he has adventures and faces danger and at the end he frees the princess and wins her. What are you going to free me from?'

'You're going to be a lot of trouble, aren't you?' said Will.

'Unless you're the princess and I'm the hero?' she said. 'Now that could work. It's mostly women who save men anyway. Of course, that's when the trouble starts. After the adventure. Men and women have different ideas about what it means to live happily ever after.'

'And what are they?' asked Will. She turned to face him, their lips inches apart.

'Her idea of happily ever after is attention, conversation, and going to splendid balls. His is watching sport, drinking beer and scratching his splendid balls.'

'How romantic.'

'I'm realistic,' she replied. 'I'm not looking for a fairy tale.'

'You're not looking for a frog, either,' he said. They looked back at the view.

'Are you thinking about sex?' she asked.

'Not exactly.'

'How about now?'

'Of course.'

'Come on then. Let's go.' She jumped to her feet. 'I think it's best to get the first one out of the way, don't you? It's always a disaster.'

'What about..?'

'What? Oh, Blake?' she said. 'That's so quaint.'

'I thought...'

'You're not going to go soft on me, are you?' She stood in the sun, hands on hips, then swung round and headed towards the gap in the trees. She had almost reached the edge of the wood when she turned back.

'If it makes you feel better,' she shouted, oblivious of the elderly couple emerging breathless from their climb up the hill, 'nothing happened with Blake. I was winding you up. He's a prick and I dumped him months ago. I had dinner and came home. Now are you coming or not?'

*

As Laura and Will raced down the hill, in Wimbledon Mary Chamberlain returned from shopping. As she entered the hall she noticed the envelope on the side table. After dropping her bags in the kitchen she returned to open it. Inside was a single typed sheet from a company called Silver Screen Locations.

Dear Occupier,

We are a company specialising in finding locations for movie and commercial shoots. Presently we are searching for a property similar to yours to act as a location for a forthcoming film production starring Johnny Depp. We urgently require a large, well-maintained, nineteenth century house in your area, suitable for a variety of interior and exterior scenes. The property has to be easily secured as Mr Depp is expected to be present on location throughout. We will pay £2,000 per day for the selected location and guarantee any restitution required.

We are impressed by your property and our representative will be in touch over the next few days to assess your interest.

Kind regards,

William Ireland CBE

Managing Director

Silver Screen Locations.

13

At Paddington Station, while the sun outside was denying the onset of evening, on platform 7 passengers poured from the Heathrow Express, holidaymakers in linen and sandals refusing to end their summer holidays and tieless businessmen on their way to or from meetings, some pale, some livid, thumbing smartphones and wheeling overnight bags.

Kracholov kept to the middle of the crowd as it flowed towards the exit, partly to pass unnoticed, though his giant frame made that almost impossible, and partly to absorb the English in their homeland. He counted two coolie hats and a sombrero bobbing in the crowd and remembered these islanders liked to escape their unreliable summer.

He stopped for a smoke in Praed Street and watched the icons of London, red buses and black cabs, as they fought the traffic. He had travelled to many places for many reasons, but this was his first trip to London and he was excited. He took photographs of shops, vehicles and street signs. His mother at home in the apartment in Sofia would want to see everything. She would be so proud when he returned. He went in search of another icon, a particular red telephone box, and finding it, photographed it from every angle before climbing inside.

He browsed the gallery of scantily clad girls and phone numbers as he waited for the call. Many of them looked Central European and one was the image of his cousin, who was supposedly working as a secretary. If he had time he would call her. If it turned out she was family he would scold her, if not he would fuck her. He checked his watch, 6.59 p.m. The telephone rang.

'Hello. This is Kracholov,' he said. A woman replied.

"In the midden, undercover

Of your horses' Monday supper,

She retrieved a dampened sheaf..." The woman finished with a question mark in her voice.

It was so Cold War, he thought, so DANS, the State National Security Agency, but then some of the guys who worked for the firm were part of the Buro in the old days; and they were conservative, they liked the old ways. Kracholov finished the poem.

"Of paper aged in days by years

And scented with the dung of twenty grazers."

'Welcome to London, Mr Kracholov,' said the voice. 'This is Best Bulgarian Cleaning Company.' Kracholov smiled. He could imagine what they might launder. He was given two addresses, the first in Abbey Road, and the caller hung up. He clenched his fists in triumph.

It was two stops on the underground to Maida Vale and a short walk to Abbey Road. Kracholov's pace quickened along with his heart as he neared the place he was seeking, a black and white striped crossing, called a zebra, with two orange beacons on top of black and white poles. He sighed. It was still there, the strange crossing on the front cover of The Beatles' *Abbey Road* album. He could see them; John in white as God; Ringo in black, the undertaker; George in jeans, the gravedigger; and Paul, Paul in bare feet because he was dead. And the music: 'Come Together', 'Here Comes The Sun', 'Maxwell's Silver Hammer'.

His father had visited London in 1969 as part of a scientific delegation and smuggled the record back for him along with a copy of the *Melody Maker*. Kracholov had become the toast of his friends as one who had touched the West, bringing the precious album to Sofia after they'd heard it on Radio Luxemburg or Radio Nis, but before it physically arrived via Western holidaymakers on the Black Sea. His status as hero and ideological subversive was assured and for a short time he became a neighbourhood celebrity. Inspired, he grew his hair to his shoulders, only to be plucked off the street and taken to the police station for a state-administered haircut. But it was worth it. And now he was standing in Abbey Road, at the source.

He photographed the crossing, he photographed people crossing the crossing; he persuaded an old lady with a Zimmer frame to photograph him crossing the crossing. She bolted when he tried to coerce others into recreating the legendary image with him as John. He completed his pilgrimage with a visit to the Abbey Road studios and stood outside open-mouthed. Not only The Beatles' final studio work, but also *Dark Side of the Moon*, the greatest album of all time, was recorded here. He felt the aura of genius and knelt to read and touch the graffiti on its famous wall. He took photographs of himself in front of the road sign; Abbey Road, NW8, City of Westminster, and added his own legend, a giant K, in black felt pen.

Temporarily sated, Kracholov walked on to the address he had been given, a white five-storey Victorian house with a chequered path, a low white wall and a privet hedge. He checked his watch again. It was time. He slipped into the property and crept along the wall. Jammed against the base of the hedge and partly covered by ivy was a black cello case. He pulled it from the undergrowth and brushed off the foliage. A keyring with two keys was taped to the side, which he removed and slipped into a pocket. He returned to the street, now a middle-aged musician wandering a legendary part of town on his way home from rehearsals.

He took the underground to the second address and watched his fellow passengers, people from all over the planet, sitting or standing in personal bubbles, blotting out the world with books, free newspapers or iPods; people on energy-saver, maintaining only the sense of where they were, how far till their stop and how easy it would be to get off when the time came. Kracholov stood wobbling with his suitcase between his knees, one arm around the cello case, the other holding a rail. For a moment he felt out of place and thought of a Bulgarian movie, *Swedish Kings*. In it a worker who has come into money goes to the seaside for the holiday of his life but, even with riches, he cannot find his feet among the white Mercedes and elegant women and returns disillusioned to his construction site because all he knows is work. Then Kracholov thought of his mother and how excited she had been when he said he was coming to London, and felt his spirits lift.

The second address was one of several flats above a parade of shops in Willesden High Street, opposite the underground station. The big man crossed another zebra, this one unexciting, merely a utility, to a door beside a local supermarket. The first key fit and he lugged the suitcase and cello up two flights. The second key opened a plain white door into a plain white flat. It smelt of paint and was empty. There was a fitted kitchen, a tiny bathroom and two rooms. He went into the largest of the rooms. It had new carpets with rising fluff, a pine bed, a chair and a cheap television on a cheaper stand. He noticed thin curtains bordering recently installed replacement windows. On the bed lay a sleeping bag.

Kracholov dropped his suitcase by the wall and laid the cello by the bed. He went into the kitchen where he found glasses, cups and coffee. There was fresh milk in the fridge and a saucepan on the counter, half a bottle of cheap cognac and a radio spattered with paint. He presumed the flat was being put to use while waiting for sale or rental. He put the kettle on and returned to the big room.

Kneeling, he opened the cello case. Within its moulded interior he found an A–Z and a tube map, which he put to one side. A long package of bubble-wrap ran the length of the void. He gently lifted it out and unwrapped it, to find a single-barrelled semi-automatic shotgun and two boxes of cartridges. It was a Franchi, an Italian hunting weapon. He had hoped for something smaller, preferably a pistol. He didn't like armed assignments at the best of times and this was a quail gun. A cello case was going to be awkward and conspicuous on the streets of London. They might have shortened it for him. But such was the efficiency of the Best Bulgarian Cleaning Company.

In the space where the gun had lain was a sealed brown envelope. Kracholov took it into the kitchen while he finished making coffee. He opened it with a knife and emptied the contents onto the counter. There were three photographs and a single sheet of typewritten paper with an address and phone number. He looked at each image as he recalled the briefing. He was on loan to the Russians for a job they didn't want connecting to them. The blonde woman was Ruby Stevens, an escort who was currently the star of a reality show, the younger woman was a photographer named Laura Valentine and the middle-aged man was her father George Valentine. Apparently they had embarrassed an oligarch, risking his lucrative government contracts and ruining his plans to redecorate his house, and he wanted to exact punishment. Laura and Ruby were to be kidnapped and sold into sex slavery. The man, George, was to learn the fate that had befallen his daughter and if he was to be mutilated along the way, there would be a bonus.

Kracholov stood the photographs against the wall and studied them as he poured the coffee. He filled a glass with brandy and took both drinks back to the room with the bed, switched on the TV and watched a news report about the British Prime Minister. Apparently someone inside his party suspected he was covering up a heart attack, while others were suggesting a drinking habit on the scale of Boris Yeltsin. An independent medical expert compared his rumoured symptoms with the early signs of dementia. Kracholov turned to another channel where there was also news, a piece about a government minister who wanted to bring back the death penalty. He switched back to find yet another story. This time a different politician was in trouble with a prostitute and some Russians. It was much like home, Kracholov thought. Then he realised the prostitute was Ruby Stevens.

*

Kracholov rose before dawn. He inspected and oiled the shotgun and repacked the cello case, this time keeping the A–Z and underground map in the deep pockets of his leather coat. After a cup of coffee and a cigarette, he made his way by tube to Pimlico then on foot to the river where he turned west. Mist hung thickly on the water, the warming sun only beginning to flex its muscles. As he walked towards Battersea Bridge the object of his journey grew out of the haze until it filled his view. Battersea Power Station, a vast industrial castle with four great chimneys, guarded by riverside cranes. He was awed but disappointed. As the front cover of Pink Floyd's 1977 album *Animals* it had been majestic and foreboding, now it was crumbling and desolate, despite hoardings that promised a new future of luxury living and retail therapy. He'd first seen it in miniature in a Virgin Records advertisement, in another smuggled copy of *Melody Maker*. Then a friend had obtained a copy of the album, which he had taped, fearing a raid at any moment. For him it was a powerful attack on communism. Only years later did he learn it was intended as a denunciation of capitalism, though based on a book that attacked Stalin, and he realised the messages you drew from music depended on which side of the wall you stood. And it wasn't a patch on *Dark Side of The Moon*.

Kracholov took photographs as the sun broke through and more as he crossed Chelsea Bridge, before turning into Battersea Park at Chelsea Gate. Inside the park was quiet, just a handful of joggers spread across the mist. A cock crowed, and he heard an unexpected muttering of monkeys as he passed a zoo. He walked on to a pagoda that rose out of the haze and a bold gold Buddha looked down at him knowingly. From there he turned into the park and walked until he was enveloped in trees. He laid the cello case on the ground and unpacked and loaded the shotgun. Glancing round to make sure no joggers were in sight he raised the gun and fired two rounds into the treetops, shattering the park's calm. Branches splintered, a menagerie of sounds erupted from the zoo and birds took flight from the surrounding trees. He swung round and fired again and a bird dropped from the sky. A dog came running at him out of the vapour then turned and fled. Satisfied the gun was functioning he placed it back in the case. It was accurate enough, he thought, just too big. He considered shortening the barrel himself and wondered where he could find a hacksaw. Certainly he would have to find a better way to carry it. On his way to the exit he stopped by the dead bird, a woodpigeon, and stuffed it in his pocket. It would make a fine dinner with cabbage and a little red wine. The zoo was erupting, joggers were running for their lives and as he climbed onto a bus the morning filled with the distant sound of sirens. He was surprised at the fuss. No one would have thought much of it at home.

A copy of a morning paper lay on the seat next to him, which he picked up to improve his English. He read a story about one of the politicians he had seen on TV the previous evening, Robert White, the one involved with Ruby Stevens and the Russians. He was proclaiming his innocence and saying he would fight to clear his name of impropriety. Kracholov puzzled over the word impropriety while his fingers drummed the head of the cello case.

14

'Hello, gorgeous,' George oozed into his mobile. 'We're here. Round the back.' He was leaning against the van, squinting in the morning sun, as he studied the Chamberlains' Wimbledon house.

'Good,' said Dot. She was in the cellar at Mersley Road, looking at the street on Google Maps while sipping a cup of tea. She flicked up Street View. There was a high brick wall, covered in creepers that curved with the road. 'There should be a green door and a sign saying 'No Hawkers".'

'I'm looking at it,' said George.

'She said the housekeeper will open the door. Her name is Edith. She's African. She'll show you round. The only thing to watch for is their detective, but she's got him weeding beds in the front garden.'

'That's helpful,' said George.

'She called *us*,' said Dot. 'She's hooked; she's desperate to meet Johnny Depp and knows the security people won't like it. I suggested she might want to be out when we call, if she doesn't want to make a big thing of it. She should have left on the school run by now.'

'You're a genius, poppet. Do you have the pony story ready?'

Dot looked at the schedule in front of her.

'Ready to go,' she said. 'I have scans of the letter, Laura's pictures and the groom's statement and phone number. It goes to the *Mirror*, Sky and a couple of websites as soon as you're finished. They're waiting for it. They know it's someone near the top of the tree and they live in South London. They're five minutes away. As soon as you text me I'll send everything out, but you don't want photographers turning up while you're in there. Be careful, George.'

'Love you, sweetie,' said George. 'I'll call when we're done.' He hung up and banged happily on the bonnet, waking Laura, Will and Luka who were dozing inside the van. He walked round to the driver's side and leaned through the window.

'Luka, you stay with the van, in case we need to make a quick exit,' he said. The singer was delighted.

'Cool. I am getaway driver,' he said. 'Do you have driving gloves like *Italian Job*?' George looked across the street to the green door then back into the van.

'No,' he replied. 'And the idea is to avoid a chase, not get into one. You stay in the van and out of sight. If their detective was at the party you're the one he'll remember. Laura, you're taking stills, Will, you're the art director. Now, let's recap on the plan. Will.' All eyes turned to the guitarist.

'Yes?' Will looked up, blankly. George let his head drop while he gripped the lower ledge of the driver's window. The art of management, he had learned, could be frustrating. Success lay in setting common goals, defining clear roles and everyone knowing their part. It was called alignment. Time spent explaining and rehearsing was time well spent, but it could be tedious. He looked at the two boys. He'd been in two minds about using them and Dot had been dead against it, but he needed manpower, so he'd taken the risk.

'This is the bit where you remind us of the plan,' said George. 'To make sure we've all got it. And then we synchronise our watches.'

'I see,' said Will.

'You have a watch?'

'I do.'

'And you can tell the time?'

'George.'

'Excellent. So?'

'So. We're scouting locations for a movie, set in the old days,' said Will. 'Johnny Depp in a frock coat. But we're really looking for signs that someone is growing weed big time. So, we want to see the attic, the basement, greenhouse, anywhere you could grow a crop. Ideally, Laura gets a shot and I'll get a couple of buds.' Will laughed. 'Joke.

Inside the house we split up and see what we can find, and if we get caught we pretend we're lost.'

'He's got it,' said George.

'I don't know why, though,' said Will. George frowned.

'We're bringing down a corrupt government,' Laura said.

'We do it for money,' said Luka. 'Like at home.'

'Quiet,' said George. He raised a finger and pointed across the road. Framed in the doorway a large African woman was peering at them. She was wearing a headscarf and a brightly patterned dress, which was partly concealed under an apron.

'That'll be Edith,' said George, 'she'll show us around. We want to be done with this in an hour.' He checked his watch. 'It's 9.05 a.m. exactly.' Luka leaned back on the bench and flipped his baseball cap over his eyes as George, Laura and Will trotted across the road to meet their guide.

Through the green door they found themselves in a vegetable garden, neatly planted in sunlit squares and surrounded by red brick walls, each bed brimming with beans, broccoli and cabbages ready for harvesting. Along one wall, behind an impressive tomato crop, George spotted a row of Victorian greenhouses. They could check those on the way out. He caught Will's attention and nodded towards them. Laura had already taken a couple of shots.

'This is fabulous, Edith,' George said. He guessed she was Nigerian and in her forties.

'Follow me,' said Edith, her manner brusque. She led them through an arch into the first of two orchards, bounded by recently clipped hedges, the first laid with apples, the second with pears.

'You think Mr Johnny Depp will like?' the housekeeper growled.

'He's going to love it,' said George. He stooped to pick a fallen apple. 'Have the Chamberlains been here long?' he asked.

Edith waited impatiently as he inspected the fruit for bruises.

'Long time,' she said. 'Since his mother died.'

'And you've been with them all that time?' George bit into the apple.

'I have been here one year,' she said.

'Oh yes?' said George, munching amiably. 'Where were you before that?'

'At home. In Lagos,' she replied. 'What is this film about?' she asked. She turned onto a brick path and led them through another arch. George nudged Will.

'Will, what's the movie about?'

Will didn't reply. He was miles away. George assumed he was in some kind of creative reverie, trying to suck a song from his surroundings.

'Tell Edith about the movie,' George said, nudging him again. Will was casting around for inspiration when they passed a plaque set in a wall that commemorated Scott, a much loved poodle who had died in 1972.

'Mr Depp plays an Antarctic explorer who lives in London around 1872,' he said. 'He lives in Wimbledon in a big house, much like this one. And he's a very keen gardener, he grows vegetables and apples and pears and...'

'Make it gothic,' Laura whispered and ran a hand down Will's back.

'He's dying,' Will muttered. 'Of cancer. But he's developed this machine, which can transpose him into someone else's body.' Edith looked at him, horrified. 'He keeps it in the attic, or possibly the basement, maybe even in a shed. And he starts to look for a handsome young boy whom he can become and live a second life. Even though it will mean death for the boy. And one day...he finds a boy.'

'In the greenhouse,' George added.

'Yes,' said Will. 'A poor lad, who works in the garden, an orphan.' Will looked at Laura who was trying to conceal her laughter. 'Johnny's plan is to adopt him, leave him his money and transpose into him at the last minute just before he dies. But he reckons without his jealous wife, played by Helena Bonham Carter, who hates the boy. And just as he transforms into him she runs in front of the boy and he becomes her instead. And she becomes him.' Edith's face betrayed a look of incredulity, but Will continued, now confident in his creative powers. 'Anyway, by some miracle, he...old Johnny, who is now his wife, goes into remission. So the rest of the movie is Johnny Depp playing his wife in his diseased body, trying to reverse the experiment before he/she dies, while Helena Bonham Carter plays Johnny Depp inside a woman, philandering all over London. It'll be hilarious.'

'What happens to the boy?' asked Edith.

'He saves the day, doesn't he, Will?' Laura said.

'He does,' said Will. 'Thank you for that.'

'How?' asked Edith, stony-faced. George could see Will's mind was a blank.

'We can't divulge the ending,' he said. 'But it involves a chase across the rooftop,' he added, pointing up at a gable.

'It sounds stupid,' said Edith, as she marched towards the house.

'It's a musical,' said George.

They were now standing on a striped lawn looking up at a great townhouse, the scent of recently cut grass filling the air. George cupped his hands as a director's lens and panned slowly around the scene, searching for secret gardens. In the distance he saw a man in a dark suit, dead-heading roses.

'Sen–sa–tional,' said George, as he finished his panorama. 'Can we get on the roof?' he asked, looking up at the house. 'For long shots. Perhaps through the attic?'

'The attic is locked,' said Edith. She turned towards the house and led them through a side door into a conservatory, through a room filled with reproduction Louis Quinze furniture and into a large hall with a crystal chandelier, marble fireplace and winding staircase. Halfway up the stairs a stained glass window streamed primary colours into the space. George presumed these were the public parts of the house where guests were greeted and entertained, the backcloth against which the Chamberlains exhibited their refinement, rank and right to rule.

'What do you want to see?' Edith asked.

'Let's start at the top,' George suggested. Edith led them up the wide stairs with great swaying hips.

'Is it a big family?' George asked, mesmerised by the sight in front of him.

'Small,' grunted Edith, apparently unimpressed. 'Only one son and one girl.'

'What's Mrs Chamberlain like?'

'Tough,' she said, with a note of admiration. 'I am nanny and housekeeper and work in the garden. I have no days off.'

When they reached the landing, an austere square decorated with equestrian prints, Edith rested for a moment to catch her breath.

'Do you always ask so many questions?' she asked. Five doors opened onto the square as well as an arch, which led into a corridor. She passed through one of the doors to another, narrower staircase with a worn green carpet, lit from a dirty skylight.

'Wow!' Laura whispered to Will. 'Servants' quarters.' They trooped up the steep steps after Edith, whose rear now had far less room to manoeuvre. For a moment George wondered what he would do if she tumbled backwards.

'What's Mr C like, the Home Secretary?' George asked.

'Weak. Like all men,' Edith growled. 'Needs a strong woman.'

'Bet they don't come stronger than you, Edith,' George said. Edith looked over her shoulder.

'Don't you try your wicked ways with me,' she said. 'I know you.'

'Not at all, but you're a radiant flower,' George said with a chuckle. They reached another small landing at the top of the house and Edith leaned on the banister, panting, waiting for the others to catch up.

'You are a bad man,' she said, with a hint of a smile.

'And the little girl?' he asked.

'She is like her mother. At home I would thrash her.'

'And the boy?' asked George. 'It's Russell, isn't it?'

'Very nice boy, handsome. Naughty boy.'

'Oh yes? How naughty?' George asked. The question hung in the air. He wondered if it was a step too far and he'd aroused suspicion. Edith ushered them into a living room with sloping eaves, from which led several doors, similar to the floor below but on a simpler scale.

'He goes out when he should do homework,' she said, her chest heaving. She waved an arm, signalling they had reached the top of the house. Along one side of the room were two windows in recesses with bench seats covered with brightly coloured cushions. There was a bookcase, a television and a sofa with a book lying open on one arm; African music was playing quietly on a portable stereo, the CD case lay on a small table nearby. It was clear Edith had not been hard at work when Mrs Chamberlain left instructions to show them around. George spotted an ageing arrangement of servants' bells above the door to the stairs made redundant by the mobile phone. He imagined Mary Chamberlain wished the old system still worked.

'This is my room when I babysit,' said Edith.

'Where is the attic?' George asked. She pointed to a door.

'There,' she said. 'But it is locked, as I said. Mr Russell has the key.'

'What's in there?' asked Laura

'I don't know,' Edith replied. 'Old things. And sometimes I hear noises.'

'What kind of noises?'

'Perhaps mice. Or bats.'

George knelt on the bench nearest the attic door and opened the window. He looked out and motioned Will to join him. Along the ledge was another window that looked into the attic. Will stuck his head out while George turned to Edith.

'We need to check we can get some long shots of the garden,' he said. 'So my colleague Will is going out on the ledge.'

'No I'm not,' said Will.

'Just as far as the next window,' said George.

'I'm not going out there,' Will insisted. There was an awkward silence and Edith watched the proceedings carefully.

'You are the art director,' said George.

'I wouldn't go if I was Johnny Depp.'

'He wouldn't have to,' said George. 'You don't expect me to, do you?'

'It's crumbling,' said Will. He looked at Laura.

'You'll need the camera,' she said. 'Here.' She thrust her Canon into his hands. 'Just point and shoot, it's all set. And if you feel yourself falling, leave it on the ledge.'

Will looked around, astonished, then climbed out on to the ledge and edged towards the attic.

'He should not do that,' Edith protested.

'It's routine. He'll only be a minute,' George said, with an idle wave. 'He does it all the time.'

Laura walked up to a large colourful print above a fireplace.

'What's this?' she asked.

'I don't know,' said Edith. Laura looked at the signature at the bottom of the picture.

'It's called 'African Celebration',' she said. 'It's beautiful. Wonderful colour. Is this home?'

'No,' said Edith. She looked anxiously towards the window. 'When is he coming back?'

'Momentarily,' said George, and momentarily Will began to appear, feet first and ashen-faced. George helped him in and took a last look across the garden before shutting the window.

'It's just a room full of old furniture,' said Will. He handed the camera to Laura and dusted himself off. George turned to Edith.

'Looking good so far, Edith.' he said. 'Excellent proposition. Is there a basement?' He looked at his watch. Edith shrugged.

'There is a wine cellar,' she said. 'At the bottom of the stairs.'

'Sensational,' said George. 'Mr Depp's character is a connoisseur of fine wine.'

George held his ingratiating smile, knowing they were extending their welcome. Edith had probably decided by now that film people were completely mad as well as nosy and wanted to get rid of them as soon as possible. She opened the main door and began the trek down the narrow staircase, George following closely, while Laura and Will lagged behind and peeled off at the first floor into the family quarters.

They listened as Edith and George descended into the bowels of the house then split up and checked each of the rooms on the floor; a pink bedroom for a princess, a black one for a teenage boy, a master bedroom with en suite and a family bathroom. Together they tried the last door, which opened into a study. Inside, floor to ceiling bookcases ranged across two walls and a window dominated the third. In front of it a large desk was piled with papers. Pictures of the Chamberlains' achievements covered the fourth wall: Mariot in pigtails winning rosettes; Russell collecting a school prize; Mary and the Secretary of State meeting Nelson Mandela and President Obama. Laura whistled.

'Do you see what that is?' she said, spotting a red leather briefcase adorned with the royal cipher. Will was looking at the photographs.

'Hey, that's The Marshall,' he said, sounding disappointed. 'Politicians shouldn't be allowed to have guitar heroes.'

Laura was leafing through documents on the desk. She ignored Will and moved to a filing cabinet.

'You enjoyed that, didn't you?' he asked.

'What?'

'Making me go out on that ledge? I could have died.'

'Don't you like danger?' Laura asked. 'I thought that was rock and roll?'

'You're an adrenalin junkie,' said Will. 'You are, aren't you?' She smiled and he advanced on her, grabbing her wrists and pulling her to him. He kissed her hard, forcing her back against the desk. 'OK. Let's get dangerous.'

She tried to push him away. They had a job to do. But she found herself returning the kiss and letting him lift her onto the desk as papers slid to the floor. His body smothered hers as he reached for the clasp at the front of her jeans. Laura stiffened in his arms.

'Someone's watching,' she whispered.

'That's the risk.'

'Someone's watching.'

'Right.'

'SOMEONE'S WATCHING US!' she shouted. She freed her hands, pulled herself into a ball and shoved him away.

'You are mental,' said Will. He stripped off his T-shirt and was fiddling with his belt when he noticed the detective standing in the open doorway. He was leaning against its frame, one hand on his hip, his coat open and exposing a shoulder holster. In his other hand he held a pair of pruning secateurs.

'Generally, we don't encourage rough sex on the Home Secretary's desk,' he said. 'Please don't make any sudden moves,' he added, snipping menacingly. 'Now, what exactly are you two doing here?'

'We're looking for a location,' said Laura.

'I could see that.'

'For a film. Johnny Depp is in it,' Will said, as he struggled back into his T-shirt. The information had no appreciable effect on the detective. Laura wondered if she should add Uma Thurman to the cast.

'There's a scene where he has sex in the study.' she said. 'We were seeing if it would work.'

'Looks like it might,' said the detective. 'I've seen you two before, somewhere.'

'We dropped off the letter,' said Laura.

'Somewhere else.'

'We're in the film business,' said Will.

'That's not it. Where's Edith?' asked the detective.

'She's in the basement with George,' said Laura. 'He's the boss.'

'Is there a sex scene in the basement?'

'No.'

'Lucky for George,' said the detective. 'You shouldn't be in here. It's the private apartment of a Minister of the Crown and off-limits. Who gave you authorisation?'

'Mrs Chamberlain,' said Laura. 'The company is called Silver Screen Locations.'

The detective punched a number on his mobile phone. He watched Laura closely.

'It'll come to me,' he said. 'It was recent. Names and addresses please.' His call was answered and he requested a background check on the company. He held out a hand for their identification, snapping his fingers impatiently, as Edith burst into the room. She was perspiring heavily.

'You must come,' she shouted and tugged at the detective's forearm. 'Now. There are men outside and a photographer in the garden.' The detective tried in vain to calm her down.

'They say Mrs Chamberlain is a horse poisoner,' Edith shouted.

She pushed the detective through the door. 'You must do something. *Maintenant!*' The detective told his colleague he would call back and ordered Will and Laura to stay exactly where they were while Edith bundled him onto the landing and down the main stairs. After they vanished George appeared around the door.

'I think we'd better scarper,' he said. The three fugitives fled down the servants' stairs, slipped out the back door and retraced their steps through the orchards and into the vegetable garden. George took a look back at the lawns to see the detective wrestling with a photographer.

'Anything in the wine cellar?' Laura asked as they jogged through the beds towards the greenhouses.

'Wine.'

'What happened, Dad?'

'I saw the detective from the upstairs window,' said George, 'heading towards the house. He must have seen Will on the roof, so I texted Dot and she did the rest.'

They found a gravel path that led behind the rows of ripening tomatoes to the first of the greenhouses. The door stuck but gave way to a shove from Will. All three crowded inside. It was dark and warm, with the sound of dripping water. The chaos outside seemed a long way off. Under the glass roof ran silver sheeting and banks of lights. Beneath, in trays, lay row upon row of plants.

'Bugger,' said George.

'What's up?' Will asked, panting.

'Roses,' said George. 'Bloody hydroponic roses.' Laura and Will looked at him, uncomprehending. 'You use exactly the same kit as you do to grow marijuana,' he said.

'Let's get out of here,' said Laura. Outside they ran along the red brick wall and through the green door into the street. As the door swung open Luka floored the van, which pitched across the T-junction and mounted the kerb, narrowly missing them, before stalling. He leaned out the window.

'We should have Mini Coopers for fast getaway,' he said. 'With driving gloves.' George pushed him aside and climbed into the driver's seat as Will and Laura clambered in the other side. They drove to the front of the house to find the photographer handcuffed to the front gate and the detective and Edith arguing with several other men as another car pulled into the drive with Mary Chamberlain at the wheel.

*

They didn't speak until they were a good way from the house.

'A bugger's muddle,' George grumbled. 'Total 'ucking fiasco.'

'I'm not so sure about that,' said Laura.

'What? I can't see a front page on the Home Secretary growing roses,' he growled.

'Did you see the book on Edith's sofa?' she said. 'It was French.'

'I saw that,' said Will. '"La Question Homosexuelle en Afrique." What was that about?'

'Nigeria was British, wasn't it?' said Laura. 'And the picture. The artist was from Cameroon. I bet it was hers.'

'So?' asked George, still none the wiser.

'When I asked her if it was home she got defensive. And the scatter cushions were green, red and yellow – whose flag is that, do you reckon? I don't think she's Nigerian. And her accent wasn't right. She's from Cameroon or Chad or Sudan or one of those places.'

'And the music wasn't Nigerian,' said Will. 'I looked at the CD.'

'Go on,' said George.

'If she's from one of those places maybe she's here illegally,' said Laura. 'And who's in charge of immigration?'

George chuckled.

'Sensational,' he said. 'You are your mother's daughter.' He slid an arm around Laura and gave her a hug. 'We've got him.'

George drove on, running through the implications of this revelation. The pony story would break tonight and would start the ball rolling, but it would be a minor irritation to a politician of Chamberlain's experience and he would ride it out. If Laura turned out to be right, this twist would trigger a scandal and he might just be hounded out of office. What he would need, thought George, was a journalist who could dig into the story, someone cunning and without scruples who would turn it into a major splash. He had just the man in mind.

'Are you going to shop her?' asked Will.

'Business is business, Will,' George replied, drumming his fingers on the steering wheel. 'She'll be fine. She'll make a lot of money, more than enough for a top lawyer. She won't be going back, wherever it is she's from.'

There was silence for a while. George was the first to break it, his mind moving to a scenario where the illegal alien story wasn't enough to bring Chamberlain down.

'I'd like to stay with the boy a bit longer,' he said. 'Russell. Just in case. She said he goes out when he should be doing his homework.'

'He's just a kid,' said Will.

'Exactly,' said George. 'A teenager with a few quid. He could be into all sorts of skulduggery.' He pulled a crumpled photograph from his shirt pocket, which he had lifted during the tour. 'Here's a photograph. He looks like his mother. See if he goes out tonight. If he does, follow him; let's see what he gets up to.' George gave a loud sigh. 'Nice work, everyone. Now let's get a cup of tea.'

Shaking his head, Will pulled up his T-shirt and extracted a document, which he tossed onto Laura's lap.

'I guess you won't be wanting this, then,' he said. Laura looked down at the document. It was a numbered copy of a confidential report. On the front cover it was marked 'Cabinet Briefing', and below it 'The London Risk Report: Top 10 Threats To Public Security. Top Secret'.

George glanced down and his eyes widened.

'It was in the study,' Will said. 'Isn't that what you're looking for? Secrets.'

Westminster Inside Track

https://www.witreport.co.uk

A Must For Horse Lovers

WIT is offering a rare first edition of The Terror of St Trinian's by Ronald Searle to the first person to correctly answer the following equestrian crime quiz.

Q1. Which flat-racing champion jockey was jailed for tax fraud in 1987?

Q2. Which National Hunt jockey became a successful writer of crime fiction?

Q3. Which politician's wife recently doped nine ponies to ensure their daughter became Gloucester's Junior Show Jumper of the Year?

Q4. What's the favourite drug of pony-dopers this year?

Q5. Why would it be odd for local police to ignore a case of pony doping?

Q6. What is the name of the sure bet horse in the film *The Belles of St Trinian's?*

Westminster Inside Track

Your eyes and ears on Westminster and Whitehall; exposing the rumours, conspiracies and whitewash at the heart of government; a virtual voice in a new age of accountability.

BREAKING NEWS: <u>Wife of Home Secretary expelled from riding school for fixing Gymkhana. Gloucester outraged/ 'I Saw It All' – Claims Jockey Sinclair/Mary Chamberlain's Doping Spree Mapped Out.</u>

WITLINKS: <u>New Cities Minister meets PM/ Ex-Cities Minister claims he was hounded from office/PM's charity fun run – in pictures</u>

[*Quiz Answers*: 1.Lester Piggott 2.Dick Francis 3.Mary Chamberlain 4.Acetylpromazine (ACP) 5.Because it is illegal 6.Arab Boy]

15

Kracholov worked his way round the shop with a tape measure, stretching and bending to assess the guitars. Behind the counter an assistant scratched his arm below the sleeve of a faded Stone Roses T-shirt. He'd seen people buy guitars for all sorts of reasons but never solely on length. Finally Kracholov seemed satisfied. He checked the measurement once more and straightened up with a groan. His choice was a Fender Precision Bass.

'That's a fine choice, if I may say so,' said the assistant. 'A mighty instrument. And as big as they come.' Kracholov tossed the tape measure onto the counter.

'I would like to buy case for this guitar,' he said, towering over the young man.

'You'd like the guitar?'

'No. Just case.'

'OK. What kind of case?'

'I don't know what kind of case.'

'Well, you can have a solid case or a gig bag,' explained the assistant. 'Solid, you can slam it around in vans, drop it down a flight of stairs, maximum protection; gig bags, light and easy, great if you're carrying them around. Or there's a flight case, super heavy duty, you can fly with it, put your guitar in the hold.'

'Gig bag is OK,' said the Bulgarian.

'Padded or unpadded?' the young man asked. 'I'd go for padded, myself. Keeps it nice and snug and it's not going to damage if you drop it. It's a little extra but worth it for the peace of mind.'

'Padded is good.'

'Cool.' The assistant went out back to find a case.

Kracholov leaned against the counter and looked around the narrow shop. He might know little about guitars but he knew their music. He pulled out his camera and took pictures of the walls and floor which were covered with shiny instruments, and through the window onto Denmark Street. More an alley than a street it was crammed with shops and basements dedicated to the mechanics of rock. He'd already taken photographs of himself outside, holding his head up at what used to be Argents and lounging in front of the 12 Bar Club and its café.

This was music Mecca. Everyone had bought guitars in this street; Clapton, Townsend, maybe even Noddy Holder. David Bowie had lived in a camper van to be close to the studio, Elton John wrote 'Your Song' nearby and the Rolling Stones recorded their first songs in the basement of this very shop, Regent Sound Studios. Kracholov imagined the scenes that must have played out here, while he was a boy in Sofia, poring over his dog-eared copy of *Melody Maker*.

A lot had happened since then. It was a few years later, after Lyudmila Zhivkova, the liberal leader of the Committee of Culture, had died in a car accident and they cracked down on rock, that he was questioned about his burgeoning collection of banned materials. They had threatened him with imprisonment and another state-administered haircut. When he laughed in their faces, they told him they would destroy his father's career. After that it was a short step to working for them, the government, and after the fall of Communism, the Mafia. Mafia, government, there was little difference in the early days. It was a chaotic time and he had done what he needed to survive. First he had taken up wrestling and built a reputation as a strongman with a heart of stone. Later, protected and affluent, he built a record collection that was the finest in Sofia, probably all Bulgaria, but by then CDs had come, and then digital arrived, and finally music, as he had believed in it, as a force for revolution, had evaporated. This visit to London was more than a job; it was a pilgrimage to a more potent time and place, when music could change the world. Before he had compromised.

The assistant returned with the gig bag wrapped in polythene.

'You exchange for cello case?' Kracholov asked.

'Sorry,' said the assistant. Apparently he didn't get a lot of call for classical instruments. Kracholov paid in cash.

He was pleased. The bag was light. It would be a lot easier to carry than the cello case. As he reached the door he recognised the track playing on the store's music system, 'Sweet Virginia' from *Exile on Main Street*, Jagger and Richards drawling about shit and shoes. As he stepped into Denmark Street, Kracholov reflected he'd picked up a lot of shit on his through the years.

16

After the examination, Sir Stephen Oliver ushered Melissa back to her chair, his hand lingering on her shoulder for a moment, before he returned to his side of the desk and settled in a high backed leather chair. Once again he was surrounded by a halo of glamorous women. Melissa looked beyond the round, bespectacled surgeon to the framed photographs on the wall behind him, a collection of rich and famous females, all radiating beauty and confidence. She felt as if she was in a theatrical agency rather than a doctor's surgery. Each portrait save one was autographed and carried a message of enduring thanks to the balding surgeon. Melissa put her nerves aside, desperate to know what each had had done, and leaned across the desk.

'Did you really work on Sophia Loren?' she whispered, looking at the unsigned image over the surgeon's left shoulder then to his manicured hands. Oliver smiled and leaned forward, tugging at his cuffs. He must have heard the question a hundred times, she knew. It was probably all part of the process: the gallery, the question, his leaning close, the answer; all designed to relax his patient long before any chemical sedation. All the same she had to know.

'No. But she's the only one,' he said. 'She is my inspiration.'

'Really?' Charles piped up from the chair next to Melissa. 'Wasn't she a bit on the chubby side?' He looked stiff and uncomfortable. An enormous basket of fruit was perched on his lap, wrapped in cellophane, rustling with every movement. Oliver frowned at the interruption in his ritual.

'Beauty and the beholder, Mr Franklin,' he said. 'To me the hourglass is the equation of femininity. And Mrs Franklin, you are a fine example since your liposuction.' The surgeon regarded Melissa, his eyes kind but huge behind bifocals. 'When I was a teenager I saw *Houseboat* on TV, did you see that movie? Cary Grant and Sophia, two of the most beautiful people ever created. And I knew my calling – to help others find confidence through beauty.' He turned from Melissa to her husband. 'But you're right, Mr Franklin, my job is to help my patients achieve *their* ideal of beauty, not mine.'

He offered Melissa a reassuring smile. This funny little man adored women and it showed.

'Do you have any more questions, Mrs Franklin, before my nurse shows you to your room? I guess you're an old hand at this by now.'

'How long will it take?' Melissa asked.

'My record for your set of procedures is two hours, forty-five minutes and fifteen seconds,' said the surgeon. 'I'll try and knock a few minutes off. Ten years ago it was twice that.'

'Please take all the time you need,' said Melissa, feeling faint.

'We'll be through by teatime. I have a gender reassignment this evening.'

'I meant how long before I look normal?' she asked. The surgeon leaned back in his chair and fretted his slim fingers together.

'I see. As you know, the results will take time to show and there will be some swelling,' he said. 'And of course, a lot depends on the individual. You'll wake up with pretty tight bandaging around your head and over your eyes and nose, to reduce the swelling, a bit like a motorcycle helmet. But please don't try to ride one while you are on medication.' He giggled and glanced at Charles who was fiddling with the ribbons on the fruit basket. 'Apologies, my little joke, but you'd be amazed at the number of patients who climb straight into a car. We don't want you back here for a tidy-up after you've hit a tree, do we?'

'No,' Melissa agreed, her eyes wide with fright. The surgeon retreated to the safety of dull process.

'We then replace it with an elastic and velcro version which you'll wear for the next few weeks, 24/7 to start with, then just night-time.' He smiled reassuringly. 'You'll need assistance for a couple of days, by the end of the week you'll be making it to the corner shop, and the supermarket in a fortnight. Have you stocked up on frozen meals?

And plenty of icepacks?' Melissa and Charles nodded. 'They're very helpful with the swelling.'

The surgeon picked up his phone and told someone Mrs Franklin was ready for her induction, his eyes never straying from his patient.

'Keep your eyes on the prize, Mrs Franklin,' he said. 'In a couple of months you'll be finished with all this. You're going to look in your mirror and see the person you were meant to be, a completely different being to the one who came to see me two years ago.'

'Will I join your rogue's gallery?' asked Melissa. The surgeon beamed.

'You're going to be my finest work and will have pride of place.' He waved in the direction of Sophia Loren as he rose from his chair. The nurse entered as he made his way round the desk to his patient.

'Have you ever had surgery?' Melissa asked.

'There's too much to be done in my case, I'm afraid,' said the surgeon. 'No, my job is to help others reach their potential.' He chuckled again and showed the couple to the door. On the way he picked up a leaflet from his desk and handed it to Charles.

'We do a lot of dental work here, Mr Franklin, the best in the country. Take a look. You might consider it. I'll see you in theatre, Mrs Franklin.'

*

The nurse led them along a white corridor with a low uneven roof, past a line of mullioned windows set within deep alcoves. Charles stopped at each to check his teeth, wondering what was wrong. His teeth, like the rest of his physique, had never drawn anything but admiration. His smile was his first line of defence and had melted secretaries, mellowed clients angry over outrageous bills, and even evaded a few parking fines. Was something out of true? He ran his tongue around the inside of his mouth, giving his face the look of a confused chimpanzee. It didn't occur to him the eminent surgeon might also be a salesman.

The nurse reminded Melissa of the Manor Hospital's history as a country lodge, cottage hospital and now a private clinic. She explained they were in the old part of the building, which housed reception, administration and consulting rooms, and were heading towards the modern extension, which boasted a state of the art theatre, minor procedures rooms and twenty-one private bedrooms with en suite facilities and satellite TV. The nurse sounded like she had learned the hospital brochure by heart and talked enthusiastically about advanced surgical procedures, caring and professional medical staff and a commitment to quality and value.

When Charles had finished feeling for uneven teeth he remembered the reason for the giant basket of fruit.

'A client of mine is staying here,' he said. 'The guitarist, Hammond Marshall? He's having some work before his tour. Could we pop in and see him?' The nurse raised her eyebrows.

'Mr Marshall? Yes, that should be fine,' she said. 'He was out of surgery yesterday.' She smiled at Charles, a big horsey smile. He grinned back, keeping his lips together. 'You're both rhinoplasty, aren't you?' the nurse asked. 'I think your rooms may be next to each other.'

They reached the new building and the smell of disinfectant. Neat teak doors replaced the ancient painted ones in the old corridor. The nurse stopped at one, the brass number plate said 66, after which another 6 had been added in lipstick.

'Quite juvenile, these music people,' she said. Charles agreed through the cellophane. Didn't he know it. She knocked on the door and popped her head inside.

'Visitors for you, Mr Marshall.' Charles heard a mumbled reply from within and the nurse pushed the door open.

Hammond Marshall was sitting up in bed, wearing cobalt blue pyjamas and a matching bandana around the white motorcycle helmet Sir Stephen Oliver had described earlier. A large plaster covered his nose on which perched a pair of Ray Bans. He was eating breakfast.

'You *are* next door,' the nurse said to Melissa. 'I'll check your bags have arrived. Please don't tire him, if that's possible.' She turned and left. Charles stood in the middle of the room with the fruit basket looking for a space among the flowers, newspapers and bottles of Grey

Goose that littered every surface. In a corner stood a pair of hinged doors repainted as a get-well card from his band mates, a spyhole in each suggesting that somewhere an hotelier was puzzling over a ravaged corridor.

The toilet in the en suite flushed and Charles and Melissa watched as a girl of about twenty came out, a blur of piercings and tattoos, and dropped to her knees to peer under the bed.

'Are you coming or what?' she shouted. 'He is not going to do it.' A moment later a pair of feet emerged encased in Nike high tops. The kneeling girl caught hold of them and pulled, and another girl about the same age appeared from under the bed and struggled to her feet. They each grabbed a bottle of vodka and staggered from the room. As the door slammed shut, their voices could be heard over the clacking of heels along the corridor.

'We didn't get a story,' said one. 'I thought your dad said he was the bollocks.'

'Yeah, we did,' said the other. 'He can't get it up anymore.'

Marshall was indifferent, flipping through TV channels past a documentary on Hitler, a property show and the latest market prices, to settle on the news. The Home Secretary was being interviewed in front of Westminster, claiming he knew nothing about wrongdoings at his local gymkhana and could they get back to the subject which was the country's need for energetic leadership in troubled times. Marshall muted the sound and squinted at his guests.

'Hello babe, with your radiant eyes so blue,' he sang, raising an arm weakly to Melissa. She waved hello and took the chair bedside the bed.

'Hello Marshall,' she said.

'I think there was a party last night,' he said.

'How are you feeling?' Melissa asked.

'Better for seeing you, babe,' he said. Marshall looked at his PR man through the cellophane. 'You got a banana in there, Charles, or just pleased to see me?' He gave a hearty laugh, which turned into a hacking cough. After it subsided he said, 'Seriously, I could handle an orange. Vitamin C.' Charles set the basket down and wrestled with the packaging.

'So, babe, what are you doing here?' Marshall asked.

'Melissa's having a procedure,' said Charles.

'Multiple procedures,' said Melissa.

'That's great, babe, you'll get multiple drugs,' said Marshall. 'Seriously, the drugs here are intense. Take a look in the minibar.'

'There are drugs in your minibar?' Charles asked. Marshall shrugged as much as he could, given he was encased in plaster.

'I brought them with me, in case they didn't have enough,' he said. 'I figured if I have to fall off the wagon I might as well go all the way. God I've missed them. My little friends.'

'Poor you,' Melissa said. She reached for his hand and patted it.

'You betcha, babe. So, are we going to be surgery buddies? That's cool.' Marshall looked at Melissa's husband. 'Think it's safe to leave her with me, Charles? You know I have a thing for this little beauty. Caviar, babe?' He raised a piece of toast coated with Beluga. When she declined he threw it into his mouth and pushed his breakfast tray to one side. 'So, Charles,' he chomped. 'Where the fuck am I?'

'What do you mean?' Charles asked, finally producing an orange from the basket. Marshall took the orange, picked up a knife from his tray and cut it in half. He reached for one of the remaining bottles of Grey Goose and twisted the cap.

'I mean, where's the fucking media?' he asked, pointing towards a pile of newspapers on the windowsill. He took his empty water glass, filled it with vodka and squeezed both halves of the orange into it. Charles leafed through the *Daily Express*. 'There's 'The Marshall Plan,' muttered the guitarist. '*Heat* magazine takes the bitch shopping. And 'The Wonderful World of Warlocks – children's book deal for Rock Witch.' And where am I? Nowhere. I'm not even missing, Charles.'

'Your sales are up on the second half of the tour,' Charles protested.

'Couldn't you knock up a rumour of an overdose? Maybe plant a photographer in the bushes.' He took a slug of his cocktail and sighed appreciatively. Charles looked out the window.

'Aren't they here yet?' he asked.

'That's pathetic, Charles. Two girls trying to raise me from the dead, they were here. Photographers in the bushes? I'd have noticed. And that Sunday coverage was crap. You said a big splash. I fart bigger bubbles.'

'It was a double page spread in the *Sunday People*,' Charles protested. 'It's your demographic.' Marshall waved at the papers.

'Everyone went with that White bloke,' he grumbled. 'The geezer at your party. He's everywhere. He's even on that new reality show. Look, there he is now.' Marshall pointed at the television and switched off the mute. A newsreader was presenting in front of a picture of Robert White superimposed over a map of the Isle of Wight.

'…disgraced politician is set to join the inmates of *Escape from Wight*, the new reality show, who were locked up in a disused holiday camp last night. White will be joining the men's team. He says he intends to prove his innocence by confronting fellow inmate and kiss-and-tell ex-lover Ruby Stevens.' Charles' jaw fell open.

'I should be on that fucking show,' said Marshall. 'Are you doing his PR?'

'Not anymore,' Charles replied. He was hardly aware of the rock star as he tried to think through the significance of the story unfolding on the screen. What the fuck was White up to? Even if he forced a confession from Ruby it wouldn't exonerate him. He *had* influenced Ledakov's planning application. But what if he made her reveal she was paid to expose him? That could lead to George Valentine and in turn to Charles and that would mean questions about who wanted White out of the picture and why. One look at Charles' client list would link it to Sir Frank Porter. White must be hoping he could muddy the waters enough to give him some wiggle room. It was a naïve strategy but it could be embarrassing at the very least and potentially catastrophic.

'Probably why he's getting so much coverage,' Marshall growled.

'It's killing his career,' Charles said. He could hear the sneer in his voice yet at the same time felt a small puncture in his vast well of confidence.

'Don't give me that,' said Marshall. 'All publicity is good. You told me that. Except paedophilia, having a small cock and maybe murder. Phil Spector hasn't made a comeback.'

There was a knock at the door. The nurse had returned to tell Melissa it was time for her to get ready. She tensed. Marshall saw her discomfort and put a reassuring hand over hers.

'Don't worry, babe,' he said. 'I'm right here. And I've got the drugs. We are going to have a blast. Listen to The Doctor.'

Melissa found a place on his bandaging to give Marshall a kiss and Charles waved as he made vague promises about making calls as soon as he got in the car. He would certainly be making calls. The first would be to George Valentine to make sure the little slut from Estonia kept her mouth shut. As they left, the PR man caught sight of himself in the mirror of the en suite. He gave his signature smile then looked at Marshall.

'Do my teeth look all right to you?' he asked. The rock star was squeezing the last of the orange into his glass, his other hand reaching for the vodka.

'Fuck knows,' he said and nodded at the fruit basket. 'Have an apple.'

17

Laura was peering through the windscreen at the same green door they had encountered that morning when Will, Luka and Johnson came round the corner into view. The light was turning, giving the ivy-clad wall behind them the beginnings of a russet glow. She leaned through the window as they approached.

'You're late,' she said. Her eyes fixed on the drummer. 'And what's he doing here?' Johnson gave an ingratiating wave.

'Rehearsal overran,' said Will. 'I said we'd give him a lift as he's on our way.'

'On our way where?' asked Laura, with a look she knew would remind Will of her mother. 'We don't know where we're going yet. He's not getting in here.'

The van was parked in the same side street as before, across the road from the Chamberlains' house. The picture of Russell Chamberlain was taped to the dashboard.

'Would it help if I apologised again?' asked Johnson, looking contrite. Laura gave him a murderous look.

'Boy is back,' said Luka. 'He went in front. And big car came back with father.'

'There's a bunch of photographers at the gate.' said Will. 'They went mental.'

'I guess everyone is on to the pony story by now,' said Laura. Luka climbed into the van next to her. Will and Johnson stood framed in the doorway with little-boy-lost looks.

'All right,' said Laura, relenting. 'But *he* goes in the back and keeps his mouth shut.' The boys piled in.

They waited, watched and grew bored as vehicles passed along the road ahead. Johnson tried a couple of jokes but was immediately rebuked, the vision of Dot squashed and covered in chocolate still fresh in Laura's memory, along with her subsequent ire which was visited upon everyone save Johnson, who had slipped conveniently into the night.

The boys were unhappy with the rehearsal. Apparently Jack Blake had breezed in, listened to their set and told them they could headline a Blake's Ride gig but they would have to play three of his songs.

'The songs are shite,' said Will. 'We'll look like morons.'

'I told you to watch him,' said Laura.

'Sure, they're shite,' said Johnson. 'But we get paid and we get to support on the next tour he puts together. Let's be morons.'

'What about musical integrity?' Will protested.

'Blake doesn't do integrity,' said Laura.

'Neither do I,' said Johnson.

'Put it into perspective,' said Laura. 'You haven't slept with him.'

A stream of passengers disgorged from a bus and one, a chubby man in his thirties, jogged across the road towards them. Laura recognised the figure from his loping gait.

'Oh, no,' she groaned. 'Leo.' The man caught her eye and quickened his pace, a shoulder bag slapping at his side. He was out of breath when he reached the van.

'Laura. Hi,' he said. 'George said you'd be here.' He smiled, showing a mouthful of crooked teeth. 'You didn't phone me.' He made a disappointed face, and then glanced into the van to divine what he could of the other occupants.

'Leo, I am never going to phone you,' said Laura. 'Believe it. What are you doing here?'

Alan Leo was a freelance hack and the blogger behind Westminster Inside Track. When his glory days in student politics hadn't led to a career in Parliament he had focused his bile on attacking the system that wouldn't let him in. He seldom ventured beyond his flat in Kennington or the watering holes around Westminster.

'The usual,' he said 'It's just one party after another. You should come with me sometime.'

'You're never invited, Leo,' Laura said. 'You hang about in pubs eating pork pies, waiting for leaks.'

He looked at her suspiciously.

'What are you up to?' he asked.

'You're late,' she said. 'Everyone's round the front.' Leo leaned against the side of the van and lit a cigarette. He looked down at a notepad as smoke streamed from his nostrils.

'I'm not chasing the pony story. That's done.' He tapped his nose. 'I'm here for Edith. The illegal alien. Very nice tip. I'm calling it 'Under the table with the Minister'.'

'You shopped her, then,' Will said. 'Another blow for democracy.'

Leo smiled. 'Don't worry about her, chum,' he said. 'She's up for it. I just talked to her. She's aching to spill the beans. Upstairs and downstairs with the Home Secretary.' He blew smoke through one side of his mouth. 'She's here with her son. Sounds like she's desperate to get asylum. Apparently he's gay and they string them up where they come from.' He looked at his watch and over to the side entrance. As if on cue the door opened and Edith peered into the street.

'There you go,' he said. 'Gagging for it.' He stubbed out the cigarette and winked at Laura. 'We have to go out sometime, girl.'

'It's never going to happen, Leo,' she said. He winked again, acknowledged the boys, and loped across to Edith who held open the door to the kitchen garden.

'Who was that wanker?' Johnson asked.

'Here,' said Laura, passing her camera to Will. 'Take this and hang around the front, just in case he comes out that way. We'll take turns.' She nodded towards Johnson. 'And take Jonah Lomu with you.'

*

Kracholov trudged along the road grasping the straps of the army pack wobbling on his back. The Franchi, now secreted in the gig bag, was fastened to one side. On his right rose One Tree Hill, the last of the sun scattering a promise of gold among its trees. On his left was the small park with neat ornamental beds and a rose garden. He turned into it and made his way through the formal garden, down a slope and into a cutting that ran past the back gardens of Mersley Road. The cutting once hosted the London, Chatham and Dover Railway; now it was a grassy walk bordered by a stone wall and tangled trees, where locals exercised their dogs and teenagers made fires and hung out after dark.

Kracholov found a dense area of shrubbery not far from number 54 and fought his way to its core. Checking he could not be seen from the houses or the cutting, he cleared a space and dumped the pack. The hit-man was pleased with himself. Half an hour in an internet café and one phone call and he had come up with the idea, found the cutting and ordered the equipment he would need from the Best Bulgarian Cleaning Company. He unfastened the pack and pulled from it a one-man bivouac tent, which he set up. He unpacked the rest of the contents, starting with the Franchi and a box of shells, and carefully stowed everything in the tent. Last, he climbed inside, filling the shelter to capacity, zipped up the tent and waited for night to fall. He flicked on a small torch, also courtesy of the Best Bulgarian Cleaning Company, and settled down to read a copy of the *NME*. Every twenty minutes or so he checked his watch and unzipped the tent to look outside.

*

Leo reappeared around nine and crossed the road to the van. It was quiet now. He boasted of his success with Edith and made another spirited attempt to persuade Laura to go out with him, only giving up when he realised it was time to meet another informant.

Laura called Will and Johnson to come back to the van for a break. She reached into the footwell for a carrier bag containing a thermos and a plastic lunchbox. When the pair arrived she broke open the seal and offered a choice of tuna or cheese and pickle sandwiches, made by Dot's fair hands. Will, Luka and Johnson agreed surveillance was a pitiful way to make a living.

Kracholov judged it was dark enough and emerged from his shelter. The cutting was silent apart from the occasional sigh of a car on the road above the gardens. There was light from a full moon only partly obscured by clouds so he pocketed his torch. He pulled a balaclava over his head and knelt on the ground, grabbing two handfuls of earth, which he rubbed into his face. Crouching and still, he listened for a few moments then crept through the undergrowth into the cutting. Staying by the trees he jogged along to Number 54 and sidled through the brush to look over the fence.

The garden was planted with mature shrubs and sloped down eighty feet to a three-storey semi-detached house in need of repair. He noticed an alarm casing he decided was a fake and two spotlights activated by movement. There was a ground floor extension with a flat roof and what looked like an open terrace on the second floor. He judged it would be relatively easy to climb to the top of the house from the outside.

There were lights in the kitchen. Kracholov delved into his camouflage jacket and produced a pair of binoculars. Inside, an older couple in matching cardigans were clearing things from the dinner table into a dishwasher. One was George Valentine. The Bulgarian presumed the table had been set for two, as the placemats and glasses had yet to be cleared. He glanced upwards across the rear of the darkened house. Through an upper window he spotted a slim line of light coming from an almost closed door. Either a light had been left on or someone else was there.

A harsh metallic noise attracted his attention. He focused the binoculars on a chalet-style shed in the neighbouring garden. There was a light inside and through a window he saw a man hunched over a bench saw, cutting a length of wood amid a spray of dust. Behind him all manner of tools hung from a rack on the wall. The noise continued for a few minutes and when the man had finished he switched off the lights and locked up. He placed the key to the shed under a flowerpot and walked down to his house. Kracholov was sure he'd seen a hacksaw.

The Bulgarian became aware of something tugging at his trousers. He looked down expecting to see a dog but found a small boy staring up at him. He guessed he was about eleven. His face was also smeared with dirt.

'What are you doing, mister?' the boy whispered. Kracholov dropped to a crouch.

'Nothing,' he said. The boy looked at him shrewdly. It was an improbable answer.

'Are you a burglar?' he asked.

'No,' Kracholov mouthed. 'Go away.'

'You look like a burglar. Are you a vandal then?'

'A vandal?' Kracholov looked across the brush to see if there was anyone else. 'My nan says *I'm* a vandal.'

'You should be at home with this nan,' said Kracholov.

'Fuck off,' said the boy, disgusted at the thought. 'So, are you a vandal?'

'I am soldier,' said Kracholov.

'Whose army?' the boy asked, suspicious.

'Your army. I am on mission,' Kracholov said in a low voice, one dirt-covered finger tapping his nose to denote extreme secrecy.

'You're foreign.'

'This is combined forces operation. Counter-terrorism.'

'Cool,' said the boy. He made a sweeping wave across the cutting. 'This is my place. We can be mates if you like. Have you got a fag?'

'I work alone,' said Kracholov. 'Go home.'

'Is that your camp over there?' the boy asked.

'You found my camp?' Kracholov was surprised. The boy smiled.

'I told you. This is my place. I know everything that goes on.'

'Please go away,' asked Kracholov. 'This is secret mission. I will have to break your legs.'

'Is it Mr Valentine?'

'What?'

'That's Mr Valentine's house,' said the boy. 'Who are you looking for?' Kracholov considered the boy for a moment then reached into a pocket and brought out the photographs of George, Laura and Ruby. The boy looked at them carefully.

'That's Mr Valentine,' he said. 'And that's his daughter. She takes photographs. I don't know the other one.'

'They are bomb-making cell,' said Kracholov.

'Fuck,' said the boy. 'What are you going to do?'

'I am assassin.'

'Wow.' The boy was clearly impressed. Kracholov stood up and from one of his voluminous pockets produced a thick roll of masking tape and stretched out a length.

'And now, I cannot let you go,' he said.

*

At ten-thirty, just as Laura was calling it a day, the green door opened. A slim figure in a black hoodie slipped into the street and walked quickly away from the house, his head down. Laura phoned Luka, who was taking his turn at the front, and started the engine.

'He's come out this side and he's moving fast,' she said. 'You'd better run.'

The figure was getting smaller so Laura pulled into the street. Luka reached the van and ran alongside it until Johnson slid the door back and helped him in.

Out of sight of the house the figure stopped under a tree and lit a cigarette. After a couple of drags he moved on at a slower pace. Laura drew up to the kerb as he crossed the road to a bus stop. He joined two more figures waiting under the shelter.

'That's weird,' said Will. 'They're wearing the same gear.' Each wore a black hoodie, dark jeans and canvas shoes and shouldered a dark grey rucksack. They talked and smoked until the bus arrived, then went up to the top deck. Laura let out the clutch and the van rolled into the street.

'Driver, follow that bus,' said Johnson. Will stifled a laugh. Laura looked at them.

'Have you two been smoking?' she asked. They averted their eyes. 'Great.' She wondered when they'd found the opportunity. It must have been at the last changeover, when Luka went to relieve them at the front of the house.

They followed the bus to South Wimbledon station, where five youths in dark hoodies filed off the bus, each with a rucksack.

'They're breeding,' said Johnson.

Hands in pockets, the five headed towards the underground.

'They're getting the tube,' said Laura. She pulled over to the side of the road and grabbed her camera as the youths disappeared into the entrance.

'Luka, come with me. Will, you take the van and drive to Clapham. It's the Northern Line, they must be heading that way. I'll call when we know where they're going.'

'Roger that,' said Will, sliding into the driving seat.

'Roger anything,' said Johnson.

The van set off at a snail's pace as Laura led Luka into the station. She bought tickets and they made it to the platform as a train arrived. The five hoodies were spread along the platform and entered the train two to a carriage and the last in a third. Laura and Luka followed the solo rider and sat a little way from him. The carriage was almost empty. Laura studied the boy. She couldn't see much of his face; a young jaw, the cable from his MP3 player trailing into his hood, the occasional glimpse of an eye as he flicked a look round the carriage. He seemed nervous, his leg shaking as he tapped one foot, a betrayal of tension disguised as an affectation of cool.

At Stockwell the five youths changed to the Victoria line. They left the underground at Brixton.

'We're in Brixton,' Laura shouted into her phone as she emerged into the night air. 'Where are you?'

'Not really sure,' said Will, 'but the cars are going really fast.' It sounded like his mouth was full.

'Are you eating?'

'We're finishing the sandwiches,' he said. She could hear Johnson making drumming sounds.

'Go to Clapham Common Station,' she said. 'Wait there.' It was central enough, she decided and safer to have them parked. Laura and Luka followed the hoodies into the backstreets until they came to a pub. Three of the youths huddled outside lighting cigarettes while the other two went inside. Laura linked arms with Luka and steered him towards the door.

Suddenly they were in Jamaica, in a dive bar with ska blasting a mostly male West Indian crowd. Hardened drinkers were strung along the bar and a group of teenagers played pool in a corner. One or two younger couples danced in front of a small stage, while older folk sat at tables talking. There was no sign of the two boys.

Laura and Luka took seats at the bar and waited for the barman who made no attempt to serve them. Laura looked round and realised it was a karaoke set up. An instrumental track, 'The James Bond Theme' by The Skatalites faded out and a fit but ageing man with white hair bounded onto the stage to give Desmond Dekker a work out. Laura felt a nudge from Luca, which she took as a sign of approval. Cool bar. She noted three exits running along one wall: Ladies, Gents and a corridor marked Garden.

'Hey, white people, Jamaica loves you,' the barman growled as he finally ambled over. 'No photographs,' he added, eyeing the camera. They ordered Red Stripe and Laura paid. Luka sipped his pint and listened to the old man, quietly adding a harmony for his own amusement, while Laura slid the camera off the bar and excused herself. Eyes followed her into the Ladies.

She spent a minute or two readying her Canon then slipped from the convenience into the corridor that led to the garden. The passage was unlit, whether through negligence or design, and led to a glass door that opened onto a courtyard. She kept to the shadows as she looked out and saw the two youths in a corner of the yard talking to several Jamaicans. A hoodie convention. She reached for her camera and began to take shots, trying to capture faces. There was light from rooms above the yard, which highlighted the group, but she knew she would need to be lucky. One of the Jamaicans produced a small bag while the taller of the two visitors brought out a bundle of banknotes.

She closed in on the transaction and, flipping the camera to series shoot, let it click away automatically. For a second the buyer's hood fell back and Russell Chamberlain was lit and recognisable. She heard footsteps along the passage and continued shooting as long as she dared, then turned towards the bar as two youths from the pool table passed her on their way to the courtyard.

Head down, she walked quickly back to the bar where she found Luka on stage singing a duet with the old man; 'I Can See Clearly Now' by Johnny Nash. The whole pub was cheering them on. She returned to the bar and picked up her drink. She thought about Will driving stoned across South London and Luka on stage and decided surveillance was probably not their calling.

'Hey, your man can sing,' shouted the barman, placing two more drinks in front of her. As the song came to a close the two hoodies crossed the bar and left. Luka was taking a bow with the old man, when Laura grabbed him by the wrist and dragged him towards the door. She was already on the phone to Will. As they left the barman came to shake hands with Luka and palmed him a small bag.

'Cool, man,' said Luka.

'No, you are cool, man,' laughed the barman. 'Come back, anytime.' Luka waved to the old man as Laura pushed him through the door. Outside they turned right and followed the five hoodies.

'They're heading back to the tube,' Laura shouted into the phone. 'Where are you now?'

'On Clapham Common,' Will said, 'getting a burger. There's this amazing food truck.' She could hear Johnson asking for more onions.

'Wait there,' Laura ordered. 'We could be coming your way.' She shut off the phone as the hoodies entered the station.

*

Kracholov stood by the bivouac and watched. Zipped inside, the boy was wrapped in several layers of tape but wriggling enough to make the shelter wobble and emitting a nasal sound that suggested a string of expletives. The Bulgarian picked up the Franchi and considered the possibilities. He hoped the combination of balaclava, dirt and darkness would be enough to conceal his identity. Also, if all went well he would be miles away within a day or so, depending on instructions, either back in Sofia and beyond reach or heading down to the Isle of Wight. That still left the question of what to do with the boy. He tried to avoid collateral damage as far as possible, particularly in respect of the young and elderly. He could arrange for the problem to be dealt with by the Best Bulgarian Cleaning Company but he was not sure they shared his sensibilities, and anyway, it would be a poor reflection on his professionalism to admit he was spotted by an eleven-year-old, no matter how streetwise. Maybe he would drop him into a skip somewhere later. It was a warm night, little harm would come to him and by the time the boy was found he would be long gone, having accomplished his mission.

'I can get out of this, you know,' said a small but clear voice from inside the tent. 'I'm not scared.' The hit-man grimaced. The boy must have wriggled free of his gag. He unzipped the shelter. The boy looked up at him with mischievous eyes.

'Is this a test?' he asked. 'Are you going on your mission?' Kracholov nodded.

'I want you to be quiet and still,' he said. 'Like you are dead.'

'Won't say another word,' promised the boy. To make sure Kracholov stuck a new strip of tape across his mouth then zipped the tent shut.

He waited for a while and when he was sure the mound in front of him would remain inert he shouldered the Franchi and made his way back to the fence. He looked down at the house, which was quiet and dark apart from the single light at the top, then across to the neighbour's garden. He was tempted. He knew he shouldn't deviate from his plan, but it would only take a few minutes. And it would improve his efficiency. And he was in Great Britain, after all. Improvisation and efficiency, wasn't that the secret to its military success in wars old and cold?

Kracholov climbed the fence and padded over to the shed. He found the key under the pot and let himself in as the moon slipped out from behind a cloud, casting a grey light inside. There was a workbench with a vice and on the wall an array of well-used tools including a robust looking hacksaw. He placed the Franchi in the vice and selected the hacksaw, a file and a wad of emery cloth. He wrapped a piece of masking tape around the barrel well short of the legal length of 18 inches and set to work with the saw exactly in the middle of the tape. A thin spray of black dust gathered on the barrel and soon he began to feel hot inside the balaclava and fatigues.

*

The five hoodies were sitting in a circle on Clapham Common a few minutes before midnight. Twenty feet away Laura was lying on the grass flicking through the shots she'd taken at the pub, deleting the failures. She showed them to Will, stopping at an image of Russell Chamberlain receiving a clear plastic bag filled with green buds from the Jamaican. Both faces were bathed in yellow light and identifiable.

'This nails him as a user and maybe a school dealer,' she said, 'and if this guy has a record we have him consorting with known villains.' She switched the camera back to shoot mode and clipped off some shots of the circle, a sniper in the shadows.

'It's not much of a deal,' said Will. 'Johnson could smoke that in an hour.'

'It looks like he has,' said Laura. The drummer was fast asleep next to them and Luka was beside him, checking for a pulse. Will rolled over and leaned on one arm.

'I thought we were after the dad?'

'We are.'

'How does this help?'

Laura fixed him with narrow eyes.

'I don't know, Will. I just get the shot. Maybe it says, 'my parents, who claim to be perfect, are too busy with their lives to bother with me, so I go out and get into trouble. My family is dysfunctional and has double standards.'

'Maybe it says, 'I'm a teenager and I like to have fun with my mates", said Will. Laura looked up at the sky.

'I need more light.'

Will leaned forward to kiss her. She pushed him away.

'Not now, Will. I'm busy.' She zoomed in on the five who were still sitting only a short distance away across the grass. Their heads were down and they were passing round a joint, their rucksacks forming an inner circle. Laura thought she heard chanting.

'Which one's Russell?' Will asked.

'I'm not sure,' Laura replied. 'The one on the right, I think.'

'Why don't we go to the pub and then back to your place?' Will ran his hand across her shoulder. Laura shrugged it off. The trouble with musicians, she thought, one trouble with them, is they just don't understand work.

At exactly midnight the five stood up and stepped forward, tightening their circle. They grasped each other's hands in a complex web of handshakes and stood silently for a few seconds, then grabbed their rucksacks and scattered in various directions, one narrowly missing Luka as he sprinted towards the north side of the Common.

'Shit,' said Laura, sitting up. 'They've gone.' She yelled at Will to follow the furthest two and took Luka with her in pursuit of the pair running north. While Will was shaking Johnson awake, Laura and Luka dashed across the main road into Lavender Gardens and past a blur of terraced houses. They stopped briefly at the junction with Lavender Hill. Opposite, a hooded figure was trotting along the side of the magistrate's court and on down Kathleen Road. There was no sign of another.

Laura and Luka followed the figure and rounding a curve in the road saw it disappear into Latchmere Road, now down to walking pace. They slowed their pursuit and recovered their breath. The figure stopped briefly at an overhead railway bridge and looked up for a few moments, reflecting on it for some reason, and then continued to another where it stopped again.

The second bridge spanned the road at an angle, its solid panels covered in layers of graffiti. Obscenities and signatures scrawled crudely in thick black marker lay on top of carefully shaded bubble lettering that in turn lay over grander typographical designs, each shout for attention replaced by another on an almost daily basis. It was a good spot for graffiti. The road was choked with traffic at both ends of the day and anyone crazy enough to drive into London via Clapham was certain to spend time at a standstill looking up at the bridge.

Laura and Luka ducked into a front garden and, shielded by a hedge, watched as the hoodie shook off his rucksack. He rummaged inside and produced a small anchor attached to a rope, which he launched skywards. Returning to earth it caught on a steel grey fence by the side of the bridge. He slipped the rucksack back on his shoulders and climbed the rope, scrabbling over the fence onto the corner of the bridge. Retrieving the anchor he moved to the centre of the structure, dropped the rucksack and knelt, disappearing behind the steel wall. He reappeared with an aerosol can in either hand and leaned over the side of the wall, stretching to reach its base. Spraying in wide arcs he obliterated the past until the bridge was turned into a yellow and red sunset.

Laura photographed the figure as he worked. Satisfied with the background he dipped beneath the panel again, this time reappearing with a stencil, which he flattened against the bridge wall and sprayed black, working in from the edges. A man in a loose suit emerged in black and light yellow, standing with his back to the viewer as if at a urinal, but looking over his shoulder. The hoodie moved along the bridge and another man appeared and then another until the expanse was filled with a line of urinating men. The artist filled the spaces around them with toilet graffiti in marker pen; phrases and cartoons with political intent, and then leaned far over the parapet and added the caption 'A Chorus Line.' Using another small stencil the figure signed the work in the bottom right corner with a small image of a parrot.

The artist dropped out of sight again, Laura assumed to pack away his tools. He reappeared and climbed over the railings, gripped an overhanging bush and slid to the pavement. From the ground he photographed the wall with his smart phone, the flash briefly illuminating the work. He turned towards Laura. She adjusted the lens, closing around the figure. The youth flipped back the hood and raised the smartphone to take a portrait of the artist and canvas. Laura hit the shutter release before she realised she was looking at a girl.

*

Kracholov had worked slowly to avoid making a noise but the hacksaw was nearly through the barrel. When it separated he laid the end to one side. He turned the gun in the vice, removed the masking tape and worked on it with the file and emery cloth to create a smooth finish. The sawn-off shotgun would no longer have a sight, but he was hardly likely to need one. The kick might be a little smarter but generally the weapon should handle as well if not more easily than in its original condition. And now it would be easier to transport and conceal. It may have been a risk but it would be worth it in the long run. Kracholov was working intently, in front of the window, when he became aware of movement at the side of the house. It was the man he'd seen earlier heading towards the shed. He released the Franchi from the vice and ducked beneath the bench. Moments later he heard footsteps outside. He looked in the direction of the door handle. If it moved he would attack. After a moment or two he heard footsteps walking away. He stood up, pocketing the file and emery cloth. He would finish the job in his camp, he decided. He felt for the door handle. It was locked.

*

'They're graff artists,' Will shouted into his phone.

'I know,' Laura replied. 'Is Russell with you?'

'No. We lost one in the street, but I don't think it was him,' said Will. 'We followed the other one into the underground. He did a nice job on a train. Wrapped it in a ribbon. Then he took a photo of himself. He was a ginger. We're back on the street now and it looks like he's heading back to the Common.'

159

Laura and Luka walked back up the Latchmere Road towards Lavender Hill. She was irritable. Will was right, she thought. She got caught up in a shot. That was her job and she was good at it. She didn't consider the rights and wrongs of it – editors did that. A job was a job; the more difficult the situation, the better the price and the better for her reputation. And people were getting to know her work. It was a tough business and you were only as good as your last shot. Conscience didn't come into it.

'Why are you angry?' asked Luka as they walked along Lavender Hill.

'I don't like to fail,' she said. She kicked the steel shutter of a shop as they passed.

'I understand,' he said. 'It is piss work.'

'What?'

'Piss work,' said the singer. 'This kind of work is not good.' For a moment, she wondered if Luka shared Will's scruples, then laughed.

'Oh, piece work,' she laughed. 'Yes, sometimes I get paid by the shot.'

'That's what I said.'

They passed a TV repair shop and stopped to look in the window. Behind a grille two televisions winked in the darkness, both showing the same black and white picture on Channel Four. It was a night camera on the *Escape from Wight* set. They watched Robert White's face grow as he approached the camera, his eyes pale and eerie. His hand reached behind the lens after which the screen went black. Laura wondered if it was live. Another camera picked up White sneaking from his quarters and crawling on his belly across the compound to the women's hut. Reaching it he skirted round the building, keeping in the shadows, and mounted the steps to the main entrance. A perimeter searchlight caught him and seconds later he was surrounded by guards and dogs. Surrendering, he was marched off to another hut, which subtitles described as 'The Cooler'. Inside he was put in a bare cell and given a baseball glove and a ball. Moments later a clock was set to count down from 10,000. Apparently, each time the ball hit a target in the wall opposite it scored a point, which was

160

reduced from the total. When he reached zero the prisoner would be released and a donation made to a charity of his choice.

Laura felt herself being pushed off the street into a doorway, where Luka pulled her close and kissed her.

'What are you doing?' she murmured, her lips squashed against his.

'I see him,' hissed Luka through the kiss. 'He is across road, behind you. He knows we are here.' They were standing in a recess made from two doorways, one to the repair shop the other to a travel firm. Still locked in an embrace, the couple shuffled round until Laura could see across the road.

Sure enough, there was a hoodie dressed in black with a grey rucksack, motionless in front of the white wall of the magistrate's court, watching them. Behind him, covering the lower part of the wall, was a caricature of a jailbreak, a gaping cartoon hole with torn bars and a line of figures climbing from the cells below: a classic burglar with a striped jersey who bore a striking resemblance to the Home Secretary; another familiar politician with a glass of champagne and a fistful of casino chips; the Metropolitan Police Commissioner recently censured for condoning excessive violence at a public demonstration; an African dictator who had siphoned his nation's wealth into a British bank; and lastly, a hoodie who was signing his name at the bottom of the picture.

Laura grabbed Luka's head and pulled him to her for a frenzied round of necking, until she saw the boy had returned to his work. She slipped her camera onto Luka's shoulder and captured the hoodie finishing his image, zooming in as he added his signature, two leaves fluttering. Cute, she thought. Rustle. Like his friends, Russell Chamberlain stepped back to admire and record his work. She was ready as he turned, having already composed the shot: Russell Chamberlain, lit in streetlight, his hood down, photographing himself in front of the cartoon, lampooned father behind, his signature at the bottom, the insignia of the magistrate's court over his shoulder. She pressed the shutter release. Job done.

Kracholov's second kick parted the shed door from its hinges and sent it flying over the chalet-style veranda into the middle of the garden, where it flattened several gnomes grouped around a pond and nearly killed the cat that was weaving among them. The cat let out a shriek that emptied the trees and shot into a rosebush. The Bulgarian came out of the hut with his sawn-off shotgun now loaded and pointed ahead. He backed around the side of the wooden hut into the darker depths of the garden, feeling behind him for the fence. Along the way, he came face to face, or rather back to front with a beehive he hadn't noticed on his way in. Perched precariously on uneven stones the hive toppled at the first contact and Kracholov found himself in a cloud of insects, angry at having their tower-block home demolished. He stumbled towards the fence and, having lost the element of surprise and to escape the bees that were now stinging, blew the fence off its posts with two shots from the Franchi. The blasts tore the night. If he'd looked over his shoulder at that moment, he would have seen the occupants of 56 Mersley Road, who were watching from the relative safety of a back bedroom, dive for cover beneath a windowsill, cracking their heads together on the way down.

Kracholov blundered through the undergrowth, waving the bees away, until he reached his camp. He grabbed one end of the bivouac tent which he pulled over his shoulder, hooked the Franchi into the loops of his backpack and staggered towards the railway cutting, dragging everything behind him, along with an accumulation of brush. With the brute force of a rhinoceros, he dragged the whole assembly through the park gardens, across the road and up onto One Tree Hill, his progress hampered by the fact the collapsed tent was once again exhibiting signs of independent movement.

Laura called it a night as the five descended into Clapham North underground. They had regrouped on the Common for a few minutes, this time in an informal circle, laughing and smoking cigarettes and comparing the images in their smartphones, then headed home at a relaxed pace, ditching their aerosols and stencils along the way.

There was little conversation as Laura drove home. Will and Luka napped, and she dropped Johnson off in Streatham. They woke as they neared East Dulwich and Luka picked up Laura's camera and switched it on.

'Be careful with that,' she warned. Will showed Luka the playback button and watched as the singer flipped through the images.

'They are good,' said Luka. Laura smiled. Luka passed the camera back to Will and pulled out the bag of grass from the pub. He smelt the contents, gave a connoisseur's sign of approval and began to roll a joint on his knees.

'He's a kid,' Will said.

'It's a job, Will. Don't personalise it,' said Laura.

'It'll be personal to him,' said Will. 'We know his mother's a twisted bitch and he obviously thinks his dad's a crook. Imagine what they'll do when they see him on the news with his portrait of Burglar Dad.'

'So?'

'The old man's fair game. I get that. He's probably done the same thing to a dozen others. But I don't see the need to go after the kid.'

'It'll probably get him an exhibition,' said Laura.

'Maybe he doesn't want to be exposed,' said Will.

'Of course he does. Everyone does.'

The argument was left in mid-air as the van rounded the corner into Mersley Road and met a roadblock. A police van was parked across the street, while two officers with flak jackets and automatic weapons guarded either pavement. Luka slipped the joint and bag of weed into a pocket as the elder of the two officers stepped up to the window to assess the occupants. Behind him, further along the road, a spotlight from a helicopter wavered over the back gardens between the street and One Tree Hill.

Laura convinced the officer they were residents and had been miles away at the times that seemed of interest to him. He signalled for the police van to move aside.

'So, what's the trouble?' she asked.

'I'm not supposed to say, but seeing as you're a resident, some nutter seems to have gone berserk with a shotgun,' he said. 'He broke into a shed at Number 56 and blasted his way out.' He asked if she had seen anything suspicious during the last few days. Laura shook her head and Will and Luka followed suit.

'I suggest you go straight home and stay there,' said the officer. 'You'll be safe inside. He's gone over the hill. We have him surrounded. He's not going to get away.'

Laura drove slowly along the street and all three looked up at the spotlight. They could hear the helicopter but hardly see it, just a dark shape above the light, hovering in the night sky. Laura parked the van outside number 54. Will handed the camera to her, with just enough hesitation to make her check the image library.

'They've gone,' she said. She looked at Will, incredulous.

'I know,' he said, with an apologetic shrug. 'I deleted them.'

*

Over the brow of One Tree Hill stood a stone church, nestled in woodland that ran down to Honor Oak. Despite damp and decay the church was host to a small yet dedicated congregation and a series of vicars who had done their best to bring it to life with concerts, services and fund-raising drives. During the day the flag of St George flew from a turret and occasional bursts of song could be heard on the hill. At night it was deserted and dark, a gothic shadow in the midst of a brooding wood. Kracholov was sitting exhausted on the church steps, concealed from the helicopter by a crumbling arch. He was reloading the Franchi as the searchlight fluttered above the trees a stone's throw away. He could see shadowy figures moving round the edge of the light, heading slowly towards him.

So this is where it would end, he thought. There had been many missions over the years and several shoot-outs, but none where the odds had been so slim. He would make his last stand by the church and, if he was lucky, create a breach in the row of policemen moving towards him, and charge through to who knows where. Surrender was not an option. There was no going back when you accepted an assignment from the firm. The Best Bulgarian Cleaning Company could reach into any prison and failure carried a severe penalty.

Kracholov looked down at the crumpled tent by his feet and noticed a rippling movement. He could use the boy as a hostage, of course, but his heart was not in it. No, he would keep it a straight fight. He propped the Franchi against the arch, unzipped the tent and prised the squirming package from its interior. He unwrapped the mummified child while he watched the shadows in the woods. The boy squealed as the masking tape came off his mouth. He looked at Kracholov with a frown.

'You are free to go,' said the hit-man, as he stripped away the final layers of tape. 'I am sorry for inconvenience, but it was secret mission.'

'Was it a success?' asked the boy, who seemed relaxed about his incarceration.

'No. I failed. You should go now.'

The boy peered about, getting his bearings, grinning when he saw the church. Clearly this was also his turf. Then he looked up at the sky.

'Is that a helicopter?' he asked, pointing.

'Yes.'

'Fuckin' wowza,' he said, gaping at the machine. He shielded his eyes and looked around the wood, getting used to the light. He couldn't fail to see the shadowy figures in navy flak jackets closing in. Kracholov picked up the Franchi and fired twice at different parts of the police ring. The figures ducked for cover.

'You should go now,' he said. 'There will be a fight.' The boy wore a grim expression, as if he had already made his own assessment of the situation and determined the odds were against the hit-man surviving.

'I know a way out,' he said.

'Go,' Kracholov insisted. He reached into his backpack and pulled out a bottle of vodka. He twisted the cap and raised the bottle. '*Naz drave!*' He saluted the boy and took a huge slug. 'Want some?' The boy took a slug and choked.

'I mean it,' said the boy, wheezing. 'I can get you out of here.' It slowly dawned on Kracholov the boy might know what he was talking about. Anyway, his options were hardly worth considering: almost certain death in a gunfight with twenty armed police or take a chance on an eleven-year-old boy's knowledge of the terrain. He twisted the cap back on the bottle.

'Go,' he said. 'I will follow.' Kracholov shouldered the backpack and held the Franchi across his chest. He left the tent.

'OK,' shouted the boy. He was excited, revelling in the chance to lead an impossible mission against a helicopter and the best the Metropolitan Police could throw at him.

'This way,' he said and led Kracholov along one side of the church, over a low wall and through thick foliage to the top of the hill. They crossed a path and descended down the other side, following a track close to the edge of the wood. As they walked, Kracholov noticed a fence to his right and beyond it rows of gravestones, the palest of which shone in the moonlight. They ducked behind a clump of trees when they saw a policeman moving up the hill, only a few feet away, and after he passed continued through the brush until they came to railings at the bottom of the wood. Beyond them lay the road, the Victorian park and the railway cutting. At the boy's instruction, they squatted and waited as a new cloud slipped in front of the moon and plunged them into darkness, and then padded across the road and down to the cutting, walking away from Number 54 until they reached a high fence. The boy led Kracholov to a small hole at the base of the barrier and through to the other side.

'It's a golf club,' whispered the boy. Kracholov looked around. He could make out a flag and a narrow chalet that might pass for a clubhouse and what could be a series of gullies, slopes and flat expanses of green. Dotted among them were louvered turrets springing from the grass. Whatever they were, he thought, they were man-made. He saw two officers with torches checking the main gate some distance away.

'We're on top of a reservoir,' whispered the boy. 'The biggest underground reservoir in Europe.' Kracholov's confidence was building. The situation was so bizarre he might just get out of it alive.

'OK,' he said, 'where now?' The boy led him to one of the turrets. He knelt and felt in the grass for a while until he found a handle. He pulled it and lifted a circular disc of grass from the ground. It hid a manhole.

'It's an emergency exit,' said the boy, as the moon emerged to reveal his beaming face. 'And the alarm's broken.' Kracholov lifted the cover.

'You go. I'll follow,' said the Bulgarian, smiling for the first time in a while. The boy gripped the sides of a vertical ladder and descended into darkness. When he had reached the bottom, Kracholov lowered his backpack into the hole and followed, carefully replacing the grassy cover. He climbed down the ladder, feeling the air growing cold and wet and sensing a vast space. At the bottom he found the boy had produced a torch. They were in one of a series of huge vaulted caverns covering vast pools of water and tiled walkways.

'This way,' said the boy. Kracholov reached in his pocket for his own torch and followed without a word.

*

A bus ride away in a Kennington bedsit Alan Leo poured the last of a bottle of Bell's whisky into a tumbler and tried to focus on his laptop, to review what he had written.

Westminster Inside Track

https://www.witreport.co.uk

The Good Life

Westminster Inside Track

They have houses in Wimbledon and Gloucester, Olympic hopes for their show-jumping daughter and run with the hunting set. We know the Chamberlains enjoy the good life.

Your eyes and ears on Westminster and Whitehall; exposing the rumours, conspiracies and whitewash at the heart of government; a virtual voice in a new age of accountability.

But it seems they live it on the cheap. Meet Edith, their housekeeper. WIT did today. Edith doesn't know how she got her name. It was a slave name handed down from her grandmother. Edith is from Cameroon. She came to England a year ago with her son, on the run from persecution – he's gay, and that means torture and a jail sentence in their hometown, if not worse.

Edith arrived on our shores to seek asylum and a better life. She found work in a well-to-do family who wanted help living the good life. Edith cleans, cooks and babysits for sixteen hours a day, in return for starvation wages and vague promises of help with her situation; just one of almost a million illegal aliens living in this country.

Edith's would be just another case for the Home Office, unworthy even of the back pages, but she is working for the Home Secretary, for less than the minimum wage, longer than the maximum hours prescribed by the European Working Time Directive and contrary to the laws relating to alien registration over which her employer presides.

Expect questions in the papers, in the House and on the streets. Meanwhile Edith will eke out her existence, hoping for justice in a land with a reputation for fair play, while the Home Secretary will no doubt continue to do his best to uphold traditional family values. Victorian ones.

[Any resemblance of this article to one of those charity campaigns that shock and twist your heartstrings is entirely coincidental. This was a strictly one-off attempt at concerned journalism.]

WITLINKS: <u>Robert White's latest gamble pays off – Ex-Cities Minister boosts reality show ratings/PM joins England training session – 'has stamina beyond his years,' says coach.</u>

18

Just before dawn Kracholov emerged through another grassy manhole half a mile away, chilled in every sense. When they parted, he gave the boy his binoculars as a keepsake and lifted him to his chest in a crushing bear hug. The two warriors pledged lifelong comradeship and Kracholov watched as the little figure swaggered down the road with the first hint of daylight. Only then did he wonder how the child came to be walking the streets alone.

When the boy was out of sight he found a clump of bushes and changed into jeans, shouldered the pack and caught a bus north. He would take a break he decided, let things die down while he came up with a new plan. He would spend the weekend making a detailed study of Soho and the places where British rock was born.

As the bus crossed London, collecting and discarding bleary-eyed workers, Kracholov planned his tour. He would start at 90 Wardour Street, the second incarnation of the Marquee Club; then on to the site of La Chasse, the drinking den where Jon Anderson had slept, swept up and poured drinks until meeting Chris Squire and forming Yes, and where Keith Moon had once arrived via the rooftops from The Who's offices in Old Compton Street. He would have a pint of English ale at The Ship, once famous for its 'lock-ins' where everyone drank before and after a gig; then on to 17 St Anne's Court, home of Trident Studios and the revolutionary 'A' Range console that allowed complex multi-track recording.

Kracholov salivated at the thought of visiting such a hallowed place. Bowie, Rod Stewart and Lou Reed had recorded there, and the progressive rock bands Genesis and Van Der Graaf Generator, the hardest music to come by in 1970s Bulgaria. A fragment of a lyric slipped into the assassin's mind:

We moved together to the West,
West is where all days will someday end.

It was from Peter Hammill's five-minute single 'Refugees'. Forty years ago Kracholov had puzzled over the words in darkened rooms sickly sweet with joss sticks. What did it mean? Everyone will one day move west? West, like the wagon trains and railways that crossed America? Or life is a journey west, for west is where the sun sets? Where we will die? Prog rock lyrics were vague, often nonsensical, but filled with portent. That was the great thing. You could read anything into them, and stoned out of your head you often did. Not that Kracholov ever caught a whiff of cannabis. He and his friends resorted to tobacco joints laced with birdseed, the occasional pop giving the impression of a badly rolled joint and a placebo effect, as they imagined what it must be like to be stoned like Western youths. They interpreted the lyric as the promise of an end to Communism and a new future filled with music and freedom and things, all the things you could possibly want, and a few you didn't know you did. West was a place where no one gave you a compulsory haircut and you could buy x-ray specs.

For progressive rock bands, he learned later, west also meant going to Wales to create a concept album based on the life of Eglantine Banks, Hobbit Mother, where they banged out twenty-minute duels between keyboard and guitar until they woke to find punk had pushed them into the discount rack and one of their number had a drug habit that had long since devoured the furniture. In the end there is failure, thought the Bulgarian. He jerked his mind back to his tour. After Trident Studios, he wasn't sure where he would go, but the possibilities were endless.

In the evenings he would cook whatever game he managed to shoot in London's parks at dawn each day, though this would be challenging now the Franchi had lost most of its barrel. His best bet would be to stalk a well-fed duck as it skirted the edge of a public pond in search of hand-outs, though the blast at close range would likely turn it into pâté. If possible he would buy tickets to an Elbow or Muse concert, as he had heard, again in a pub, these were the bands closest to progressive rock and one had even written a symphony, albeit only thirteen minutes long. And all the time, in the back of his mind, he would be planning his next raid on Mersley Road.

*

While Kracholov had wandered the watery catacombs of Honor Oak Reservoir, George slept soundly. Incredibly, he missed Laura and Will's ferocious argument on the pavement outside Number 54, where each battled for the last word until police officers at either end of the street had readied their weapons and started towards them, whereupon the lovers had fought along the path and up the stairs and slammed into their respective rooms. Dot, who was aware of the burgeoning romance between her daughter and the musician, woke and listened intently, then rolled over and went back to sleep, relieved things might be ending as quickly as they had begun. To her mind Laura was destined for greater things and she drifted back to chiffon dreams of a white summer wedding in a grand house to an impossibly rich, aristocratic and malleable groom, though it was not altogether clear in her dream whether the handsome hero was marrying Laura or her glamorous mother.

Will woke on Friday morning with something like a hangover. After Laura had stomped into her room he and Luka smoked a joint while he vented. Halfway through a second they forgot what they were talking about and wrote a song, imagining the crazed gunman outside was chasing a pair of young lovers on the run, kind of *Romeo and Juliet* meets *The Godfather*. They made a stab at recording in the dead of night and called the song 'Running for Love'.

Will breakfasted to the realisation he was likely to be evicted as soon as George found out about the previous night's debacle. Laura blanked him on the stairs while he was taking out the rubbish; not even the hiss of 'arsehole' under her breath. Clearly they were over. After a promising audition he hadn't got the gig.

He wondered what had possessed him. He'd seen the dustbin icon on her camera and become fascinated by what would happen if he pressed it. He had touched the button as if placing a bet and a choice popped up. For a moment he was a contestant on *Who Wants To Be A Millionaire*. Will, is the answer: A. Delete This Image; B. Delete All; or C. Do Nothing? He'd chosen B and Deleted All. The way Will saw it his parents might have lost the right to control their destiny, but the boy hadn't. His mistake lay in thinking Laura would see it his way. Instead, she had flown at him. Women. Wired differently. He had fucked it up again.

*

Luka spent most of Friday with Johnson sightseeing. This consisted of visiting pubs of marginal historic interest, an hour at the Trocadero and a peek in the door at Ronnie Scott's after a liquid lunch. Will spent the day in the flat, recording guitar parts into his Mac which Luka could add to later, all the while waiting for the knock at his door that would trigger their homelessness. When the singer returned in the evening there had still been no knock, so Will dragged him to the pub, where they re-lived their first meeting in Brac and shaped the immense future they would build together. Afterwards they worked on the rough track from the night before.

Saturday was punctuated by minor chores for George, which Will carried out with trepidation, and rehearsals. Will and Luka travelled into town and met the rest of the band at the studios and after rehearsals the boys moved on to a pub. Laura didn't show at either place.

*

Charles Franklin visited his wife on Friday, the morning after her surgery, and pulled up a chair next to The Marshall who was already at her side. After the flowers and platitudes of a hospital visit the two men settled down to drink coffee laced with brandy and catch up on the news while Melissa drifted in and out of a drugged reverie. As the surgeon had predicted, Melissa looked like a character from a fifties sci-fi movie, as did Marshall, their heads encased in white egg shaped helmets, though the guitarist had moved on to the more flexible velcro and elastic version. Charles took the first two newspapers from a stack he had brought, tossed the *Mirror* to Marshall and settled down with the *Daily Mail.*

The pony story had been running for twenty-four hours and was covered in all the papers and on morning TV, which was playing on the set bolted to the wall opposite Melissa's bed. Charles smiled. It was all over the web too. The story had received an ironic treatment: ambitious wife of the Home Secretary, selfish and unpopular on a scale not seen since Imelda Marcos, had doped all the ponies at the local gymkhana, robbing a bevy of well-bred young ladies of their dreams. The *Daily Mail* was outraged by the decline of motherhood, the *Mirror* by middle-class mischief, and *The Guardian* quoted an animal rights activist who called for an equine equivalent of the Court of Human Rights. The story was proving an embarrassment for the Home Secretary, but not career-threatening. As a spokesperson put it, 'This is a family not a Cabinet matter.'

Now the story was taking another turn as Billy Sinclair, stable-hand and hopeful jockey, was interviewed on Sky TV. Looking directly into the camera he told the viewing public he suspected a cover-up. He claimed all the toffs involved had been paid off to keep them quiet and questioned why the police had not investigated the matter and in customary fashion leaked it to the media. Charles, Marshall, and in a rare moment of lucidity Melissa, watched the perky lad suggest himself as the hero of the hour and protector of democracy. The story moved up the political Richter scale and statements were made on behalf of the Home Secretary, denying a cover-up and any personal knowledge of, or interest in, equestrian matters.

Charles assumed the spin machine in Whitehall was now in overdrive. He chuckled when, just as the pony scandal seemed under control, Sky broke the second story, the altogether more damaging allegation that the Home Secretary was harbouring illegal immigrants to run his London home. Charles imagined Chamberlain locked in a room with a handful of trusted advisors, sweating over his next utterance. He wondered if he could order champagne as he relaxed in his hospital chair, triumphant. George had delivered big time. His phone rang. It was Sir Frank Porter calling to congratulate him. Charles preened and left the room as Melissa pushed a button on one of her tubes to deliver more pain relief.

By evening the BBC was all over the story and outraged members of Her Majesty's Opposition were calling for the Secretary of State's resignation. He in turn was leaving his wife to carry the can. Family friends commented how the situation, on top of the pony fiasco, was putting an intolerable strain on their marriage. The same friends admitted Mary Chamberlain handled all aspects of the household's management, including expense claims, due to her husband's pressing schedule. One journalist promptly dug up how much she was paid by her husband for her help in mismanaging his political life.

By Saturday she was in hiding in Gloucestershire. Ken Chamberlain appeared on television in London, looking exhausted, and stressed again the difference between marital and Cabinet responsibility. Later, on the steps of their country house, his wife made a tearful apology for the shame she had brought on her family and blamed the pressure of standing in the shadow of such a great man. Meanwhile, another anonymous 'friend' revealed Mary's long-standing mental health problems and praised Ken Chamberlain's saint-like devotion to his wife's wellbeing.

Laura watched the story unfold while she catalogued the shots from the book launch and the recce round Chamberlain's house. As far as she was concerned, the Chamberlains were exposed as the arrogant and conniving leeches she was sure they were. Wasn't arrogance the fatal flaw of all who felt they should stand above the crowd? She wondered if the graffiti story would have finished them. It certainly added texture to the picture emerging of a massively defective household. She remained furious with Will but had not told George. She had simply described what they'd seen and said she'd missed the shot. George was more surprised than disappointed. He had patted her on the shoulder and said they could try another night if they needed to, but first they would see how things went with the two stories that were running.

As she flipped through the figures on her screen, playing with exposure, contrast and temperature, Laura sensed something else nagging at her. Her thoughts drifted back to art school, remembering work with grand themes and dreams of breaking new ground in photography. Moreover, she found herself looking at the images in front of her, questioning what they said about her as well as their subject.

*

George spent most of Saturday in the cellar listening to Radio 4, absorbing the news while tidying up from his investigations. The Home Secretary was wounded, that was certain, wounds worsened by a conspicuous silence from the Prime Minister. In most cases the PM would have pledged confidence in his colleague even if he intended to throw him to the wolves later. George assumed the Great Man was waiting for the latest polls to reveal the extent of the damage to his adversary as well as their relative popularity before making a move. Only then would he know how far to plunge the knife. No matter, thought George; of one thing there was no doubt. They would be rubbing their hands with glee inside Number 10.

He bagged up the rubbish from the Chamberlains' house and had Will and Luka carry it out to the dustbins. The most incriminating items he kept and filed for future use. He filled the crate Dot had left at the bottom of the cellar steps. All the time he ruminated. Though cornered, the Home Secretary would, George suspected, wriggle his way out of the avalanche of bad news. He was a wily operator. If so, they would need to come up with something else. And the quicker the better, given the pace of developments on *Escape from Wight*. It might only be a matter of hours until White cornered Ruby. What would happen then? Would she expose them all in front of millions of viewers? He was fairly confident she would honour their bargain and stay silent, unless of course a large amount of money was on offer.

When the cellar was cleared, George opened a drawer and pulled out the report Will had taken from Chamberlain's study, placing it on the bench in front of him. 'The London Risk Report: Top 10 Threats To Public Security. Top Secret'. He spent a long time reading. It was dynamite. The report detailed the greatest dangers to the capital and detailed the security arrangements for each of them. Lying on the desk in Chamberlain's study and guarded by detectives it was a bomb without a detonator. A simple leak to the papers would result in an investigation into its theft and blame would likely fall on the security services. It would not polish off the Home Secretary. However, found elsewhere, somewhere public, where the minister was shown to be negligent, it could have devastating consequences.

George considered the report from every angle, always returning to his grand plan, the details of which he had been filling in over the past few days. Was this just a way to put the final nail into Chamberlain's coffin, or could it be the catalyst for the last and most spectacular achievement of his career? The risks of using it were great. He assumed the report was the last thing on the Home Secretary's mind at present, but if its disappearance had been logged and an investigation was underway, detectives might already be trying to track down the mysterious Silver Screen Locations.

More certain, Dot would kill him. It broke their single ethic. They exposed the truth, they did not distort or manipulate it. Nor did they judge. The media might do all these things but that was their business. This was the creed he and Dot had agreed and they had never wavered from it. At Valentine Competitive Insight they uncovered information, albeit by illegal means once in a while, but it was just that – fact, occurrence, a secret truth. White *was* with Ruby and Anton Ledakov in the casino, he *had* made representations about the planning application; Mary Chamberlain *had* doped ponies; Edith *was* an illegal alien. These were facts, albeit concealed, which George and Dot placed before the court of public opinion. The London Risk Report on its own was innocent, saving the fact it had been stolen. To be useful it would require the single manipulation of their business partnership. George balanced ethics, Dot's rage and the risk of exposure against the potential reward.

Whether the report became part of it or not, George realised things were heading rapidly towards a conclusion. He resolved to pack a few more crates over the weekend and when he heard Dot descending the cellar steps with a mug of tea he slipped the report back into the drawer.

*

Over the weekend *Escape from Wight* became a phenomenon. The programme satisfied the nation's craving for fly-on-the-wall entertainment and millions became addicted, captivated by the idea of celebrities incarcerated in a World War Two setting without access to hair straighteners. Newspapers selected their favourites and *Heat* magazine luridly profiled each contestant, including an interview with Ruby conducted before she was helicoptered to the camp. William Hill opened a book on who would be most likely to escape, favouring the swarthy lead of a long-finished soap.

By Friday afternoon, Robert White had completed 10,000 throws on target, winning a sizeable donation to his nominated cause, a charity with a mission to bring opera to the unfortunate. He was escorted back to the Men's Hut, rubbing his elbow and nodding appreciatively at the smattering of applause from his fellow contestants. The following day he managed to get close to Ruby in the Catering Hut as they queued for dinner. As their meagre rations were slopped into bowls on wooden trays, White begged her to confess that she had set him up in the casino. An argument ensued that ended with Ruby emptying the contents of her tray over him and stealing his cutlery, after which the guards intervened and marched him back to the cooler, gave him the ball and glove and reset the clock to 10,000.

Later on Saturday the Women's Escape Committee split into two teams of three, each allocated to one of the tunnels they had discovered. They would finish them before the end of the weekend and make their escape. Ruby led one team which included the bitchy lead singer of a girl band whose career had tanked after going solo and an elderly cookery writer who had been the model for modern celebrity chefs, but had earned little, drunk much, and needed to promote a book to get her by in old age. The three intrepid tunnellers disappeared into their hole with forks, spoons and a stolen saucepan for the rest of the weekend. Minute cameras along the tunnel recorded their animated conversations about husbands, celebrity, and a range of addictions led by shopping on Amazon. Meanwhile, the men found a pair of wire-cutters and a map of the woods and spent the weekend arguing over their escape plans.

Chamberlain's chaotic private life and *Escape from Wight* dominated the media throughout Saturday. But news ebbs and flows, and as one story plateaus, awaits a new twist or dies, another rises, and by evening both were trumped, for the time being anyway, by events in the West Midlands.

19

The smell of frying bacon drew George to the kitchen in his dressing gown, to find Dot juggling pans as she made his favourite breakfast, the Full Monty; eggs, bacon, sausages, mushrooms, toast and Marmite. Laura always joined them on Sundays and was already down, sitting at the kitchen table among the morning papers, chewing toast and tapping her Samsung, while the news ran on a small TV on the wall.

'One egg or two?' Dot asked, giving an unconscious shake of her hips. She was wearing a flowery apron and waved a slotted turner. George stuck two fingers in the air, grabbed a mug of steaming tea from beside the kettle and sat down. He was grumpy this morning, having worked late into the night, and knew his best strategy was to smile and keep quiet.

'Chamberlain gets a roasting,' said Laura, tossing the *Sunday Mirror* to him. 'And they're making a big thing of the Prime Minister not supporting him. They say he'll have to resign.' She stopped for a slurp of tea.

'We'll see,' said George. He peered over the paper at his daughter, admiring her ability to eat like a truck driver but never gain a pound.

'And Edith is putting the boot in,' she continued, reaching for the Marmite jar. 'She's illegal all right, came in on a lorry across the channel. She's been working for the Chamberlains for a year. They didn't even check her address. She says Mary Chamberlain promised to help with her papers if she worked for less than the minimum wage.' Laura examined her toast to ensure it had the correct combination of butter and black sludge. '*She* sounds a delight. And the police are considering prosecution over the ponies.'

She pointed her toast at the TV.

'But that's the big story. It started breaking yesterday after *Escape from Wight*.'

'What happened?' asked Dot.

'Big riot in Birmingham,' said Laura.

'On *Escape from Wight.*'

'Oh, the girls finished the tunnels,' said Laura. 'Now they have to find their escape clothes which are hidden somewhere in the camp. Trouble is the boys found them instead and are planning to go over the wire in drag. It'll never work. Have you seen the size of that DJ from Capital Radio?'

'Did Robert White get to Ruby?' Dot asked. George caught the look of concern that flickered across her face. She'd been more confident than he that Ruby would keep to their deal but even she knew the Estonian could be fickle if it came to money.

'No. He's still in the cooler,' said Laura, through a mouthful of toast. 'He had a thousand throws to go when I switched off.'

George reached for the handset and turned up the volume. A reporter was standing in front of a group of demonstrators in Birmingham's city centre. Beneath her ran the caption: 'Birmingham Riots LIVE'. George forked a sausage as she gave her report.

'Police regained control of the city centre late last night, helped by heavy showers which affected much of the West Midlands. This morning it emerged that a group of protestors, thought to be Asian Muslims, have taken over the building behind me in Broad Street and are barricaded inside. They are believed to have at least two hostages and may be armed. So far they have made no demands.'

'Country's going to the dogs,' George grumbled.

'It's already gone,' said Dot. She squirted Fairy Liquid into the washing up bowl.

'Trouble started after the Aston Villa and Birmingham City derby,' continued the reporter. 'Fans clashed with demonstrators from a local factory which closed last week, with the loss of a hundred jobs.' There was a montage of the previous evening's violence, rioters clashing with police in the rain and dark. 'Scuffles broke out along Broad Street and turned into a pitched battle on Birmingham's Walk of Stars. Bottles and concrete slabs were thrown and the area was sealed off. More than thirty arrests were made. Protesters on both sides stayed in the area and conducted an all-night vigil.' The broadcast cut back to the reporter as a cow walked up and nuzzled her curiously. 'Participants in a third, countryside march were also caught in the chaos.'

The reporter interviewed a clergyman who said Birmingham was a tinderbox that might ignite the country, and then a retailer who said he was ruined. The first called for calm reflection, the second for the return of borstal training. The reporter turned back to the camera.

'This morning we have reports of a build-up of demonstrators,' she said, 'with anti-fascist and nationalist groups travelling to the city. It is believed the West Midlands Police are drafting in additional resources from neighbouring counties. At the siege site armed police and negotiators are trying to make contact with those inside. A police spokesman said all options were presently open and they could not rule out the possibility of a terrorist act.' The reporter looked squarely into the camera. 'Where this will end, no one is sure, but one question being asked this morning is, why did the West Midlands Police allow three marches to take place on the same day?'

George looked up from his empty plate.

'That was magnificent,' he said. Dot smiled indulgently. He flipped through the rest of the *Mirror*. There was a picture of Hammond Marshall's wife being squired to an occult convention by two young men. "Warlocks To The Marshall!' says Wife', roared the headline. Beside it was a smaller picture of two young women standing outside the Manor Hospital, above the caption: "He looks like a Martian and is limp as lettuce,' claims Marshall fans'.

George rose from his chair, tucked the newspaper under his arm and picked up his tea.

'I think we should pack a few more crates,' he said. Dot and Laura looked up in surprise. 'We're going to be on the move. I can feel it in my waters. I've started in the cellar.' Wife and daughter watched bemused as he walked from the kitchen. He stopped in the hall to pick up a leaflet from the table beneath the mirror. It advertised Blake's Ride at The Rialto, King's Cross. He pocketed it and started humming as he descended the steps to his office.

20

Shortly after two the phone rang. George took the call in the cellar, then went up to Laura's room and knocked on her door. She opened it guardedly, half expecting Will.

'You're going to Birmingham,' he said. 'That was Charles Franklin. Eleanor Porter is going there and they want a photographer.' Laura frowned. 'A car is coming to take you to the airport.'

'Can you fly to Birmingham?' she asked.

'She can.'

Fifty minutes later Laura was sitting in the rear of a Learjet 45 on the runway at London City Airport in a seat that reeked of new leather. Behind her, in an area that doubled as a bar and washroom, a gilt mirror crammed eight plush seats, the cockpit door and a world of maple cabinetry into its reflection. Laura glanced at the frayed edges of her jeans and fiddled with the rucksack on her lap.

She looked up to find the co-pilot greeting Charles Franklin as he stooped to enter the cabin, stabbing at his iPhone. When he saw Laura the PR man grinned and made his way down the narrow aisle.

'Hello,' he said, with a flash of white teeth. He was dressed in a blue suit with a white shirt open at the neck. He relaxed into the seat opposite as if he owned the plane. Laura returned the greeting, trying to find a tone that combined dislike with recognition he had given her the job.

'I'd offer you a glass of champagne,' said Charles, 'but I suppose we're working.' Laura looked over his shoulder to see Eleanor Porter and two middle-aged men climbing aboard, one in a crumpled pinstripe, the other in jeans and a blazer. They settled in the seats nearest the cockpit. Eleanor was wearing a soft grey suit, with a narrow black belt and ballet pumps, offset by a black satchel bag which she placed on the fourth seat. She acknowledged Charles and Laura before sitting down.

The co-pilot closed the door and gave the briefest of safety instructions. They would be five in all. Flying time would be less than thirty minutes, the challenge being to slip in and out of two busy cities. Laura leaned across to Charles.

'Shouldn't we be taking the train?' she whispered.

'Why?'

'Taxpayer outrage at MPs' expenses?'

'This is a crisis,' said Charles. 'Anyway, it's not on the taxpayer. This is Eleanor's plane.'

'Oh.'

'Well, it's her husband's, which amounts to the same thing.' He smiled as a thought occurred to him. 'Think of it as a banker giving something back to society.'

'Did you just think that up?' she asked. 'Is that spin?'

'It's being prepared,' Charles replied.

'I'd never have taken you for a boy scout,' she said. 'I bet it comes so naturally, you don't even notice. The spin thing, it just oozes from every pore.' Charles looked at her quizzically. Laura guessed he was trying to work out if he had received a compliment or an insult.

'It's my gift. Anyway, let me explain,' he said. 'Have you been following the situation in Birmingham?'

'I saw the news.'

'Eleanor is Minister for Cities and our second city is in trouble so she's going to see what she can do about it.'

'And what's that? Host a fashion show?' Charles looked at her blankly. 'I thought she was a model?' Laura looked across to the minister. And the rest, she thought. Robert White gets ousted and Eleanor Porter gets his job. Now the Home Secretary is getting the same treatment and she's off on a rescue mission. She had to be in on the scam.

'She was,' said Charles. 'She's also a First in Economics, past Chairman of the Employment Select Committee, and an MP for an inner city constituency. She's a very smart lady.'

'I get that.'

'I want you to take lots of pictures of her, wherever we go,' he said.

'What can she do about it?' Laura asked.

'It doesn't matter. If she succeeds she will be the hero of the hour.'

'Heroine.'

'Exactly. And if she fails…well, she tried, and the Home Secretary gets the blame,' said Charles, looking smug. 'This is all about Eleanor.'

'I thought it was about race and urban decay.'

Charles frowned and Laura wondered if she'd gone too far. After all, he *was* her dad's biggest client. Maybe he was having second thoughts about his choice of photographer. Why had he chosen her, she asked herself. Maybe he'd been impressed by her work at the launch party and thought a woman might be sensitive in portraying another woman in a taxing situation. Or maybe he just wanted to get into her panties. Either way now he would be thinking she was high maintenance.

'I have absolute rights over all images,' he said. He had dispensed with his smile. 'You give me everything at the end. In fact you give me the camera and I'll get you a better one.'

'I like this one.'

'Then I'll send it back to you after I've finished with it,' he said. 'That's the deal. You're going to be very well paid and the pictures will make your career.'

Charles strapped himself in and Laura followed suit. 'I wanted to see your portfolio,' he said in a lighter tone, his smile returning. 'Now I'll see you in action. It's going to be exciting.'

Laura looked through the window as they took off and watched the river and city shrink beneath them. They flew low, just above a bank of white cloud. When they were airborne Eleanor Porter came to the back of the plane.

'You must be Laura,' she said, offering a hand. 'You come highly recommended. Charles insisted.' She had the most captivating eyes Laura had ever seen.

'Why don't you come up front?' Eleanor suggested. 'We're having a briefing and it will give you an idea of what's going on.' She checked herself momentarily in the gilt mirror at the back of the plane before returning to her seat. Laura pulled out her camera and a spare lens and followed, taking the seat now cleared of Eleanor's handbag. Charles swivelled so he could sit in on the briefing. Eleanor introduced her two companions.

'This is Sir Michael Kerrigan from the Cabinet Office and Chris North, my speechwriter. Chris was at *The Times*.'

'Before I moved to the dark side,' said the man in the blazer, leaning across to shake Laura's hand.

'Until you saw the light, you mean,' said Eleanor. 'Laura will be taking some pictures for the record.' The minister turned to her civil servant.

'So, Michael, what's the latest?'

'Can I ask a question first?' said North. 'What's the deal, Eleanor? Shouldn't this be Chamberlain's gig, if it's anyone's?'

Sir Michael Kerrigan leaned forward.

'The Home Secretary is distracted at the moment,' he said. 'And it was felt his presence might be counter-productive. Given the situation may involve race issues, the current allegation about using illegal aliens as sweatshop labour is how shall we put it, unfortunate.'

'I suggested it to the PM,' said Eleanor. 'Someone needed to do something and everyone was dithering. And I have Cities.'

Laura was impressed. As Eleanor Barry she'd been a fabulous model. As Eleanor Porter it looked like she had balls. Laura clicked the shutter.

'And you're bored with cocktail parties and speaking to the Women's Institute,' said Charles. 'I always thought life as a junior minister was a witless existence.'

'Anyway, we're here now and we must do what we can,' said Eleanor. 'Michael, put us on track will you?'

The civil servant opened a file and began the briefing, raising his voice above the noise of the aircraft. After a while Laura moved from her seat and took photographs of Eleanor from as many vantage points as she could find in the cramped cabin.

'It looks like a crisis born of coincidence,' said Kerrigan. 'According to the police report there were three separate situations. The first was the Birmingham City – Aston Villa derby, which they were ready for. The ground was well managed and any trouble was contained, though they noticed an unusually large number of casuals.'

'Casuals?' repeated Charles.

'Football fans who wear designer gear and are usually affiliated to hooligan groups. They often turn up at anti-Muslim rallies. But none of them were known faces and there had been no traffic on the web. The second group were employees of a local firm in Sparkwood that had been closed down the week before, Sparkwood Sparks and Cables. It makes automotive components for the car industry. Apparently they had a full order book but the bank foreclosed on them. It had about a hundred employees, mostly British Asians, probably Kashmiri. They were planning a demonstration in Victoria Square.'

'Sparkwood's an unemployment black spot, right?' asked North. Kerrigan nodded.

'What about the third group?' Eleanor asked.

'That was a planning protest. Residents from a village called Rownley protesting against the siting of a waste incinerator. They came in on the A38 in a coach. Mostly pensioners, according to the report. They were led by an old farmer called Ted Eggleston who brought his cows with him.'

'Cows?' Eleanor smiled.

'Forty Holstein-Friesians, in two cattle trucks. He claimed he had the right to take them to the Bull Ring, which used to be the old cattle market. It was a ruse. They were heading for Victoria Square as well, where they were to hand a petition to a representative of West Midlands Councils.'

'So what happened?' Eleanor asked.

'The casuals went on the rampage inside the Bull Ring after the match. When they heard about the Asian protest they marched on Victoria Square. They broke through a police cordon and were about to attack when Eggleston and his Holstein-Friesians arrived. They created a barrier between the two sets of protestors, which allowed the police to re-form and the Sparkwood contingent to escape down

Broad Street. Unfortunately, the casuals broke the second cordon and there was a running battle down the street, cows, police, and protestors – all the way to the Walk of Stars.'

'Walk of Stars?' queried North.

'Birmingham's version of the Hollywood Walk of Fame,' said Charles. 'It celebrates such immortals as Noddy Holder, Ozzy Osbourne and Jasper Carrott.'

Kerrigan continued, 'There was a riot by the canal and some of the Asians took over a shop. No one knows how they got in. The police have the area locked down. Now there's a build-up of Asians and a contingent from Unite Against Fascism as well as nationalists coming from all over. The siege is the flashpoint. One side says they are there in sympathy with the Muslim protest, the other to support law and order. There's about three hundred protestors in Birmingham now and a lot more on the way,' he said. 'The army is on standby, but using them would be a public relations disaster.'

'Do we know who is inside the shop?' Eleanor asked.

'The police were still to confirm that when we left. They're assuming it's some of the Sparkwood employees.'

'What about the hostages?'

'They want to brief us on that when we get there. Their big worry is that gunshots were heard at the time the building was taken over.'

'So what's the plan?' asked Charles. Laura snapped a shot of Kerrigan's reaction. She sensed the two men had little time for each other.

'The usual practice is to secure the area, try to negotiate; after that the police will go in,' said the civil servant. 'The level of force will be determined by the degree of threat and how trigger-happy the commanding officer is. Apparently, there has been no communication from the protestors. After the police briefing I've arranged for us to meet with the Sparkwood factory's bank and the planning authority.'

'Well done, Michael,' said Eleanor. 'I'd like to visit Sparkwood and the site.'

'We'll need to arrange that with the police,' replied Kerrigan.

'So what's the message here?' asked North. 'The answer to

questions like: 'What do you think you're up to, minister? And why? And how do you think you can make a difference, exactly?"

Eleanor thought for a moment.

'I'm not sure yet,' she said. 'I know we have several issues. If we can rule out extremism there's still public order, but underlying that we've got unemployment, multicultural Britain and a side issue on environmental planning.'

'You've also got two by-elections coming up,' said Charles. 'Both inner cities with similar issues.'

'Right now the questions that really puzzle me,' said Eleanor, 'are who exactly is in there and what do they want? And why the gun? It doesn't make sense. Let's hope the police have some answers.'

The door to the cockpit opened and the co-pilot popped his head out to tell them they would be landing soon. Laura returned to her seat and strapped herself in. She glanced through the window as they dropped through the cloud to see Birmingham's rooftops and then back into the cabin as her fellow passengers readied for landing. She felt pressure in her ears as Charles caught her eye.

'Hopefully, we'll find time for dinner,' he said, the trademark smile spreading across his face. 'The hotel has a passable red.'

21

The briefing took place in a hot and airless conference room over glasses of tepid water and untouched cups of tea. Laura sat next to Charles Franklin at one end of the minister's party, facing a row of uniformed police officers across a long table. A plate of digestive biscuits lay in the centre, undisturbed. She felt uneasy at first, sure she had committed a heinous crime she couldn't quite remember and was about to be dragged to the cells. Then she realised it was the police who should be nervous as they faced their government masters. They were introduced as Assistant Chief Constable Donald Rudd, Chief Superintendent Sara Lane, Chief Inspector Richard Saunders – the Silver Commander in charge at the siege site – and a junior officer whose name was promptly forgotten. Apparently, the Chief Constable was on holiday in Thailand pulling what strings he could to get a flight back and a pair of long trousers.

The atmosphere was tense. Laura wondered if this was because Eleanor Porter was not the bimbo either she or the police had expected. The minister was well briefed and had fired a fusillade of questions on the way to the conference room. Why were there three marches at the same time? How did the police respond when they saw the number of casuals in the crowd? Was a single police helicopter sufficient for the country's second city?

Rudd invited CS Lane to lead the briefing. Nice move, thought Laura. Working the girl-on-girl thing. She peered past the officers at the pin board behind them. There were a dozen photos of Asian men, along with shots of the shop, and a map of the siege area. It would have made a good picture but Charles had instructed her to keep her camera out of sight and her mouth shut.

Sara Lane was a no-nonsense stocky blonde in her mid-forties. She started the briefing by telling them the siege site was a women's fashion store called Ego Central, well known for its Intimate Id line of lingerie. Laura noticed a dreamy expression spread across Charles' face and assumed he had fused images of the policewoman with notions of feminine apparel and was struggling to separate the two.

Meanwhile Lane continued. The protestors inside the shop were believed to be members of the Sparkwood march, mostly Kashmiri Muslims, led by local councillor Sultana Choudhury and two brothers, Mirza and Khalid Khan.

'Mirza became famous a few weeks ago,' said Lane. 'He chased some youths off his estate who were beating up an old man. He made the local news and now they call him The Have A Go Fellow. He's the production manager at the factory. Mid thirties, family man, no police record. He was the spokesman. Khalid is his younger brother. He's single, militant and was arrested in the 2009 riots, as was Choudhury. The demonstration itself went off without incident.'

Two marchers from the Rownley protest were also missing; Ted Eggleston, its leader, and Josephine Donna Smith, known as Donna, an eighty-year-old spinster and treasurer of the Rownley Operatic and Dramatic Society. They also believed there was a third hostage; Alfred Little, a sixty-four-year old from Dudley, the odd job man responsible for security at the shop, was also missing. Apparently Little had not returned home the previous night, and more importantly, according to his wife, he had not been seen in his local pub. Lane said thermal imaging confirmed there were twenty-one people inside the building and a Holstein-Friesian cow.

'Eggleston and Smith may be subject to charges in relation to yesterday's events,' added Rudd, conscious he should contribute, 'for contravening the Public Order Act.' He nodded at Lane to explain.

'We stopped the countryside protestors at the edge of the city pending the outcome of the match,' she said, turning to the map behind her. 'Here, at a vacant lot on Harborne Road, with an officer guarding each of the cattle trucks. It seems Eggleston persuaded two of his party, two elderly women, both members of the Rownley

Operatic and Dramatic Society, to distract the officers while he let the cows out. One of them was Donna Smith.'

'Distract them?' asked Kerrigan.

'Apparently they exhibited signs of distress,' said Lane. 'The women that is. One ran her wheelchair over a drain and got it stuck in the grate; the other, Donna Smith, collapsed on the ground and rolled around in the gutter. When the officers went to their aid Eggleston let the tailgates down and the cows escaped. We have a witness who says it's characteristic of Miss Smith's behaviour. Apparently we should have seen her Madame Arcati. They call her Prima Donna. Eggleston was last seen herding his cows towards the city, reciting 'The Charge of The Light Brigade.''

'Why do you believe this is a hostage situation?' Eleanor asked.

'We can't be sure it is. The media ran that,' said the Assistant Chief Constable. 'It could be worse. We have to assume they have at least one weapon. A gunshot was heard late yesterday afternoon outside the boutique at the time we believe they gained entry – possibly to frighten Little into opening the building. We don't know if anyone was injured. It means someone brought a weapon on the march, presumably with intent. It may be stretching it but it's possible occupation was always the goal.'

'We have a witness who says she saw one of them with a gun,' said Lane, 'though we haven't been able to corroborate that yet. Also, they are refusing to communicate, and until they do and we can eliminate certain scenarios we have to keep all options open. Finally, as well as an arrest record, we understand Khalid Khan and Choudhury have links to known terrorist organisations.'

'Which organisations and what kind of links?' asked Kerrigan.

'We're checking. We can't be certain of any of this but it's enough for us to proceed with extreme caution,' said Lane. She looked to her superior but it was CI Saunders who spoke.

'We have imaging of two people who appear to be sedentary and apart from the rest of the group,' he said. 'They could be bound and possibly injured.'

'What about the cow?' Laura asked. She felt cold stares from the officers across the table. Officers, she assumed, who had risen to the heights of policing through their ability to prise confessions from serial killers with just such stares. She felt similar looks from her own side and a pinch from Charles, an inch above her knee, which could only be interpreted as 'shut up, right now, or you will be hitchhiking back to London with your camera wrapped around your neck.'

'I just wondered,' she said. 'Is it a hostage?'

'The cow is relevant,' said Kerrigan. 'The animal rights lobby will have a field day if something happens to it.'

'I suppose it could give rise to a charge of theft,' said the Assistant Chief Constable. 'We've rounded the rest up.' For an instant Laura imagined the Assistant Chief Constable for Operations on a police horse with a lasso and chaps.

'What are they doing in there?' asked Eleanor.

'Sitting mostly,' said Lane, 'and singing.'

'You've made no contact at all?'

'No, ma'am,' said Saunders. 'They haven't responded all day. Their mobiles are switched off, all except Khalid Khan's, which is on voicemail.'

'We know he's made calls to Pakistan,' said Lane. 'We're trying to find out who he's talking to. We think it's someone in Mirpur. Kashmir.'

'They made one communication,' Saunders said. 'At two o'clock they hung three banners from the upstairs window.'

'What do they say?' asked North.

"Don't Let The Spark Go Out' and 'Banks Are Bad for Business."

'Nothing to do with race there,' observed the speechwriter. 'Or terrorism.'

'And 'Go Shit On Your Own Doorstep," Saunders added. 'We're not sure what to make of that one.' Eleanor looked at him.

'Maybe they've joined forces with the Rownley group,' she said. 'I'm not sure this is a hostage situation. Shouldn't they be making demands? There's no point having hostages unless you use them.'

'They could still be working out what to do,' said Lane.

'What if they hid from the trouble last night and are using the situation to continue their protest?' Eleanor asked.

'Then why aren't they talking to the media?' asked CI Saunders.

Laura looked at the Chief Inspector. He seemed perplexed. Richard Saunders was tall and blond, a rugged specimen of homo sapiens, and a man in uniform. She assumed he saw himself as the archetypal protective hero. Don't worry, madam; I will rescue your cat/child/car/stolen items. The minister might be a famous former supermodel but she was the same age as his usual worshippers. How could he not enthral her? Laura imagined he had felt a frisson on meeting the politician and was arrogant enough to assume it was reciprocated.

'Silence is a dangerous game to play,' he added. Move along, madam, leave it to me. Let the big strong policeman take care of this.

Kerrigan shuffled in his seat.

'So what options are you considering?' he asked. 'Strategic and tactical?' Rudd intervened.

'There are other threats to consider,' he said. 'There's a build-up of Asian sympathisers and far-right demonstrators. Both sides are hijacking the siege for their own purposes and some are just there for trouble. We've managed to keep them apart and a good way from the site, so far.' Sara Lane rose and turned to the map.

'Here and here.' She indicated two points on the map. 'There's a group of Asians at the junction of Gas and Berkley Streets and the casuals are located on Broad Street further west.'

'We hope it will settle down for the night,' said Rudd. 'But tomorrow could be a different story.' His hands opened in a gesture that implied this was a guess rather than a calculation.

'CI Saunders will brief you on the situation at the site,' said Lane. 'He is leading operations there, under my command.'

The Chief Inspector took his turn in front of the map. Laura decided to hate him.

'The site itself is locked down,' he said. 'Broad Street, Gas Street and Berkley Street are blocked off. We have eight cars there and armed response teams. We're running operations from an incident caravan on the site with a link to Gold Control. There's a hostage and rescue team in place with a police negotiator and a psychologist, as well as paramedics.'

'You haven't answered my question,' said Kerrigan. Saunders looked to his superior officers.

'One option is to wait it out,' said Lane. 'Sooner or later they will need food and that will make them talk. They'll have to let the cow go soon, unless they're planning to eat it, which could give us a chance. Or we can go straight in. It all depends on the threat level to the hostages. Assuming they are hostages.'

'The other factor is the build-up of demonstrators,' Rudd said. 'We need to finish this quickly; otherwise it could get very ugly indeed.'

'Not just in Birmingham,' said North.

'What's your preferred course?' asked Eleanor. Lane waited for a signal from Rudd before she spoke.

'We will keep trying to negotiate for the time being,' she said. 'If we don't hear anything by dawn, we'll go in before the crowds build up again. Saunders?'

'We'll cut off the electricity and go in with tear gas, through the first floor window and the rear entrance,' said the Chief Inspector. 'We haven't decided yet on tasers or live ammunition.' Laura had no doubt about his preference. 'We're also considering using an air-raid siren,' he said. 'Wear them down through the night, so they're nodding off when we go in.'

'Terrific,' said Charles, 'the media will love that. Birmingham Blitz. People will write songs about it.'

'What time is dawn?' asked Eleanor.

'Just after six.'

'And what if they're not armed?'

'They'll be fine if they surrender immediately,' said the Chief Inspector. There was an uncomfortable silence. Laura watched as the others considered the implications of what they had heard.

'When can I visit the site?' Eleanor asked.

'We'd rather you didn't, just yet,' said Rudd. 'In fact we'd rather the media wasn't aware of your presence until afterwards. We appreciate as Minister you are showing how serious the government is taking this, but the fact is you're very well-known and we believe it will only inflame the situation.'

'It'll leak,' said Kerrigan. 'We've set up briefings with the bank and the region's environmental team.'

'I want to visit Sparkwood,' Eleanor said. Rudd squirmed in his seat.

'We also advise against that,' he said. 'We can't be responsible for your safety or the effect it will have on the situation. I suggest you visit after we've resolved things tomorrow morning. And to be frank, I'd leave it a while longer.'

Eleanor asked for a break and the officers filed from the room.

'I don't think they have hostages,' she said, after the door shut. 'It's just a protest gone wrong.'

'Whether they do or not this is a fucking minefield, Eleanor,' North growled. 'Everyone is watching this. If the police mess it up we could have riots in every major city in Britain. It'll make Brixton and Toxteth look like tea parties. We should get out of here, now.'

'We're here to stop that happening,' Eleanor said. Laura wished she could use her camera.

'I agree with Chris,' said Charles. 'Let it all burn down and then hold an enquiry. Come up and visit then. That's the safest way. We should be in London. If we leave now we could be back before anyone knows we've been away.'

'That is bollocks, Charles,' said Eleanor. 'We are here, we are staying here and we'll do what we can. In the meantime, you and Chris had better start writing.'

The two men baulked. Writing was clearly the last thing on their minds.

'Think two scenarios,' she said. 'One where it all ends well, another where it's chaos. There's a theme that works for both.' She stood up so she could pace while she thought aloud. 'This government will not allow Britain's cities to break down. We have three messages. One: there is no going back on a tolerant Britain. Tolerance is a value that must apply to all citizens. Two: we will solve the economic causes of unrest. This is about jobs. We must bring Britain back to prosperity. And three: those who choose violence must know we will preserve public order. We support our police force, the best in the world...'

'Present company excepted,' said Charles.

Only now Eleanor showed a hint of insecurity.

'What do you think?' she asked.

Laura realised she had Eleanor completely wrong. Whatever she had been in the past she was something else now; a politician certainly, maybe something more.

'It's good,' said Charles. 'Caring, but something of the Iron Lady about it. And it'll work for the by-elections. But we're still in the shit if this all goes tits up.' Kerrigan leaned forward.

'You're largely in line with policy,' he said. 'Of course it will stir the immigration issue. And it could raise the police funding debate. Should we spend to protect against terrorism or militancy.' He looked over his glasses. 'And I agree with Charles, about the tits up thing.'

'Over to you, boys,' said Eleanor. 'Turn it into Shakespeare.'

'Ant and Dec might be better,' said North.

'Whatever. Weave your magic,' said the Cities Minister. 'We'll be doing a lot of talking tomorrow.'

'So what do we do now?' North asked, looking through the glass door at the officers waiting outside. Kerrigan was cleaning his glasses with a handkerchief.

'My recommendation is we proceed with the briefings,' said the civil servant, 'but hold on visiting the site and Sparkwood. Let's see how things look after dawn.' He looked at Eleanor. 'I'm sorry, Minister, but I think we need to follow the line on that one. It also means we can see how things turn out before declaring our hand.'

'That's why he's the highest paid mandarin in the land,' said Charles.

Eleanor pouted but said nothing. Laura could see she felt cornered. Kerrigan's opinion was obviously important and the other two were in agreement. Eleanor looked at the senior officers in the corridor.

197

'OK. Let's wrap this up. I need to phone the PM, and my husband.' She looked at Charles, who was winking at Laura. Under the table the hand had returned to her knee, this time it seemed with mischievous intent.

'And you should phone your wife.'

22

The next two briefings took place in Eleanor's suite at the Crowne Plaza hotel. Two nervous bankers, one from the city's largest branch and another from London perched on chairs covered with purple velour and explained the long history of cash flow problems at Sparkwood and the inevitability of the bank's decision to foreclose. Laura thought they looked like worried mice. They rambled on about bank policy, lending rates, risk profiles and their duty to shareholders. Charles asked them what percentage of their chief executive's bonus would be required to bail out the factory. North asked if they wanted to be blamed for the next English Civil War. The bankers laughed anxiously then expressed concern about creating dangerous precedents based on unsafe lending. Eleanor asked them to explain what lending they were referring to, as she hadn't noticed much recently. She asked them to consult with their bosses and think again, if they didn't want to court the government's displeasure. North went further by suggesting that if they didn't think again they might be blamed for the breakdown in society that followed, as they were already for the economy in general, and this might lead to lynch parties roaming the cities stringing bankers from streetlamps. As they backed away, feeling for the door behind them, looking even more like mice, they apologised for being unable to do more.

The chairman of the local planning committee brought his planning director as well as a technical team, who crammed into the suite using every available sofa, chair and stool. The chairman clearly viewed the meeting as a peer-to-peer conversation and, relaxing in an armchair, invited Eleanor to lunch and a guided tour of the city when times were quieter. Eleanor froze him with a glare and focused on the technical team who were sitting on the edge of their seats. Ted Eggleston emerged from the briefing as a greedy and manipulative adversary. It appeared the old farmer had lobbied to have the new incinerator sited on his land from the first, but had raised his price at the last minute, threatening to stir up the local community and environmentalists if his demand was not met. When the local planners called his bluff and proposed a neighbouring site he had made good his threat.

The meetings finished before dinner and Eleanor excused herself, choosing to go to the gym and have supper in her room. The rest ate in the hotel restaurant, where Charles tried to flirt with Laura, North drank two bottles of burgundy and Kerrigan tapped away on his BlackBerry, preparing his team for the chaos he felt the following day would bring. After dinner Laura escaped to her room while North staggered to the bar with Charles for a drunken brainstorm, hoping to soak their way to a few soundbites. Michael Kerrigan retired to write a paper.

By midnight the Downing Street mandarin was tucked up in bed reading Proust and Chris North was lying across his, fully clothed and snoring. Charles was taking a call from Eleanor's husband and trying to shrug off the evening's alcohol.

'You'd better be right about this,' growled Sir Frank Porter.

'It wasn't my idea,' said Charles. 'I think she's insane. This place could explode any minute.'

'Well, you'd better make sure it doesn't,' said Porter. 'She needs to come out of this on top otherwise Chamberlain will be all over her. He'll say it was his job and she buggered it up.'

'I know.'

'And what about Chamberlain?' Porter asked. 'We need to finish him.'

'He's struggling.'

'Exactly. Struggling. I want him inanimate. I'm paying you a lot of money, Charles. I expect results. Do you realise if we pull this off Eleanor could be the next Home Secretary? Do I need to say what that could mean for both of us?'

'I'm working on it,' said the PR man. In fact he was flipping channels on the TV set between *Escape from Wight*, the news and the hotel's porn channel.

'And keep an eye on her,' said Porter. 'She just called to find out about the media in Mirpur. She's up to something.'

The banker hung up. Money people never say goodbye, thought Charles. They deliver the message and end the transaction. No sense of relationship. No EQ. But Charles knew Porter was right. They had embarrassed Chamberlain but there was every possibility of a comeback, particularly if things went wrong in Birmingham. He looked at his watch. It was too late to call George. He would try him first thing.

He was about to switch channels when Ted Eggleston's ruddy face filled the TV screen, in an interview filmed the previous day. Under his face ran the caption: 'Local farmer held hostage. Last interview'. Eggleston was in full flow, stabbing the ground with a shooting stick.

'We have an entire police force, the second largest in the country, ensuring that a bunch of ill-bred hooligans get to watch a football match, while everyone else, salt of this earth, have to give up their rights and wait for them. It's despicable.'

'You're objecting to a new waste incinerator?' asked a young reporter.

'Another erosion of liberty,' spluttered the farmer. 'Jumped-up planners deciding where to site a major environmental disaster, based on a strategy created by head-in-the-cloud boffins who report to an unelected, unaccountable body.'

'I thought waste incinerators with energy recovery were supposed to be better for the environment?' suggested the reporter.

'Better for your environment,' growled Eggleston. 'You probably live in Birmingham. Did you know that fifty per cent of the waste produced in the West Midlands comes from its cities? It's your rubbish, not ours. You should be taking care of it rather than driving it out to the country and dumping it on us.' Behind him, as if to underscore his point, two marchers raised a banner that urged Birmingham to 'S*** On Your Own Doorstep'. The reporter continued his questioning.

'So there is no truth in the rumour that you are against the plant because they didn't agree to site it on your land?' he asked. Ted Eggleston froze. After a moment of disquieting stillness he began to vibrate and his eyes bulged, resembling a volcano at the moment of eruption, an instant away from a flow of boiling lava. The reporter took a step back as the blast began.

'That's an outrageous suggestion, young man,' the farmer barked, 'and if you broadcast that you will hear from my lawyers.' He grabbed his shooting stick and waved the young man to one side. 'Now out of my way, I need to get on.' The camera followed Eggleston as he staggered off towards his fellow marchers, muttering something about dogs, how he wished he'd brought them, and if he had he would set them on the TV crew.

Charles changed channels. On the Isle of Wight, the girls' team had found a suitcase of men's clothes in 1940s styles and were trying them on in their hut with much gaiety while Robert White spied on them through a window, until he was caught by the camp guards and carted back to the punishment hut for another 10,000 throws. By coincidence, and for a relatively small fee that Charles would set against expenses, the porn channel featured two girls in 1940s lingerie stripping off in an aircraft hangar for two British fighter pilots, played by glistening Swedish bodybuilders.

In the hotel corridor, oblivious to the nocturnal fascinations of his charges, a police constable was stationed by the lift, while another patrolled the reception below.

23

Laura woke to a tap on her door and rolled over to check the time. The digital clock on the bedside table read 1.45 a.m., its lurid green lines slicing the dark. She had no idea who it could be and wondered why the thought of Will had slipped into her mind. He had no clue she was in Birmingham and even if he did he wouldn't be here, would he? Did she want him to be? She shook the idea from her head and slid out of bed, pulling on a T-shirt as she crept across the carpet to the door. She squinted through the peephole. It was Eleanor Porter.

'Fuck,' she said, and opened the door to stand blinking in the light from the corridor. 'And hi.'

'Can I come in?' asked Eleanor. Laura flipped the light switch and widened the gap to let the minister pass, noticing she was without make-up, wearing silk pyjamas and trainers and looking fantastic. She was easy to hate.

'Sorry to wake you,' Eleanor said. 'Can I borrow some clothes? I'm going out and don't want to attract attention.' Laura cocked her head and Eleanor laughed. 'Sorry, that didn't come out right. I mean I don't want to look like me.'

'I've a spare pair of jeans,' Laura said and went to her rucksack, which was lying on a chair alive with purple velour. She pulled out a crumpled garment. Eleanor's eyes lit up.

'Black, that's perfect,' she said. 'Can I borrow your hoodie?' Laura shrugged. Whatever.

'Where are you going?' she asked.

'I want to see what's going on.'

Laura was intrigued. Bent politician or not, the woman in front of her grew more interesting by the moment.

'Can I come?'

'You shouldn't,' Eleanor said.

'*You* shouldn't,' replied Laura. 'Nobody will notice me.' She watched Eleanor change while she pulled on her jeans. She still had the figure of a young woman, showed few traces of age and none of her two children. Laura was struck by how gracefully she moved even when tying shoelaces. A few minutes later she was dressed for the street, only her designer footwear standing out, but then everyone spent a fortune on trainers. Laura zipped her boots. On the way out she reached for her camera.

'No photographs,' said Eleanor. 'We're bystanders.' They left the room and crept along the brown corridor to the lift. Eleanor giggled.

'There was a policeman,' she whispered. 'But I sent him to get cocoa.' Laura wanted to pinch herself. Here she was sneaking out of a hotel with a government minister, once one of the world's top models, on some secret midnight adventure. It was surreal. By the time the lift arrived they were both giggling.

They missed the only other guest wandering the hotel in the dead of night. As the lift doors closed Charles Franklin turned into the corridor and padded along to Laura's room. He was carrying a bottle of champagne and two flutes. When he reached her door he leaned into it, listened for a moment then knocked, casting a shifty glance along the hall. After the call with Porter he knew he should be listening at Eleanor's door if anybody's, but reasoned she would be getting her beauty sleep and this could be a lot more fun. He waited and knocked again, straining to hear stirrings within. Meanwhile Eleanor and Laura slipped out of the lift on the first floor and took the stairs to the basement car park.

*

The siege site was ten minutes' walk from the hotel and the night was still warm. When they found the exit from the car park, Eleanor consulted a map she had picked up at the front desk earlier. They turned right into Holliday Street, which was deserted, and walked downhill tracing a path that would take them south of the siege.

Once she had her bearings Eleanor became chatty, somewhere

between a girlfriend on a shopping trip and a head-hunter. She asked Laura where she lived, where she'd studied and questioned her knowledgeably about photography.

'How long have you worked for Charles?' she asked.

'Just a couple of jobs. I mostly work for my dad, George Valentine.'

'The caterer,' Eleanor said.

'That's one of his things. He has a finger in a few pies.'

'Oh yes?' Eleanor asked. She quickened her pace. Laura stared after her. Maybe she had no idea about George's more nefarious activities.

'Research is his main thing,' Laura said, as she caught up. 'Charles is his biggest client.'

'That's interesting,' Eleanor replied, with a look that suggested it wasn't. Laura was certain it wasn't an act. If there was a connection between George's work and the minister, she wasn't aware of it. Laura changed the subject.

'Why did you stop modelling?' she asked. Eleanor looked thoughtful for a moment.

'It was time,' she said. 'You can't do it for ever. And I never intended to. I fell into it. I was at university, reading economics and a boy I was dating took some photographs of me. He got them published and before I knew it I had an agent and was modelling part-time. It was great. I made ten times what I could in the union bar. Next thing I knew I'd dropped out and was in the Maldives shooting a commercial.'

'Awesome,' said Laura, trying not to sound impressed. They crossed Bridge Street and walked under a red brick aqueduct that carried a canal into the city. Their passage was lit by Victorian-style lamps, which threw a sepia glow across patterned pillars and damp walls. But for the tarmac road and its painted lines they could have slipped back more than a century.

'It was,' said Eleanor. 'And I had money, clothes and went to fabulous places. And for a time I was the one everyone wanted. Then I woke up. A lot of it was pretty seedy; drugs, eating disorders, creepy people. It's a vanity industry and completely self-absorbed. And there were younger girls coming up all the time, all of them hungry. And I wanted to eat again.'

'Why politics?'

'I was a goodwill ambassador for Unicef and loved it. I thought I was making a difference. But celebrities are on the outside at the end of the day. And some like it that way – you can play the agitator. But you're not around when the aid is being loaded into the back of government trucks and sold to the highest bidder. I realised I wanted to see things through. So I quit and went back to university. That's where I met my husband. He was Chancellor.'

They walked in silence for a while.

'I just want to take photographs,' said Laura.

'That's good. You're young, you'll do many things,' Eleanor smiled. 'Just make sure you take great ones. Particularly if they're of me.'

They heard the murmur of a crowd as they emerged from the aqueduct and the road inclined, new buildings rising either side of them in red brick with blue metallic window frames; a developer's stab at empathy with a waterside industrial past. The junction of Berkley and Gas Streets was blocked by barriers and patrolled by yellow-jacketed policemen. Two police cars were parked close by. Twenty or thirty demonstrators, all Asian, were gathered by the barriers, chatting rather than chanting. Laura saw Rudd had been right, numbers were dwindling for the night leaving only a hard core keeping vigil.

Two young men on the edge of the crowd had noticed them and seemed to be wrestling with ancient and conflicting urges; solidarity and male bonding or the chance to chase girls. Eleanor bowed her head, letting the hood fall around her face, while Laura put on a 'don't even think about it' expression that promised a public put-down for any who dared approach. They linked arms and picked up their pace, passing before the youths realised they had dithered too long.

The two women walked on to a mini roundabout and turned north into Granville Street, which Eleanor judged was past the siege site. They would walk up to Broad Street and double back. As they rounded the corner there was a ping from inside the minister's hoodie. Eleanor pulled her phone from a pocket and read the text with a smile.

'Good boy,' she murmured. She signalled Laura to wait while she made a call. Moments later a flicker of disappointment crossed her face. Laura guessed whoever Eleanor was calling was on voicemail. She watched as her companion took a deep breath. She seemed nervous. When Eleanor spoke a new voice emerged, a dark and husky whisper.

'Khalid, it's Eleanor Barry. The Lady Eleanor. I need to hear your voice. Call me. Call me now.' She left her number, hung up and continued along the street. Laura ran to catch up, open-mouthed. Eleanor made no attempt to explain the call. 'Do you have a boyfriend?' she asked, returning to girl chat and interview.

'No. Maybe. I don't know,' said Laura.

'It sounds complicated.'

'There's a musician.'

'That's complicated.'

Laura was not to be distracted. The Will thing was too difficult and something strange was happening right here and now. She placed a hand on Eleanor's arm and brought her to a standstill.

'Just hang on a minute, Minister. Eleanor. Whatever,' she said. 'What was that just now? Was that Khalid Khan? The one with the terrorist friends? How did you get his number?'

'His friends don't make him a terrorist,' said Eleanor.

'And what was all that about Lady Eleanor? What are you up to?'

Ahead, there were lights at the junction with Broad Street and another barrier. People were milling about. Eleanor smiled.

'My husband got the number.'

'How?'

'He's a powerful man.'

'And who's Lady Eleanor?'

'Maybe you're too young. It was my perfume. I guess I was at my peak then. I had my own fragrance, *Lady Eleanor*. I did a couple of commercials, where I played an aristocrat getting ready to elope with my olive-skinned lover. It caused quite a stir at the time. And that was the line. He's late, trying to fight his way to me and I call him. 'I need to hear your voice. Call me. Call me now.'' Laura's thin brows furrowed. She remembered it.

'I was twenty-nine,' Eleanor explained, 'which would make Khalid

Khan about fourteen at the time. And it was big in the Asian community. My olive-skinned lover was a Pakistani film star. I thought it was worth a try.' Eleanor drew an imaginary veil across her face and fluttered her eyes. 'What do you think?' she asked, suddenly a skittish maiden. 'Will he call?'

'You're bad,' Laura said. The phone rang. Eleanor checked the number then looked at Laura and mouthed, 'It's him.'

'Khalid?' she whispered. The husky voice again. Laura moved closer. Eleanor looked puzzled. She shook her head. He wasn't saying anything. She tried again. 'Khalid, this is Eleanor. Eleanor Barry. Is that you?' She tried the siren tone one more time. 'I need to hear your voice. Khalid?'

Still nothing. Laura nudged Eleanor who let her listen but motioned her to keep her mouth shut. They stood like girlfriends teasing a potential date.

'Hello,' he whispered. Not much more than a croak.

'Hello,' Eleanor replied.

'I can't talk,' he said. A deep voice, young and strong, thought Laura.

'That's OK, then listen. Can you listen?' Eleanor asked.

'Yes.'

'It's me, Eleanor, and I want to help you. All of you.' Silence. 'I'm a government minister now. For Cities.' Nothing. 'I know you don't have a gun. Your auntie told us. Your auntie in Mirpur.' There was a sigh. 'But the police think you do,' Eleanor said, the huskiness gone. 'They're coming to get you in the morning. With tear gas and tasers, maybe guns. We have to talk.' Still no answer. 'Maybe you need to talk to some people first?' she asked. 'Talk to them. But call me back, please. There's not much time. And Khalid, I promise I can help. Call me soon.' There was a pause and the caller disconnected. Eleanor pulled a pack of cigarettes from a pocket.

'You smoke,' said Laura. Eleanor shrugged apologetically and ducked into a doorway where it was dark and lit up. Laura followed.

'That was some bluff,' she said.

'I wasn't bluffing.'

'Then how do you know they have no gun?'

'My husband lends money to a media baron,' Eleanor explained, exhaling smoke. 'And he knows a man who knows a man who knows all the media in Mirpur. And one of them went to see Khalid's auntie. Apparently, Auntie had called Khalid when she heard on TV they had a gun. He promised her they didn't. '

'And you believe him?'

'I believe he wouldn't lie to his auntie.'

'And he called you. How did you know he would call you?'

'I didn't,' murmured Eleanor. She drew on the cigarette again and exhaled slowly. 'There's something funny about fame. People either run from you or to you. Some run a mile. Maybe they can't think of anything to say. Maybe you unsettle them in some way and they'd rather you stayed on the pages of a magazine. Others run to you. They think they know you, like a best friend, and they imagine you will be who they want you to be. Sometimes you're part of their dream, someone they imagine knowing; sometimes you are their dream, and that can be a problem. Others just want a little stardust.'

'Stardust?'

'Sure. People talk about the people they've met. You'll talk about me. They can love you or loathe you, it doesn't matter. The point is, the more famous the person the more interesting it makes the teller in the act of retelling. They run from you or to you. Assuming they recognise you in the first place.'

'So you were betting he was pulling his plonker over you when he was fourteen,' said Laura.

'I wouldn't put it quite like that,' said Eleanor, taking another deep draw, 'though if my son is anything to go by, fourteen-year-old boys pull their plonkers to anything that moves. Let's go,' she said, pointing to the top of the street. She stubbed out the cigarette and started towards the junction. 'Now tell me about your boyfriend. And I don't mean his plonker.'

'Why do you want to know?'

'I'm interested and we have time to kill before he calls back,' said Eleanor. 'My guess is there are others in there who will take convincing.'

'He's a musician. We had a row. This job came up. Not much more to tell,' said Laura.

'You like him. What did you fight about?'

'A matter of principle.' Laura was surprised she was still angry.

'That's better than a matter of chemistry.'

'Anyway, I don't want a relationship right now.'

'Sweetie, they don't come to order,' said Eleanor. Before Laura could reply the phone rang. This time Eleanor didn't share the call.

'I want to meet you,' she said. Her lips were pursed and her eyes narrowed. She was having to think quickly. 'I'm coming now. I'll be at the rear entrance in fifteen minutes. I'm wearing a dark blue hoodie and black jeans.' Laura nudged her hard.

'There will be two of us,' Eleanor added. 'I'm bringing Laura, my assistant. You'll like her. Is there anything you need?' Apparently Khalid had a shopping list. 'And please open the door,' Eleanor pleaded. 'We'll all look very silly if you don't. Fifteen minutes.' This time Eleanor hung up. She lit another cigarette. Her hand was shaking.

'So?' Laura asked.

'They want cigarettes and tea. And they wanted to negotiate on the phone. It sounded like someone else is calling the shots.' Eleanor blew smoke into the night air. Laura looked up at the sky. It was as starry a night as you could find above a city centre. This was a night she'd remember. The thought of Will slipped into her head. What had he said? Leave a trace. This was a night that might just do that. Up ahead, beyond the barrier, there were two police cars and several officers. Before it a young white crowd were milling about on the corner in front of O'Neill's bar. Most were looking east towards the siege site.

As they drew closer Laura noticed placards lying against the wall, ready for the next day's provocations.

Eleanor walked up to the senior policeman at the barrier. She presented her Cabinet Office pass and asked to be taken to Silver Command where she wanted to speak to Chief Inspector Richard Saunders. The policeman made a brief call on his radio, after which they were escorted through the barrier to the other side of Broad Street, then along the pavement, past yellow-jacketed policemen and another barrier into a loading bay where a white caravan was tucked into a space behind a wall. As they jogged towards the vehicle Laura looked back across the road to the siege site. Arc lights flared across the face of the shuttered building, spilling into the empty restaurants on either side. Above a sign proclaiming Ego Central three grimy banners flapped gently in the softest of summer breezes.

Chief Inspector Saunders came smartly down the steps of the caravan and acknowledged the two women with a half-hearted salute.

'Good morning, ma'am,' said the policeman. 'I had a feeling you'd turn up.' Eleanor flipped her hood onto her shoulders and shook her hair free.

'I've arranged to meet the Sparkwood protestors in a few minutes,' Eleanor said.

'That's not possible,' Saunders replied, his grin deleted.

'Which? That I've arranged a meeting, or that I'm going to have it?' Eleanor asked.

'Certainly the second,' he said. Laura saw he was bolder than in the briefing room. This was his turf, she supposed, his battle – and maybe he suspected Eleanor was acting beyond her powers, a politician chasing glory.

'I had a conversation with Khalid Khan a few minutes ago,' Eleanor said. 'I've also ascertained they're not armed.' Ascertained was a good word for a policeman, thought Laura.

'And how did you manage that?' Saunders asked, his tone patronising.

'I did a little police work,' she said and explained her unusual connections. 'I'm surprised you hadn't thought of that.'

'We had, but we don't have an answer from Mirpur yet,' said the chief inspector. 'In any case, I can't let you go.'

'I don't believe you have the power to stop me,' Eleanor said. 'Correct me if I'm wrong but the police force reports to the Home Office. The Home Office reports to the Prime Minister and I am here on his authority.' Authority was a good word too. The Cities Minister held up her mobile. 'Would you like to speak to him?'

'I am responsible for your safety,' Saunders said.

'Your plan is to go in at dawn, right?' Eleanor asked. "Yes, Minister" is a sufficient answer.'

'Yes, Minister.'

'So, we have four hours to resolve this peacefully. And avoid riots in Birmingham, and possibly all over the country. I have a channel of communication which makes me the best person to achieve that.'

A junior officer emerged from the caravan with an anxious look on his face. Eleanor looked at him, then back to the chief inspector.

'He's about to tell you the Assistant Chief Constable and your chief superintendent want you to get me out of the area as soon as possible,' she said. Saunders looked at the junior officer, who nodded. 'We have a situation here that is about to escalate,' Eleanor continued. 'If you go in there, guns blazing, you could be responsible for a bloodbath and the biggest outbreak of civil disorder in this country since the Gordon Riots. This will not be good for your pension. Particularly if it comes out, and trust me it will come out – because I am a politician and I specialise in information coming out timed to suit me – if it comes out they were unarmed and someone could have resolved this.' Laura decided if she had to place a bet on the outcome of this contest she would back Eleanor.

'I am going over there in about two minutes,' Eleanor continued, 'which means your only other course of action is to arrest a Minister of the Crown, which wouldn't be good for your pension either.' She pointed at the armed officers in flak jackets stationed at various vantage points. 'And I suggest you tell your men that shooting one wouldn't be good for theirs.'

'Get the picture?' Laura added. The opportunity to kick a policeman while he was down was simply too good to resist.

'Now, do you have any cigarettes?' Eleanor asked, her face suddenly beatific.

'Cigarettes?' asked Saunders, confounded.

'I said I'd bring cigarettes. And tea would be nice.'

Saunders looked helplessly at the junior officer who was still standing on the steps.

'PG Tips do?' asked the officer.

'Perfect.' Eleanor smiled at him sweetly.

'Just get on with it,' Saunders grunted. The officer disappeared into the caravan.

'You'll take an officer with you,' Saunders said.

'No, they're expecting two women.'

'It's not negotiable,' he said. 'You'll take an officer. Or it all stops right now, we'll call the Assistant Chief Constable and everything gets wrapped up in red tape. And I keep my pension.'

Eleanor said nothing.

'It'll be a woman in plain clothes,' Saunders added. 'But I want her armed. Her job will be to protect you, not to make an arrest.' Before Eleanor could protest he had stomped up the steps into the caravan.

Within minutes the junior officer returned with an assortment of cigarette packs unified by their health warnings, a lighter, a box of tea bags and a tower of plastic cups, all of which he handed to Laura. Moments later a heavy-set woman wearing jeans and a leather jacket joined them. She introduced herself as Detective Sergeant Freda Lincoln. Uniformed officers escorted them across the road into the arc lights and down Gas Street to a covered alley that ran parallel to Broad Street. This was the delivery entrance for all the shops facing the main street, a line of evil-smelling refuse bins running its length. Inset halfway along was the back entrance to Ego Central, its steel doors lit like a film set. Police barriers formed a square in front of it and Laura noticed armed response officers in the shadows.

When they reached the barrier Saunders wished them luck. Laura followed Eleanor across the square with the trembling tower of cups, and DS Lincoln brought up the rear. Eleanor hit last number redial on her phone as they reached the door. She spoke briefly then caught Laura's eye.

'They won't let us in,' she said. 'Because there's three of us.' Laura looked above the door. They were using the CCTV.

'The police insisted,' Eleanor explained into the phone. She signalled her companions to wait. For a moment Laura had no idea what was going to happen. They heard the thud of a bolt and the door opened slightly. DS Lincoln tried to widen the entrance with her shoulder but the door held fast. Laura looked inside to see a thick chain taut across the gap at shoulder height. They were regulating the width. Eleanor pressed the phone against her ear then looked at Laura.

'They've opened it to a size 10,' she whispered. She stepped under the chain and Laura followed, but no matter how she tried to compress her breasts, belly or buttocks, DS Lincoln could not pass through. Laura had some sympathy as she watched a lifetime of disappointment flood the detective's face. As she must have found in so many shops over the years, despite every conceivable diet and punishing exercise regime, she would never make a size 10. When she stepped back, exhausted and dejected, the door slammed shut in her face.

Suddenly, Eleanor and Laura were in darkness. They heard the door lock behind them and were shoved forward, along what they both sensed was a corridor, into a large dark space. Laura gasped as she felt warm, wet breath on her forearm. A large animal snorted beside her and she heard the clack of hooves on the concrete floor. The animal issued a long low moan and another set of lights flashed, this time neon strips, bathing Eleanor, Laura and a Holstein-Friesian in blinding white light. All three blinked, trying to understand their surroundings. It was yet another square, this time bordered on three sides by clothes racks and manikins. Laura sensed people beyond the racks, behind the clothes and lifeless figures.

'Hello,' Eleanor said, and stepped into the light. Laura realised she was witnessing the supermodel at work, feeling for the heart of the light, the hottest spot, as if it was just another catwalk. Eleanor found the centre and struck an assured pose. If the light was supposed to intimidate her it had the opposite effect. Politicians and models walk into the light no matter the circumstances. Laura followed her, while the cow wandered off and nuzzled a sequinned top in the style of Versace.

'We come in peace,' said Eleanor.

'What do you want?' shouted a woman from somewhere behind the racks. Laura guessed this must be the councillor.

'Sultana Choudhury?' Eleanor asked. 'I'm Eleanor Porter and this is Laura Valentine, my assistant. We've brought cigarettes and tea.'

'Not so fast,' said the voice. There was a sigh from the rack to their left. Laura could hear whispering, like the hiss of a snake sliding along the rack, and made out the words 'white dress'. Eleanor turned to her.

'I wore a white dress,' she whispered. 'In the commercial. It was my signature.' Apparently some were disappointed she was wearing jeans. Eleanor opened her pack of cigarettes, pulled one out and held it up.

'You don't mind, do you? It's been a long day.' She lit the cigarette and inhaled deeply. Smoke rose from the tip and curled in a tantalising pattern. 'Sultana, I want to help you,' she said. 'The police are coming at dawn. And they will come in force. You are in a dangerous situation.'

'We are not armed,' said the voice.

'I know that, but they don't believe it,'

Clothes parted on the rack in front of them and Sultana Choudhury stepped into the arena.

'Have you come only to taunt us?' she asked. This one, Laura realised, Eleanor would never impress. 'Are we on television?' the councillor asked.

'You're everywhere,' said the minister.

'In Mirpur?'

'Mirpur, Pakistan, India.'

'You're all over America,' said Laura. Sultana Choudhury nodded, apparently satisfied.

'We have demands,' she said.

'Tell me about them,' said Eleanor. She drew on the cigarette as elegantly as you could these days.

'We want to be heard,' said a male voice. Another rack parted and a man in his thirties joined Sultana in the arena, handsome save for the paunch of a comfortably married man. Laura assumed this was Mirza Khan, the Have a Go Fellow. Khalid would be thin and wiry.

'You have been heard, Mr Khan,' Eleanor said.

'Something must be done,' he insisted.

'Something has been done,' she said. 'It's time for you to go back to work.'

'We have no jobs,' shouted a voice from behind the racks.

'You all have jobs,' Eleanor said. 'The factory is re-opening this morning.' There was silence then a murmur.

'How?' asked Sultana Choudhury.

'I asked your bank to review the situation and while they were not very helpful to start with they changed their minds. It seems they owe money to another bank and that bank takes a different view of your situation.' Laura had an inkling the second bank would turn out to be run by Eleanor's husband. 'You can phone the factory manager. He's expecting you in at 8 a.m. You have orders to make up.' The murmur was on all sides now. Even the cow was chewing the Versace with renewed enthusiasm. A solitary growl sounded amid the cautious celebrations.

'What about the incinerator?' barked a wizened old man who had blundered into the light through a tangle of fashion knock-offs. He was followed by an ageing woman with a walking stick and a Hermès scarf.

'Mr Eggleston?' Eleanor asked. 'So glad to know you are well. Can I assume you and Miss Smith are not hostages?'

'Hostages? Absolute rot. We are holding a legitimate protest,' the old man grumbled. Sultana grimaced.

'We tried to persuade them to leave but he demanded equal opportunity,' she said.

'So what about the incinerator?' he asked.

'Less good news there, I'm afraid,' said Eleanor. 'It seems you've been a little naughty, haven't you, trying to blackmail the planning authorities? You'll have to continue your discussions with them and I suggest you do that on an open and honest footing in future.' Eggleston's faced reddened.

'Will we be arrested?' asked Sultana, cutting through the rising noise.

'I don't know. Have you done anything wrong?' asked Eleanor.

'We didn't trespass. Mr Little let us in to escape the riot.'

'That's right, I did that,' said an eager voice with a thick Brummie accent. Another pensioner joined the throng in front of the racks, a short sprightly man in the blue uniform of a security guard. 'It were havoc out there. I was locking up when it all kicked off, so I locked myself in. Then they were about to be murdered, so I let them in. I call it a Christian act. Though they're telling me it's a Muslim one too.'

'What about the gun?' asked Laura.

'That was Mr Eggleston,' said Choudhury. All eyes shifted to the farmer whose face turned purple.

'Absolute rot,' he growled. 'It was a ruddy farmhand. Welshman named Jones. Took my Purdey from the cattle truck and let it off to frighten people. Beggar's buggered off to Swansea by now.'

'Why didn't you give yourselves up?' Eleanor asked.

'They were going to tear us apart,' said Mirza Khan. 'And we didn't know they'd gone until Mr Little fixed the CCTV. By then police marksmen were everywhere and they were saying on the radio we were armed and dangerous.'

'Why didn't you phone the police?'

'We didn't know what to do. That's when Sultana and Khalid came up with their plan.' The racks moved once more and a younger, slimmer version of Mirza Khan joined the group. Khalid.

'Oh yes? And what was that?' Eleanor asked.

'To wait,' said Sultana. 'To say nothing and wait until our story was everywhere.'

'Until we had leverage,' said Khalid. His expression was tough but his eyes were shy.

'They confiscated our phones,' said a voice behind the clothes.

'All except Khalid's,' said Sultana. 'He was in charge of communications.'

'So, now you are everywhere,' said Eleanor.

'And that's why you're here,' said Sultana.

'What happens next?' asked the minister.

'That bit we hadn't figured out,' said Sultana, smiling at last. 'I was rather hoping you were our exit strategy.'

For a moment Eleanor looked bemused and Laura realised the councillor was the leader, the strategist, and that Eleanor had been played. They had been waiting. Simply waiting it out.

'Very clever,' said Eleanor, inclining her head, more a bow than a nod.

'Does that mean we can we go now?' asked Mirza. 'I could do with a shower.'

'First, we have to get you out of here without a bloodbath,' Eleanor said. 'Or arrest.' Laura looked around at the anxious faces peeping through the clothes racks.

'We have caused no damage,' said Sultana.

'Apart from the cow,' said Little. 'She shat on some stock.'

'And we ate what was in the fridge,' said Mirza.

Eleanor pulled out her phone and tapped in a number. 'Wake up, Michael,' she said. 'It's time for you to justify your immense cost to the public purse. I want you to phone the Assistant Chief Constable and broker an amnesty.' Laura imagined Michael Kerrigan in his pyjamas, trying to gather his wits. Eleanor looked around at the group.

'So, shall we have a cup of tea?' she suggested.

The space filled with excited chatter as the racks were rolled aside and people came into the square, slowly at first, laying aside makeshift weapons of manikin arms, coat-rack poles, wire coat hangers, and a pink umbrella.

Sultana Choudhury and Mirza Khan shook hands with Eleanor. Alfred Little took the tea and cups from Laura and headed for the kitchen. Khalid Khan hung back. When the tea was brewed Laura brought him a cup.

'I was prepared to fight,' said Khalid.

'I believe you,' she replied. 'I'm curious. Why did you call her? Was it just an exit strategy?'

Khalid laughed. 'The second time was strategy. The first time it was her voice. She is astounding.'

'I'm just beginning to realise,' said Laura.

Eleanor joined them and Khalid offered a shy smile. He was a good looking man. Laura wondered if the minister found him attractive. 'You were right,' said Laura. 'About your perfume and his plonker.'

Khalid's face grew serious.

'I have to thank you,' he said, looking into Eleanor's eyes. 'About the jobs. That might never have happened.' For a moment Laura thought Eleanor was going to kiss him but at the last moment she offered a ministerial hand.

'All part of the service,' Eleanor said. 'Something for all those taxes you pay.'

24

Just before dawn a police van arrived at Granville Street and ten officers piled out. Within minutes they had moved the barrier and thirty weary nationalists to the corner of Berkley Street, giving them a view of the siege site and a wide avenue of retreat west along Broad Street. Simultaneously, a contingent of officers opened the barrier to Gas Street and invited the Asian supporters to move to where they too could watch developments.

The protestors stepped into the street warily, as if it was laid with land mines. At Broad Street they found a new barrier, forming one side of a square, with Ego Central on their left and the loading bay and incident caravan on their right. Opposite they could see the barrier at Berkley Street and the nationalists. The sides were evenly matched but too tired to respond to the sight of each other. On both sides protestors craned over the barriers to see what was going on in the loading bay and were rewarded with the sight of several police cars, two more vans and an air-conditioned coach. Those who stretched furthest also witnessed a vigorous debate between the policeman in charge – a uniformed chief inspector – and three civilians, who comprised the highest paid mandarin in Whitehall, a ministerial speechwriter with a hangover and a top London public relations consultant.

Over the next forty minutes the area changed complexion. Armed units were withdrawn apart from a handful of marksmen left out of sight on rooftops or inside the upper floors of the surrounding buildings. A steady stream of Asians arrived on the Gas Street side of the square; men, women and children who were directed into position behind the barrier. Television crews and photographers with long lenses and stepladders appeared and selected their spots. Benches were delivered and more lights were set up until the square became an arena flooded with white light. The loading bay filled with senior uniformed officers, Assistant Chief Constable Rudd and Superintendent Lane arrived in police cars, and the mayor came in a black Daimler, complete with his mayoral chain and the manager of Sparkwood Sparks & Cables. The Chief Constable would miss the denouement; he was presently finishing a chilled breakfast tray after a sleepless night in the back of economy on a KLM flight from Bangkok, now on its final approach to Schiphol airport.

At ten to six two cordons of officers marched into the square and took up positions in front of the barriers. At three minutes to six Assistant Chief Constable Rudd joined them, his buttons and badges polished, holding a red loudhailer. A sharp metallic voice filled the air.

'Ladies and gentlemen, we can confirm we have successfully negotiated terms with the occupants of 255a Broad Street,' he said. 'The negotiations were led by Superintendent Lane of the West Midlands Police,' he paused briefly before adding, 'working closely with the Minister for Cities, who is presently inside the building.' There were cheers from within the Asian crowd and bemused looks among the nationalists. The media already knew. Charles Franklin had painstakingly briefed them on what was going to happen. It wasn't just a question of turning out for a scoop, he had said. Not only would they have the top story of the year, he guaranteed they would be making history. Feeling the pressure, photographers rechecked their shutter speeds and depths of field.

'We confirm this is not a hostage situation and no arms are involved,' Rudd continued. 'The occupants were taking refuge from the events on Saturday and waiting to be sure it was safe to leave. They also wanted to draw attention to their cause.' The journalists knew all about Sparkwood and the car factory and had biographical details on Sultana Choudhury and the Khan brothers. Charles had worked hard during the past few hours, waking staff from his office to put together a press pack, and what they couldn't do, he and Chris

North had, waking residents on the Sparkwood estate to fill in the back story.

'We expect them to vacate in a few minutes,' blared the loudhailer. A wave of excitement ran through the Asian crowd, which had swollen and massed along the barrier, and now vastly outnumbered the sulky assembly opposite. 'We will take them to a private location for debriefing, where doctors will be on hand to check no one is suffering as a result of their ordeal.' After that, the press pack promised they would return to work at the Sparkwood factory, which was re-opening as a result of a loan by an investment bank in a deal brokered by the Cities Minister.

'There will be a full investigation,' said Rudd. 'But no prosecution of the Sparkwood protestors is anticipated.' There was a round of applause from the Asian supporters. 'There will be a press conference after the building has been evacuated.'

Rudd walked back to his colleagues, masking his irritation. If he'd had his way he would have charged the lot of them with wasting police time and thrown the minister in jail for a day or two, but this was politics, not policing.

A hush fell over the square at one minute to six and a countdown began in the minds of everyone present, and on screen on TV stations around the world. All eyes fixed on the steel shutters in front of Ego Central, which were now bathed in a fusion of natural and artificial light. At three seconds past six, the siren sounded. Unused through the night it filled the air with a wail, conjuring images of aerial bombardments, huddled families and the best of being British. Both crowds were stilled. As the wail died away the shutters rippled, jerked upwards a notch, and then rose slowly but steadily to reveal thick black drapes. Music issued from within, escaping into the square; a synthesiser and a single plaintiff voice singing of love in Hindi; then a rhythmic chant and thumping dhol, tabla and pipes, a driving Bollywood hit, 'Madhubala', by Pakistani pop idol Ali Zafar.

The shutter reached the top and Eleanor Porter stepped through a slit in the drapes. She was wearing a midi-length dress, blinding white and backless, and sling-back heels, her make-up pastel. She walked to the centre of the square and turned to the audience on each of the three sides, waving and smiling. The square erupted; cameras whirred and a crackle of flashes leapt along the line of photographers like a cartoon fuse. The Asian crowd started to cheer as Eleanor turned back to the opening. She beckoned towards the black drapes while her foot tapped the pavement.

Mirza, Sultana and Khalid emerged in a line holding hands aloft, triumphant, before breaking their chain to wave. Sultana had also raided the clothing racks, choosing a more conservative outfit than Eleanor's, combining western and Asian styles; its sales would rocket the following week and in Whitechapel and Mirpur the pattern would hastily be copied to meet demand at home and abroad. The three leaders made V's for victory and peace and the crowd went wild, waving and chanting. The nationalists watched silently, realising this was not to be their day.

Charles was waiting at the barrier with Mirza Kahn's wife and four small children. He ushered the children into the square and they scampered towards their Have-A-Go father. The last, a toddler, got lost along the way and Eleanor scooped her up in an unintentional yet perfect photo opportunity. Charles tried to punch the morning sky in a salute to his genius. It had to be a *Time* front cover. This was better than sex, he decided; except maybe that time with the pizza delivery girl who looked like Beyoncé.

Next came Eggleston and Prima Donna, ambling either side of the cow. Prima Donna had gone for haute couture, or the closest to it she could find, a full-length red gown with sequins and matching lipstick. She waved regally. Eggleston simply glared at the photographers in his tweeds, his cap pulled down over his forehead. Ought to be horsewhipped, he seemed to be saying.

The cow was unperturbed. Had she an interest in anything other than food and an inkling of what her brush with fame would mean, she might have shown some excitement. But then, she didn't even have a name. This would all change in a few days when an American dairy food company would call to hire the cow to promote its products and offer Eggleston a seven figure sum to name her Philly.

Laura and Alfred Little were supposed to be next, Laura looking chic in a black top over her jeans, her old clothes in an Ego Central shopping bag. At the last moment she gave Alfred a kiss and pushed him forward while she slipped quietly around the edge of a barrier. In her line of business it was best to remain the observer, not the observed. Alfred did a sprightly jig and bowed to the crowd. The rest of the protestors emerged in a line, fifteen bedraggled men and two glamorous women, their arms linked. They danced as if they were in a Bollywood musical, the tabla player thumping in time with the music. The applause was thunderous, the crowd inspired, captivated by the spirit of their neighbours, conquerors and heroes all. They would go down in folklore as Birmingham's Balti Brigade. Some of the women wiped tears from their eyes. It was a day to celebrate and in Sparkwood festivities might stretch to a week.

At a signal from Rudd a group of officers who had assembled in the loading bay split into two lines and formed a tunnel into the square. With a final wave Eleanor led the protestors into the tunnel. Khalid was the last to leave, blowing kisses to the crowd until the police closed around him. The Asian crowd continued to cheer and dance as another track replaced Ali Zafar. The nationalists turned away along Broad Street, vanquished and dejected.

In the loading bay the police separated the protestors. Eleanor and the three leaders were escorted to meet the senior officers; Eggleston, Prima Donna and Alfred Little were taken away for interviews; the cow was led off for milking and then to a sack of feed; and the rest of the crowd climbed aboard the air-conditioned coach and departed for the debriefing. Charles was with Sir Michael Kerrigan and Chris North, following the first group to the caravan, when he spotted Laura waving from behind the barriers. He arranged for her to be allowed into the compound and hugged her. Right now he loved everyone. When she disentangled herself she handed him a piece of paper.

'It's a list of clothes we borrowed and their prices,' Laura said. 'Eleanor wants you to pay the bill so no one can accuse us of stealing.'

Charles pocketed the invoice.

'Are you all right?' he asked, flashing the signature smile.

'I'm great,' she said, and offered him a packet of Wrigley's gum, which he refused. 'Pictures, idiot. Of inside,' she said, flicking her thumb towards the shop. 'Though I wasn't supposed to take them.' Charles' face lit up.

'Good girl,' he said, emphasising each word. Now he had the montage to go with his cover feature. He slipped the camera into a pocket.

'You can be a real prick,' Laura said. 'But that idea for everyone to dress up and do the catwalk thing – that was sick.'

'I know,' he said. Charles was pleased with himself. 'Kerrigan wasn't keen. Unorthodox. I convinced him a party atmosphere would make sure nobody did anything silly.' Charles nodded towards the marksmen on the rooftops who were now standing down, the morning sun glinting on their rifles.

'And you knew it would be massive.'

'That is my genius,' he said. 'News is the new reality show. *X Factor* was news, now news has the X factor. Someone should give me a prize.' Prize or not, he thought, as he surveyed the scene, Sir Frank Porter was going to get a humongous invoice.

'The sad thing is they probably will,' said Laura. 'Who got all the people?'

'The factory manager. I rang him after Michael woke me. He called everyone in Sparkwood. I reckon we'll reach a billion people.'

'Congratulations,' Laura said as she mounted the steps. 'But you're still a prick.'

*

An hour later, after Alfred Little had verified he opened the shop voluntarily and Eggleston and Prima Donna admitted they were not and never had been hostages, the Assistant Chief Constable agreed to proceed with the press conference. By now the crowds had thinned. Most of the Asians were heading to the factory or to Sparkwood to prepare for the celebration that evening, and the nationalists to pubs with round-the-clock football where they would plot their revenge. The remainder joined the journalists queuing to gain entry to the banqueting suite at Jury's Inn in Broad Street.

Immediately prior to the conference Eggleston was arrested and charged with two offences: carrying a firearm in a public place contrary to section 19 of the 1968 Firearms Act, and defecating on the public highway, the latter offence being contained in the same ancient statute that allowed him to bring his cows to town. The charges would later be dropped, following a new agreement to site a waste incinerator with energy recovery on his land, at a reduced price. Some would see this as collusion, others as coincidence, yet others as a rare example of public authorities working together seamlessly for the common good. It mattered little to Eggleston. His modest accommodation would be more than offset by the earnings of his prize cow. By the time planning for the incinerator was granted Philly would be an established star of TV commercials, a regular on children's television and on the threshold of a film career.

Rudd started the press conference by repeating his earlier speech, this time without the loudhailer. Subject to a review by the proper legal authorities, he said, there would be no charges relating to the Sparkwood protest or the temporary occupancy of Ego Central; Alfred Little was recognised for his selfless act of bravery in harbouring the protestors who would otherwise have faced serious assault and injury; and his officers were commended once again for their dedication to duty. Having established the force's ownership of the success he introduced the Minister for Cities, whom he thanked for her small yet vital role in resolving the situation.

Eleanor said little about her activities during the previous twelve hours and talked about the larger issues at stake: tolerance in multicultural Britain; employment; the responsibility of banks to small business; and law and order. She congratulated the West Midlands Police Force on their handling of the crisis, and praised the bravery of the Sparkwood protestors and their leaders. Kerrigan and North nodded from the second row as their minister hit each of her key messages.

Charles had primed several of the journalists, knowing the real story would come out in the question and answer session that followed. Rudd opened the floor with a satisfied smile, only to reel at the barrage of enquiries directed towards the Cities Minister.

'How did you come to be inside the shop, Minister?'

'How did you know it was safe?'

'How did you get the bank to change its mind?'

'Is it true you brokered the deal?'

With each short reply, Eleanor became the story, and try as she might to deflect it, deferring to Sultana, Mirza and Khalid, the more she was cast as a modest heroine on a par with St Joan. She should not have worried; the story was big enough to go round. When she was at last allowed to pass the baton to the Sparkwood leaders there was a fresh round of camera flashes.

Afterwards Eleanor visited the factory, where the media were already encamped waiting for the coach to return with its cargo of local heroes. There were interviews with Eleanor, the Khans, Choudhury and the factory manager in front of the gates and inside along the production line. Later Eleanor visited Sparkwood and stayed for the party, sponsored by the owner of a chain of balti restaurants. By the time the limousine arrived to take her to the airport she had six messages to call the Prime Minister and three from her husband.

Sitting beside the driver Charles debriefed his voicemail and was quiet for the rest of the journey. When they reached the airport he slipped off to buy a magazine and made two phone calls, the first to George Valentine the second to Sir Frank Porter.

'We have a result,' he said when he heard the banker's voice

'I'm watching it,' said Porter. 'Now, what about Chamberlain?'

The man was insatiable, thought Charles. Chamberlain would be publicly humiliated by Eleanor's success, but Porter wanted a death-blow. Charles took a deep breath.

'He called me,' said Charles.

'What?' said Porter.

'Ken Chamberlain. He left a message, twenty minutes ago. He wants a meeting tomorrow morning.'

'Jesus Christ,' said the banker. 'Watch him, Charles.'

'Don't worry. I have a plan,' he said. 'By the end of tomorrow he'll be toast.'

*

Once airborne, Charles snapped his seatbelt open and found a bottle of champagne. Eleanor convened a debriefing session and they sat as they had on the outbound flight with Charles playing steward. Laura took photographs.

'The opposition are on the attack,' Eleanor said. 'They're saying I was endangering lives in a flagrant act of self-promotion.'

'That's ridiculous,' said Charles as he filled his glass.

'And that a minister should never be in the front line. They're comparing it to Churchill at the Sidney Street Siege.'

'That's good,' said Charles.

'Except he ordered in artillery,' said Kerrigan, looking over his glasses. 'And people died.'

'They're also asking where the Home Secretary was,' Eleanor smiled. 'The PM is over the moon. And the pollsters think it might just swing the by-elections.'

'I guess it'll be his idea now,' said Chris North.

'Who cares?' said Charles. 'The media love you. The *Mail*'s website is calling you the Platinum Lady.'

'We had a call from the White House,' said Kerrigan. 'The President wants to give you a dinner. You also have an invitation to Mirpur.'

'Good for the Kashmiri vote,' said Charles. Eleanor declined a refill so Charles topped up his glass. 'Also, L'Oreal wants to revive the Lady Eleanor fragrance. And you have two movie offers. Zac Efron wants you to play his mother and a director in Mumbai wants you to play yourself in a movie about the siege. That's Harvey Nicks, Hollywood *and* Bollywood. I'd say that makes you triple A-list.'

Kerrigan held up his glass.

'It's not for me to say,' he said, 'being an impartial civil servant, but all in all I'd say it's been a rather successful day.'

'Eleanor, you're a star,' said Charles.

'What about the protestors?' she asked.

'They'll be fine,' Charles replied. 'That irritating councillor will probably be the first Asian mayor of Birmingham, the Khan brothers will get a book deal and the Brummie, the security man, he'll end up doing voice-overs when they can't afford Noddy Holder.'

'I mean what happened on the streets?'

'They melted away,' said Chris North. 'In Birmingham. Everywhere. You saved the world.'

'*Time* want to profile you next week. We have the front cover,' said Charles, opening another bottle. 'The big question is what happens next. We need to maintain momentum.' Eleanor looked at her colleagues.

'I'll only do things that focus on the issues. Mirpur maybe, if I have a reason to go there.'

'The White House?'

'No.'

'OK. I've got it,' said Charles clicking his fingers. 'We leak it you've turned down two movie offers and the White House *and* the re-launch of your perfume to concentrate on rebuilding our cities. That'll cause a frenzy.' God, he was hot. Did his brilliance have no end?

'Charles, don't you ever stop?' Eleanor said and swivelled her chair, indicating the meeting was over.

Charles retired to the back of the plane with the champagne and sat opposite Laura. He reclined his seat and watched her for a while, but she was unaware of him, staring out of the window into the night sky, deep in thought.

'Penny for them,' he said.

'What?'

'You were miles away. What are you thinking about?'

'Matters of principle,' she said. 'They matter.'

'I see.'

'And honest politicians. There are some.'

'Yes,' he said. This was all a bit deep to his way of thinking. He'd assumed she'd been reflecting on the amazing events of the day and realising just what a genius Charles was, which thought was now acting as an aphrodisiac. She'd obviously spent too much time with Eleanor.

'It's not something I believed,' said Laura.

I'm sure of that, thought Charles. After all she was a Valentine. She was an odd fish, he decided, not at all what he'd hoped, and something about her had changed in the last twenty-four hours. Something fundamental. Maybe she was a lesbian.

Laura's eyes drifted back to the window. Charles finished his glass and poured another. He would celebrate alone. Today he had created a star. Tomorrow he would put one out. He looked across at Eleanor and considered the nature of fame. It was like a fire. Once lit it could rage, consuming everything in its path, but equally it would fade without fuel. A disaster or triumph was like a breath of wind across its embers. Eleanor Porter was back on top of the A list, and though she may have fanned the flame, Charles had thrown on dry logs, sprayed it with accelerant and created a conflagration the world could see. And no matter what Eleanor wanted he didn't intend to stop now. He hadn't mentioned it, but he had leaked they would be landing at London City Airport in thirty minutes. As he drifted into a snooze, a contented smile spread across his face. It was going to be like The Beatles.

25

Charles arranged himself on the sofa for convenience and effect. He'd reserved the drawing room of the Meard Street Hotel because it afforded privacy as well as prestige yet opened onto the lobby, which was ideal for his purpose.

The Meard Street was Soho's latest boutique stopover, blending contemporary and classic design to deliver conservative surroundings with an up-tempo twist, the perfect setting for a PR guru holding court. Two pink sofas faced each other over a low table laid with the morning papers, coffee and place settings for a breakfast no one would order. Charles sat facing the lobby with his back to striped curtains.

Apparently relaxed, his stomach was in turmoil. This was way beyond pitch nerves. He glanced at the papers. He should have been ecstatic. Eleanor Porter née Barry, aka the Lady Eleanor, *was* the news. Journalists had scrambled over each other for epithets: 'New Model Minister', 'Queen of Jobs' and 'When Eleanor's Cross'. The *Daily Mail* trumpeted 'Winston Returns!' turning the Opposition's accusation into an accolade. Charles checked the monitoring service on his iPhone and confirmed she was as prominent online and around the world. The choreographed exit from Ego Central was the most viewed video on YouTube followed by the rock and roll frenzy at London City Airport. It was his finest hour, his masterpiece. Yet, he knew it was a transitory glory and that everything would turn on this next meeting. A line from Shakespeare slipped into his head, one learned for A levels that he was surprised was not lost. *This is the night that either makes me, or undoes me quite.* It was Iago, somewhere at the back end of Othello, his ghastly plot reaching its climax and everything wagered on the next turn of events.

What was Chamberlain up to, Charles wondered. Why a meeting now? He'd been wrestling with the thought all night. Even the craziness at London City Airport hadn't entirely pushed it out of his mind. He looked up to see the Home Secretary standing in the doorway.

'Hi Ken, *great* to see you,' Charles said, rising and channelling his nerves into an enthusiastic greeting. 'Coffee?' Chamberlain took the sofa opposite. He looked exhausted.

'Congratulations, Charles,' he said, with a wave at the papers. 'You've pulled off a remarkable coup.'

'Thanks,' said the PR man.

'Eleanor must be delighted.'

'You know Eleanor,' said Charles. 'She's more interested in what happens next up there.' He jerked a thumb skywards as if Birmingham was somewhere on the floor above. 'She is amazing.'

'I imagine she's cock-a-hoop,' said Chamberlain, pouring himself coffee. 'She couldn't be in a better position. I suppose I should be thanking you too.' Charles pushed the sugar bowl towards his guest.

'Me?'

'You've taken me off the front pages. I'm buried under Eleanor, which is what *The Times* is saying should happen to me.' Chamberlain dropped a lump of sugar into his cup.

'Sorry, you've been having a time of it,' said Charles.

The politician looked at him squarely. He was about to speak when a waiter arrived to take their order. Both declined.

'Someone's having a go at me, Charles,' Chamberlain said when they were alone again.

'You think so?'

The Home Secretary leaned across the table.

'I'm not stupid,' he said. 'A private letter from a pony club which was destroyed mysteriously reappears? A groom who only uses newspapers to wipe his arse suddenly sells his story? My housekeeper is exposed immediately after a visit by a film company that doesn't exist? It doesn't add up.'

Charles glanced nervously over Chamberlain's shoulder into the lobby.

'Who would do that?' he asked.

'I have my suspicions,' said Chamberlain. Charles felt the Home Secretary's eyes boring into him. 'And if I connect it to the Robert White affair – you remember he was supporting me over this thing with the PM? Well, what if he's a victim too? It could go all the way to the top.'

'I can't believe that, Ken,' said Charles. He hoped his tight mouth read as an expression of incredulity. 'What about White? Maybe it's him. After all, he thought you betrayed him. Maybe he wants revenge.'

'Unlikely,' said Chamberlain. 'For one thing, he's on the Isle of Wight, in a cell, doing a poor impression of Steve McQueen. And he's not that bright.'

'He escaped,' said Charles. 'Last night.' He picked up one of the tabloids in front of him and handed it across the table. Robert White had indeed escaped, as had Ruby Stevens. Late the previous evening the men's team had found a clue hidden behind a pipe in their washroom that gave the precise location of a cache of bicycles outside the camp. At midnight all except Robert White, who was still in the punishment cell, had changed, broken through the wire and found the bikes. They were now cycling across the Isle of Wight in drag.

Meanwhile the girls had changed into their stash of male clothing, crawled along the two tunnels and made a run for it into the woods. The first group were caught almost immediately and placed in the punishment hut just as White was being released. However Ruby, the bitchy pop star and the drunken cookery writer had escaped detection and hiked across the fields with the moon above and the sea behind them. White had returned to an empty camp and, still in prison clothes, made his way to the break in the wire and started to walk north, nursing his arm, which after 30,000 throws of a baseball was virtually useless.

Chamberlain threw the paper on the table.

'That doesn't prove anything,' he said. 'He's trying to find the prostitute, to get her to confess it was a put-up job.'

'Possibly,' said Charles.

'Anyway that's why I wanted to see you,' said Chamberlain, his voice low and determined. He leaned further forward. 'I'm going to fight, Charles. All the way and whatever it takes. You should know that and so should whoever is behind this.'

'I see,' Charles murmured, his mouth dry.

'And I'm going to need help,' said the Home Secretary. 'Are you available?'

'Of course, Ken. Happy to,' Charles said, without missing a beat. He had guessed this was coming and had already decided on his response. And anyway, it was a reflex. Whatever a client wants, whatever he asks, the answer is yes. You figure out how to deliver it later. 'Love to. Let's get the bastards.'

Charles picked up his cup, spilling coffee in the saucer. He attempted an earnest nod but his stomach was still churning. Things were getting out of hand, positively medieval in complexity. He wished he could take the request at face value. That would mean he was still in control. But Chamberlain was an intriguer of the first order. Did the politician suspect him? Was that it? He would know who had the most to gain from his ruin. After the Prime Minister, Eleanor was in the ascendant and he knew Porter as an implacable foe. And that led to Charles. Was this a ploy to divide his enemy or simply the act of a desperate man seeking help? Either way Charles had to say yes. Refusal would mark him as an enemy and pretty much confirm a conspiracy. Also, better him than a competitor who might dig up who knows what.

His hand was shaking as he put down the cup. There was also the Ruby and White factor, which he'd been trying to ignore. The significance of their escape was not lost on him. Would Ruby stay quiet when White caught up with her or spill the beans? And if she did could it be traced back to him? Had George mentioned him to her? Had *he* mentioned Porter to George? He couldn't remember. The risks were piling up. Hadn't someone once said the seed of destruction was sown at the moment of triumph? Some Greek no doubt. Or Shakespeare again. He needed to put an end to this or it was going to explode in his face.

Charles calmed himself. After all wasn't this why he was here, he reasoned. Why they were having this meeting? He had a plan, didn't he? A plan that would finish things. And anyway, who would believe Chamberlain right now? Everyone loved Eleanor and the Home Secretary was humiliated. Anything he said would sound like sour grapes. His confidence returning, Charles looked over Chamberlain's shoulder once more, to see George Valentine standing in the lobby holding a battered brown briefcase. Things would be fine, Charles assured himself. He was touched by genius. And this was his time. He looked at his watch.

'I'm in your corner, Ken, really,' he said. 'But I'll need a bit of time to get organised. I've a lot on with Eleanor and Marshall's tour. Let me see what I can do. I'll call you later.' He stood up as did Chamberlain, the meeting over. Despite his worry Charles couldn't help savouring the shift in power. A month ago Chamberlain wouldn't have given him the time of day.

Charles walked his new client to the door, where their drivers were waiting along with Chamberlain's detective. They shook hands and climbed into their cars. Charles drove straight to his office to provide himself with an alibi for what was to happen next. His mood darkened again. It had better work, he thought. Once this development broke Chamberlain would know for sure he was involved. Charles was gambling on it being too late for him to do anything about it. When he had rung George after Chamberlain's voicemail in Birmingham, and George had suggested the idea, it had seemed flawless. The wave of enmity against the Home Secretary would turn into a tsunami and wash him out of office into exile and disgrace. Now he wasn't so sure. He reminded himself once again of his luck, his gift and his certainty that this was the move that would place him at the top table.

As he arrived at his office it crossed his mind to call Melissa. He'd been meaning to but, what with one thing and another, hadn't. He had texted. Wasn't that enough? 'V busy. Stay in hosp. Have fun xx'. It made sense. The boys were at school and he wasn't around. And anyway she'd still be groggy, wouldn't she? And if he visited he'd have to deal with Marshall who would only complain about his media profile. How long had she been in there, anyway? He would call later. Once he was done with this.

*

While Charles and Chamberlain were shaking hands at the hotel entrance, George took a deep breath, slipped into the drawing room, pulled the report on domestic security threats from his briefcase and stuffed it among the cushions in the sofa previously occupied by the Home Secretary. Then he walked to the Gents, locked himself in a cubicle and sent a text, after which he sat down racked with regret. But the deed was done and there was no going back. There were a lot of plus points, he reasoned. It would finish the job, they would get paid and he and Dot could disappear to Spain. Even if there was trouble they should be long gone. Bathed in soft lighting designed to relax the bowels he listened to someone urinating. It wasn't quite the ending he'd imagined. His original concept had been far more ambitious. But it would never have flown with Dot. Though neither would this. As it was, he had broken the cardinal rule and she would exact cruel and lasting punishment. For the first time in ages he longed for a cigarette.

While George wrestled with his conscience Alan Leo, who had none, walked into the hotel straight to the drawing room and sat in the exact spot Charles had occupied earlier. The waiter was clearing the table.

'Was that the Home Secretary I just saw here?' Leo asked.

'Yes sir,' the waiter said. He sounded proud, his status elevated by the company he served. 'Can I help you, sir?' he asked.

'No hurry,' said Leo. He relaxed into the pink sofa as if waiting to order breakfast. 'What's that?' he asked, pointing to the corner of a flat red object peeping above a cushion in the sofa opposite. The waiter lifted it free.

'Interesting,' said Leo. 'What would you say it is?' he asked, pulling a face that fell short of cherubic.

'A document of some kind,' said the waiter. 'He must have left it behind.'

'Was that where the Home Secretary was sitting?'

'Yes sir,' the waiter held the document between a finger and thumb. He bent at the neck to read it. 'The London Risk Report: Top 10 Threats To Public Security. Top Secret.' He looked at Leo.

'Are you a resident, sir?'

'No. I'm a journalist,' said Leo. He produced the voice recorder that had been switched on since he entered the building. 'And you are no longer just a waiter, my friend. You are news.'

*

In the gent's toilet George's mobile rang.

'Yes?' he whispered.

'Where are you?' It was Dot.

'I'm with Charles,' he said.

'It sounds like you're in a toilet.'

'I am.'

'Well, come home. I've cracked it,' she said. There was a note of triumph in her voice.

'Cracked what?'

'The whole thing,' she said. 'Chamberlain. I've found the secret that will bring him down.'

'Ah,' George sighed.

'Well, don't sound so pleased,' she said. 'And I've packed three crates. It's all very exciting.'

You don't know the half of it, thought George.

*

Two hours later the line of light that had lanced Will's curtains and advanced across the bedroom floor reached his face. He kicked the duvet into the air and sat up in bed.

He was late. He banged on the wall behind him and shouted for Luka to wake. Hearing him groan, Will made for the bathroom, but moved too quickly in the tiny space. Within moments the toothpaste was in the toilet bowl, he'd run scalding water over one hand and shot gel over his chest, which he sponged off with one of Luka's T-shirts, mistaking it for a towel. He peered through the steam. Why was the place full of Luka's shit? And how come he had so much of it? His duffle bag must be like the Tardis. When Will was finished he slid the door open and exchanged places with his bleary-eyed flatmate.

Will scavenged breakfast while Luka complained he couldn't see. There was the same plop of the toothpaste and a cry as scalding water claimed a second victim. Scooping dry cereal from the box, Will went bare-chested into the living room, sat at the desk and opened his laptop. He logged into YouTube to watch the Birmingham video again, the one of the choreographed exodus from Ego Central.

'Awesome,' he murmured. It was as remarkable as it had been at three o'clock that morning. He turned to the bathroom and shouted. 'Hurry up, we're late.' Luka always took forever.

Will took the laptop into the bedroom and watched the video again while he struggled into skin-tight jeans. He froze it at the moment Laura left the clothes shop. It *was* her. What was she doing in Birmingham, he wondered, inside a siege? He let the clip play on and grabbed a shirt. The camera followed the Sparkwood protestors as they boarded the coach, turning and waving, laughing into the lens. Must be a friend filming, or a relative, Will thought. The camera swung back across the loading bay past busy policeman. He paused the video again. He couldn't be sure, but wasn't that Laura again, standing in front of a police caravan, talking to the big-shot PR man from the party? What was *he* doing there? And Eleanor Porter was involved. It was all kind of weird.

Will shut down the laptop and returned to the kitchenette.

'We gotta bounce,' he yelled. 'I'll see you downstairs.' He leaped the steps two at a time and was jogging along the first floor landing as the bathroom door opened and Laura emerged in another cloud of steam, once again wrapped in towels.

'Hi,' he said, having come to an abrupt halt.

'Hi,' she replied. She stepped aside to let him pass. At least she'd spoken to him.

'What were you doing in Birmingham?' Will asked.

'Avoiding you.'

'You were with that PR guy, Franklin.'

'Do you have me under surveillance?' she asked.

'You're the one who does the surveillance,' he replied. Laura turned in the direction of her room. He cringed. Just once, why didn't he think before he opened his mouth? 'No, wait. I didn't mean that.' She stopped and looked at him, her head cocked, eyebrows raised. Everything about her said he had about five seconds to say something that would make a difference. 'I didn't mean to start that way,' he said. Four seconds. 'I didn't expect to see you and if I did, I didn't think you'd speak to me. So I said the first thing that came into my head.' Two. 'And I just saw you on YouTube and was surprised.' One. Oh, fuck, just go for it. 'I'm surprised by a lot of things about you. What I really wanted to say was…can we talk? Maybe have coffee? I'd like to talk. Maybe even listen.' Just in time.

She smiled.

'You missed me.'

'OK,' he said.

'OK what?'

'I missed you.'

'OK then,' she said, her hand reaching for the door handle.

'OK what?'

'OK to coffee.'

'OK,' he said. 'Cool.' Luka arrived on the floor, with a flat-footed thud, struggling to button his shirt. He grinned at Laura.

'Only not now,' Will said. 'Later. We have to be somewhere.' Will and Luka raced down the stairs and wrestled with the front door.

'Are you still playing Blake's tunes?' she shouted. 'He's a shit.'

When the front door was opened Will looked back to see Laura leaning over the banister.

'I will find you,' he shouted. He could hear her laughing as he shut the door.

Westminster Inside Track

https://www.witreport.co.uk

Top Secret Report Found In Soho Hotel

Westminster Inside Track

Your eyes and ears on Westminster and Whitehall; exposing the rumours, conspiracies and whitewash at the heart of government; a virtual voice in a new age of accountability.

A 'D' notice issued by the Home Office means you won't be hearing about a Top Secret report found at a Soho hotel this morning. Detailing the gravest security threats facing London and the measures taken to protect the city, the report was left in plain view in one of the hotel's public rooms. It was found moments after Home Secretary Ken Chamberlain left the building following a meeting with London PR guru Charles Franklin. According to the waiter who served them, the document was found in the room where the meeting took place. WIT is wondering, is Ken Chamberlain the most careless Home Secretary in history? And is the request to restrict reporting really to protect national security or cover a cock-up? Maybe the 'D' in this notice stands for Dunce.

ADVERTISEMENT: Vacancy for Housekeeper

Housekeeper required by prominent family following revelations that previous incumbent was an illegal alien. Benefits include board and lodging, a fair wage by 1950s standards and complimentary citizenship after twenty years' servitude.

Hoovering and dusting are essential as this is a family that desperately needs to clean house. The role includes some childcare as the lady of the house may face a spell away from home following criminal charges for fixing her local gymkhana.

An appointment is sought immediately as current arrangements, whereby Cities Minister Eleanor Porter does the master's job while he fulfils domestic responsibilities, are unsustainable.

WITLINKS: Cities Minister Eleanor Porter – model for our times/ Accident prone Home Secretaries – a league table/ 'D' notice secrets we couldn't share/ White on the run and headed for Cowes

26

Marshall and Melissa made a curious couple, gliding through the Berkshire countryside in an open-top Rolls-Royce, wearing matching elastic head-wraps and hospital gowns, their heads bobbing to ZZ Top. Each wore sunglasses lodged in their bandages and, impossible to detect, both were laughing. The minibar lay on the back seat enthroned on white leather. Melissa tilted her head in the breeze.

'Are you sure we should be doing this?' she shouted.

'Sure,' Marshall yelled back. 'We're not in rehab. Bit of fresh air will do us good.' The Rolls purred and the wind whistled as the needle wavered around sixty. 'You know, the only sound you can hear in a Rolls-Royce is the clock,' he shouted. 'When the roof's on, of course; down it's like a fucking Spitfire.' Marshall erupted into a fresh burst of laughter. Melissa looked at him. He was clearly wasted and loving it.

'I meant drugs and driving,' she shouted.

'You're right,' he replied. 'We're running low. Take two of these.' He passed her a small plastic container. 'There's a can of Red Bull in the back.'

'What will they do?' she asked.

'You won't sweat the small stuff,' he shouted. She took one.

'You're a bad boy, Marshall.'

'That's my job,' he said, peering through the windscreen. 'Anyway, we've had five days in there. We need a decent meal and I know exactly the place.' Melissa glanced at him again. He was doing his best to affect nonchalance, one hand lightly touching the steering wheel, his arm resting on the calfskin armrest, though underneath he was obviously wired. He turned to face her and she looked into his mirror sunglasses, shocked to see an alien staring back.

'It's by the river and has a spectacular wine list,' he said. 'And I promise you tablecloths.' The road wound through trees that locked overhead and sunlight spattered the car like a disco ball.

'Just remember, I'm a married woman,' she said. 'In case you have ideas. Not that I'm saying you do, of course.'

'Oh, I have lots of ideas about you, Melissa,' he said. 'And I'm a Rock Star. Rock Star and Married Woman go together like Jack and Coke.'

'A bad, *bad* boy.' She swept her head from side to side, not appreciating she was stoned. Marshall fiddled with his iPod and ZZ Top cut to Nazareth and a song about bad, bad boys. He sang along, drumming on the steering wheel.

'Worse than bad. Wicked,' she shouted into the wind.

'I'm a pirate,' he yelled, and flipped on the cruise control so he could climb onto the seat. Astride cream leather he drove with one hand and waved at the road ahead. 'And these are my seven seas.' When the car swerved he dropped back onto the leather seat. 'The only trouble is I'm an *old* pirate,' he panted, worn out by the exertion.

'You need to eat more spinach.'

'I need a fag,' Marshall said. He slowed down while he rummaged for a cigarette and, finding one, popped it into the opening in his head-wrap. Melissa reached out and turned down the music.

'Do you remember Northampton Fields?' she asked.

'Sure,' he said, blankly. "82 wasn't it?'

'Marshall,' she said, disappointed. 'That's when we met.'

'Hey babe, the eighties were a bad time. I was using a lot. There are gaps. I remember meeting you. We did the festival on your dad's land and went to a party at his house.'

'You wrecked the place,' she said.

'That's a pirate thing.'

'I was seventeen. You were thirty.'

'Age is in the mind, babe,' said Marshall. 'We're forever seventeen.'

'You were outrageous,' she said, and smiled. 'I'd never seen anything like you. You *were* a pirate.'

'And we did, didn't we?' he said, the comment somewhere between a statement and a question.

'We did. Don't you remember?'

'I remember a wine cellar.'

'There was the wine cellar, the summer house and the helicopter.'

'The summer house. Of course,' he said, appearing to relish the memory as it resurfaced. 'I thought the helicopter was someone else.' Melissa looked at him angrily. 'Sorry, babe. Difficult decade.'

'And then you left,' she said.

'Another pirate thing. You didn't get pregnant?'

'No. I fell in love and got married,' she said. 'And now I'm a respectable wife and mother.' Melissa could feel herself straightening out. She shuffled into her own space on the large cream seat and watched the landscape pass by. She reflected on her brief entanglement with the guitarist and how surprised she'd been when he turned up years later on Charles' client list, burned out and rehabbed. They'd met occasionally since and she could tell she still attracted him, even at her peak weight, though she couldn't imagine why. Maybe he was just a brunette-and-big-boobs man, as the various women who flowed through his life and into the newspapers had demonstrated. Present wife excepted.

'So where's your husband?' Marshall asked.

'Working.'

'He should be here. With you.'

'I expect he's busy,' she said.

'Because you're beautiful, sweet Melissa.'

'Don't be silly.'

'He should look after you, or someone else will.' Marshall looked at her, but any sign of a romantic expression was masked by medical wrapping. He took off his sunglasses to reveal his pirate eyes, heavily bruised from surgery.

'When did he last call you?' he asked.

'He texted. On Friday.'

'To tell you to stay in hospital.'

'The boys are at school,' she said, excusing her husband even though it rankled. 'And he's busy. He thought it would be good for me.'

'Today's Tuesday, Mel,' said Marshall. 'And I warned him. He shouldn't leave you alone with me.'

'Don't be ridiculous,' she scoffed. What would a rock star want with a frumpy housewife who looked like a character out of Dan Dare? The Mekon, that's who she looked like, she realised. The green-headed super-intelligent ruler of the Treens, Dan Dare's arch-enemy. Only her head was starch white. Suddenly she felt paranoid.

'Because we're going to have fun,' he said. 'You're going to laugh. You're going to laugh so much.' He opened his eyes wide, and she tried to guess what expression he was making. 'See. And we're going to fall in love.'

'Oh yes?' she smiled.

'That's how it's going to be, babe,' he said, as if it was already a fact. 'That's my prophecy. I'm looking for love, babe. And I'm looking at you. And you're going to run away with me. And we'll live a country life. No rock and roll crap. One more tour and I'll retire and we'll raise little trout together.'

'Marshall, you are off your head,' she said, laughing. 'Why would I do that?'

'Because you'll want to. Melissa, be my MILF.'

'That's disgusting.'

'The Mom I'll Love Forever. Kiss me,' he demanded.

'No,' she replied. 'We might get stuck.' The Rolls slowed as they reached a village. They passed a church, rolled over a stone bridge and into a car park at the back of a thatched pub. Marshall switched off the engine and they sat quietly. The Rolls simmered after its run in the sun, the only other sounds the birds and the breeze. Melissa looked into the garden which sloped down to the river's edge where there was a boathouse. On the bank opposite there were green reeds, then fields with grazing sheep that swept up to an ancient village. It was perfect.

'Best grub for fifty miles,' said Marshall. 'And it's all mine. The Witch Bitch doesn't know about this one.' He slipped from the car, his gown fluttering, and skipped round to open her door. 'I keep some clothes here, so we can change,' he said. As she stepped down she looked up at the sign that hung in front of the pub. The Jolly Roger.

'Welcome ashore, milady,' he said in a passable Long John Silver, bowing and flashing a smile of yellow and gold. 'And after lunch we'll take a punt, you and I, and I'll find a willow by the riverbank, where I will show you my ardour. Ah-har!'

27

The tarmac was bubbling as a Mr Ripple ice-cream van turned into Mersley Road. Immaculate in white coat, bow tie and hat, Kracholov straightened the wheel and slipped a cassette into the ancient stereo system. It was one of a job lot he'd bought at the weekend, trawling old record shops. A loud electronic raspberry issued from the horns on top of the van and segued into a majestic and melancholy classic of progressive rock, 'Back Street Luv' by Curved Air.

Nineteen seventy-one, Kracholov remembered. The same year the wily Zhivkov, father of Zhivkova, achieved absolute power and told his countrymen to love Bulgaria for itself and Russia for its oil. It was Curved Air's only song to reach the top ten in the UK music charts. Classical roots, Kracholov observed, like so much progressive rock. Almost a requiem. The music settled into a swaying rhythm and Sonja Kristina's acid folk voice floated onto the street.

The van whirred along the tarmac turning the heads of hot and lazy children who puzzled over the battered vehicle with its faded clown emblazoned on the side and the depressing drone of a shy girl's vain search for love in place of the usual bright jingle. Kracholov pulled up opposite number 54 and peered across at the house. A double-fronted Victorian semi stared back, its upper windows winking in the sun. It was set back from the street and built on a rise, which made it appear bigger than it was. He saw it was run-down as it had been at the back, which he took as a good sign, meaning a weakness was likely, something broken or poorly maintained that might provide an easy means of entry. A post was attached to the front wall hosting a For Sale sign.

By the time the song finished, and despite its gloom, a crowd of children and several mothers had gathered around the van. Kracholov switched off the cassette and sighed. He'd asked for a surveillance vehicle, expecting an anonymous car, but Mr Ripple was the best the Best Bulgarian Cleaning Company could come up with at short notice. Apparently a lot of surveillance was under way in London and everything else was in use. He climbed from the driver's seat into the back and opened the sliding window. A small girl looked up at him expectantly. Behind stood her mother in a tank top, her shoulders sunburned, her arms crossed, one fist gripping a purse.

'Are you Mr Ripple?' asked the little girl.

'Yes. I am Ripple.'

'You don't look like him,' she said, looking at the side of the van. 'I want Mr Ripple.'

'I am brother,' said Kracholov. 'Mr Ripple had accident.'

'I want a Super Ripple with a Cadbury flake,' the girl said. Kracholov pulled a cone from a stack, placed it under a spout and pulled the lever. Nothing happened. He should have checked the stores, he realised. The Best Bulgarian Cleaning Company was not known for its attention to detail. He'd even heard tales of guns supplied with the wrong bullets. He slid open the icebox beneath the counter and peered inside. All he could find were boxes of small rectangular blocks wrapped in silver foil.

'We have choc-ice,' he said.

'I don't want a choc-ice,' said the little girl, with a look of profound disappointment.

'That's all there is,' he said. He refrained from adding they were Best Bulgarian choc-ices rather than the brands advertised on the van. Not that there was anything wrong with Bulgarian ice cream.

'Mum.'

'Where's Mr Whippy?' asked the mother. The muscles on her upper arms flexed and an angel tattoo appeared to flutter heavenwards. 'It's usually Mr Whippy.'

'I don't know Mr Whippy,' said Kracholov. 'I am Ripple.' The news that Mr Ripple only had choc-ices spread along the queue and one or two mothers left with their children in tow, the youngsters looking back at the van, distraught. Kracholov peered over the crowd to Number 54. The commotion was making any form of surveillance impossible. He looked down at the little girl.

'You want one or not?' he barked, which caused her to look as if she'd swallowed a cork. She nodded vigorously as her eyes filled with tears. He produced a choc-ice and slammed it on the counter.

'Three quids,' he growled. The mother gave him a ten-pound note and a look of disgust. Kracholov opened the cash drawer to find it empty. 'No change. Three quids exact, please,' he demanded. The mother and child peeled off from the queue, the mother complaining loudly and warning the rest of the experience ahead, while the little girl burst into tears, unable to comprehend why Mr Ripple could not give her what he advertised on his van. Others followed to avoid facing disappointment at the end of a long wait. One angry parent muttered something about the Trades Descriptions Act and threatened to phone the council. Kracholov looked down at the next customer in desperation.

'Hello, Agent K,' said a young boy. It was the lad who had led him to safety on his last visit to number 54. 'You in trouble again?' Kracholov frowned. That was all he needed, to be pinpointed as the gunman from the previous week. He picked up a tea towel to wipe his brow, forgetting it was covering the Franchi, and quickly replaced and straightened it. 'Bit of surveillance from the front this time?' The boy winked after a peek back at the house. 'Don't seem to be going too well, does it? Here, let me in. I'll sort it out for you.' Kracholov studied him. The boy had proved useful before and he was ready to try anything. He opened the door at the back of the van and the boy climbed inside.

'Tell you what,' said the lad, his face set firm. 'I'll sell the ice-cream and you do the watching. But I want commission.' Kracholov told him he could have everything he made and climbed into the driver's seat while the boy checked the cupboards. Inside one he found a box and pushed it into place under the serving hatch, stepped on it and, filling the opening, his hands flat on the counter, he bellowed across the street.

'Roll up, boys and girls. Roll up. Special deal today – a one-time only collector's item. Limited edition. Mr Ripple's Retro-Choc. Try the ice cream your dad had as a boy. Going cheap. Come on, who's first? I'll give you two for a fiver, five for a tenner. Come on, mums. Don't sulk, buy in bulk, and get enough for your Incredible Hulk. Go on, treat him indoors.'

Kracholov glanced at the lad and wondered just who was whose apprentice, then watched the house while the boy did brisk business. There were no signs of movement in or around the property.

'Maybe no one's in,' the boy called over his shoulder while he served a customer. 'Why don't you call the estate agent?' He pointed at the signboard. Kracholov looked at him, mystified, and the boy explained, as far as he could, about estate agents. Kracholov made two calls. The first was to the Best Bulgarian Cleaning Company for a tutorial on how the English property system worked; the second was to the number on the signboard.

Twenty minutes later an eager young man in a shiny suit arrived in a shiny car with the agent's details printed on its side. He sprang up the steps to the front door and stood jangling the keys in the doorway, a clipboard under his arm. Leaving his coat and hat on the seat Kracholov slipped from the van, brushing his hands as if finishing a cone. He waved at the agent when he was halfway across the street.

'Mr Levytski?' asked the agent, consulting his clipboard. He offered an open hand, which Kracholov shook vigorously.

'Hot enough for you, Mr Levytski?' the agent asked. 'Is that a Russian name?'

'Ukrainian,' Kracholov answered, looking up at the front of the house. The agent made a sound that suggested he appreciated the difference.

'We have a lot of Russians buying property in London just now,' he said, following Kracholov's gaze.

'It needs repairs,' Kracholov said. 'Which is good. I am builder.'

'It says here you're an accountant.'

'And builder. It's my passion.'

The agent gave Kracholov a potted history of the property. Late

Victorian, it was currently owned by a couple who were planning to retire, and were looking for a quick sale, so might take an offer. The agent gave Kracholov a knowing wink, which the hit-man assumed was a signal that a valuable piece of insider information had passed between them. The couple lived on the ground floor and had tenants on the first and second floors. The tenant on the first floor was their daughter and there was a commercial tenant at the top who was on a monthly contract, so there would be no problems with vacant possession. For cash he could take the keys within four weeks. The agent put the key in the lock. 'Shall we take a look?' he suggested. 'It's a superb period property. Just needs some TLC.' As the door swung open, Kracholov brushed past into the hallway. 'Take your time,' said the agent. 'Have a good look round. No one is in. The only place we won't be able to see today is the cellar. That's locked. But it's fine. No damp. The owner uses it as a workshop.'

28

While Kracholov surveyed their bedroom, his eyes lighting on a Spanish property brochure on the bedside table, George and Dot were travelling at fifty-eight miles an hour in the slow lane of the M40 heading towards Oxford. They were passing Postcombe, one of the villages with see-saw fortunes that lined the turnpike road from London, once host to stagecoaches until the railway displaced them, then motorists until the motorway bypassed them again.

A driver passing the white van and glancing in would have seen a balding, middle-aged man hunched over the steering wheel and peering through the windscreen, his ample wife turned towards him, her forefinger stabbing the air, as if conducting Stravinsky. The same driver would be forgiven for thinking the woman was giving instructions on road safety, as the van seemed to slow and accelerate in direct correlation to her finger. In fact George and Dot's conversation was much more bizarre. Inside the fan was on full, but George was feeling hot and uncomfortable.

'What on Earth were you thinking?' Dot demanded, frowning behind her sunglasses.

'I don't know. It was our last job.'

'And you kept it?' she asked. 'This report. These ten security risks or whatever?'

'Yes.'

'Kept it in a drawer. Without telling me. For days. And I bet you were going down to that cellar every night, looking at it and thinking, weren't you?' she asked.

'Yes.'

'Hatching this silly idea.' Dot sat back in her seat, her face a picture of indignation. George looked out to the road, wondering how long this would last. He knew there was a way to go. Dot's anger was like a mountain range, it rose to an icy peak and then fell away slowly, and every excuse he made, every word he uttered would lift her to a new peak, until there was a snow-capped sierra of furious outbursts. He would say as little as possible, he decided, and aim for the Brecon Beacons over the Himalayas.

'You lied to me,' she said. 'Every night. You lied.'

'I didn't lie. I just didn't say anything about it,' George said, and cringed, realising this could lead to a frozen summit where the air would be thin.

'There's more to lying than what you say. You lied by not telling me,' she said. 'So, you took it from that house. Where was it?'

'On his desk. In the study,' George said. 'Will took it.'

'You took it from his desk and then you hid it. And then you came up with this…this ridiculous idea.'

'Yes.' There was a short, ominous silence, then a new and dangerous tone. A glacier.

'How can I ever trust you again?' she said. 'How can I?'

'Come on, Dot…'

'You've put everything we have at risk,' she said. 'Spain. Our retirement. Everything. This is more than pinching someone's dustbins, George. You could get time for this.'

'Dot.'

'Don't you want to come and live in Spain?' she asked. 'With me. Is that it? You'd rather be in a prison cell, so long as you can live dangerously?'

'No.'

'Have you done this before?' she asked, in the hurt-beyond-repair tone.

'No.'

'How do I know?'

'I haven't.'

'Why should I believe you? You could have been doing it for years. Planting things.'

'You know I haven't,' said George. 'We agreed.'

'And you've broken the agreement.' The fact was in front of them, indisputable as a block of granite. 'It was the number one rule, George. We reveal, we never conceal, we do not manipulate. The subject gets what's coming to him. Or her. Nothing more. We do not intervene. We do not interpret. We do not judge.'

'I know.' George looked at his wife with a hangdog face.

'Who did you use?' she asked.

'Leo.' He screwed his eyes tight, awaiting a ski-lift ascent.

'Leo?' she snorted. 'You used Leo? George, he's a moron. If that man was standing by a lake with his balls on fire he'd search for a tap. I am sorry. You are unbelievable.'

'I should have told you,' he said.

'I would have said no.' There was another silence. 'Can you get it back?' she asked.

'It's too late,' said George. 'He wrote the story before we did it. It's probably already started. We could see if it's on the radio.' He reached out to the dashboard and received a slap on the wrist.

'I don't want to hear it on the radio, George,' said Dot. 'It will not help me to hear about this fiasco on the radio. If you can't say anything sensible, just be quiet while I think.' She picked at her nails.

'We weren't getting anywhere, love,' he ventured. 'The pony story wasn't enough to hang him and he was wriggling out of the immigration thing.' Dot looked aghast.

'That's because he's a cunning and clever man, George,' she said. 'He must have known something was up from the start. And he certainly will now, won't he?'

'I suppose so,' said George. Dot gave him a withering look.

'Yes, George. Unless he has dementia. I mean, he's likely to remember whether he took a top secret report and stuffed it down the back of a sofa or not. That's if he hadn't noticed it had been nicked in the first place. And if he knew it had been nicked, he'd be a bit surprised to find it turning up there, wouldn't he?' She hardly paused for breath. 'He knows the ropes, George. Do you think he got to the top without a bit of jiggery-pokery? He's shredded a reputation or two in his time. I cannot believe you could be so…so…' Dot looked out at the motorway, as if she expected the perfect word to appear on the horizon. George glanced at the speedometer. They were travelling at forty miles an hour.

'He'll think it was Charles,' said Dot. 'He set up the meeting.'

'It *was* Charles,' said George. 'He liked the idea.'

'Then he's a fool too,' she said. 'We have to be careful, George. The risks are piling up. Chamberlain's a tough nut, be sure of that, and if he puts Charles under pressure…well, I'm not sure he's got the bottle. And if he goes for Leo, *he* can finger us on Edith and the ponies.'

'Leo won't reveal a source. It would ruin him.'

'You think he'd notice?' said Dot. 'Prison would be a step up in his living standards. Then there's Ruby. We don't know what will happen when she and White meet up. I think she's OK but she'll do anything for money.'

'I'm sorry, Dot. I was doing it for us.' George realised too late he had whisked them back up the mountain.

'Don't give me that,' she said. 'You were doing it for you. You wanted to go out with a bang. Slipping quietly out of the country wasn't good enough for you. No, you had to end on a great big stunt. Well your big stunt could land us in jail.'

'At least we're ready to go,' he said. 'Apart from the house. Maybe this foreign bloke will offer on it.'

'I'm not worried about us, George,' said Dot. 'I'm worried about Laura. Ruby knows her. So do Charles and Leo.' George ranged over the events of the last two weeks. They were secure as far as everything else was concerned: the fake film company had never been used before, the bike had false plates, and the number the jockey had for Laura was for a disposable phone.

'She'll be fine,' he said.

'If worse comes to worst, she'll just have to come with us to Spain,' said Dot. 'She won't like it but there it is.'

She squinted at a road sign coming towards them.

'It's this one,' she said, jabbing a finger in the air. 'I guess I'll have to sort it all out, as usual,' she added, with a sigh. 'It's just as well I found this little lot.'

'What have you found?' George asked, aware they had spent more than the requisite twenty minutes on her topics of conversation. In fact the one-sided discussion had lasted since he arrived home and confessed. In theory he was owed two hours of uninterrupted listening. Maybe the rule was suspended in these circumstances.

'You'll see,' she said. 'It's not nice when someone has a secret, is it?'

George bit his lip. He wondered if this was the moment for total honesty, the time to reveal the rest of his grand plan, his idea about the files. It would mean a new ascent but further deceit would result in him being left without oxygen on the upper reaches of K2.

'There is one other thing,' he said, taking a deep breath, but he was interrupted by another woman's voice chipping in from the satnav and commanding him to take the next exit.

'This one,' said Dot, her tone implying he had ignored the instruction a second earlier. George took the slip road and switched off the electronic voice, wishing he could achieve a similar result with his wife. The road rose and fell, snaked right and left, shedding HGVs and coaches and then those who only wanted fuel, until the van rolled into a car park, black and baking and littered with vehicles. In front of them was a steel and glass building with a metal quiff for a roof. It proclaimed they had reached a Welcome Break.

George pulled up in front of a large bin overflowing with rubbish. He regarded it with a professional eye. A connoisseur of waste, he was glad he wouldn't have to go through it, with its crushed cola cups, masticated burgers and melted ice cream, the boxed and cellophane-wrapped detritus of the modern staging post. He wondered what it would have been two hundred years ago – apple cores and beer dregs perhaps, animal bones and grease for lubricating coach wheels. And horse shit everywhere, if not in the bin then all around it. Though there wouldn't be a bin, of course, just an inn and a dirt road; and not a fuel station, just a horse trough. And it wouldn't be here but in Postcombe. This would have been a quiet field or wood. George climbed from the van and opened the door for Dot who descended regally.

She led them along a pavement, past sunburned shrubbery. They passed a picnic area with wooden trestle tables and bench sets, and George watched as an obese family forced themselves into its intractable structure. There was a pond with carp to amuse small children and a row of fountains that spattered its surface.

The place was heaving with travellers, enticed onto the roads by the sun, now seeking a diversion from driving ten feet behind the car in front at eighty miles an hour. Outside people queued for the cash point and smoked and inside they lined up for toilets, fast food, or the games arcade. There wasn't much rest at a rest stop, George thought, unless you counted the Days Inn, which offered an overnight cubicle for tired travellers and cheap trysts. Rest was the ten minutes you sat in an uncomfortable seat to scoff your KFC. All in all, he concluded, a stop at an eighteenth-century coaching inn would be preferable, even with the odd weevil.

'Wake up, George,' Dot snapped as she scanned the seating area in front of Starbucks, the outlet at the heart of the building. 'I'd like a cappuccino.' She motioned for him to join the queue.

'What are we doing here?' he asked.

'Wait here,' said Dot. George watched as she walked over to a woman who was sitting alone at a small table. She was of a similar age to his wife, but taller, and as slim and angular as his wife was robust. She was clutching a man's leather shoulder bag and looked nervous. The two women exchanged words and Dot made signals to George, which he interpreted as an order for Earl Grey tea and biscuits in addition to the cappuccino. He ordered, waited and paid, then carried his tray to the table.

'Don't sit down,' said Dot when he arrived. He stood awaiting further instructions, wondering how much public upbraiding he had to absorb before this morning's events would be forgiven. Dot and her companion stood up, gathering bags and coats. The tall woman smiled weakly but Dot whisked her away before George had a chance to say hello.

'We need somewhere we can talk,' said Dot. She stomped off across the floor, an imperious wave signalling George to follow.

They found a table on the deck outside, overlooking the fountains, and sat in plastic chairs that received a cooling hint of spray.

'Lovely day,' said Dot, fanning herself with a menu as beads of perspiration formed on her brow.

'Sensational,' said George. The woman repeated her weak smile. George laid out the refreshments. Dot sipped her cappuccino with pursed red lips and finally relented, introducing the woman as Mrs Tom Howard. Mrs Howard was a librarian and the widow of a journalist who had worked for Gloucester's leading newspaper. George learned her husband had died a year ago.

'So, Tom covered the '92 election?' Dot asked, with a softness her husband thought had disappeared forever.

'Yes,' said Mrs Howard. 'He covered everything at different times. You do on a local paper. He had a career in Fleet Street but he wasn't good at corporate politics, so we moved to the country and he got a job with *The Citzen.*'

'He covered Chamberlain's campaign?' Dot asked. George began to see where this might be going.

'Yes. His seat was a marginal and it was a tough fight.'

'Chamberlain won, though,' said George.

'Yes, but he shouldn't have. The favourite was the Labour candidate, Ben Wheeler, who was way ahead in the polls, but he was involved in a scandal two weeks before the election. You might remember it?'

'Something about a boat,' George said. Mrs Howard nodded.

'Tom found out something about Chamberlain that happened two years earlier,' she said. 'It was a rumour that had been around the news desk for a long time, but no one knew where it came from, and nobody had followed it up.' She stopped to sip her tea before continuing. 'Apparently Chamberlain owned a river cruiser, which he kept on the Thames. It was called the *Greta Garbo*. Two years earlier it had been involved in an accident, a hit and run. It collided with another boat, hit a mooring bollard and then careered off up the river. A woman was seen at the wheel waving a bottle of champagne and yelling at everyone to get out of the way. Everyone assumed it was Mrs Chamberlain.'

'It sounds like her,' said George.

'Anyway, two children on the damaged boat were thrown into the river and nearly drowned, while Chamberlain's boat disappeared. It was found moored a few miles upriver. Whoever was on board had done a runner. When the manager of the boatyard rang about it Chamberlain claimed he wasn't on board and that it must have been stolen. He threatened to sue the yard for not taking care of it. The owner of the other boat complained but nothing could be proved. No one saw Chamberlain take the boat out in the first place so that was where it was left.'

'How did your husband get involved?' Dot asked.

'Tom investigated the story and found a witness who'd seen Chamberlain and his wife on the boat that day. He thought it stood up, so he ran the story.'

'Wasn't it discredited?' George asked. He offered Mrs Howard a biscuit, which she declined. She nodded.

'Three days later Chamberlain proved he and his wife were on holiday in Cornwall that week. Then the witness changed his story and admitted he couldn't be sure who was on the boat. We assumed he was got at,' she said. 'Then Chamberlain claimed it was all part of a smear campaign by Wheeler. And lo and behold, a lot of damning evidence turned up at a rival paper.'

'What sort of evidence?' asked Dot.

'Invoices to Wheeler from a firm of private detectives for work they had supposedly undertaken for him, trying to dig up dirt on Chamberlain. It included copies of Chamberlain's credit rating and criminal checks, all of which showed an unblemished past, of course. They'd also come up with a record of the boat's ownership, which implied Wheeler had known about it and stirred up the story.' Mrs Howard covered her eyes momentarily. 'Then, in the last week of the campaign an envelope arrived at the paper addressed to Tom. Inside was a large amount of cash. Three times his monthly salary. Someone checked and the taxi that delivered it came from Ben Wheeler's campaign office. Everyone assumed he'd been bribed by Wheeler to fabricate the story.'

'I remember that,' said George.

'The voters sided with Chamberlain and Wheeler lost the election,' said the widow. 'Wheeler was finished after that. It's a sad story, he took to drink and drugs and two years later threw himself into Cheddar Gorge.'

'What happened to Tom?' Dot asked.

'He didn't lose his job immediately, but he might as well have. A year later he was made redundant. They said it was the recession. It was the end of serious journalism for him. He wrote for the free sheets and taught at the local FE College. He drove a taxi for the last few years. I suppose he was one of those people who get trodden on by those climbing to the top.' Mrs Howard turned and looked into the fountains, her face displaying an age of anxiety. 'I can't see that man without feeling sick,' she said.

'So where does this get us?' George asked, looking at Dot. Mrs Howard returned to her story.

'Tom got depressed,' she said. 'but he never gave up. The thing about my husband, he was a terrier. He would never let things go. And he was a good journalist. He had a nose for things. So he kept on looking, very slowly, very carefully. For years. He knew Chamberlain had set it up, to cover up the truth and ruin Wheeler. Tom was just a pawn in the game.' She picked up the brown leather bag and placed it on the table. 'These are his files,' she said.

'What's in them?' Dot asked.

'Everything. He was about to publish them when he died.' George pulled out a lever arch file and flicked through the contents. He whistled.

'Sensational.'

'He was pleased with it,' said Mrs Howard. 'He thought it would exonerate him.'

'And the rest,' said George. He looked through the contents again, more thoroughly this time. There was a record from the same firm of detectives of work undertaken for Chamberlain at the time, including references to surveillance on Wheeler, the agency's entire file on the Labour candidate and an internal memo reporting an unusual request

260

for 'an additional, special and positive report on the client'; there was a bank statement from Mary Chamberlain's account showing a cash withdrawal of the same amount Tom Howard received, one day before it was placed in his account; then a Land Registry certificate for the property Chamberlain claimed to be staying at in Cornwall at the time of the boating incident, with a note that identified the owner as his lawyer and a statement from a local cleaner saying the villa was empty that week; next, a written affidavit by a witness who saw Chamberlain and his wife climbing up the river bank from their boat on the day in question; and finally, a photograph of Ken Chamberlain aboard the *Greta Garbo*, in the right hand corner the red digital imprint of the day of the accident.

'Chamberlain's wife must have taken it,' Mrs Howard said. 'Don't ask me how Tom got it.' George could guess. Obviously Tom Howard could trawl through a dustbin or two when it was necessary. He and Dot were silent. Mrs Howard took another sip of tea. 'Then Tom went back over other elections, in the past and more recently. Chamberlain used the detective firm many times. You'll find a lot of interesting information in there,' she said, pointing at the file. 'You might look at the section on his first term as a borough councillor. The leader of the council was forced to retire in favour of Chamberlain following concerns about his health. Concerns first raised by Ken Chamberlain.'

The three of them sat quietly listening to the hiss of the fountains and children's laughter beyond.

'How long have you had this?' asked Dot.

'Since he died,' said Mrs Howard. 'A year. I couldn't face it. Not without him. I didn't know what to do. Chamberlain is a powerful man and he's discredited us before. I was frightened. Then you called, asking if I had any information that could help your investigation.'

'Investigation?' George mouthed to Dot.

'Into election malpractice,' Mrs Howard said. 'And I thought it might be time. Does it help?' she asked, as she finished her tea. 'I hope it's enough. We didn't have many friends, and we don't have children, but I would like to get his reputation back.'

'Don't worry,' said Dot, patting her hand. 'It's enough,'

Later, sitting in the car park, George paused before releasing the handbrake.

'That was sensational, Dot,' he said. 'I think you've saved our bacon.' Dot smiled but said nothing. George realised she wasn't going to let him off the hook just yet. His mobile rang. It was Charles Franklin. He answered it and listened, the colour draining from his face.

'The police have arrested Leo,' he said when the call was finished. 'And Charles has been questioned. He's in a state. Apparently, Chamberlain reported the dossier missing immediately after our visit. And it was a numbered copy, so when it turned up in the sofa they knew it was fishy.'

'I told you,' said Dot, ascending the nearest peak.

'We're all right for now,' George said. 'They've issued a D notice, so there won't be anything in the papers for a day or two.'

'That won't stop the bloggers,' said Dot. 'Bugger.'

George turned to his wife, his lips bursting with his last secret.

'There's no time to argue any more, Dot,' he said. 'We've got to think fast. So I need to tell you the rest. There was another part to my plan and I think you need to hear it.' He released the brake and drove towards the motorway slip road, thinking his story was best told while driving. That way he wouldn't have to look Dot in the eye and she would have part of her mind on the road.

After he had finished, she asked a few questions then said nothing. They spent the run home in silence, George on tenterhooks, expecting an eruption at any moment. Meanwhile he mulled over the threats that were circling and the chances of avoiding their consequences. They were banking on Ruby, Leo and Charles keeping silent. It would need only one of them to talk and the path would lead to 54 Mersley Road. There were two other factors that would determine the success or failure of their adventure. The first was the dossier that sat in Dot's lap. It was big enough to deal a fatal blow, but would it remain credible if sentiment shifted towards Chamberlain? The second was the speed of their getaway. George considered how long it would take to pack the remaining boxes and wondered how they would persuade Laura to come with them without sparking a row.

As they pulled into Mersley Road Dot was the first to spot something was wrong. The front door was ajar but the lights were off. She bustled up the path ahead of George, bristling, ready to start an investigation into who had gone out without locking up and find a target on which to vent the day's frustrations. Initially George was relieved as it made a diversion from his misdemeanours, but once inside he realised things were serious. The hall mirror was askew and a flower vase upturned. Had Laura and Will had another fight? George switched on the lights as Dot checked their rooms. Nothing was disturbed on the ground floor except for the French doors in their bedroom, which were open. Dot headed upstairs while George fetched a golf club.

Laura's floor was silent and empty but they could hear muffled sounds above. They made their way to the top of the house, Dot in front and George behind, brandishing the club above his head. Dot slid open the door to Will's flat and peered inside. Sitting on the floor in the kitchen area, surrounded by pots and pans and broken crockery, were Will and Luka, back-to-back and bound together with electric cable, duct tape plastered liberally over their mouths. Laura was nowhere to be seen.

29

Surfacing, Laura grew conscious of the sound of television, a constriction around her wrist and finally the blindfold. She fought the urge to move and tried to gather her wits before betraying she was awake.

She remembered being bundled into an ice-cream van after the mad scramble downstairs. The man had bound her hands, blindfolded her with airline eyeshades and forced her to lie face down on the floor. They had driven for what seemed hours then stopped and waited. A door had squealed open and she was dragged from the vehicle, across a pavement, up a flight of stairs and into a room. He had shoved her onto a bed and tethered her wrists to the headboard, muttering in some Eastern European language. There was vodka on his breath. It was the one moment when she had lost it and, fearing the worst, lashed out with her legs until she was exhausted. But nothing happened. He must have gone to park the van.

As she recovered from the panic and exertion she noticed the smell of fresh paint and new carpets. Rubbing her head against her shoulder she pushed the blindfold above her eyes. The lights were off but the glow of a streetlamp the other side of thin curtains was enough to suggest a sparsely furnished room. From the noise outside she judged they were still in the city, on the first floor of a building, most likely flats. She wondered who might live above, below or to the sides, and was about to scream for help when the man returned and checked her fastening and blindfold. He told her to be quiet like a mouse and sleep. The room quietened until she couldn't tell if he was still there or not, and despite her anger and fear she found herself obeying his command and drifting into oblivion.

It was noisier now and she could smell coffee as well as the paint and carpets. On TV an insistent voice was making claims about a rejuvenating face cream. Apparently it was so effective people no longer recognised you when it was applied. Laura rubbed her head against the mattress, as if asleep but dreaming, gently easing the blindfold onto her forehead. The curtains were still drawn, holding back the morning sun, but it was light. She could tell the bed was pine and the plastic ties around her wrists white and attached to struts in the headboard. A light bulb hung from the ceiling and the room was bare apart from the bed, a chair and the television, a pre-plasma box on a plastic stand. A heavy camouflage jacket hung over the chair back and a copy of the *NME* lay on the seat. Laura guessed her assailant had spent the night there keeping watch. By the wall she could make out a pair of army boots, a kit bag and a cello case. She heard the rifling of cutlery somewhere beyond the door. He was in the kitchen. Laura tugged at her wrists, but the ties were unbreakable, then she tried to loosen the struts in the headboard with even less success. Eventually her attention drifted to the television.

'It's a new twist to reality TV that has the nation enthralled,' claimed a bubbly presenter. 'This was the scene last night shot by a local resident on his mobile phone.' The programme cut from the studio to an unsteady picture of a country road at night, where a group of men dressed in women's clothing were riding ancient bicycles. The presenter continued, 'The boys' team was ahead of the girls' and within sight of Newport when they were spotted by the driver of a removals van. The man alerted his friends and pursued the celebrities.' The shaky mobile was replaced by CCTV footage of cyclists racing through a shopping centre chased by a posse of vehicles, plate glass crashing around them.

'After a chase that one eyewitness described as Bradley Wiggins meets Jason Bourne, the escapees were captured and held until the driver could claim his reward.' Professional video showed the driver proudly opening his truck to display the boys' team, bruised and gripping mangled bicycles, after which he received a giant cheque from the programme's producer.

Ruby's team had been more successful and while spotted by the programme's helicopter unit, no one else had noticed them. They had walked across open land until Ruby negotiated a lift to Cowes on a truck, driven by an ageing farmhand who apparently did not possess a television and was too deaf to hear the chopper. Ruby rode up front while her companions lounged in the back on straw bales and basked in the sun. They reached Cowes in the evening to find their faces on wanted posters all over town. Ruby spent another ten minutes in the cab negotiating the driver's silence while her companions took a walk by the sea. After she emerged, refreshing her lipstick, they hid in a bus shelter until morning, waiting for the first ferry.

Robert White meanwhile had also hiked across open country, exchanging his prison clothes for a scarecrow's in the middle of the island. Happily, in addition to sporting a face-mask of the Prime Minister and the caption 'Bullocks to Politics,' the scarecrow was dressed in a decent suit and tie. Years later, as chairman of a charity providing hunting experiences for the disadvantaged, White would say this long commune with nature and chance encounter was a turning point in his life. At this moment, however, he was captured on CCTV arriving in East Cowes and heading for the harbour. Laura shook her head. She couldn't believe people watched this shit.

She sensed her captor in the doorway and worked the eyeshade back into place while feigning restless sleep. The next thing she knew he had removed it and was towering over her, a mug of coffee in one hand and a plate of toast in the other. He placed them on the floor beside her and released one of her wrists.

'White will win,' he said and made his way back to the kitchen. He returned with his own coffee, turned the chair to face the screen and sat down. 'Even with damaged arm. He is amateur sailor. English are good sailors. He will steal boat.' He looked at his watch.

Laura examined her kidnapper. A giant of a man, he had changed from the camouflage fatigues he wore last night and now looked like a nightclub bouncer in Armani trousers and a black T-shirt. She judged he was fifty-something but still in shape, with biceps like

Popeye tattooed in Cyrillic script. Laura remembered he had a shotgun and wondered if it was in the kitchen. Not that it mattered – her chances of overpowering him even unarmed were less than zero. She thought hard about her first question, discarding anything that might sound a note of anxiety.

'What does your tattoo say?' she asked, mustering a hint of flirtation. The muscles in his neck bulged as the big man turned towards her.

'It is national anthem of my country,' he said.

'What is it in English?'

"Dear Motherland, you are paradise on Earth. Your beauty and your charm, they have no bounds."

'That's nice. Sort of 'I Love Mum',' she said. He turned back to the screen.

'Tattoo also says: 'Countless fighters gave their lives for our beloved people. Mother, give us manly strength to carry on their course."

'And this is the manly thing, is it?' Laura asked, now sitting up, bristling. 'By kidnapping me you're doing your bit for the Motherland?' She glared at the back of his head.

'This is business,' he said. 'You are noisy woman. You should keep mouth shut.'

She decided not to.

'What country is it?' she asked. 'Romania?'

'No.'

'Poland?'

'No.' She worked her way around Eastern Europe as best her knowledge served.

'I am Bulgarian,' he growled, apparently frustrated by the interruption to his viewing.

She looked at his other arm which had the letter K tattooed thickly just below the sleeve of his T shirt. She thought back to the night before and the game he'd played with the boys, after he burst into Will's flat with the shotgun. What was it? 'Mr K says...' Like 'Simon says' but it had ended up with the boys bound with plastic wrist ties and electric flex and gagged with duct tape. Then he'd bundled her downstairs. So. A Bulgarian called K. It was progress.

'So what happens next?' Laura demanded. 'We can't stay here all day.' The kidnapper sighed.

'You do not stay all day,' he said. 'Tonight you leave.'

'Leave? Where am I going?' she asked. 'And *who* are you?'

'I am contractor,' he said, his eyes not straying from the TV. 'And you are contract.'

'Why? What have I done?'

'It is not my business,' he said. 'You made enemy.' Laura was shocked.

'Who?'

'I am watching TV,' he growled.

'Who is this enemy?' she insisted. 'And what does he want? I assume it's a man.'

'It's a man.'

'Does he want money?' she asked. The Bulgarian laughed. On screen White was climbing aboard a dinghy.

'I told you. He is stealing boat.'

Laura knew she had to keep him talking. She looked across at the cello case and *NME*.

'Are you a musician?' she asked. She wanted to scream 'let me go you fucking monster', but guessed it might not help.

'I am music lover,' he said. 'You know FSB? Gentle Giant?' Laura nodded though she hadn't the faintest idea what he was talking about. 'UK best at progressive rock,' he added.

So. He liked music. It was another fact. Maybe it would prove useful, something on which to build. Mr K, Bulgarian kidnapper and music lover, fumbled in his jacket for his phone and stood up.

'I make call now. You be quiet please.' He left the room and moments later she heard him talking in the kitchen. In Russian. It was definitely Russian. The conversation grew heated. After a few minutes he returned and resumed his position in front of the television. He seemed irritable.

'They don't sound very pleased with you,' said Laura. 'Have you fucked up?' He ignored her. 'Sounds like you fucked up.' Russians. Why were Russians after her, she wondered? She didn't know any Russians. Except one. The oligarch at the casino. The one she photographed and George had splattered all over the newspapers. Anton Ledakov. Maybe that was it. Hadn't she read the publicity cost him a big deal? Or maybe he'd lost allies in government, or it had embarrassed him somehow in Russia. *And* she'd turned him down. Was this his idea of revenge? Kidnap her. And then what? Another thought occurred to her.

'You've only done half the job, haven't you?' she asked.

'What?'

'I bet he wants Ruby too. Ledakov. Is that it? But you can't get her, can you?' She wondered if she was worse off knowing who was responsible for her plight. 'Because she's down there,' she said, pointing at the television. 'On the Isle of Wight.'

'You talk too much,' murmured the big man.

'Are you going to kill me?' she asked. Mr K looked at Laura with narrow eyes.

'He has job for you,' he said.

'Job? What kind of job?'

The burly Bulgarian looked back at the screen. Robert White was struggling to raise a sail as he floated into Cowes harbour.

'Job with no breaks. Will keep you busy day and night.' He clenched his fist and held his forearm erect in the universally accepted sign for a cock. 'Service industry. Tomorrow you will be on container ship to Gulf, with horny crew.'

Laura got it. She opened her mouth to scream. But didn't. Instead she wrenched her thethered wrist away from the bed until the tie bit into her skin and the pain distracted her. Then she waited. She waited a long time. Until she could trust herself, until she was in control again, almost calm, her breathing approaching normal. She forced herself to watch White as he navigated out of Cowes. It was almost as if they were watching television together, the oddest of couples, a mafia goliath and his contract bound to the bed. When she was confident her voice would not tremble, that she could keep it light, she spoke.

'So, are we going out, then?' She knew her only chance of escape lay in somehow persuading her burly captor to unshackle her. 'Now that I'm here the least you can do is take me out,' she said. 'It's going to get very dull otherwise. And if this is my last day of freedom, maybe we could go to a pub or a club or something? Or see a band?' The big man ignored her, still watching the screen, holding his mobile in front of him, a large finger hovering over the keypad.

*

Dot made them go through it again while George handed out mugs of tea. They were in Laura's workroom and Dot was sitting at her daughter's PC sifting through her emails. Will repeated the tale. He, Laura and Luka were having dinner together in the top flat. Luka had wanted to cook to thank Will for letting him stay. They were eating a typically Croatian meal washed down with a cheap Merlot when the big man burst in with a shotgun. Luka thought he was Bulgarian. Will explained Mr K's curious game which had left them bound and helpless, and how Laura had disappeared through the door and down the stairs.

'And he didn't say what he wanted?' asked Dot. She logged out of Laura's mail.

'No,' said Will.

'Was there anything else about him, the way he behaved?' she asked.

Will and Luka thought. Meanwhile George's mind was racing over the two questions that had plagued them all night. Who would kidnap Laura? And why? It made no sense. They had considered Chamberlain but it didn't fit. He might be after them but he wouldn't send a Bulgarian in camouflage fatigues with a sawn-off shotgun. Special Branch, maybe. And anyway, he would come after George.

'Who is it, George?' Dot asked. Her voice was plaintive and she looked drawn and close to tears. He shook his head. The trouble was a lot of people had reason to hold a grudge against the Valentines, their lives and careers cratered by a well-timed photograph or dossier. But most had no idea of their involvement and few would connect Laura with their work. And none were Bulgarian.

'Let's go through it one last time,' he said. 'Laura didn't have any enemies?'

'No,' said Dot. Will shook his head. Luka shrugged.

'A stalker?'

'She would have said,' said Dot.

'And nothing strange happened in Birmingham?'

'She didn't mention anything.' said Will.

'What about a jealous ex?'

'George,' Dot snapped, striking the shrill note that never failed to sear his brain. 'He's over fifty, Bulgarian, with a sawn-off shotgun. He's a pro. It has to be us he's after.'

There was a name. It had been at the back of George's mind for a while and he had kept it there, small and nondescript, seeking all other explanations, fearful of its consequences; but as the hours had passed it had grown in size and distinction. And now it was elbowing forward in high definition. 'What is it George?' Dot asked.

'Ledakov,' he said.

'What?'

'It's Ledakov.'

'Ledakov?' Will echoed.

'The Russian,' said George. 'The one we set up with White.' It made sense. Laura took the shot at the casino. Then he lost a lot of government contracts.

'He'd go after Ruby,' said Dot.

'What if he's coming after us too?'

'How would he know about Laura? She was just the photographer.'

'She said something about her ID not working,' said George, remembering the conversation while he was under the bike. 'When she got back from the casino. Maybe she used her real name. If she did it wouldn't take him long to find us.'

'What would he want?' asked Dot.

'Revenge.'

Dot shuddered. George guessed she was thinking of the Russian and

271

the dark deeds he might be capable of, a man who had stripped his people of their assets and maybe some of their lives. It was spooky, he thought, when you'd been married to someone for thirty years how often your minds followed a parallel track. Shame this was such a dark one.

'What do we do?' she asked. 'We can't go to the police.'

'Why not?' asked Will. Dot and George regarded him with the same uncomprehending gaze. Did they have to explain? It was too dangerous for one thing. They might never see Laura again. And the police would ask questions, lots of questions. They would want to know about the family, their occupation, they might wonder about their past or their taxes; they would certainly search the house. They would probe George and Dot's affairs and might even uncover their forthcoming disappearing act. No, involving the police was out of the question.

'Someone will contact us,' George said. Dot looked unsure. 'Someone will contact us and they will want something. And we will give it to them. Whatever it is. If it's money we will pay.'

'Ledakov won't want money,' said Dot.

'Maybe not. But the person who calls might. And who knows? Russians like bribes. Maybe he'll let us pay a fine.'

Dot sank back in her chair and burst into tears.

'She's my baby,' she sobbed. George moved close and folded her in his arms.

'I know,' he said. 'Someone will call.'

'What if they don't, George?' Dot said. She seemed small and helpless in his arms, and far away, as if her vast personality had shrivelled inside her. Luka offered to make more tea.

'They will,' said George. 'But in case they don't we'll start an investigation. We'll buy information if it costs us every penny we have. We'll go back over every case, every file, anyone who could have something against us. Starting with Ledakov. We will find her. I promise.'

'You're a good man, George,' said Dot. She clung to him, tightly at first, then gradually relaxed her hold and George felt her slowly inflating in his arms.

'We're going to need a lot of cash,' he said.

'How much?' she asked.

'Half a million? Maybe more if we have to pay off Ledakov's people.'

'Alright, then,' said Dot. She wiped away her tears, her fingers still trembling.

'Alright?' asked George.

'Alright to your plan,' she said. Her voice was strengthening. 'The nonsense you were talking about yesterday. The retirement plan. We'll go ahead with it.' She was matter-of-fact, almost herself again.

'We will? I thought...'

'Things have changed,' she said. 'Do you have a handkerchief?' He did. Will and Luka looked confused. George smiled. It was understandable. They were witnessing the indomitable Valentines at work. It would be a peculiar sight to outsiders, a glimpse into their private chemistry and its power to overcome adversity. A lot of people had underestimated them over the years.

'We'll need to move quickly,' he said.

'OK,' said Dot.

'First, you get the money from the bank. From the safety deposit box. I'll start the ball rolling on the other thing. I'll see Charles today.' He turned to the boys, who were still looking puzzled 'We have a plan,' he said, beaming. 'And the less you know about it the better. Now, is there anything else you remember?'

'There was one thing,' said Will. 'It's probably nothing. I thought I heard an ice-cream van.'

George despatched Will and Luka to make enquiries in the street and was about to head down to the cellar to phone Charles when he noticed Dot standing by the doorway. She was misty eyed, staring around the room.

'Come on, love,' he said. 'We're not going to find her in here.'

'I was looking for clues,' said Dot, 'but I can only see memories.'

30

The ninth-floor boardroom of The Reputation Works was in the midst of a makeover. Its table had disappeared under a starched white cloth topped with crystal glasses and glittering silverware. Two waitresses were bustling about, placing menus and name cards. The chairmen of Britain's two largest companies were to be bookends and along one side would sit an American film star who was making her London stage debut, then Charles, Eleanor, the Mayor of London, a duchess and Sir Frank Porter. Opposite, with a view of the skyline, would sit other London luminaries and in the centre, in pride of place, a very special VIP.

Charles watched the preparations from a corner of the room. Apogee was the word that slipped into his mind. Odd word, he thought. Greek. He could have chosen crown or culmination. But it seemed the right word, the furthest point of orbit from the Earth, the most distant as well as the highest. And tonight he, Charles Franklin, was hosting an impromptu dinner to honour Eleanor Porter and discuss Britain's urban crisis, in the presence of the Prime Minister of Her Majesty's Government. To call it a coup would be an understatement. For Charles and The Reputation Works, this was the apogee. Theoretically secret, the whole agency was aware of the dinner and excitement was palpable throughout the building. The public relations business was about connections and they would dine out and sell-in on this particular nexus for months, even years to come. There was only one problem with apogee, thought Charles. Didn't it imply you could go no further? He picked up a glass and examined it.

He should have been ecstatic but his overriding emotion was fear. He was troubled by the stunt with the Home Office report. It should

274

have finished Chamberlain but now looked like a blunder that might turn the tide in favour of the politician. The mainstream media might be on hold for the time being, but the police were suspicious. The fact that the report had been stolen from Chamberlain's office was documented and could only lead to the conclusion it was planted among the cushions in the Meard Street Hotel. And that Charles was probably involved.

He was shaken. When detectives had arrived at his office the day before he assumed it was a security check for tonight's dinner, but they had grilled him for two hours. Why was he meeting Chamberlain that morning? When had he arrived? Who were his clients? Did he know anyone with a grudge against the Home Secretary? He wanted to say, 'Guys, get real, he's Ken Chamberlain. Apart from the PM and every politician he's stabbed in the back on his way up the greasy pole, there are dozens of criminals, immigrants, and nutcases who've had their appeals rejected or rights discarded who just might want to stick it to him, and that's before you start on the idea of a terrorist plot.' Instead he played innocent and curious. They had seemed satisfied when they left but had returned this morning to repeat their questions.

Now he was getting calls from journalists. They had realised their crusade against the Home Secretary might turn into something bigger, a criminal conspiracy reaching into the heart of government. So far the D notice was holding, restricting reporting, but people were beginning to smell a rat and it was only a matter of time before he and that runt of a journalist Leo would be fingered. On the plus side the Prime Minister had not cancelled. That was probably down to Eleanor. Her star was in the ascendant and as long as he was hitched to it he was safe. He looked uneasily at Sir Frank Porter's place card, realising he would be unhitched at the first sign of trouble and from apogee he would fall from orbit and burn up on re-entry.

Charles watched the waitresses at work. Something was definitely wrong. In other circumstances he would have made a pass at the flightiest of the girls and ended up in a broom cupboard for a pre-prandial appetiser. His phone rang. It was his wife. He remembered she was leaving hospital on Friday and he still hadn't called.

'Mel, I am *so* sorry,' he said, oozing contrition. 'It's been one hell of a day.' He let her bleat for a while. 'I can't pick you up, darling. I have to be in Birmingham. Eleanor's getting the freedom of the city and we're launching an Inner Cities Trust sponsored by Frank's bank.' More bleating. He put on his I'm-so-sorry-but-I'll-make-it-up-to-you tone.

'It's a big deal, sweetie,' he said. 'Look, I'll send you a car. I'll be back in the evening.' He looked at his watch. 'Darling, I'm expecting the Prime Minister any moment, can I call you back?' He heard a snuffle at the other end, followed by silence and a click as she hung up.

He looked out at the skyline. It was all beginning to unravel. What was that quote? 'Things fall apart; the centre cannot hold.' Who was that? Some African writer? It was in a book he'd skim-read, or maybe he'd found it in a dictionary of quotations. Either way it seemed apposite. His PA popped her head around the door.

'Charles. There's a Mr Valentine in reception,' she said.

And now George. What was this about? He'd called earlier and said he wanted a meeting, which was unusual as he never visited the offices. Hopefully he'd dug up something on Chamberlain, the more lurid the better. Charles turned from the window and told her to show the man into his office seven floors below, well away from this glittering scene. He didn't want the evening contaminated by anything other than the orchids now arriving and the case of Clos d'Amonceler sitting on ice in the kitchen.

*

Charles found George in his office overlooking the square, sitting at a glass-topped table set with refreshments. He was studying the ebb and flow of life outside, as the workday melted into a balmy evening. On the floor, by his feet, was his brown briefcase.

'Charles,' he said, rising to his feet as the PR man entered. Charles shut the door carefully, motioned George to sit and took the chair opposite.

'George, we've got to do something,' he said, his nerves bubbling over. 'The police were here again, and the media have shifted; they know someone is after Chamberlain. They're putting together a conspiracy story. If that blogger twerp cracks I'm fucked.'

'Relax Charles,' said George, 'it won't happen.'

'And George, if I'm fucked, everyone's fucked.' George selected a cup and saucer and reached for the jug of tea. A tag dangled from its handle identifying it as Earl Grey.

'Well, we wouldn't want that, would we?' he said. 'Do you have builder's tea?' Charles ignored the request. Unable to settle he made for the drinks cabinet behind his desk and poured himself a stiff one, offering the bottle to George as an afterthought. George declined.

'At least that Ruby woman has been caught,' Charles said. 'On *Escape from Wight*. She was arrested for getting on a ferry without paying. I'd sooner have her locked up while White is free. Even if he is stuck on a boat.'

Charles watched transfixed as George poured his tea with a calm and precise hand, the liquid streaming slowly and steadily into the cup.

'You've found something, haven't you?' he asked.

'Everything you could possibly need,' said George. 'It's sen–sa-tional.'

'I knew it,' said Charles, mastering his universe again. 'Thank Heaven. I knew I could count on you, George. What have you got?' George dropped two lumps of sugar into his tea.

'That's only part of the reason I'm here, Charles,' he said. 'There are a couple of other things first.' Charles hovered by his desk. 'This might sound odd, but did anything strange happen in Birmingham?'

'What do you mean? It was all strange,' said Charles.

'With Laura, I mean.'

'Laura?'

'Did you notice anything? Did she make any enemies? Or friends? She's disappeared.'

'Disappeared?'

'Abducted,' said George.

'George. I'm sorry. But I haven't the faintest idea what you're talking about. She spent a lot of time with Eleanor and some demonstrators who think she's Wonder Woman's sidekick and the rest of the time she was surrounded by police.'

'You can't think of anything?'

'Nothing,' said Charles. 'Last time I saw her she was fine. Exuberant. Maybe she's eloped with one of your musical waiters.'

'This is for real, Charles,' said George. Charles felt uncomfortable. More things falling apart. And now he was trapped in some kind of relentless staring match. It was as if George had decided he was one of the X-Men and was applying his telepathic powers to determine whether Charles was hiding something.

'I don't know anything,' Charles insisted.

'I think it may be Ledakov,' George said. Charles choked on his drink.

'Ledakov. Jesus, George. We don't want him poking about. We've got enough trouble as it is.' He looked at his watch. 'Look, I'm sorry about Laura. I really am. But I'm sure she'll turn up. There'll be a perfectly reasonable explanation. Now, can we talk about Chamberlain?'

'There's one other thing,' said George. 'Dot and I have decided to retire.' Charles wondered if George was having some kind of breakdown.

'I'm very happy for you, George,' he said. 'But can we sort Chamberlain out first? Otherwise we're all going to retire. To Wandsworth. And I don't mean the fucking Common.'

'I'm sure we can, Charles,' said George, 'but it's linked.'

'Linked?'

'You see, we're selling our businesses and we've got buyers for most of them. In fact we're almost ready to go.'

Good for you, thought Charles. Right now he wished *he* had an exit strategy. He looked at the figure across the table. There was something different about him today. Something deliberate. It dawned on him George was playing a game, laying down a card at a time, each a trump, but Charles couldn't see the game yet or his own hand. Just what was the bastard up to?

'It's just the investigations business left,' said George. 'It's proving difficult to find a buyer. I'm not surprised. The technology has moved on. No one wants to go through dustbins anymore,' he said. 'These days you outsource that to the same blokes who do your car wash. No, the big thing is electronic intelligence: hacking, phreaking, that sort of thing. I dabble but I'm not a native. The new kids on the block think I came out of the ark.'

'Is this going somewhere?' Charles asked.

'You see I have to get what I can for it. And the only assets we have are our records.' Charles recognised a high trump, but still didn't see the game.

'Records?' he said.

'The records of all the work we've done, for you and others. Our files.' George paused. 'So, we've decided to have a Clearance Sale.'

'A what?'

'We're 'Closing Down. Everything Must Go.''

'Go? Go where?" Charles asked. 'What the fuck are you talking about, George?'

'Our retirement plan,' said George. 'We're offering our clients first refusal to buy their files. The White case, all the others, everything we've done over the years.' Charles looked at the man in front of him, sensing tables turned. He'd always seen George as a supplier, a low life provider of commodity services. Now he was lounging in his office as if he belonged there, looking around at Charles' paintings and furniture, enjoying the smell of expensive leather, probably imagining himself as a wheeler-dealer, making it in Charles' world, a world where the dirt didn't stink.

'You can't do this, George,' Charles said. 'They're already mine. I paid for them.' George reached for the briefcase and placed it on his lap. Apparently he had anticipated the objection.

'They're not, actually,' he said. 'If you look at our contract...'

'What contract?'

'Our original contract.' George extracted a document from the briefcase, which he placed on the table and pushed towards Charles. 'Dot and I retain all the intellectual property of Valentine Competitive Insight.'

'Intellectual property?' Charles blanched. 'You dig up shit on people, there's nothing intellectual in that. This is blackmail.' George looked up at him calmly.

'It's just an offer,' he said. 'You don't have to take it up.'

'And what if I don't?' asked Charles.

'We'll archive them. But of course, we can't guarantee their safety. And there would be a small fee to cover the cost of storage. Personally, I think you should buy them.'

'What are you playing at, George?' Charles saw betrayal. The centre cannot hold.

'We're sixty this year,' said George, a coy smile on his face. 'And what with everything else, it's time to pack it in. I promised Dot.' Charles was open-mouthed.

'I don't care how old you are,' said the PR man. 'Or what you promised your wife. You can't do this. I will crucify you, George.'

'There's no need to get upset.'

'What's the collective noun for lawyers? An army? An addendum? I'll have an inn-full of the bastards after you. You'll be summonsed and *sub judice* before you can say subpoena.'

'You'll find another supplier. I can make recommendations. There's a fantastic hacker in Sweden, though I've heard she's picky with her jobs.'

'I could have your legs broken.'

'You don't know anyone who does that, Charles.'

'And you do, I suppose?'

'I do, as a matter of fact,' said George. Charles looked out onto the square, realising lawyers could not help him and the man in front of him was as close to the underworld as he got.

'How much?' he asked.

'For storage?'

'For the files. All of them.'

'A quarter of a million,' said George. 'In cash. On Friday.'

'I don't have that kind of money.'

'I hope we can part as friends, Charles,' George smiled. 'We have a lot of water under the bridge, you and me.'

Charles' head filled with images of rats and sinking ships, of George and Dot retired to a caravan on the Norfolk Broads, of himself in handcuffs. He put a hand on his desk to steady himself, to remind him he was in his office, at the heart of his company, the brightest star in the sky.

'I assume it includes what you've got on Chamberlain?' he asked.

'No.'

'No?'

'That's the other part of the retirement plan,' said George. He had produced another card, this time from his sleeve. 'We're going to auction that one.'

'Auction it?' Charles shouted. 'For fuck's sake, I hired you to do that job!'

'You pay by the day, Charles, not for the result,' said George, pointing at the contract. 'And we're resigning that job as of now.'

'And when did you find out whatever it is you found?' Charles asked.

'Dot did that on her own time and it comes from an independent source. The auction is Friday night.' George dipped into the briefcase again and pulled out a leaflet, which he placed on top of the contract. 'Here,' he said. Charles stooped to look at it, nonplussed. It was some kind of music venue. Blake's Ride. The Rialto, King's Cross. The man was clearly stark raving mad.

'I'm supposed to be in Birmingham,' Charles said.

'That's up to you,' said George. 'You'll need a ticket. When you get inside someone will find you and tell you what to do next. Ask for the auction. Be there at 9.30 p.m. We'll exchange the past files first, then move on to the auction. The reserve is another quarter of a million.'

'How do I know there's enough to bring him down?'

George dipped into the briefcase for a third time and returned with a single sheet of paper.

'That's a summary,' he said. 'The file covers almost twenty years of work.' Charles scanned the paper quickly. You could never fault George on quality. It was priceless, a comprehensive catalogue of corruption. Chamberlain would not survive and the Home Office report would become a side issue. But it was expensive. He would need to talk to Porter. Always on cue Charles' PA appeared at the door.

'Just to let you know Sir Frank and Lady Eleanor have arrived and our VIP will be here in fifteen minutes,' she said and disappeared, closing the door.

George snapped his case shut and stood up, the meeting at an end. Charles was looking out over the square. Neither offered a hand.

'I'd best be off,' said George. 'It sounds like you're busy and I have to find Laura.' When he reached the door he turned back. 'One more thing,' he said. 'There'll be two other bidders.'

31

Kracholov and Laura turned heads as they arrived at the Dominion Theatre for the evening performance of *We Will Rock You*. They emerged from a cab holding hands, Kracholov first, dressed in the white thobe of a Gulf Arab, his head covered with a red-chequered ghutra held in place by a black wound iqal. The Franchi lay hidden beneath the crisp folds of the dishdash, lodged in his trouser belt. Laura followed, wearing a black abaya and hijab in the latest Dubai fashion. Kracholov had wanted her to wear a burqa but that had met fierce resistance. It was probably enough, he conceded. They might create a minor spectacle but it was unlikely anyone would notice the plastic tie binding their wrists, and if they did they would put it down to some cultural practice designed to keep women in bondage. A problem would only occur if they encountered a real Arab, which he judged he would see coming.

Kracholov was still in two minds whether this was a good idea. It was a risk he wouldn't usually take, but Laura had spent the entire morning badgering him. First she tried to persuade him to call her mother, assuring him her parents would make it worth his while to return her unscathed. This was, of course, impossible. A breach of contract on that scale would result in a loss of face for the Best Bulgarian Cleaning Company and a prolonged and grisly end for Kracholov. She switched tack after an hour, and spent the rest of the morning complaining of boredom and suggesting places he should visit while he was in London. Kracholov was not wholly averse to the idea. He wanted to see more of the city and particularly its music scene. If all went well this would be his last night in the capital and, whether he headed south to the Isle of Wight or back to Sofia for a while, he had no idea when he would return, so he was keen to make the most of it. One thing was sure, staying in the flat and being subjected to this woman's constant nagging was not an option. He might batter her to death, which was not his brief.

This left him with a conundrum. Whether to leave Laura in the flat unsupervised while he went out, or find a place where he could take her without drawing attention to her predicament or affording her an opportunity to escape. The idea of Freddie struck him in the middle of the afternoon and he called the Best Bulgarian Cleaning Company to make arrangements, including the provision of a disguise.

He paid the cab driver with some difficulty and led Laura into the great art deco foyer, past security only interested in tickets and ostentatious bags. People were filling the vast cavern with its twin staircases, brass balustrades and pillared balcony, all cast sepia in the cream light from six gilt chandeliers.

Kracholov bought a souvenir programme from a concession in the centre of the foyer and again fumbled in his robe for money. Laura reached out with her free hand to take the item from a fresh-faced young man behind the counter. Leaning into his ear she whispered, 'Please help me. Call the police. I've been kidnapped.'

Kracholov thumped a handful of notes on the desk.

'Ignore woman,' he said. 'She is first wife. She is jealous of new wife.' The concessionaire blinked nervously. 'She has made bed. Now she must lie in it,' said the Arab. 'Though not so often,' he added with a wink. 'Come,' Kracholov growled, giving his 'wife' a tug. He led her past more concessions into the auditorium.

Inside, the atmosphere was more stadium gig than West End show with loud music and an excited buzz. They passed a huge mixing desk and walked down the centre aisle, following a girl selling bottles of beer from an ice-cream tray. Their seats were halfway from the stage under the Dress Circle. Kracholov shuffled into the row and sat on the inside, leaving Laura on the aisle, which he reasoned was safer than letting her sit next to anyone. He settled into his seat, repositioning the Franchi, which momentarily suggested a huge and steely erection to the consternation of the lady next to him. Unabashed he peered around the dark red space.

The audience comprised all ages and nationalities. Tourists and students jostled with couples and coach parties from every corner of Britain. A few rows in front a group of girls giggled and took photographs of each other and behind them a French party arrived and agitated its way into the centre of a row as the lights began to fade.

Kracholov's attention was drawn to the stained and faded front curtain, which he took at first for poor quality then realised it was a symbol of degradation and the long passage of time. His mind slipped back a quarter of a century to July 1986 when he had driven 770 kilometres from Sofia to Budapest via Belgrade, sleeping in his car, to the Nepstadion, where he and 56,000 Eastern Europeans watched Freddie Mercury and Queen for the first and only time. The Magic Tour. It was an epiphany for Kracholov on several levels. First and most obvious was Freddie as a manifestation of rock deity. Second, he realised his marriage was over – he had left his wife behind after a bitter row over the one ticket he had been able to acquire and it proved the final twist in their short and tempestuous relationship, but one of the best concerts of his life. Love came and went, he concluded, but music was eternal. Last, but in some ways most profound, he realised he could enjoy music without a prolonged instrumental.

In the darkness he heard a desolate whisper of wind and the controlled whine of a guitar, a drum roll, and the sinister march he recognised as 'Innuendo', then the merging of a choir and distorted guitar that could only be Queen. Moments later he was listening to 'Radio Gaga' and witnessing an Orwellian world where people were marching automatons controlled by a corporation, Globalsoft, their every thought and desire prescribed, where deviants were rooted out by a brutal militia and music had died. Kracholov's stomach tightened. This was a world of consumers rather than communists, but it was his youth set to music, his world before the wall came down, before the mafia. He gave himself to the show, even harbouring a faint hope of redemption as the young hero Galileo arrived on stage to begin his two and a half hour journey to freedom, via Queen's back catalogue.

*

Laura paid little attention to the show but was grateful her captor was absorbed. She spent the next twenty minutes considering ways to escape. She flirted with the idea of standing up and screaming hysterically until they were bundled from the auditorium, but realised there was no guarantee the security people would listen to her story or call the police, and anyway Mr K had his shotgun and would make a bloody mess along the way. Then she wondered if she could attract the attention of someone in the row across the aisle and spent several minutes making grotesque facial expressions, but only succeeded in making a small boy cry and switch places with his mother.

Next she noticed a jacket belonging to the man in front of her, folded over his armrest. The inside pocket was exposed as was the top of a ballpoint pen. Checking the burly Bulgarian was still entranced, now by a lust–hate relationship with the Chief Executive Officer of Globalsoft, the Killer Queen, Laura leaned forward in an improvised coughing fit and extracted the pen, hiding it in the sleeve of her abaya. She leafed through the glossy souvenir programme, trying to find a page with clear white space on which she could write a message. Finding none and growing angry, she tossed the brochure on the floor, which temporarily attracted the big man's attention, so she dutifully bent to pick it up, the back of her hand brushing past a used and dusty ice-cream cup from a previous show. Ordinarily she would have been disgusted, but Laura gripped the cardboard with excitement, hiding it under the programme as she retrieved both from the floor. She waited a long time, until her kidnapper was settled again, this time with tears welling in his eyes.

The Bohemians, keepers of the flame of rock but terrorists in the new world, who lived hidden in the remains of Tottenham Court Road underground station, were lamenting the lost heroes of rock, when Meat, a bawdy free spirit in stockings and punk make-up had stepped forward to sing the one song Freddie had never sung, recorded by his band-mates on his death. 'No One But You (Only The Good Die Young)'. She sang with professional poignancy and a wave of quiet nostalgia swept through the crowd and in some cases grief was revisited. Laura checked on the Bulgarian who appeared to be infatuated and lost.

Under cover of the glossy programme, and careful to keep her tethered wrist still, Laura unwrapped the cup, smoothing the surface with her thumb, unconcerned by dust and dirt, intent only on creating a surface ready for a brief ballpoint message. As she worked the cardboard she composed a line in her head: 'Girl with Arab kidnapped. Help. Laura Valentine.' She would add Dot's telephone number and try to hand it to someone in the interval or leave it in a prominent place. Checking Mr K was still spellbound she clicked the biro and began to write. She felt a scrape rather than a smooth roll and knew instantly the ink was not flowing. She scratched a corner of the flattened cup with growing intensity and random patterns, but still the ink would not come. She clicked the biro several times to see if made a difference. It didn't. It was a cheap throwaway that should have been thrown away long ago. Desperate, she wondered if she could scratch a message deeply enough to be read before she gave up, cardboard and pen still resting in her lap under the programme.

The first half of the show ended in an anti-climax, with a Bohemian slain and the hero and heroine on the run to a soundtrack that finished in the high-pitched vocal wail that defined 1970s rock. The Bulgarian sat motionless after the last drawn-out chord, apparently stunned by what he had seen.

'I'd like an ice cream, please,' said Laura, seeing a woman with a tray making her way to the front of the stage. The big man ignored her. She repeated the request. 'Come on, Mr Ripple, you're the ice-cream man.' People in the row in front turned to look.

She had created a dilemma for her captor. He would need to quieten her, but would he point the Franchi, which might be interpreted as indecent exposure? Or drag her into the queue to be gawked at by all in the auditorium, only one of whom needed to become suspicious to cause mayhem? Laura felt the big man grasp her hand and followed him down the aisle to the queue. She dropped the pen on the floor but brought the programme and card with her in case another opportunity to create a message presented itself. While they stood in line the Bulgarian made frequent sweeps of the auditorium, checking they were not attracting attention, each time finishing on Laura to make sure she was not trying to engage anyone in conversation. Her heart quickened, she knew she had little time. She looked at the theatre-goers around her, in the queue and nearby seats, scanning coats for pens, for the first time in her life dreaming of a nerdy clerk with a ballpoint in his shirt pocket, until she spotted a woman sitting at the end of the row in front of her, talking on a mobile phone. As they moved slowly up the queue she wondered how she could give the woman a message or borrow the phone without her captor knowing. Mr K made another sweep coming to rest on her face.

'Rum and raisin,' she said. That might buy a moment. There was no way they'd have rum and raisin. As they inched forward the woman placed her phone on her armrest while she delved into her handbag. In the next moment it was in Laura's free hand hidden at her side. When the big man made his next sweep he didn't seem to notice the woman searching the floor around her feet.

Laura waited until he was the next in line and becoming impatient, his sweeps less frequent as he looked over the customer in front at the selection in the tray. She raised the phone, punched in her mother's number and dropped her hand to her side. She waited the amount of time she felt it would take for Dot to answer. The Bulgarian made another sweep. The customer in front of them was paying. She had to move quickly. He would be distracted for a few seconds at most and then they would be on their way back to their seats. At that moment the customer turned and gave the big man a hefty slap across the face. He stepped back in surprise to reveal a tent in his dishdash. Apparently the Franchi had slipped once again and prodded the woman between the buttocks. As the Bulgarian protested his innocence Laura turned away from him and lifted the mobile to her face. She heard the cue to leave a message. She gave the name of the theatre, the fact that Russians had abducted her, that her assailant was armed and looked like an Arab and that she would be sold into sex slavery later that night. Mr K was still occupied so she also told Dot she loved her then dropped the phone to the ground, near its owner, the line still open.

The aggrieved lady stomped away from the queue and the big man made his selection, groping inside his robe for money.

'Tottenham Court Road,' Laura shouted at the floor, hoping the phone was still live. She turned to a man behind them in the queue and asked what time the show finished.

'FINISHES AT 10.20,' she repeated at the floor before feeling the tug that signalled her captor's transaction was complete.

The second act passed slowly. The burly Bulgarian was again sucked into the drama while Laura waited nervously for it to end, feigning sleep, praying Dot would check her voicemail and imagining her mother and George fretting over what to do. She would have to be alert and ready to move quickly if the moment came. She was vaguely aware of the pantomime on stage as it twisted through Queen's songbook until hero, heroine, music and the world were once again free. The big man dragged Laura to her feet for the last few numbers, clapping over his head to 'We Will Rock You'. This posed something of a challenge for Laura who made rhythmic Y shapes as Mr K clapped. The waving of imaginary football scarves to 'We Are The Champions' was more of a success and the free for all of 'Bohemian Rhapsody' allowed for any variant of expression. And then it was over, with a shimmering gong and a standing ovation. The big man, looking drained and elated, made the sign of the horns with both fists.

Five minutes later Laura and her captor were standing outside, Laura clutching her programme, as the audience dispersed. She examined the crowd for any sign of rescue. Her kidnapper brushed fellow theatre-goers aside to take the first available cab, despite Laura's resistance, and they sped off into the night. Laura looked back. Three cars behind them a familiar white van dropped into sight.

32

'We could have taken him,' Johnson muttered. He was sitting on a box in the back of the van opposite Luka, brandishing a garden hoe. 'When he switched to the ice-cream van.'

'He has a gun,' said Will, looking doubtfully at the crowbar in his hands.

'There are five of us,' said the drummer. 'We could've blocked him off in that alley and rushed him. Some of us would've made it.'

'We could have made him an offer,' said Dot. She was sitting up front between George and Will, clutching her handbag and the black holdall containing half a million pounds. George sighed. Much as Johnson irritated her he knew Dot and the drummer were of a mind at that moment.

'Sssh!' he hissed.

Witnesses have different perspectives, he reflected as he peered over the wheel into the dark. In George's mind it had all happened too quickly to do anything. They had followed the taxi through the city into Old Street where the kidnapper and Laura had climbed out on a street corner. Dot had screamed when she saw her daughter and urged George to step on it. Unfortunately they were five cars behind and by the time they reached the cab the pair had vanished into a side street.

George had pulled up to consider the options. He could turn into the alley and risk being spotted – would the assailant know their van? He'd obviously had them under surveillance. They could get out on foot, but they'd be instantly noticeable, armed with makeshift weapons borrowed from his neighbour's shed – George with a cordless nail gun in addition to Will's crowbar and Johnson's rusting garden hoe. Luka alone might pass scrutiny, his choice of armament being the top half of a microphone stand from Will's flat, which at a pinch could be taken for a walking stick. The last option was to go unarmed with the element of surprise. Flesh against gun. Whichever, he needed to decide before the kidnapper dragged Laura into one of the buildings in the side street and they disappeared forever.

He was still calculating the odds when an image of Mr Ripple flashed in front of him, swerved left and roared off along the street ahead. George slipped the handbrake and with a crunch of gears the van lurched forward.

They had followed Mr Ripple south then east into the Docklands passing Canary Wharf with its jigsaw of blazing lights, then on to the Royal Docks past City Airport and the old leviathan Tate & Lyle, which lay slumbering by the river, puffing offset carbon into the night sky. At last the ice-cream van had turned into a lane beyond the airport runway and driven past a basin, now Gallions Point Marina, to a lock that marked the end of the docks.

Mr Ripple had ascended a concrete ramp and stopped at the top, its engine still running. George had switched off his lights and coasted the white transit into the parking area below, stopping in the shadows. Now, looking up through the windscreen, he had a clear view of the ice-cream van, its brake lights flaring and exhaust burping fumes. It was waiting but not settled, a predator waiting to pounce. His fellow passengers craned forward to peer through the windscreen, like a curious but cautious Victorian family posing for their first photograph.

'What's he waiting for?' Will asked.

'I don't know,' said George.

'Who are they selling her to?' asked Johnson.

'Could be anyone,' said Luka. 'After drugs, human trafficking is most profitable illegal industry in world. And fastest-growing.'

'Really? What do you think she'll fetch?' asked the drummer.

'Do you mind?' said Will.

'Sorry. It makes you wonder though.' Johnson looked disparagingly at Luka's mic stand. 'What are you going to do with that?' he asked. 'Sing him to death? At least I can give him tetanus.'

'I bet she's in the back,' said Will, turning to George. 'I could creep up there and let her out.'

'What do you think, George?' asked Dot. George could see she was impatient for something to happen. He weighed it up, this time with a bias for action.

'OK. Let's do it,' he said. 'But quietly.'

Dot stowed the holdall under the front seat and George locked the van. Moments later they were tiptoeing up the ramp, weapons ready. As they reached the top, George waved Will to the front. The rest took positions either side of him and prepared for battle. George levelled his nail gun, which he knew sprayed 90mm nails at three per second, and wondered how far they would reach compared to 12 gauge shot. Johnson held his hoe like a medieval pike-man and Luka raised his mic stand *en garde*. Even Dot looked ready to swing her handbag with devastating consequences.

As the crowbar slipped into the groove in the rear door the ice-cream van started down the other side of the ramp, dragging Will after it. George and his team were left standing on the crest with an unrestricted view of the river, wide and dark before them, stretching east towards the sea. They were on the river wall by a lock, on the side that curved west towards the city. In front of them Mr Ripple was trundling along a concrete path between the lock and a railing fence, past blue-and-white mooring bollards. George froze. If the kidnapper chose that moment to look in his rear view mirror he would see the silhouette of a strange set of superheroes, a B&Q Four, their DIY powers profiled against the sky. He would also notice the fifth of their number with his face pressed against the rear window as he struggled to dislodge the crowbar. The concrete path gave way to a wooden quay and the ice-cream van continued on its course, juddering as it crossed uneven planks. George decided the driver was still oblivious to their presence but that Laura, bound and bouncing around on the floor, might be aware of them and filled with hope.

The B&Q Four followed the van as it rattled along the quay until it reached the end and came to a stop. George signalled his troop to congregate in the shadows by the fence under cover of a convenient shrub. The group squatted. Will had now freed himself and loped across the planking to join them. George took stock of the situation.

The van was parked at the river's edge. To its left was the lock entrance, to its right the river wall stretching towards the city. There was no way a vehicle could go further. Beside the ice-cream van a narrow lattice footbridge, like a cattle grid, crossed from the quay to a concrete path which ran along the river wall and where railings offered the only protection against stepping into the river. Mr Ripple was still and silent. This must be the end of the journey.

The driver's door opened and the burly kidnapper stepped out, his Arab disguise discarded in favour of a suit. The Franchi was in his left hand. He had a torch in the other, which he flashed across the footbridge and out to the river beyond. The B&Q heroes lay flat on the wooden quay, praying the moon would stay hidden and the torch wouldn't flicker in their direction. George weighed up the enemy. He was Bulgarian, whatever that entailed, built like an all-in wrestler armed to the teeth and he dispensed violence for a living. It didn't look good.

The man opened the back of the van and climbed in to release Laura. Dot stifled a groan as her daughter emerged, still in the black abaya and re-attached to her captor. The pair stood waiting in front of the footbridge. The kidnapper flashed his torch towards the river again.

'They're waiting for a boat. Coming from the city,' Will whispered. George signalled his troop to huddle close. He had a plan. As the Bulgarian swung his torch in its pre-arranged arc, Dot, George and Luka trotted across the quay to come round behind him, the other side of the ice-cream van, while Will and Johnson took the more dangerous course and crept along the fence towards the footbridge. George's group gathered by the van and peered over the bonnet at the kidnapper. He had finished signalling but was still looking out to the river. A light flashed back from a small launch, which was heading slowly towards them. A man was standing on the foredeck with a rope coiled in his hands but the light was coming from the cabin.

At least two aboard, thought George, possibly more. The captain cut the motor and the boat drifted towards a steel ladder set in the river wall. Above its top rung a chain connected a gap in the railings. This was the handover point.

Will was the first to step from the shadows onto the footbridge. With a menacing swing of the crowbar he turned to face the Bulgarian. George had instructed him to 'hold the bridge for one minute' and he looked intent on doing just that. Johnson joined him, barring the garden hoe across his chest.

'Will,' shouted Laura as soon as she recognised him.

'And Johnson,' said Johnson. George was relieved to see his daughter looking elated, though her expression hardened when they heard the safety catch slip on the Franchi. Her captor shook his head.

'Very good, boys. You are heroes. Girl is impressed. Now Mr K says get off bridge and go home to Mummy.'

'We can't do that,' said Will.

'No fucking way, Mr KKK,' added Johnson. The Bulgarian sighed. He placed the torch in his pocket, shifted the Franchi into his right hand and gripped Laura's wrist as he advanced onto the bridge. He lifted the Franchi and brought it down on Johnson's shoulder. The drummer collapsed while the shotgun continued its arc, the sawn-off barrel coming to rest at Will's groin.

'Go home. Or I blow your testicles.'

'Wanker,' groaned Johnson. His assailant peered down at the drummer and kicked him in the crotch, as if demonstrating he knew where to find his genitalia. Meanwhile Will's lips were moving. George wondered if he was praying then realised he was counting. They were to hold the bridge for another twenty seconds.

'Do as he says, Will,' shouted Laura. George looked past the Bulgarian to see the boat was now moored and three men were climbing the steel ladder. It was now or never. He nudged Luka and they crept past the van towards the kidnapper.

'Say goodbye to testicles,' said Mr K. He was about to pull the trigger when George slipped the nail gun between the big man's legs.

'You blow his testicles and I'll nail yours,' he said. A moment later Luka brought the mic stand down on the Bulgarian's arm and the Franchi dropped to the ground. The singer took a second swipe across the big man's shoulders and a third across his chest. The kidnapper sank to his knees. The mic stand was now useless for its original purpose. Johnson climbed unsteadily to his feet and joined Luka. After he had recovered his composure he set about his assailant, kicking him in the groin while cupping his own in his hands. Still the burly kidnapper would not topple. George stooped to pick up the Franchi.

'Let's chuck the fucker in the river,' Johnson shouted as he delivered another boot to the man's genitals. The Bulgarian appeared insensible now, his chin resting on his chest and eyes closed as if asleep, but still he didn't fall. Dot was hugging Laura. Both were crying. George nailed the big man's trousers to the quayside from knee to ankle.

The three men from the boat were now approaching the top of the ladder.

'Let's get out of here,' George shouted. He freed Laura by shooting a nail through the wrist tie and tugging at the split plastic, and then all six fugitives started towards the ramp, only to find their path blocked by another man with a gun sitting on a mooring bollard, smoking a cigarette.

'Nice try,' said the man

Two guns in a day and another foreign accent, thought George; where did they all spring from?

'Albanian,' Luka whispered, as if reading George's mind. That figured. The man was in his twenties, swarthy and attractive in the oily Mediterranean way that Dot so admired, and dripping gold. He was wearing a black leather jacket despite the balmy evening.

'Drop your weapons, please,' he ordered. There was something about him that left no one in doubt he would open fire on any laggard. One by one they laid their implements on the ground. George placed the nail gun and the Franchi in front of his feet.

'Quite a collection,' observed the young man. 'Are you gangsters or gardeners?'

By now the men from the boat had arrived, also armed. They exchanged words with the man on the bollard. Though the youngest, he seemed to be their leader.

'My brothers would like to know what you are doing?' he asked. Dot stepped forward.

'We are taking my daughter back,' she said. She pointed at the Bulgarian, who was struggling to free his trousers from the quayside. 'That man kidnapped her.' The young man translated for his siblings who laughed.

'My brothers and I have deal with him. For this woman.' He pointed at Laura. Dot bared her teeth.

'Well, the deal is off, young man,' she said.

'It's not as easy as that, Mother,' said the Albanian. He seemed relaxed, holding his pistol lightly as if it was merely a tool to emphasise a point. 'This is prearranged deal. She is purchased by very rich man. For lot of money.' He waved the gun and his brothers separated Laura from the group.

'How much to buy her back?' asked Dot. The Albanian smiled.

'This is not option, Mother,' he said. The Bulgarian joined them, breathless, his trousers in tatters.

'I am Kracholov,' he said. He pointed at Laura. 'You have woman. I want my money and I want him and him.' He indicated Johnson and Luka then looked at George. 'And him.' George imagined the Bulgarian was bent on retribution and after the sale of his daughter would take the three men to a dark and desolate place where he would inflict slow and cruel punishment before killing them. He thought of the scene in Marathon Man where Laurence Olivier tortured Dustin Hoffman in a dentist's chair. And Dot. What would happen to Dot? She'd be all alone, with God only knows what fate in store. Kracholov picked up the Franchi and checked it for damage.

'I will double your price,' said Dot. George marvelled at her composure.

'I am not for sale,' said Kracholov.

'Not *your* price,' said Dot. She looked at the Albanians' leader. '*Your* price. What are you selling her for?'

She had his attention. The young man explained the new offer to his brothers.

'And these three idiots,' said Dot, indicating George, Luka and Johnson. 'They come with me.'

There was an argument among the brothers.

'That's three hundred thousand dollars, Mother,' said the young man. He seemed amused by the negotiation. He nodded towards his siblings. 'But not all my brothers agree.'

'Three hundred and fifty then,' said Dot. 'That's my final offer. Paid in cash sterling and I will give you a fair rate.'

'And where is money, Mother? In your handbag?' The young Albanian laughed. He obviously found the prospect of Dot wandering around with a small fortune highly unlikely.

'It's nearby,' she said. 'We came prepared. It's hidden.' This time all the Albanians laughed, until Dot opened her handbag, pulled out a bundle of fifty pound notes still in their bank wrapper, and chucked it onto the ground beside the nail gun. Clever girl, thought George. She *was* prepared.

Kracholov raised the Franchi and pointed it at Dot.

'Don't listen to her,' he growled. 'We have deal. And remember *who* you are dealing with.' There was further chatter among the Albanians after which they pointed their guns at Kracholov.

'We're not afraid of Russians,' said the young man. 'We have new deal now.' He waved at one of his brothers. 'Give him his money.' The brother pulled an envelope from his jacket and threw it at the Bulgarian's feet. Kracholov bent to pick it up.

'What about agreement?' he asked.

'That's your problem,' said the Albanian.

'It will be your problem too.' said Kracholov. George imagined any default on their deal would be a big step backwards in Russian-Bulgarian-Albanian criminal relations. Maybe even fatal for Kracholov. Anton Ledakov probably had connections that reached from the dark underbelly of Moscow into every capital city. A contractor who failed to deliver would no doubt pay a heavy price, considerably more than the money in Kracholov's envelope, most likely including an unpleasant end in an evil smelling alley, preceded by a session with Laurence Olivier's dentistry drill.

The young Albanian smiled. He was a Young Turk challenging the old guard, thought George, though he wondered if ambitious young Albanians should be referred to as Turks.

'You did your part,' said the young man, smiling at the Bulgarian. He exhaled into the night. 'You brought her to us. And you have your money. It's up to us what we do with the merchandise.' It was a contractual and philosophical point on which he looked set to remain firm. 'We'll find someone else for His Royal Highness. He is short-sighted anyway. The sheik can wait.'

'At least let me kill that one,' said Kracholov, pointing at Johnson.

'No,' said Dot. 'It's all or nothing.'

The young man turned to her.

'You drive hard bargain, Mother.' He stubbed out his cigarette. 'So, where is money?'

'Wait here,' Dot said. She looked at George who tossed her the keys to the van. The Albanian motioned for one of his siblings to accompany her.

'I go alone,' said Dot. 'Or not at all.' The young man laughed. He looked at the group in front of him.

'Go on then, Mother. We have collateral.'

While Dot returned to the van, the men waited, the Albanians with their guns trained on Kracholov, Kracholov's gun veering between Johnson, Will, Luka and George. George presumed Dot would count out wads of fifty pound notes to the agreed amount and then find somewhere to hide the remainder. An argument broke out among the brothers which did not diminish as Dot returned with the holdall. As she approached the young man smiled.

'They want to kill the men,' he said, nodding towards his brothers. 'Then take the girl and put you to work on cannabis farm or giving oral sex to retired bodyguards. That way we make more money and leave no evidence.'

'Then you would have no honour,' said Dot. She handed him the holdall. 'This is what we agreed.' The young man counted the money.

'You are something, Mother,' he said. 'You remind me of my mother.'

'And you, young man, you could be something,' said Dot. 'You're good-looking, a natural leader and I am sure very talented. You find a better way to make a living than this. Make your mother proud.'

He laughed.

'My mother is proud,' he said. 'This is family business. She would shoot you all.' George watched as the young man looked in turn at his murderous brothers, the murderous Bulgarian, and Laura, her family and friends. Mercy was probably rare in his line of work. Would it be dead bodies drifting with the tide or everyone left to go their separate ways? Was he savouring the power of life and death and considering the nature of honour?

The young man looked at George and nodded towards Laura.

'Is she like her mother?' he asked. 'Maybe I am saving His Royal Highness much trouble.'

'Oh, exactly like her mother,' said George.

'Go then,' said the man. He seemed surprised at his decision. 'Before I change my mind.'

'No,' shouted Kracholov. He raised the Franchi to the Albanian's head. The brothers re-sighted their guns on the Bulgarian.

'Go, now,' repeated the Albanian.

The six walked as calmly as they could towards the concrete ramp. They were spread in a line across the quay and after a few paces joined hands. They didn't look back. When they reached the top of the ramp they heard the blast of a shotgun followed by a fusillade of small-arms fire. Anyone in the vicinity would have looked up into the night sky expecting to see fireworks.

33

Two hours later 54 Mersley Road was busier than its neighbour's bee hives at peak pollination. On every floor suitcases and bags were open, perched on beds or chairs, their owners flitting from one room to another, plucking clothing and prized possessions and returning to fill their chosen receptacles.

The journey from the docks had been emotional with George stoic at the wheel while Dot and Laura held a sobbing reunion. Will sat in the back marvelling at their achievement while Johnson nursed his genitals, claiming he deserved greater recognition for his death-defying courage. Laura told her story, growing in animation until she reached the point of her rescue. All six were euphoric. Will said it reminded him of the drive back from a blinding gig.

When they reached the house Dot and George took Laura into their living room and sat her on the sofa. Over a drink they explained the plan they had devised during the past twenty-four hours. It was sketchy at best, they admitted, with far less detail than usual for one of their projects, but it was what it was. They were bringing their retirement forward. They would stay in a hotel for a few nights, something large and anonymous in west London, until Project Clean Up, as they had code-named George's plan, was completed. They would remain in the hotel just long enough to complete the transaction on the villa in Spain and have their belongings put into storage. Then they would move to another hotel in their new identities, John and Hannah Ward, and from there they would make the jump to Malaga.

George refilled their glasses and continued. They would deal with the house in Mersley Road later and from a distance. It would sell when it sold and there was nothing they could do to hurry things.

When the time came they would help Laura set herself up in a flat out of the proceeds. It wasn't optimum but it would have to do. Things were moving too fast, George said, with too many moving parts. He cited one of his management books which said the test of a great business leader is how well he or she performs when the situation is uncertain, and this, he asserted, was such a situation. It needed quick and dramatic action and improvisation would be key.

Laura had rarely seen her parents so excited. She supposed it was relief at the end of one adventure mixed with anticipation of the next. Most of this was not a surprise. She knew they wanted to retire. She was puzzled by the sudden timing, even in the current circumstances, and the change of identities, but she had experienced enough of her parents' business affairs to know a moonlight flit was an occasional feature. Just what Project Clean Up was her father didn't exactly define but this was also par for the course. She assumed it was one of George's famous brainwaves, a ruse to recover the lost money.

Laura reflected on the chaos that was life in the Valentine household and the prospect of moving on. She'd always known when the house was sold she would need a place of her own and as far as she was concerned it was time. She hadn't intended to stay so long, just until she got on her feet after college. Maybe she'd grown lazy. Working for her parents was good money and it was too easy to put difficult dreams on hold, dreams like striking out as an artist. It would be good for her. What she was not prepared for was Dot's suggestion she join them.

'Just until things settle down,' said her mother. 'Until this Chamberlain thing is over and we're sure that gangster has gone.'

'He's gone, Mum,' said Laura. 'He's dead.'

'We didn't see that,' said George. 'And maybe that Russian friend of yours will send someone else.'

'*My* friend?' said Laura. '*You* got me into that. I want to stay here, Mum. My life is here.'

'It's that boy,' said Dot, with the hint of rancour that never failed to drive Laura into the stratosphere.

'He's part of it,' she said.

'He'll have to go too,' said George, with a nod to the upper floors. 'For his own safety as well as yours. He's in it now. They all are.'

'Come for a few weeks,' said Dot. 'It'll be fun. You can help us move in. We'll shut up the house for a while. When they realise it's empty they'll give up and try something else. Then you can come back.'

Laura said nothing and watched as a stubborn look spread across her mother's face. She guessed it was a mirror of her own. At moments like these George generally tried to calm things by laughing and saying she was her mother's daughter. Only then did they tell her the full story. She knew all they wanted was to protect her, but as usual their emergency measures were the result of chaos they had created but would inconvenience her the most. Her parents, she had to face it, were irresponsible.

George sighed and slowly the tale unfolded. The Chamberlain affair was heading towards an unpredictable end, with the fiasco of the Downing Street report about to explode in their faces, and that could mean jail for everyone. Then there was the possibility Ruby would reveal all before the cameras. That would mean embarrassment if not more jail. Finally, the risks associated with Project Clean Up were significant. And if that backfired you might as well throw away the key. Add the prospect of extreme violence by a wounded Bulgarian or the Russian mafia and they all had to leave and they had to go now.

'You're better off not knowing anymore,' he added. 'That way, if the worst happens they'll see you as a hired hand and not a conspirator.'

'Trust us on this one, Laura,' said Dot. 'We've been here before.'

Laura went upstairs to her room. George followed, climbing to the top flat to tell Will and his friends to clear out immediately. Then he headed for the cellar to check the floor plan of The Rialto for the following day as well as pack his business into crates.

Dot stayed in the living room and switched on the television. The room was littered with packing cases and over the past few days she had stowed away many of their belongings. Up to this point she had done so painstakingly, each object wrapped in paper or bubble-wrap and placed carefully in one of the clearly marked crates. Now she moved around the room quickly, wrapping only the breakable objects and then haphazardly.

She hardly noticed the stories flitting across the screen. There was a preview of the ceremony to be held in Birmingham the next day, where Eleanor Porter would be given the freedom of the city. This had been moved to the steps of the Council House in Victoria Square, due to media interest and expectations of a large turn-out, not least from Sparkwood. It was reported the police did not expect problems but would be present in large numbers to pay homage to the Minister for Cities as well as ensure public order. While in the kitchen Dot missed a story about the Home Secretary's continuing struggles. His ex-housekeeper was selling her life story for a record advance at the same time as he was launching an investigation into the theft of a secret report from his house and its mysterious appearance at a Soho hotel. Evidently a D notice that banned reporting had now been lifted.

She returned to the living room to hear that further south, on the Isle of Wight, Ruby Stevens was now in a cell at Cowes police station. Robert White had also been captured after a spectacular hue and cry. Her wrapping slowed as she watched the story. Apparently, he had stolen a small dinghy and headed into the Isle of Wight Sound early the previous morning, making for Chichester. Unfortunately, other yachtsmen had spotted him and, offered a competitive challenge, had changed tack, radioed their friends and given chase, forcing White to head west and then south. The pursuit had turned into a round-the-island race. White sped through white water as the few boats following him grew into an armada, British sailors imbued with the spirit of their forebears, some with a little rum and a reward in mind, others for sport, with a jug of Pimms and sunburned girlfriends plastered on their foredecks. The chase lasted late into the afternoon until White was almost back at Cowes when a second fleet, a Dunkirk flotilla of dinghies, motorboats and kite-surfers met him head on. Moments later he was surrounded, with helicopters buzzing overhead capturing all for the early evening news and live broadcast on *Escape from Wight*.

Robert White was now secured at the police station in Cowes

awaiting transfer back to the camp. Dot felt a chill as she learned he was in the cell next to Ruby Stevens and they would be moved together. Ruby was now alone, after her girl-band companion had walked off the show after ten minutes in the police cell, and the elderly chef was taken to hospital suffering from nervous exhaustion. Even more reason to make themselves scarce, thought Dot.

She heard George climb the steps from the cellar and go into the bedroom, and guessed he'd be packing a few things for the hotel. When she reached the doorway she found him puzzling over a drawer full of her brassieres, with a tell-tale look on his face. She marvelled how men could think of sex at the most inappropriate moments.

'Tell me it's going to be all right, George,' she said.

'Dot, it's going to be sensational,' he replied and without a beat he moved across the room to enfold her in a hug.

*

Upstairs Will was packing while Luka collected his things from the bathroom. Will stuffed underpants into the sound box of his acoustic guitar, slipped socks around its neck as he laid it in its case and threw the rest of his clothes into a battered suitcase. Essential objects such as his laptop, effects pedals and notebooks filled a duffle. He found a Morrisons carrier bag and went into the living room, where Johnson was keeping watch for Russians.

'There's one under your streetlamp,' said the drummer. 'Real KGB type.' Will glanced out the window.

'That's Mr McDonald, he's a neighbour.'

'He could be a sleeper.'

'He's eighty.'

'Maybe they got him in the sixties,' said Johnson. 'What's he doing under a lamp post at three in the morning?'

'Walking his dog,' said Will. 'He's an insomniac.' Will glanced out the window and saw the man held a lead that disappeared into a hedge. He left Johnson scanning the street for suspicious activity and flipped through his vinyl collection.

'I don't know why you're bothering,' said Johnson. 'You can get all that stuff for nothing online.' Will would have said something but knew he owed the crazy drummer. Quite apart from his earlier bravery Johnson was bailing them out. A room was free at his place, while one of his housemates was saving dolphins from a clubbing in Japan. Luka and Will would share the room.

'You know possessions are slavery,' Johnson continued. 'Have you ever thought about that, Will? Imagine you had no possessions. Do you think you can?'

'Very funny. Fuck off,' said Will.

'In fact, I have less than no possessions,' said the drummer. 'I have debt. He didn't cover that, did he?' Will placed half a dozen albums in the supermarket bag as Luka joined them, his worldly goods crammed into a backpack.

'Where the fuck have you been?' asked Johnson, looking at the bathroom.

'Singer,' said Will. 'We should get out of here,' he added, looking round the room for anything he'd forgotten. For an instant he wondered if George was on the level. Maybe he just wanted him out? Will wouldn't put it past him. But his story made sense. What if the Bulgarian had survived or another set of heavies were on the way? Kracholov knew where they lived. Maybe he'd told someone about it. Who knew how mafias worked? And then there were the Albanians. What if they lived and had changed their minds? Getting out was a smart idea.

The three bandmates were halfway down the stairs dragging their bags along the landing when Johnson brought it up.

'Are we still doing the gig tomorrow?' he asked. 'Because every time we go on stage we won't know if someone's going to take a pop at us.' Will stopped. He hadn't thought of that.

'It's not a problem for me,' Johnson continued. 'It could be good for sales. How old are you, Luka?'

'Twenty-seven,' said the singer.

'There you go,' said Johnson. 'The next in line for the myth of twenty-seven. He'll be the one. We will be immortal but only he will die.'

'It was you who kicked him in the nuts,' said Will.

'Yeah, but he'll go for the singer first. They always do. We can keep on the move. Get a caravan or something.'

'I don't believe this,' Will said. He wondered if he was the only one concerned about musclemen bent on mayhem heading their way this very moment. He let go of his bags and stood up straight. 'OK. Band vote. What do you want to do?'

'I need the money,' said Johnson. 'So I can get my possessions back.'

'Luka?'

The singer shrugged.

'I came here to sing.'

Will looked at them, more amused than amazed. Something had happened between them. Somewhere along the line things had gone beyond music. Even Johnson, obnoxious as he was, had put his life on the line for the cause. They were comrades now, bound by crazed events.

'OK then,' he said. 'We play. Now, can we please fuck off out of here?'

As Will grabbed his bags Laura rounded the stairs. She was holding two bottles of Cava.

'This is for you,' she said. 'We wanted to thank you. Even Mum.'

'You don't have to thank us,' said Will.

'I wouldn't say that,' said Johnson. He took the bottles. 'Possessions. I will prize them.'

'They're happy to have their little girl back,' she said. 'And George is over the moon for some reason. Something to do with a project Dot didn't like, but they're doing anyway.' The four stood on the landing, embarrassed. Will knew they should go but he couldn't move. 'You guys are an adventure,' she added.

'Come with us,' said Will.

'I can't. I have to go to Spain.'

'Come on, babe,' said Johnson. 'Get with the programme. We'll find room.'

'We'll be your Band On The Run,' Luka suggested. 'You can shoot us.'

'Someone should,' she said.

'Forget them,' said Will. 'Come with *me*.' He held her gaze. 'And no, I don't have a funny line.'

'You risked your testicles for me,' she said. 'You must love me.'

'They're yours,' said Will. 'Anytime. And I wish I hadn't said that.'

'I'm glad you didn't lose them,' she said. Will kissed her, to shut himself up as much as anything else.

"Unchained Melody' moment,' shouted Johnson. In an instant Luka and he had quiffed their hair, mimed rolling their sleeves and approximated a clean cut 1950s grin. They launched into 'Unchained Melody' on the cramped landing. Acappella. Laura pulled Will towards her and they kissed properly.

When they came up for air Laura vanished into her bedroom, reappearing a moment later with a suitcase and a string of cameras. The boys were still singing.

'So. Where are we going?' she asked.

*

When Kracholov made his assault just before dawn he was flanked by two Russian bodyguards. The house was dark and silent.

He was the sole survivor of the gunfight at Gallions Point. Having fired a shot which killed one of the traffickers instantly, he had dropped to the ground and in the volley that followed the rest had liquidated each other as well as the family business. He had come through it with a criss-cross of bullet grazes to the head and profound tinnitus in one ear, in addition to the ruined suit and bruised groin. The damage would have been considerably worse had he not been wearing his Reebok 10k genital protector. He had used the device for several years now, with its twin benefits of protection against shock and appearance of enhanced manhood, and was delighted with the results.

He had also recovered a blood-stained bag of money from the dead Albanians, the sterling equivalent of three hundred and fifty thousand dollars. It was enough to change his life, and his mother's. It might even be enough to bargain for his life if his mission failed, but for the time being the bag was hidden behind the boiler in the flat in Willesden High Street.

The Russian heavies had been provided at the insistence of Anton Ledakov once the oligarch learned of the evening's fiasco. Their official remit was to assist the Best Bulgarian Cleaning Company in completing the assignment and restoring corporate relations between their two organisations. If this failed, however, Kracholov knew they were to kill him.

Once inside, the three men found the house empty and little to help them identify the whereabouts of its former occupants. The Russians looked at the Bulgarian menacingly and one of them cracked his knuckles. Kracholov noticed something on the floor by the front door and squatted to examine it. It was a flyer for a gig at The Rialto in King's Cross the following night. He slipped it into his pocket. It looked like he was going to be in London for an extra day or two at least, until he'd tracked down his quarry. And if he didn't succeed there was every possibility he would finish up in a quarry. So, maybe he'd go. It might produce a lead, maybe even a great gig. And what the hell, life is short and Russians liked rock music. It might put them in a good mood. He hoped his ear would clear by then.

34

The Rolls pulled up in front of wrought iron gates set on vast pillars in a moss-eaten wall that circled the estate. The car shivered imperceptibly, its engine purring unheard beneath the rain spattering its roof and the ear-splitting rock that bled through every pore. Inside Marshall and Melissa were still encased in velcro, though this time dressed to travel.

As the song ended the window on the driver's side slid down and Marshall reached out to the entry-phone. A moment later the gates began to open, one faster than the other, the second juddering, as if out of breath trying to catch its partner.

Melissa gazed along the asphalt road to her home, a turreted stone edifice rendered gothic by the rain.

'Wow, babe,' Marshall cooed. 'It's been a long time.'

'Thirty years,' she said. Marshall turned the stereo down and switched tracks. Guns & Roses, 'November Rain'.

'I got to experience this,' he said. He removed his sunglasses, but even grey daylight was too much, so he replaced them. He drove at a stately pace and Melissa watched him absorbing the view.

'We played over there,' he said, nodding to a hollow in front of a wood.

'Over there,' Melissa laughed, pointing in the opposite direction. 'There's a lake somewhere.'

'Behind the house. Well done, you remember something.'

'Got any fish in it?'

'Some.'

'We'll start a trout farm,' he said. Melissa laughed.

'Marshall, I am not going to marry you.'

'Yes you are, babe.'

'We're already married. To other people.'

'Not for much longer.' He scanned the rolling hills and trees stretching into the distance then seemed to tune into the ballad. 'We love each other, babe,' he said, 'it is written in the pouring rain.'

He parked in front of the house by crumbling steps and a stone arch that sheltered an oak door. He switched off the engine and waited, rain pattering on the roof.

'Where are the flunkies?' he asked.

'No flunkies,' said Melissa. 'Just a gardener and a daily help, but he's deaf and it's her day off.'

'Babe, you got to have flunkies, a pad like this.' She placed a hand on the door. She would make a dash for it.

'Thanks for the lift, Marshall,' she said. 'And the rest. It was fun. Really.' The guitarist climbed from the car and stood with his face upturned to the rain, his arms outstretched.

'This is so cool,' she heard him say. Marshall ambled to the rear of the car, popped the boot and grabbed a bag. Melissa opened her door and joined him in rushed steps, one hand over her head to protect her bandages. She tried to take the bag.

'Thank you. Really,' she said, and offered him a kiss on the cheek. He pulled back.

'No way, babe,' he said. 'I'll bring the gear. That way you have to make me coffee.' He stood, immovable, and Melissa realised they were both getting soaked.

'Come on, then,' she said, with the indulgent frown she reserved for a naughty yet charming child, and started up the steps. He called after her.

'Want anything from the minibar?' She looked back and laughed.

'*No.* I have to get back to normal.'

'Normal is overrated, babe,' he said. He followed her to the door and they stood close to each other under the stone arch as Melissa fumbled for her keys. He was only a kiss away and she wondered if he'd try. But he didn't. Maybe she'd misinterpreted him or he'd decided it was a moment for doing nothing and was hoping for another, different kind of moment later. Maybe he was that rarity of men, one who could wait.

The door swung open and they tripped into the hallway. They shook off the rain and he placed the bag where she asked, by an oak-panelled wall.

'Great crib,' he said. 'I remember this.' Melissa watched as he peered at the rich panelling, mullioned windows and broad staircase, the family portraits and heavy Jacobean furniture. It didn't take much to imagine the place filled with men in capes and jewel-encrusted swords plotting war, and she knew Marshall had a vivid imagination.

'Where is everyone?' he asked.

'The boys are at school, Charles is in Birmingham and the gardener could be anywhere in a hundred acres.' Melissa placed her keys on an oak table. She wondered how she was going to get rid of him before her husband came home.

'Kitchen's this way,' she said. She would make him coffee, show him the house and send him on his way. She led him along a panelled corridor into a bright modern kitchen.

'Think about it, babe,' he said, as she switched on the coffee machine. 'You have money, I have money. Well, I will have money after the tour. So, no problems there. We'll have mutual pre-nups. Then we can buy each other presents that mean something.' She took off her Jackie Kennedy sunglasses and placed them on the counter, then plucked mugs from a cupboard and moved to the fridge.

'You're forgetting one thing,' she said.

'What's that, babe?'

'I love my husband.'

Marshall seemed to ponder the point.

'Maybe you did,' he said, 'before children, before it got boring, before he was never here. But it's burned out, I can tell. Maybe it didn't crash, it just slipped away without you noticing.'

'We're fine,' she said, hearing her voice sharpen. She put on the radio and he was quiet while she poured the coffee. She handed him one and their fingers touched.

'I'm not going away, Melissa,' he said. 'You see, it's you, you're the one that I want.'

'Ooh-ooh-ooh,' she replied.

She started the tour in the hall beginning with the history of the baronetcy. He listened for a while to the well-honed tale.

'Don't you see, Mel? You can be free,' he said. 'With me. We can have adventures.'

'Adventures?'

'I'm a pirate. Wherever you want to go, I'll take you. Whatever you want, I'll get it for you.'

'Anywhere?'

'Anywhere. Everywhere. I will show you the world,' he said. 'Or we can just veg out here, mow the lawn and raise little brown trouts.'

'Trout,' she corrected.

'Whatever.' Marshall's arms were outstretched again. 'See. I need you. I've always needed you. It's always been you. I just didn't see it.'

'Marshall. You were out of your head when you met me.'

'But you slipped inside my mind,' he said. Melissa groaned in frustration. He had an answer for everything and mostly they sounded like half-familiar lyrics. She showed him the dining room, which boasted a mahogany table with carvers at each end, and an open fireplace that smelt of its last fire.

'I have children,' she said, leading him into another corridor.

'They'll love me,' he said. 'My fan base is bald guys and teenage boys. We'll take them out of school and play with them. I'll teach them how to shred. And if you don't like the noise we'll shred in the shed.'

'Marshall. Stop it. You are amazing and you make me laugh. But it's not going to happen.' She opened another door and showed him into the TV room, a panelled snug with comfortable sofas, a state of the art entertainment system and a window seat overlooking striped lawns.

'There's one more thing,' he said, taking the window seat. Outside, a stone lion reared behind him, its skin flaking. She saw his confidence had evaporated.

'Yes?'

'It's sensitive,' he said. 'That stuff the witch wife said – that I couldn't get it up any more. She was right, Mel. Nothing. For more than a year. And rock years are like dog years. Not so much as a tweet from old Woody here. But Mel…you stir me.'

'Thank you for sharing that,' she said. He was on his feet again, coming towards her.

'And I stir you,' he said. 'I know I do. I have to. I'm a rock god.'

'You are funny, Marshall,' she said. 'And that is attractive.'

'Whatever it takes, Mel. I love you,' he said, moving in for a kiss. 'And fuck me, that's a big one.'

He had noticed the television built into the wall behind her and promptly left Melissa to examine it. 'It must be a hundred inches. Fucking amazing.'

'Charles thinks big is best,' she said.

'How do you switch it on?' he asked. He was gone. Melissa sat on the window seat, bemused as he played with the handset, his jaw dropping as the device sprang to life. He sank into one of the sofas, obviously dazzled by the scale of the image. Melissa looked at the screen. They were in a city somewhere and there were crowds. It felt like they were in the room, the sound was everywhere; cheering and Asian music. Then a helicopter shot of people. It was sunny wherever it was.

'It's Birmingham,' said Marshall. 'The Council House. I went there once, before a gig, to meet some of the nobs.'

Now they were looking at a podium and the mayor was speaking. Marshall's feet were on a footstool now, his arm along the back of the sofa. The mayor welcomed Eleanor Porter to the podium and presented her with a key to the city.

'They did the same thing for Ozzy once. Or was it Noddy? I think I was there.'

Melissa looked for Charles but couldn't see him anywhere. Usually he liked to be in the shot, like Alfred Hitchcock, somewhere in the background but visible, just for a few seconds. They had dozens of recordings of his appearances on the sidelines of great and sometimes notorious events.

The camera cut away to a group of Asians in traditional dress in front of the podium. They were smiling and clapping. Marshall clapped his hands as he remembered something.

'Hey, that's those guys who holed up in the clothes shop,' he said. 'And we met *her* at that book launch, didn't we? Cool. What did you make of her?'

Melissa sat watching him. Is this what life would be like with Marshall? Passionate declarations of love interrupted by sudden fascinations, followed by feet-up domestic bliss? She should have been annoyed with him, breaking off from lovemaking to watch television, but she wasn't. He made her feel comfortable, he made her laugh, and he asked her opinion. When was the last time Charles had done any of these things? Marshall jumped to his feet.

'Sorry. I was telling you I love you.'

'And I was going to show you the library.'

She led him back along the corridor to Charles' inner sanctum. Marshall was quiet in the great room, reverential, apparently awed by walls filled floor to ceiling with learning. He looked up at the portrait of Melissa's father.

'The old man?' he said. She nodded. 'I remember him, he was a pistol – said he'd seen better dressed poachers when he saw us, and threatened to shoot down the helicopter for scaring the game.'

'That sounds like him,' said Melissa.

'He took a couple of shots. Luckily he'd been at the brandy and soda.'

'You do remember.'

'I remember you,' he said, green eyes blazing from within his white helmet. Melissa felt breathless, fixed by his gaze until he broke it and looked around the room. 'And I remember the booze was kept in that globe,' he said.

'Do you want a drink?' Melissa asked and moved towards her father's favourite antique. 'One for the road?'

'Let's make it one for the old man,' he said. 'Brandy and soda.' Melissa tried to slide the upper half of the globe open but it was locked. She crossed to the desk in front of the window and tried the centre drawer.

'Charles keeps the key in here,' she said, 'but he keeps this locked too.' She tapped her nose with her index finger. 'But Number One son says he keeps the key for it in here.' She opened a cigar box lying by the PC and rummaged inside. The rich smell of Havana tobacco filled the room. She produced a small key with a flourish and in moments the desk drawer was open. She was searching for the second key, her eyes ranging over the drawer's contents, when she saw the photograph.

She picked it up and studied it carefully. It was the face of a woman, taken a long time ago. Beneath this photo was another, the same woman from a different angle, and a third. It was a woman she knew well. On each photograph there were markings and measurements, of the subject's eyebrows, cheekbones and nose. Beneath them was a full-length picture of the woman, naked by a lake, with measurements of her waist, hips and breasts. There was a heavily notated close-up of the breasts with precise dimensions of cup, nipple and degree of uplift. It reminded her of a Leonardo da Vinci drawing. Beneath them were photographs of Melissa, with similar markings.

She let the pictures drop onto the desk and looked up at Marshall, her mouth falling open. It was like a sudden death, the death of everything. She could see nothing else, only the pictures and then Marshall with a look of horror on his face. She couldn't breathe. She felt denial, rage and despair; she wanted to be sick.

'Are you OK?' Marshall asked. 'Have you been at the mini bar?'

She looked at him uncomprehending, and then laughed. Mad, lovable man who desired her. He was probably trying to remember what he was supposed to do in case of an overdose.

'Mel?'

'Do you want me, Marshall?' she whispered. She felt numb, unbelieving of the idea that had just entered her mind.

'What?'

'Do you want me?'

'Of course I want you, Mel. I said. You're all that I want.'

'Then take me,' she whispered. 'Now. Here.'

'Is something wrong?' he asked.

'You could say that,' she said. 'My bastard husband is trying to turn me into Lucy Lowe.'

'Lucy who?' Melissa showed him one of the pictures.

'My best friend thirty years ago,' she said, her head spinning. 'His first girlfriend. The bitch. I knew he still fancied her. He's been redesigning me as her. Now, do you want me or not?'

Marshall looked nervous as a schoolboy. She swept the offending pictures into the drawer and slammed it shut.

'There's just one thing. I want to know your name,' she said.

'My name?'

'Hammond Marshall is not a real name. I want total honesty.'

'Henry Herbert.'

'Herbert? Henry? Really?'

Marshall nodded.

'OK,' said Melissa. She turned away from the guitarist and bent low over the desk, each hand grasping a corner. 'I want you to take me, Henry Herbert,' she said. 'Now. Over his desk.' She waited, readying herself for revenge. Marshall said he wanted her; now she would see whether he meant it. It was only at that moment, committed and splayed over Charles' desk that she began to worry that her suitor might not be able to perform, that her allure might not be strong enough and his demons too powerful. That would be too embarrassing. She gave a wiggle of encouragement, let out a seductive sigh then waited and hoped, holding her breath. A moment later she felt her dress rising and his hands on her waist, firm and intent, and then lower down she felt him stirring behind her. She looked past her father's portrait to the rows of books and up to the panelled ceiling, then closed her eyes and gave herself to Henry Herbert, sometime superstar, who was a buccaneer once more.

Outside, fifty feet from the house under cover of a hedge, Alan Leo was waiting. He'd been stationed there since early morning. Rain was running off his waterproofs, water had permeated his clothes and his feet had lost all feeling. At first, he'd wondered why George Valentine had asked him to do this job and not his daughter. It wasn't really his thing. Granted he'd waited in the rain for a story once in a while, but he wasn't a photographer and he didn't get out of London much. Still, George was his best source and had offered good money. How difficult could it be? Leo adjusted the zoom lens realising he'd hit the jackpot. Instructed to capture anything that might incriminate Charles Franklin, he was about to catch the man's wife in flagrante with a rock star who was in the midst of a very public divorce and of uncertain ability in the shagging department. Front page *Sunday Sport*. He zeroed in on the tattoo on the star's right buttock. It read 'Made in Lewisham'.

At the same time the sound of sex was filling the long corridor outside the library, coming from the empty TV room. On the hundred-inch screen, in high definition and surround sound, Robert White and Ruby Stevens were fornicating on the floor of an ageing police van, hired by the *Escape from Wight* production team to transport them back to the camp. There had been no forced confession when they met, no revelations, no apologies for selling out the former minister and no recriminations from him. In the moment he saw her White realised he had been drawn to the Isle of Wight by lust or love or both. All else was deception. For Ruby it was the chance to keep him silent and an eye for ratings. They had looked at one another in silence then leapt on each other and now four cameras were capturing their every rutting intimacy and broadcasting them live to ten million viewers. It was a first for daytime television.

35

The Rialto sat on a corner of King's Cross and, like many of the souls who wandered the streets beyond its doors, had found a few ways of scratching a living through the years, following London's fads and fortunes, failing more times than not and bankrupting more than one set of investors. By turns a factory for airplane parts, labour exchange, silent picture house, adult movie centre, even an ape house, it had been a live music venue twice. Timing is everything in the entertainment industry and these days it was cool again and turning a profit, riding on the death of record royalties and the comeback of the live gig.

Inside, Jack Blake sat on a stool in the centre of the music room, capacity 800, running final checks for Friday night's Blake's Ride. Stationed behind a mixing desk beside an engineer, he was surrounded by the technology of sound, light and vision. In front of him two computer screens showed live feeds from every part of the building. There were miniature cameras covering the stage and audience, green room, bars, stairs and entrance. If the action was dull on stage he could cut to interviews and happenings anywhere in the building, and stream them live to the Blake's Ride site as well as a screen above the stage. The site had half a million members who watched gigs, downloaded tracks, listened to Blake's Ride radio, chatted in rock suites and tried to win VIP tickets to Friday Night Live at The Rialto. The live show was fast becoming the hottest ticket in town and the web-cast drew a bigger audience every week. Bands that broke here could break the UK and maybe the world.

Blake reviewed the camera feeds while Don't Know Yet plugged in their instruments on stage, getting ready for their sound check.

One of his staff, wearing a Blake's Ride T-shirt, approached the mixing desk.

'Jack, couple of old folks say they have an appointment,' he said, jerking a thumb over his shoulder. Blake peered into the shadows at two figures, one carrying a canvas holdall. He smiled, climbed from his chair and padded over to them.

'George, Dot. Great to see you.' He exchanged a handshake with George and a hug with Dot. 'You guys are looking great.' The impresario shielded his eyes to look beyond the lights. 'Laura's around here somewhere,' he said.

Dot smiled at the young man. She couldn't for the life of her understand why Laura preferred the ragged musician on the stage, who was currently trying to stop screeching sounds emitting from his amplifier, to the tanned urbane man in front of her, or why she and Blake had broken up. He had it all. He was good-looking, rich and successful and he was going to be more of all three, maybe the biggest thing in music. He was charming, always polite to Dot and showed no signs of drugs or deviancy. She loved his cars, the Aston, the Ferrari, even the Porsche, and the easy way he had of making her feel young and attractive, quite apart from what he did for her daughter. She found herself tilting her head, exposing her neck, unable to resist flirting. So what if he was arrogant, he had reason to be; and had she been a few years younger, well maybe a few decades younger, she would have soon knocked him into shape, pricked that little bubble. Instead, Laura chose a noisy scruff destined for penury. And now she had chosen to follow him to God-knows-what squalor rather than come with them to Spain.

Dot shook her head wondering if she were to blame. At the same time she noticed she was slipping one foot in and out of her shoe and feeling just a little skittish. George thanked Blake for the floor plan.

'Could we see the room?' he asked.

'Sure.' Blake told the engineer to take a break and led the couple over the stage and through the Green Room. George winked at the musicians as they passed, while Dot sniffed with disapproval. They continued down a flight of stairs to the basement and along a narrow corridor with doors either side. Had he looked back Blake might have noticed an additional sway in Dot's hips. He unlocked one of the doors, pushed it open and switched on the light.

'Will this do?' he asked. 'It may get noisy, but you won't be disturbed.' George and Dot looked around. The room was large and square, a little-used office that doubled as storage space. Metal shelving lined the walls, joined to flaking plaster with cobwebs and filled with dusty files. There was an old desk with a 1980s red telephone and an angle-poise lamp. An animal cage occupied a corner, a leftover from The Rialto's days as a primatarium. Inside stood a stuffed gorilla, speckled with dandruff from the ceiling and brandishing a roll of wallpaper. The room was lit with a single un-shaded bulb. Dot wrinkled her nose, detecting a faint smell of urine. George checked if the phone worked.

'Not much in the way of frills,' Blake conceded.

'It's perfect,' said George. 'We don't need it for long. How much do we owe you?' He pulled out a roll of banknotes.

'Forget it,' said Blake, shaking his head. 'Old time's sake. Is there anything else you need?' George and Dot looked at one another.

'We're expecting two or three people,' George said, while Dot thought how to arrange the room for their purpose. 'Men. They'll be older than your usual crowd and look out of place. They'll be asking for the auction. It would be good if your people let them through without a fuss.'

'That's easy,' said Blake.

'And maybe one of your staff could bring them down when we're ready?' Dot asked, in the voice she reserved for charming her way to an upgrade. Blake winked conspiratorially.

'I'll send someone down. You just tell them what you want, Dot.' He handed George the keys. Dot mouthed her thanks as she fingered a pendant. Blake pointed out the fire exit which was the last door along the corridor, and left them to it. George swung the holdall onto the table, unzipped it and widened the aperture. He carefully lifted out a pile of documents and laid them on the table, then unzipped an inner compartment and produced two black balaclavas, two pairs each of

320

dark glasses and woollen gloves. Dot looked at him and then the gorilla.

'Showtime,' she said.

*

Back behind the mixing desk Blake clicked his fingers.

'Time to get the party started,' he shouted. He cranked up the volume on the sound system and switched to the exterior cameras. A street scene appeared on the monitor in front of him as well as the screen above the stage. Two hundred music fans lined the white walls of The Rialto, waiting for the doors to open, chatting in the warm rain, some with hoods up, others brazening out the weather, knowing they would soon be inside and sweating, steam rising from their sodden T-shirts.

Charles Franklin and Sir Frank Porter were twenty feet from the front, trying to blend with the crowd. Porter was irritable. Charles guessed it had been a long time since the banker was at a rock concert and even longer since he'd queued for anything. He'd turned up in jeans with miniature rips bought for him by his daughter last Christmas which he'd earmarked for gardening but had never worn; cowboy boots and a hat from a business trip to Dallas; a white shirt, dark jacket and sunglasses. Given his squat stature and the scowl frozen on his face the overall effect was late period Van Morrison. Only the City umbrella jarred. Charles sported shirt tails that hung over his jeans and below his blazer, which he believed was cool but most would take as mid-life crisis.

'Isn't there a Fast Track?' Porter grumbled. He craned to see over the queue. Charles knew in the banker's world people who kept him waiting soon found themselves jobless. 'This file had better be as good as you say.'

'It'll finish him, Frank,' Charles whispered. 'It'll mean an investigation into the '92 election *and* show he's behind the PM's health scare. He'll have to resign. Nobody will care about the report once this gets out.'

'You hope,' Porter muttered. A pair of beefy security men came down the line checking tickets. They looked the two middle-aged men up and down but said nothing. Porter waited until they passed. 'I assume Chamberlain is a bidder, the other must be a newspaper,' he said.

'So long as Chamberlain doesn't get it,' said Charles. 'The media will do the job for us.'

'No. I want it,' Porter snapped. 'I want this shambles under control. This isn't going to make the news, Charles. We're going to buy this file and bury everything. We'll use it to make him kill the investigation and retire. I want him to disappear. I want him gone. He can fuck off to the country and make up some memoirs. He can sodomise his fucking ponies for all I care.' Charles nodded. He knew Porter well enough not to contradict him when his blood was up. The banker's face flushed. 'He can have a consultancy with the bank. I just want him out of the way.'

'Where exactly is the money?' asked Charles. It had been puzzling him for a while.

'Don't worry about money, Charles. I'm a banker. I have all the money.' Porter patted one of his pockets. 'I think a million in diamonds should more than cover it, don't you? White, ponies, illegal aliens, leaked reports and this bloody file.'

Charles looked up and down the queue to see if he recognised anyone. Most were in their late teens or early twenties, a good-natured, tattooed army in jeans, T-shirts and hoodies. He noted those who stood out from the norm: the three middle-aged women a few rows behind, whose breasts jiggled as they giggled loudly and claimed they'd seen the headliners rehearsing in a pub and then argued over who fancied the drummer most; the man in a leather jacket, his arm lolling over his girlfriend's shoulders as he told his companions he used to sing with one of the bands, but they were rubbish since he left; the group of Africans he recognised from Eleanor's book launch; the three burly men wearing Armani suits and impassive faces who looked Russian; and in the distance, a second man with an umbrella, leaning against the wall, his hat pulled down around his head, another Van

Morrison lookalike, but this time taller and thinner, in jeans and a full length coat, the collar up around his ears. Tall Van. If he'd been closer, Charles would have noticed the angular music fan carried an attaché case and might be taken for the racy twin of the present Home Secretary.

The doors swung open and Blake's Ride went live, streaming indie rock beneath images of a sodden yet enthusiastic crowd pouring through the entrance and past the box office, up the steep staircase painted hellish red and into the foyer bar, to fill up on beer and wine in plastic tumblers. Two staff in Blake's Ride T-shirts, a sparky blonde and a black dude, waited with microphones to carry out pre-show interviews with the punters. They accosted anyone who looked interesting and extrovert, following a pre-set formula: a compliment about their dress and a quick-fire barrage of questions: where are you from? Who have you come to see? Why? And what's your Blake's Ride message? This last was a philosophical soundbite in five words or less that summed up their take on life. Bon mots ranged from 'Tantra Tarot Turns Me On' to 'I Think Therefore I Wham!' and were published instantly on the site in a league table called Blake's Riders, an internet compendium of Wildean wit in the Twitter age.

The interviewers scoured the foyer as if amphetamined, challenging anyone to match their in-your-face energy. Those in the know had a message prepared and went for their smart phones immediately after delivering it to see if they had made the list. The African dance band couldn't come up with anything but were forgiven because they looked awesome. The middle-aged women chased the dude to be included, only to be deleted when Blake saw their lined faces and sagging chins. The shorter of the two Van Morrisons ducked into the Gents when the dude approached him, apparently thinking this might be the Man himself checking out new talent. He tried to interview Charles instead who followed his master into the toilet, leaving the interviewer wondering to camera what they might be up to inside.

At precisely 8.30 p.m. Blake cued the first band, an anorexic group led by a self-harming waif who sang in a scrawny voice, 'My Life Was Over Before It Began'. Her devotees swayed haphazardly in front of the stage.

A few feet away Kracholov and his two colleagues leaned over a rail on a raised section of the floor, plastic pints in hand, puzzling over the lead singer's allure. Kracholov loved the venue and the crowd, but wasn't so sure about the music. His practised eye swept across the audience, noticing the two Van Morrisons leaning against the wall some distance apart.

Blake had also noticed them and picked them up on the monitor, just in case one turned out to be the real thing. He discarded the short one immediately, but kept coming back to Tall Van. He clearly wasn't the Man, but he looked familiar; someone from television maybe? It would come to him. He re-focused on the waif who was coming to the end of her set, but kept a camera and an occasional eye on Tall Van.

The room filled over the next hour, becoming dense with people and expectation. A second band played a tight rock set, which Kracholov and his companions enjoyed, while the man who claimed to have sung with one of the bands slagged them off in a booze-boosted voice. The Vans stayed in exactly the same positions against the wall weighing each other up with sidelong glances, while the plump middle-aged women drank and gyrated, edging unsteadily towards the stage. The Africans danced, loose-limbed and careless, playing with the simple rhythms of western rock.

In the Green Room the boys grew nervous. The band onstage was good. They'd have to raise their game. Will, Luka and Johnson huddled together and were joined by their keyboard player Little Malcolm (so named because he was six foot six) and bassist Norway (after his place of birth.) Laura wished them luck then checked her camera. They readied themselves by the stage door as the current act finished to thunderous applause. Three minutes of commercials and five more of interviews ran on the Blake's Ride site while the equipment was re-set and they waited. Will was nauseous.

When the door opened again, to another burst of applause, the boys strode into the light, plugged in and tuned up. Laura followed.

'Good evening, Rialto. How do you feel?' Luka yelled into the microphone. He waited for the crowd's roar to subside before adding, 'Because we… Don't–Know–Yet!' They kicked into their first song, 'Time To Fly'. Will thumbed dampened strings, hammering a note, almost a drone that gave the song its tone. They looked good and Luka was breathtaking in the centre spot. He sang, strong and confident, with a hint of pathos. Will was excited to hear the song, conceived in the street and written on a bus, flooding the space.

Kracholov was compromised from the moment Luka opened his mouth. One of his targets was framed in front of him, open and vulnerable, prey displayed in its habitat unaware of threat, to be cut down without a thought: business to be taken care of. Yet here was a voice that touched his soul, a sudden treasure from the gods, and he was frozen in admiration, rooted and mute. He hardly noticed as his two companions tapped him on the shoulder and pointed to Laura taking photographs from the side.

The audience was also making its judgement, moving forward slowly, packing together then advancing on the stage, their decision made. The band was accepted and now the dance could begin.

Across the room a roadie with a beer belly and a beard introduced himself to Short Van and Charles Franklin who asked for the auction. They followed as he led them along the wall until they reached Tall Van, where a similar ritual was observed, after which they congaed to a side door that led to the staircase Dot and George had descended earlier.

Tall Van examined Short Van as they trooped down the stairs, while his wine-buff nose twitched, scenting damp and possibly worse. As they reached the basement he touched the shorter man on the shoulder and the banker turned. The two men squared up to each other, Ken Chamberlain looking down on Sir Frank Porter, an angry curl winding across his lips as he recognised his nemesis.

'Porter,' said the Home Secretary. 'You cunt.'

'Home Secretary,' said Porter, with a surprised look, 'I didn't know you were a music fan.'

'So it was you,' said Chamberlain, his voice rising. 'Why? For God's sake?' Porter pulled down the brim of his hat.

'It's business,' said the banker.

'But why? Is it some kind of upstart priest thing?' whined the politician. 'Are you doing it for the Man?'

The roadie was baffled. In his mind Tall Van seemed upset with Short Van about doing something for *the* Man. Were they talking about the hallowed Belfast Cowboy himself?

'It's not personal,' said Porter.

'Not personal?' shouted the Home Secretary. 'Of course it's fucking personal. You've pilloried my wife and daughter, you've ransacked my house. And now you're buying my past?'

Porter glared at the roadie.

'Can we get on with this, please?' he snapped.

The roadie continued along the narrow corridor. He had no idea who these people were, or what they were talking about. He dispensed with the idea they actually knew Van the Man. They weren't cool enough; just a couple of middle-aged geezers with a thing about him. They probably wanted to buy a joint and someone was dealing in one of the rooms.

'It's Eleanor, isn't it?' Chamberlain shouted as they filed along the passage. 'It's all about Eleanor. You're doing this to shove her up the greasy pole. You bastard!'

The roadie showed them into the office. He'd be glad to have them off his hands. After all, there was good weird and dark weird. And these two were seriously weird. The Vans quietened when they saw two figures in black balaclavas and dark glasses standing behind a desk, a single bulb glowing in front of them and light from an angle-poise shining directly into their faces. Behind them stood a gorilla. More weird shit, thought the roadie. He cupped one hand for a tip, which went unnoticed, and headed off to the fire exit for a smoke. Upstairs the band were starting their second number and sounding hot.

The two Vans, Charles Franklin, the two figures in balaclavas and the gorilla stood in a circle around the table.

'Good evening,' said the larger of the two masked figures.

'What the fuck is this, George?' asked Charles. 'Some kind of minstrel show?'

'I said they'd recognise us,' said Dot.

'Just being professional, Charles,' said George. 'Giving it a bit of decorum.'

'Is this the caterer?' Porter asked, looking askance at Charles.

'Maître d', actually,' said Dot.

'Is that thing alive?' asked Chamberlain, looking nervously at the gorilla.

'That's Damien,' said George. 'He's with us. Now, let's get down to business, shall we?' He ran his gloved hands over the documents on the desk, ensuring a neat and ordered pile. 'This is the sale and transfer of all rights and materials in past cases relating to Valentine Competitive Insight.'

'You're the muckrakers,' said Chamberlain. He turned to Porter and Charles. 'Are these the people you've had digging up shit on me?'

'This sale covers all past cases up to this week including the White case,' continued George.

'White?' said Chamberlain. 'You did that? Here, I'll buy that,' he said, making a grab for the file. The Home Secretary had seen a chance to buy his way out of trouble.

'This is a pre-agreed sale,' said Dot, shielding the document. 'The auction comes next.'

'But I'll buy it,' insisted the Home Secretary. 'How much do you want?' Porter stepped forward. He pulled a small black bag from his pocket.

'Don't be ridiculous, Chamberlain,' he sneered. 'You're a politician. You don't have money.' Porter spilled a number of diamonds into the palm of his hand and held them to the light. Chamberlain turned pale and the rest were silent, in awe as the light played on the stones, a handful of brilliance in the gloom. Even the gorilla seemed to be watching, a tiny glint in his black eyes. Porter placed them on the table.

'That's a quarter of a million. And one for luck,' said the banker.

'Pick up the files, Charles,' he added with a smirk. Franklin pulled a thin folded nylon bag from inside his jacket.

'Just a minute,' said Dot. She scooped the diamonds into her hand, held them to the light again and examined them. Her mouth widened from a pout to a smile. 'That'll do nicely,' she said. George pushed the files towards Franklin who slipped them into the bag.

'Next item,' said Dot. 'The Chamberlain File. To be auctioned.' George picked up the red telephone and dialled a number. He spoke briefly into the mouthpiece and nodded to Dot. The mystery bidder was on the line. Dot shuffled to a central position behind the desk, flanked by George and the gorilla. She opened the holdall at her feet, took out the dossier prepared by Tom Howard and placed it on the table. She flicked through the pages with the look she would have worn if flashing a garter, and summarised the contents.

'One lot only, a truly unique item: the complete political history of Kenneth Chamberlain in the period 1985-2005, with original documentary evidence and signed statements, prepared by the late Tom Howard. Now who will open the bidding? Do I hear one hundred thousand?'

*

Upstairs the crowd was transformed into a writhing mass. A trance state had drifted back from the early converts by the stage to the next level behind the rail on the raised floor, where the interested but detached had abandoned their shouted conversations, and finally to those at the back, who rarely lost themselves to music or anything else. When staying on the periphery became too embarrassing the final rows either surrendered to the crowd or slinked off to the bar. The whole place was heaving and the band looked out on faces that appeared contorted in pain or ecstasy. The boys were astounded. All save Luka. He knew this would happen one day, and showed no surprise it was this time, this place, with this band. He was an explosion of energy, strutting and preening, inciting the mob to greater heights. He turned and smiled at his band-mates, as if to say,

'Chill guys. This was written. It was always written. Didn't you know?'

Kracholov stood stock-still at the rail, buffeted by all around him. It was as if he could read Luka's mind. This was a powerful destiny at work, and it made his dilemma worse. If he was looking at a god in the making, what did that make him? Was he the Judas to make a martyr? He looked behind the singer to the drummer, the one who had dented his Reebok 10k. He had no qualms about him. Drummers were ten a penny. He would happily impale him on his sticks, but not until later. He would not ruin the music. Not yet. The two Russians were thumping his shoulder now. Forget the band, they shouted. Get the girl. He reassured them, now was not the moment. They would act later. And maybe he would kill the drummer first.

Jack Blake was exultant as he watched the audience, in the club, on the screens and streaming on the site. The comments coming in on the chat forum were peppered with superlatives. These guys were a hit. He glanced at the monitors noticing one of them frozen in a still of Tall Van, standing in front of the wall, and it hit him. Ken Chamberlain. Ken Chamberlain the Home Secretary and pariah, dressed as Van Morrison, in The Rialto, watching rock while his world burned. It was priceless. Silently Blake gave thanks. Jubilant before, now he was euphoric. This would be a night in a million. He had a new hit band and a fabulous publicity hook for Blake's Ride. Within seconds he was streaming the frozen image onto the site with the caption, 'Can You Name This Van? Win a Year's Pass to Blake's Ride'. Answers started to come immediately, and aside from suggestions of Van Helsing, Van Diesel and Rip Van Winkle, most correctly identified the politician. He reached for his iPhone and called the Sky news desk. With a little luck Blake's Ride would make the nightly news as well as the following day's tabloids.

After the call Blake scanned the crowd again, seeing arched eyebrows, tops stained with sweat and fists held high. All eyes were fixed on Luka, wide open, expectant. Where next, they seemed to be asking. Politicians, media and business may fuck us, but in you we trust. Take us where you want, we will come. Blake sat supreme at the mixing desk, intoxicated by success. Now for the crowning glory, the band would switch to his songs, as arranged. Not just the biggest thing behind the scenes, he, Jack Blake, would soon own the music too.

He looked towards the stage and saw Will turn his back on the audience to face his band-mates.

'What next?' shouted the guitarist, his voice clear in Blake's headphones. The impresario was puzzled. They all knew what came next. It was a done deal. They would play Blake's songs and get paid. And then they'd get to open for someone big on a tour, maybe even a record deal. Blake was giving them a free ride. What was the little shit up to?

'No, Will,' shouted Little Malcolm. 'Don't do it.' Blake could see the keyboard player pleading with the guitarist. He had been the first to buy-in to the plan and the easiest to convince, the one who only wanted money.

Next Will turned to Norway and Luka. Their shrugs said it was his call. He was the leader. Last he turned to Johnson, the mad one. The drummer's sticks flourished around his kit.

'Fuck it. Let's do it,' he yelled, his voice and drums exploding in Blake's ears.

"Not For Sale", Will shouted. Little Malcolm's eyes went to the ceiling and he shook his head as the rest prepared for the song.

They were twenty seconds into the number before Blake realised he was betrayed, that they had broken the deal, thrown away a guarantee of commercial success and gone with their own material. It made no sense. A second later he went berserk. But no one could hear or cared. The number was hard, fast and loud, a notch or two up in tempo and the crowd was going wild. Blake dropped back into his seat, bent on vengeance.

'Cut to the audience,' he shouted at the engineer, who looked at him in astonishment. 'Keep the sound but I want them out of the picture. Get them off my fucking site.' The visuals on the website transitioned to the audience, the bars, and exterior shots of the building, anywhere the engineer could think of to diminish the band's impact.

'Where's Chamberlain?' Blake shouted as an idea occurred to him.

He would follow the politician's story, use it to promote Blake's Ride and reduce the band to the soundtrack to a media sensation. He scanned through the cameras, looking for Tall Van, but he was nowhere to be found. Only then did he think of George and Dot in the basement and their bizarre auction. 'They'll be older than your usual crowd,' George had said. Blake knew George was an operator, a ducker and diver, dodgy to his dirty fingernails. Just what was he selling? And to whom?

'Are there cameras downstairs?' Blake yelled. The engineer appeared not to understand. 'Cameras,' he repeated, pointing to the floor. 'In the basement. In the office?'

'No.' The engineer shook his head.

'There's one in the gorilla,' shouted Blake. 'We used it for that jungle fever gig. Is it hooked up?'

'I don't know.' The engineer shook his head again.

'Yes you do. That's where they go for a spliff and a shag,' Blake yelled. 'And you film them and sell it to porn sites. Don't lie to me. I've seen them. Now where the fuck is it?' The engineer shrugged. He hit a button on the desk and an image of the Green Room melted into the office, where the two Vans and Charles were viewed through bars, looking across a desk at two figures in black balaclavas. Between them on the desk lay an open file.

'Is there sound?' Blake bellowed.

'Should be,' said the engineer, fiddling with a fader. 'It's not working.'

'Well, fix it,' shouted the impresario. 'And stream it anyway.'

While the engineer messed with cables and connections Blake scanned the screens in front of him. Outside, the doors were shutting as they were now at the fire safety limit and security at the door were holding back a queue. He watched as a Rolls-Royce drew up to the kerb. A man and a woman climbed out and walked to the entrance. They were dressed in white, the man in a suit, both their heads encased in white velcro. When the doormen realised one of them was Hammond Marshall the couple were escorted into the building.

'Reckon I've fixed it,' the engineer shouted. He slid one fader up and another down and Blake heard a woman's voice in his headphones, which he recognised as Dot's. On screen Tall Van was looking anxious and Short Van was beaming.

'Stream it,' shouted Blake.

Inside the basement room the auction was drawing to a close.

'Now do I hear any advance on five hundred and twenty thousand pounds?' Dot asked. 'Come on, gentlemen, this is a very valuable property, including a complete dossier of Mr Chamberlain's 1985 and 1992 smear campaigns, and several documented cases of blackmail and bribery.'

'I can go all night, Ken,' Porter laughed.

'Give in, Ken,' said Charles. 'He has more money than God.' Chamberlain hung his head. Dot looked to George who shook his.

'Sold to Sir Frank Porter for five hundred and twenty thousand pounds,' she said. Porter produced the little black bag from his pocket and poured a stream of diamonds into his palm, which he lifted to the light. Once again they glittered in the gorilla's eyes. For a moment Blake forgot his anger, astounded by what he was witnessing.

'Did that go out on the site?' he asked.

'Yep,' said the engineer. Blake sat back in his chair, triumphant.

'Put it on a loop and play it again,' he said, as the crowd around him erupted. He reached for his iPhone. It was ten-fifteen.

*

Porter and Charles were the first to leave the basement room, the banker clutching the dossier to his chest. They lumbered up the steps and slipped into the venue as the band started its last number. Sensing the finale, the crowd surged forward, pinning the two deserters against the wall and crushing the breath out of them. When they recovered, they had to inch their way towards the exit signs at the back, easing past one person at a time, shoving and apologising. It was going to take hours.

Close by, directly in front of the stage, the man who claimed to have sung with one of the bands danced wildly with his girlfriend, giving Will the finger whenever he could catch his eye. Next to him the three middle-aged women were waving at Johnson. Moments later Melissa and Marshall arrived, dead centre, through a path cleared by the heaviest-set roadies who now formed a protective circle around their charges. Porter knew a VIP enclosure when he saw one, mobile or otherwise, and signalled to Charles to make for it. He had already decided to bribe one of the heavies to escort him out of the building, confident that diamonds would be a roadie's best friend. As they neared the group Charles spotted Melissa and, despite the fact he was supposed to be in Birmingham, waved at her cheerily, his mind searching for an explanation for his presence at a London rock venue with a Secretary of State. Melissa waited patiently for her husband to arrive. One call to his office was all it had taken to establish his whereabouts and while Marshall was keen to see the show, she had come to find her spouse. She smiled as he struggled towards her, and offered an inviting glimpse of her décolletage.

On the other side of the VIP circle Kracholov and his companions had made their way to the front through the discreet use of violence, leaving several members of the audience temporarily disabled, who, when they recovered, would puzzle over what had happened and marvel over the absence of marks on their bodies. Kracholov had snapped out of his reverie. A job was a job. He was what he was, this was what he did, and he always completed what he started. If his destiny was rock Judas, so be it. While he stayed in front of the stage his companions made their way along its edge, their sights set on Laura who was still taking photographs from the side. He was to create a diversion while they snatched her. He looked around for a weapon that would accomplish his task.

What happened next was captured on five cameras in addition to Laura's and would become rock folklore, the defining moment in the histories of Blake's Ride and Don't Know Yet. It began with the man who claimed to have sung with one of the bands. He had taken to conducting, an imaginary baton in one hand while the other was cupped in a circle and offered to Will as a suggestion the guitarist spent much of his time in solo sexual practices. Enough was enough, thought Will. He strode to the edge of the stage, dropped to his knees and slapped the round back of his Stratocaster into the man's face, dislodging a tooth and causing him to collapse on the floor. His girlfriend tried in vain to prevent the audience from trampling him underfoot.

More significantly, the moment acted as a starting pistol for a number of seemingly unconnected events. When Charles and Porter reached the apparent safety of the VIP circle, Melissa leaned out and grabbed her husband by the hair, releasing the scream she had suppressed since catching sight of him. Within seconds she had torn handfuls from his scalp and landed a right to his eye worthy of a champion. Seeing the roadies' attention diverted, Kracholov grabbed a mic stand from the front of the stage, inverted it and made ready to bring its heavy base down on Luka's skull, his aim being to kill the singer with a single blow. Then he would charge on stage and spear the drummer. However, at the moment of attack, he felt a blow to the side of his head which made his strike fall wide by a foot and the base of the stand thud onto the stage floor. He turned to the source of the blow to find Hammond Marshall, who had seen him grab the stand and knew only too well what kind of nutters you found at the front of an audience. Kracholov recognised him and was star-stuck just long enough for Marshall to land a second blow. Two roadies piled in and grappled the Bulgarian to the floor as Marshall dived on top of him.

Kracholov's mistimed blow was the signal for his companions to rush at Laura. However, the altercation with the man who claimed he had sung with one of the bands had put the musicians on alert. As the two Russians grabbed Laura, Norway swung his bass into one and Will hit the other. At this point Little Malcolm waded in, grabbing each dazed Russian around the neck and, with their heads sticking out from his armpits, he ran them straight across the stage into the wall behind the drum kit, after which he turned them to face the audience. Johnson meanwhile had detached his Zildjian crash cymbal and applied it to each of their heads, maintaining the song's pulse while rendering them senseless. The three middle-aged women could contain themselves no longer and helped each other onto the stage.

They ran across to Johnson and smothered him with admiration and the softer parts of their anatomy.

Somehow, the band played through the chaos into an extended ending, the screaming feedback from Will's amplifier only adding to the anarchic crescendo. Security from the back met with the roadies at the front and regained control, relieving Little Malcolm of his twin burden, adding reinforcements to those trying to restrain Kracholov, and rescuing the man, now crushed, who claimed to have sung with one of the bands. Marshall prised Melissa from her husband and Porter and Charles continued their push to the exit, Charles clutching his head, his shrieks of pain going unheard among the ecstatic cries of the crowd.

*

Chamberlain staggered past the doormen and collapsed against the wall in the rain, exhausted and desperate, his chest heaving. He was finished, he realised. He would be humiliated, rejected and ridiculed, his office stripped from him. He would be consigned to exile as a country solicitor and even then he would have to live with the laughter of children outside his office window. He might even be struck off.

Rain dripped from the brim of his hat. He slid down the wall, racking his brains for a strategy. He'd always found one in the past, a way to confound, undermine or obfuscate. He thought of past manipulations, so many deceptions that had ruined others and left him on top, smiling in triumph. But nothing came. There was no bright light. He could see no way out and felt nothing but a throbbing pain in his head and fatigue that engulfed his body.

He must run, he thought. Get away from this place. Perhaps if he could find somewhere quiet, somewhere he could think, just for an hour, a few minutes even, he might find a flash of brilliance that would turn the tables. There had to be a way. He knew he had minutes, hours at most, before Porter destroyed him. Whatever, he had to leave no trace of ever being in this place. He was about to run into the night when a gravelly voice called from the queue.

'Oi, Home Secretary.' Chamberlain looked into a flash of light.

'Hey, Van the Man,' called another. Suddenly there were flashes all around.

'You'll be needing a man with a van,' called the first voice, 'to move your stuff out of the Home Office.'

He was in the middle of a viper's nest. He'd mistaken a bevy of press photographers for a queue of music lovers. Flashes crackled like electricity.

'Tell us about 1992 and all that,' a third photographer called. Suddenly there was a journalist in front of him. Leo. The one who'd found the report in the Meard Street Hotel.

'So, Minister,' said Leo with a huge grin. 'What's worth half a million quid?'

For the first time in his career Chamberlain was speechless. He couldn't understand how they could know about the dossier so soon, or the price paid. Worse, he couldn't conceive how he might pull these diverse strands together and turn them into something that made him look heroic and sabotaged his enemies. He was tongue-tied. It was as if he was slowing, aging, while everything around him grew faster, and others assumed control. Maybe this was the start of dementia, the moment you could no longer match the pace needed to survive the world. For a split second he wondered whether it might be the answer. Hadn't it worked for that corporate fraudster in the eighties? The only known case to recover from Alzheimer's. He looked up at the night sky. There was an answer, he knew it, but it was just out of reach. There were words if only he could find them.

Chamberlain remained slumped as the doors behind him swung open and Porter and Franklin stumbled into the street. They stood dazzled and frozen as they were also bathed in flickering light.

'It's the diamond geezer,' shouted a photographer.

'Did you get them from the bank, Frank?' chuckled another. Porter clutched the file to his chest.

'Does your wife know you're out?' shouted the man with the gravelly voice. 'And how much money *have* you got?' Porter and

Charles turned back to the doors, hoping to regain entry, only to find them barred by a line of security.

Chamberlain mustered the strength to stand and rushed at Porter with a terrifying scream, knocking him off his feet. They rolled on the wet pavement, scrabbling for the dossier, which Porter dropped by the kerb. As they wrestled in the rain Alan Leo picked up the file. He found a streetlamp and flicked through the contents. He couldn't see much but realised he had found the biggest story of the year and the scoop of his lifetime: a dinner-jacket awards story, a permanent job with pay-rises-and-promotion story, maybe even a shift-into-TV story. Leo couldn't believe his luck. All he'd done was follow Hammond Marshall and Melissa Franklin to London to get a few more shots for the double divorce story and then, while he was waiting for the couple to emerge, the place had been surrounded by photographers. He had traded what he had on the lovers for the scoop on Chamberlain and for once he had been in the right place at the right time.

It was payback time for the hours and days spent waiting in the shadows, for the thousand red herrings and blind alleys, and for his rejection by the political establishment. He'd won the lottery, was on the footboard of the gravy train. Who knows, maybe he would finally be taken seriously, become the star that others admired: maybe the doors would open at last. He didn't notice he was soaked to the skin. Coming back to Earth he realised Charles had fled and Porter and Chamberlain were now searching the pavement together, having realised the dossier out of either man's possession was a far worse proposition than in the other's hands.

The entrance opened once more and Hammond Marshall and Melissa stepped into the rain under a Blake's Ride umbrella. The photographers had everything they needed on Chamberlain and Porter and swivelled to catch the rock star and his new girlfriend.

'Hey Marshall,' shouted the gravelly voice. 'We hear you can get it up again!'

Marshall hugged Melissa and paraded in front of the photographers, smiling and waving. He admitted he was in love, and yes he hoped he and Melissa would marry after the tour, but it was all up to the lady. Behind them, during the photo session, the man who claimed he had sung with one of the bands was carried out on a stretcher and two Russians and a Bulgarian were escorted from the building in handcuffs, neither incident diverting the photographers' attention as they weren't famous.

Inside, Don't Know Yet played another set to a now dedicated fan-base and even Blake came round to the idea this band could be seriously big without his interference. He grew philosophical about it; after all, whichever way things went he had a percentage. Later, out of curiosity, when the night was almost over, he slipped down the narrow staircase to the basement, a rum and coke in hand, and made his way to the office. The room looked no different to when he'd shown it to George and Dot at the beginning of the evening, the same shelves and cobwebs, same desk and red phone, same gorilla in a cage. He picked up the telephone and put his ear to the receiver. It was disconnected. He looked around the room for a few moments more. There was no sign they had ever been there. Not a trace. Except, and maybe it was his imagination, didn't he detect a glint in the gorilla's eye?

Westminster Inside Track

https://www.witreport.co.uk

Number 10   Whitehall   Around Westminster   @witreport

TWEETS:

WIT@witreport Live from
@TheRialtoKX.
@KenChamberlain_MP is
going down. Twenty years of
bribery and corruption. Read
all about it in #WIT tomorrow.

> ### Westminster Inside Track
>
> *What's going down in
> Westminster and Whitehall;
> the rumours, conspiracies and
> whitewash at the heart of
> government.*

WIT@witreport Sod #WIT. This is going to the highest bidder.

WIT@witreport I'm going to be rich. The name is Leo. Alan
Leo. Remember it. #fameandfortune #Iminthemoney

WIT@witreport Arrested by Special Branch. Sitting in the
back of an unmarked car between two dudes in plain
clothes. Fuck.

WIT@witreport They say if I don't stop tweeting they'll <@ *&
f%v(

36

By morning the rain had stopped, the outlook for the weekend was sunny and for once an English weather forecast was not blown off course by changes in pressure. Across the country the sky stayed a cloudless blue for two whole days and millions migrated to lakes, lidos or the seaside in case these were the last days of summer.

Luka spent the weekend alone, wandering the city and digesting the gig. Strange things began to happen to him almost immediately, tiny signs at odds with the way an individual should be absorbed and ignored at London's core. In a café he felt he was being watched. On the street someone across the road pointed at him. When he came across a busker on the underground and joined him for a few minutes, he tripled the take in the old man's hat. On Sunday he went to a municipal festival in Camden to watch his African friends play. After the third girl approached him for an autograph he realised something material had changed in his life. This was confirmed when he was invited to perform with the band and introduced as the lead singer of Don't Know Yet and a mighty cheer rang from the crowd.

Johnson, blissfully unaware of his spreading fame, spent the weekend in the Holiday Inn King's Cross, around the corner from The Rialto, with the three middle-aged ladies, slipping out occasionally for supplies of Doritos, cream cakes and bottles of Absolut. Norway dragged Little Malcolm up to North Wales to find rugged land and dense forest where they could camp and hunt; land as close as he could find to home, where he would be free to roam naked with a spear if he chose. Little Malcolm was not entirely at ease with the proceedings.

In Northamptonshire, Marshall and Melissa spent the weekend quietly, driving across her estate in an ageing Land Rover and making plans for their new life together. Marshall finally met the gardener, who turned up his hearing aid as the two men stood by a stile discussing the finer points of breeding sheep, Northamptonshire sandstone and Saxon churches. Melissa watched them talk; two aging rustics, one by birth the other by dissolution. She looked at her new beau affectionately. Charles wouldn't have given the gardener the time of day. She thought about time and destiny. Twenty-five years ago she and Marshall had coupled momentarily, albeit repeatedly, and she imagined a deposit had been made on a future relationship and now they were of an age, and Marshall mellowed enough, 'burned out' his friends would say, when they were matched. She was still in a daze from Charles' betrayal and had no idea where things would lead, but the craggy-faced rock star seemed to love her, and he was kind, funny and periodically attentive. And let's face it, he *was* a rock star. Was this, she wondered, some kind of twisted modern fairy tale?

On the Isle of Wight another twisted modern fairy tale played out. Released from custody and back in the POW camp, Robert White and Ruby engineered opportunities to meet as often and in as many parts of the camp as they could, inside and out of the buildings. Each rendezvous turned into a frenzied union until they had made love in every imaginable location and position and in front of every camera in the compound. By ten-thirty on Sunday evening it was as hot in the nation's living rooms as it had been in the parks and streets outside.

Those who were kept indoors for one reason or another had to make the best of it. The man who claimed to have sung with one of the bands spent his weekend in the University College Hospital in Euston Road, traumatised by his trampling. His girlfriend sat beside him reading aloud or watching television. She changed the channel anytime there was a mention of anything that might upset him, which was a frequent occurrence given the variety of storylines emerging from the Friday night gig at The Rialto.

Kracholov and his companions spent Friday night and most of Saturday in police cells, initially on charges of causing an affray then on suspicion of illegal entry and racketeering, and were eventually released on bail after the intervention of lawyers hired by the Best Bulgarian Cleaning Company and an anonymous oligarch.

While his wife and Marshall played house, Charles went to ground in their London flat with the curtains drawn. He surfed, watched TV and read the newspapers in a deepening gloom. By Sunday afternoon he was so low he called the red-headed graduate trainee and invited her out for supper. He knew he was ruined, his reputation razed. Not only was he labelled the 'Dung-Meister' and demonised for defining a new low in spin-doctoring, he was universally condemned as an unprincipled fixer bent on corrupting government. Moreover, he was outed as a cuckold, rendered such by a wizened old freak fifteen years his senior and supposedly impotent. The very least he could do was be seen on the town with a woman half his age. This last hurrah might have transpired had he made a reservation. Unfortunately, when he and the graduate trainee arrived at the restaurant, the most pretentious of his haunts, he had no booking and his privileges to turn up unannounced had been revoked. They dined a street away at Pizza Hut, unnoticed.

Chamberlain had also gone to ground in Gloucester, but he still had a wife and children in tow and chose to throw himself on their mercy, by turns confessing and justifying his many sins, to tearful recriminations and catharsis if not forgiveness. On Sunday, at his wife's suggestion and to the shock of regular parishioners, the family went to church for the first time in years. They walked through the village on foot, dressed in black, running the gauntlet of a dozen photographers, before surrendering themselves to the tender mercies of a genial parson, his less forgiving congregation and the Almighty.

Eleanor Porter returned from Birmingham on Saturday morning and knew long before she reached their Mayfair house that her husband was involved in something known as The Rialto Incident. She pushed past the photographers camped outside. Inside, she found a note from Sir Frank saying he had flown to Brazil on urgent business and from there would tour some of the world's developing economies before returning. He promised he would call soon and pledged his undying affection. Eleanor tried to call Charles but couldn't track him down. Later she switched her mobile off, its voicemail overloaded.

Throughout the weekend she played with the children while answering calls on the house line from friends, her constituency team, and the government press office. All the time she kept a weather eye on the news and the growing posse of press and paparazzi outside her door.

Alan Leo was busiest of all. Almost all his weekend was spent in airless rooms helping either the police or the media with their enquiries. The initial discussions with the police were tricky. They questioned him closely about his involvement with Chamberlain. Hadn't he been tracking the man for some time? Why? And wasn't it he who had revealed the story about the illegal alien, Edith? Then there was his suspicious appearance at the Meard Street Hotel, just in time to find the stolen report. How did he explain that? And how did he come to be at The Rialto? Did he know the two auctioneers in balaclavas? Who was he really working for? Leo held firm under pressure, knowing his brilliant future was on the line. George would be proud of him. He simply repeated his name, rank and social security number: Alan Leo, freelance journalist and blogger, acting on a tip-off from a confidential source. No, he would not reveal his or her identity nor could they compel him to do so.

As the officers grew frustrated, he suggested they might like to concentrate on the file in his possession, a file that revealed the habitual corruption of one of the most senior figures in the government and a lifelong disruption of the democratic process. Wasn't this the big issue, he asked, innocently. And wasn't Chamberlain the fish they should fry? The detectives, sweating in shirtsleeves, gradually came round to his point of view, a view encouraged by their superiors who were receiving pressure from editors anxious to talk with the young man they'd previously considered a nonentity, and senior figures in government who believed the best course was to keep things simple and let Chamberlain receive his just deserts. By the end of the weekend Leo had never been in such demand, treated so reverently, nor offered so much money.

*

Will and Laura spent most of the weekend in bed, her bed at number 54 Mersley Road.

Jack Blake had taken them all to a club after the show, their dispute apparently forgotten, and while Johnson danced with his girlfriends, the impresario had slurred over a martini about the wonderful future they would share. Will and Laura left around three and took the night bus, staring out at London's inebriated streets and realising things would never be the same. It was Laura's idea to go home rather than to Johnson's place, partly through tipsy bravado, partly because she'd seen the police take Kracholov away, and partly in case George and Dot were there, though she knew deep down they would be gone. Sure enough the house was empty and they stumbled up the stairs to her room, fell on her bed and went to sleep in each other's arms.

They slept until midday despite the almost constant vibration of Laura's iPhone on the windowsill and urgent voicemails from Blake coming from the phone in her workroom. Laura was the first to wake to a room flooded with light. She lay still for a long time, looking at the man sleeping next to her and listening to his steady breathing. His skin was soft and clear, still boyish, the lines that would age him only beginning to emerge. He was wrapped in her white duvet, a great cowl around his head. She fancied he was an Arctic explorer or astronaut and almost gave in to the urge to fetch her camera. But she didn't disturb him. When he woke they would have to talk, sober and in the sunlight. Until then her mind was free to roam. She wondered why she felt so relaxed. He had slept the night in her bed, invaded her realm. Last time had been daytime and they hadn't slept. This was different. She thought back over the past few weeks to his pathetic pass on the stairs, the visit to One Tree Hill, and the long, languid afternoon in this room. She smiled at the thought of him on the window ledge, his passion for music and their argument over the boy. He had been right about the boy and the music. She watched him, still sleeping, and thought how quiet he was compared to his band-mates and yet so determined, and now he was going to be famous. Despite her best efforts she had let him in.

She looked around the room, her attention caught by the jumble of cosmetics on the mantelpiece. Blake hadn't made it here to see her things and guess her secrets. She noticed the places where her favourite things had been, the ones she'd taken to Johnson's, and made a note to take a few more: an extra lens, her sketchpad and the picture of George, Dot and her at London Zoo when she was four, the one with the heart-shaped sunglasses which she had loved so. Her thoughts drifted back to Will and to Birmingham, where she had missed him and Eleanor had seen it, then the crazy kidnap, the rescue and the gig. She didn't know why but she wanted to laugh.

The doorbell rang and she slipped from the bed, into a dressing gown and downstairs, fetching a heavy saucepan from Dot's kitchen before unbolting the front door. She found two men on the doorstep dressed in overalls and noticed a van parked beyond the gate. The elder of the two was about to try a key in the lock. His mate leered at her.

'Morning luv,' said the older man. 'George gave us the key. But I thought we'd try the bell, just in case.' Laura kept a firm hold of the saucepan. Just in case. The man held up an order form. 'We've come to collect everything from the ground floor and cellar for storage.'

She let them in and sat on the stairs, watching as they carried Dot and George's belongings out. She was hardly aware she was crying until she felt a hand on her shoulder. Will sat next to her and handed her a cup of coffee. He was dressed.

'Are you all right?' he asked.

'It's happened before,' she said, holding the mug with both hands. 'We had the bailiffs round once and another time they had to do a runner when I was at school.'

'Where have they gone?' he asked.

'Underground. They'll be in touch. It's not that. I was remembering. I came home for a weekend and somebody else was living in our house. I waited outside for six minutes, looking through the windows. I didn't know what to do. And then I saw Mum and Dad behind a van, waving. I remember every one of those minutes.' Will placed his arm around her.

'Come on,' he said. 'Let's go to the pub and then we'll go to the supermarket.' She managed a smile. 'It's a plan,' he said. 'Look.' He opened his fist in front of her, almost a magic trick, to reveal a crumpled banknote. 'I went upstairs for a T-shirt and found a twenty behind the radiator. Don't know how I missed it.'

They walked across Peckham Rye, through the ornamental gardens and across its sun-baked plain to the Clock House, where they sat outside. Will fetched two pints. They sat either side of a table watching the customers, traffic and life spread across the Rye. As the terrace filled no one made an attempt to join them; it was as if their table was reserved. They carried an aura as did the world to them. Every character and situation was comical or profound: the men with dogs excusing their pints; the bus stopped in traffic filled with hot and irritable passengers; the ragged football match on the Rye with jackets as goal-posts. They were characters and settings in their movie, and today their movie was a rom-com. Things that would normally irritate were funny: the queue at the bar, the wasp crawling into Will's beer, the wailing child throwing chips to the ground.

Then, from looking outside as one, they would become intensely aware of each other: the shape of her face, the colour of his eyes, the slope of her neck, the movement of his throat as he spoke. Time slowed, the sun burning images into their memories like old-fashioned photographic plates. Then anxiety as each pulled back in turn, a momentary retreat before diving deeper into a narcotic-free ecstasy.

'You OK?' he asked.

'Yes. Why?'

'It doesn't come often.'

'What?'

'This.'

'What's that?' she asked, cornering him to commit first.

'You know what I mean.'

'It was an amazing night,' she said, avoiding it again.

'It was, but I don't mean that. You know what I mean,' he said. They looked into each other's eyes, each seeing blue.

'It doesn't last,' she warned.

'It lasts as long as we want it to.'

'And how long is that?' She swore silently. She'd given herself away. 'Longer than today,' he said.

The feeling was too intense so they looked outside again, beyond the traffic at dog-walkers, children on bicycles and the football match, where jubilation had followed a goal. Neither would admit what was happening between them but they knew it was the one thing everyone around them had lost, never had or was yet to find.

'Let's go back,' she said.

'Shopping first,' he said. 'And that's the first and only time you'll hear me say that.' They stopped at a grocer's along the Forest Hill Road and bought pasta and pesto, and then returned to her rooms, made love, laughed and listened to music.

It was only after the sun went down that they started to reconnect with the world. Laura wandered naked into her workroom to debrief the voicemail. When he heard laughter Will joined her. They listened as Jack Blake's voice leapt into the room, urgent and enthusiastic.

'Laura, are you with Will? They're the most downloaded videos on YouTube – the band and the auction. We need to record the songs and get them out quick. Call me.' The next message was panicky. 'Hey, Laura, where are these guys? Hammond Marshall's agent called. He wants them to support on his tour. This is big. Call me.' The last was terse. 'I know what you are doing. It'll be there tomorrow. This is your moment, Will. Put her down and call me.'

Still naked they logged onto YouTube. Everything was there, the band, number by number, the auction, footage of the scuffles inside and out, everything branded Blake's Ride. They scanned a few sites to catch up on the news and at ten o'clock watched TV.

Chamberlain was the top story. The BBC's political correspondent was camped outside the Home Secretary's Gloucestershire house, in front of a scrum of photographers, while a handful of African protesters chanted 'Asylum, asylum, Edith needs asylum.'

'There is no sign of the Home Secretary this evening,' said the reporter, his eyes bulging. 'However, he is thought to have talked with the Prime Minister and insiders say he will resign tomorrow. Many are asking what role was played by top banker Sir Frank Porter in all this, and what it means for his wife, Birmingham heroine and Cities Minister, Eleanor Porter. Meanwhile, the police would like to hear from anyone who can identify the two mysterious auctioneers.'

Back in the studio a younger reporter explained how the story had unfolded on social media. She interviewed Blake and showed a montage of Blake's Ride, the band and the scuffles outside, all to the soundtrack of 'Time To Fly'.

Will cooked and they drank white wine, ate and went back to bed, by which time Luka had also left a message. On Sunday morning Will rose early and logged on. Laura made breakfast, coming in to look over his shoulder. They chewed bacon and toast spread thick with marmalade and drank coffee as they browsed the news.

Chamberlain was still the top story, his history of smearing opponents laid out in full, highlighting his use of health scares. One article reported on the sad decline and death of the journalist Tom Howard, another speculated on what Porter and Charles Franklin had been up to, suggesting Porter was hell-bent on protecting the Prime Minister from his enemies and implying there was connivance from Number 10. Yet another recorded the banker's meteoric rise to power by lending to countries with questionable records on human rights.

Cooler sites focused on Jack Blake and suggested Blake's Ride could make him the first mucanet (music and internet) billionaire. They turned to the tabloids, which fought their readership battles with Hammond Marshall and Robert White. The *Sunday Sport* went with the rock star. 'Marshall! Back On Top! And From Behind!' bawled a banner headline. The site boasted exclusive pictures of his new love taken outside The Rialto and intimate scenes in the library of the Franklin residence. Under a close-up of a buttock stamped 'Made in Lewisham' ran the caption, 'Star's new mate gets seal of approval'. The *Sunday Mirror* went with 'Ruby and White Go All Night at Camp Wight'. Will turned to the blogosphere. On the one hand bloggers lauded The Rialto Incident as the latest example of social media as a check on corrupt government, while others bemoaned a Britain under surveillance. They also counted four mentions of Don't Know Yet as a band to watch and two rumours they would be joining the Hammond Marshall tour.

The lovers repeated their routine of the previous day, with a walk through the Rye, a drink at the Clock House and the afternoon spent in bed, but this time they were more engaged with the world. They played a game that lasted through lunch, where they tried to predict what would happen to each of the characters involved in The Rialto Incident. Will started on the way to the pub by forecasting that ticket sales for the Hammond Marshall tour would rocket on news he was still a hell-raising womaniser and therefore a continuing inspiration to balding men and teenage boys. Laura decided his witch wife would get the marital home in the divorce, which she would fill with young warlocks, but Marshall would think it a small price to pay for Melissa and a reputation for potency. Will predicted Don't Know Yet would be hired as support for the tour and become a spectacular success, their Rialto EP gaining a Brit Award. Furthermore Laura would become official photographer for the tour, which would lead to an exhibition the following year. She would also be the photographer at Marshall and Melissa's wedding, which would take place on the Northamptonshire estate, with the Reverend Al Green officiating and four Elvises as ushers. Thereafter Marshall would retire and he and Melissa would open the estate to the public, start an organic farm and build a recording studio, conference centre and luxury accommodation.

At the pub, over a glass of wine, Laura fancied Don't Know Yet would become the biggest band in the land, acquiring its own clothing label and entourage, complete with wellbeing and singing coaches. They toasted a future of mind-boggling multi-platinum sales, sell-out tours and breaking China. They decided not to dwell on Blake because his future was already foretold. He became the mucanet billionaire everyone assumed he would be and collected houses, cars and expensive divorces on five continents.

On the way home they stopped in the park and sat under a tree. Laura mimed her hands running over a crystal ball and turned to Ruby and White. In the absence of a successful breakout they would be declared joint winners of *Escape from Wight*, then hire a publicist and announce their engagement. Anton Zakharovich Ledakov, always a pragmatist, would be White's best man, having forgiven the couple, reasoning a comeback politician and a reality star were useful items to have in his pocket. The couple would be in demand for public appearances and host an afternoon chat show until White re-entered Parliament. As he rebuilt his political career Ruby would stay in television, finding work in soaps where she would feature as the hooker with a heart of gold. She would star in pantomime at the Orchard Theatre Dartford, and gradually become Britain's best-loved Eastern European and a national institution.

In a rare act of magnanimity Ledakov would also forgive Kracholov. Laura promised she would personally broker a deal with Ledakov who would cease hostilities against the Valentine family and agree to Kracholov becoming her and Will's personal bodyguard. In return he would receive the supermarket bag of ransom money and Marshall would add a private concert in the Kremlin to their tour. There the oligarch would entertain a gathering of the Russian ruling elite and the President would play air guitar alongside his favourite rock hero in a pre-election publicity stunt. Kracholov would be happier than he ever thought possible. He would wear his tour T-shirt with pride and play 'Laura and Will say' at every opportunity with venue managers, media and concessionaires, his Franchi exchanged for a nail gun.

On the gentle slope beyond the ornamental garden they grew serious and considered how the political story would unfold. In it Chamberlain resigned as Home Secretary and was suspended as an MP pending a full investigation of the 1992 election. It required all his political skill to secure an ambiguous result. After this he was subject to criminal proceedings as well as prosecution for contravening a number of regulations relating to England's waterways. Following conviction, appeal and exoneration on legal grounds, he retired to the country to eke out a living as a country solicitor and devote his life to charitable endeavours. Long after the dust had settled, following years of penance spent protecting endangered species in Gloucestershire, and conspicuous success in improving the life and habitat of the water vole, he was promoted, broke, to the House of Lords. His wife Mary, who left him after his conviction, returned on his elevation to the peerage. Their son went quietly to art school, while an anonymous graffiti artist known as Rustle emerged as a popular satirist.

In Sir Frank Porter's scenario, the errant banker failed to return from South America and, despite regular sightings on all continents, never resurfaced. Aside from an elderly lady who became convinced he was living a Spartan existence in a crofter's cottage on the Isle of Skye, most reports suggested he was living a life of extreme luxury, moving around the world with relative ease and coinciding with the most important dates in the sailing calendar. This tallied with the investigation into his past, which revealed his bank was riddled with fraudulent investment schemes, each of which siphoned vast sums into offshore accounts around the world. These were accorded to various named individuals all of whom bore a striking resemblance to the London banker.

Eleanor Porter offered to resign as Cities Minister, and the Prime Minister vacillated, but after a campaign by supporters, many from the Sparkwood area of Birmingham, she was persuaded to stay. She commenced divorce proceedings, making no claim on her husband, but as his affairs unravelled she did her best to ensure his diverse pots of gold were discovered and the money returned to those he had cheated. As Minister for Cities she became a pivotal figure during the unrest and demonstrations that followed government cuts, mediating between every combination of interest group. She was responsible for introducing many improvements to urban Britain, including energy-saving transportation, better financial support for small businesses, and education and employment schemes for deprived areas. Sultana Choudhury became her advisor on the concerns of minority communities.

Eleanor would hold the post of Cities Minister for another eighteen months, developing a reputation as a no-nonsense politician, adept at knocking heads together and intolerant of departmental bureaucracy. She was romantically linked with film stars, writers and industrialists but remained unmarried, preferring to focus on her children and career. Following two standing ovations at successive party conferences she was promoted to Home Secretary and in some corners it was whispered she would one day make a fine Prime Minister.

As for the Prime Minister, he faced a spirited challenge from the Opposition who tried to implicate him in a conspiracy to bring down his own Home Secretary. There was even a suggestion he was behind Robert White's disgrace. But in the absence of Porter or other credible witnesses, and in the face of the opprobrium heaped upon Ken Chamberlain, they switched to an attack on his judgement in appointing such sleaze-balls in the first place. The Prime Minister's role in the affair remained an enigma. Later, following a bold swim across the Channel, which put an end to rumours about his health and raised a huge sum for charity, and a perfectly timed upturn in the economy, he was returned to power at the next general election.

In most good stories the villain ends unhappily. With Porter absent and Chamberlain free, Laura and Will decided Charles Franklin would be brought to book. An initial idea to try him for treason was dropped and he was charged, tried and found guilty of conspiracy to steal the Downing Street report as well as several dustbins of rubbish and sentenced to eighteen months in an open prison. His fellow conspirators were never found. While he was on trial Melissa divorced him and, as the sole owner, sold The Reputation Works to a large communications group. 'Doing a Franklin' became a popular idiom synonymous with an ambitious plan bungled and leading to criminal consequences. While in prison he mixed with captains of industry and aristocrats and made useful contacts among the numerate but misdirected and wealthy but addicted. He studied theology, was born again, and achieved a double page spread in *The Sunday Times* on his conversion and rehabilitation. When he left prison he would help his local community, he said, though as he was ostracised from his home of twenty years, he would have to find a local community to help. He assumed this would be in Fulham where his red-headed girlfriend lived.

As they reached the house, they raced to finish the game. Laura imagined Alan Leo, crusading journalist, would be given a permanent job with a national tabloid, a first step in a newspaper career which would lead him to become editor of the *Daily Express* and a judge on a television talent show. Later he would have his own TV chat show in America and go down in history as the first such host to be shot dead by a guest. Billy Sinclair became a jockey of sorts, parking cars at an elite hotel in Dubai. Edith and her son were given asylum and ultimately British citizenship and Edith became an agony aunt with her own highly rated blog. In Birmingham Sultana Choudhury one day became Lady Mayor. Will and Laura reached the gate, gasping.

The only prediction they wouldn't make was about them. They had now and they had tomorrow; that would do for the moment. At the end of the day, as the sun was setting, they took a bottle of chilled white wine, a Clos d'Amonceler, and walked to the top of One Tree Hill. They sat on the bench near the gun emplacement that some mistook for a bandstand, in front of the torch erected for a King's Jubilee and looked north, beyond the trees to a pink sky above London's horizon, and watched the long white trails of planes coming home.

Westminster Inside Track

https://www.witreport.co.uk

Westminster Inside Track is now closed.

The proprietor is on holiday. When he returns he will have moved on to bigger things. Instead of grubbing around for titbits of gossip in draughty rooms around Westminster he'll be rubbing shoulders with the glitterati and mega-rich, wolfing down canapés and drinking champagne. He'll be making loads of money and have no need to take pot shots at the great and good as he will be one of them.

Applicants are sought to take over this blog. If you are disenchanted, distrusting and disenfranchised, barely making a living and would like to disgrace the disreputable or just crap on them weekly send a mail to **witreport@outlook.com**

Westminster Inside Track

Your eyes and ears on Westminster and Whitehall; exposing the rumours, conspiracies and whitewash at the heart of government; a virtual voice in a new age of accountability.

37

Charles Franklin gathered his few things together. He had to admit it hadn't been so bad. There had been moments. He'd met a famous footballer and a wild young musician, and his sons had been impressed when he produced their autographs during a visit. He imagined it was cool to have your dad in jail if you were a Northamptonshire baronet at a top public school.

In fact it had been a lot like his own schooldays. There was ritual, regulation and hierarchy, but once you figured out who the prefects were and knew who to avoid in the washrooms you were fine. One or two warders were odd but no worse than his old English master, the one with the collection of carriage whips who used the boys for target practice. The food was not exactly Michelin, but it beat school rissoles and tapioca pudding. And there were no cold showers, cross-country runs or midnight beatings of whole dormitories for talking after lights out. All in all it was probably no worse than one of those budget hotels that seemed to be springing up everywhere.

There had been some memorable parties too. Booze had been easy to come by and Viagra, though he didn't quite see the point of that until he managed to get away to a hotel on the pretext of meeting lawyers and found the red-headed graduate waiting. No, on balance open prison was not such a big deal. He might even say it was a positive experience. He felt broadened, fitter and relaxed.

There had been a fair amount of slopping in and out, of course, but that was only to be expected. Much of his time had been spent working in horticulture, enjoying time in the gardens and library. He'd become something of an expert on biodiversity and the effects of climate change. Aside from the incident in the hotel he had been a model prisoner, and his eighteen-month sentence had meant he was eligible for a conditional release after serving only half that time. And he wrote. There had been plenty of time for writing. Initially he wrote to his lawyers to find out what he had to do to get his sentence reduced. It was shortly after their reply that he started to look for God, found Him remarkably quickly and expressed his remorse. Then, again on the advice of his lawyers, he had written to all he had wronged seeking forgiveness. It was an embarrassing and tedious exercise and had taken some considerable time, due in part to the numbers involved and the resistance of some to his pleas. But his lawyers said the more letters of support he received the greater it showed his commitment. In the end he wrote the last few dozen himself. Then he turned to the book. This had come quickly and easily and, who knows, he might have found a profitable calling.

He picked up the large manuscript and flicked through its four hundred and forty pages of double spaced script before stuffing it in his bag. His signature smile spread across his face. It would set the record straight. The book, written as a novel, was the unexpurgated and true account of Porter's plot to bring down Ken Chamberlain and all the characters involved. He had taken pleasure in writing it. The great thing about being a penitent was he could reveal, and revel in, his lust, greed and vanity in all its gory detail, and the more he did the more he guaranteed a mass readership. He hoped it would make a great deal of money, but more importantly it would exact revenge on George Valentine and his wife by revealing their central role in the whole affair. It would also be his way back. He had an agent, a publisher and plans for its promotion. He would present himself as a convert and model of contrition, a serious writer and commentator on climate issues, a campaigner for a better world as well as a novelist, and re-launch himself in society. He would become a pundit and a regular on afternoon TV, and who knows it might even open the door to politics.

Charles walked through the cell door and on to the end of the corridor where an elderly warder was waiting.

'Ready, Mr Franklin?' said the old man, taking his bag and escorting the prisoner all the way to the front gate. 'We've got a new boss,' he said. 'Old friend of yours, I believe; Eleanor Barry, or Porter as she used to be. She's the new Home Secretary.' Charles had heard. 'Shame she wasn't appointed earlier. She might've done you a bit of good.' The warder had a twinkle in his eye.

Not much chance of that, thought Charles. Eleanor had dropped him like a hot brick when the pendulum swung. He could understand it; he would have advised her to do the same. Porter was the one who could have helped, but he had disappeared with a pile of cash and without a trace.

As they neared the gate his thoughts turned to Melissa. He'd read she had opened the estate to the public, with tours of the house, conference facilities and accommodation, a working farm and a recording studio; a rural retreat with the occasional superstar flitting across the landscape like some rare bird. What a waste. It could have hosted the finest parties and political discussions that might have shaped the world. But what could you expect of a musician. No class, no respect for the proper order. Still, no point dwelling on what might have been. There was no room in his new life for bitterness.

'So, what happens next for you, Mr Franklin?' asked the warder. 'I expect it's back to the finer things in life? Will you be keeping up with the religion?'

'I've got a book coming out,' Charles said, as the gate swung open and he saw freedom in the shape of the pretty red-headed graduate and a convertible BMW.

'Good luck with that, sir. What's it about?'

'*George Valentine's Retirement Plan.*'

'We all need one of those, sir. Very smart, I'm sure.'

'That's the title,' said Charles. The pretty graduate ran towards him. He flashed his signature smile and opened his arms, confident this moment marked a beginning.

END…

38

A WEEK LATER

The pool lay still and glittering in the midday sun, waiting for someone to leap in and create drama in the silent landscape. The concrete edge was hot but not scalding as a month ago, as was the sun-drenched patio that ran to the villa's whitewashed walls. Behind the building lay a garden of olive trees and beyond them a hill. In front the beach stretched along the coast to the nearest town three miles away.

There was a flash of colour behind the French windows, bright red and gold, and Hannah Ward padded out to the pool, her curves straining a glamorous one-piece bathing suit. She wore sunglasses and a wide-brimmed hat, held a drink in one hand and a phone to her ear with the other. She settled herself on a wooden lounger under a giant version of the umbrella in her strawberry daiquiri and sighed as she relaxed on the blue cushions.

'No, darling,' she said. 'I'm fine, just fine. It's beautiful.' She curled her legs out of the sun. 'Laura, darling, don't worry, it's a present. It's what we wanted to do.' She tweaked her sunglasses and sipped the cool drink as she listened. 'Now you'll need to get the boiler serviced,' she said. 'And the council tax comes up soon. Have you told them it's changed hands?'

As the conversation continued, roaming over the domestic details involved in running a house, Hannah cast her eye across the beach to the town. It was change-over day. Each week was growing quieter as the English school term approached. One more and they would celebrate the end of their second year in Spain.

'And you'll come and visit sometime?' Hannah asked. She bristled slightly at the reply. 'Of course you can bring him,' she said and then, with mild indignation, 'I'm always nice to him.' They talked a while longer and when they were done Hannah put the phone down, lay back and closed her eyes.

A few minutes later her husband plodded out to the pool. He was wearing vast swimming shorts and a Hawaiian shirt, John Lennon sunglasses and Crocs. He took the lounger next to his wife and stretched out.

'Was that Laura?' he asked.

'Yes. She's so pleased about the house.'

'Good. Best thing to do, all ways round.'

Number 54 Mersey Road was now legally the property of Laura Valentine. John Ward had reprised his former role of George Valentine twice in the last two years to make visits to England: once to deliver half the proceeds of the auction to Mrs Tom Howard, the second to arrange the transfer of the house.

'The exhibition went well,' Hannah said. 'She's been hired to photograph the fifty most influential people in the world for an American magazine. Our girl's doing well.'

'Sensational. And how's that boyfriend of hers?'

'He's fine.' Hannah sniffed.

'We'll have to get that plaque,' chuckled her husband. 'He's turned out to be a star.'

'Stars explode,' said Hannah.

'Any news?' he asked.

'Charles was released,' she said. 'Frank Porter was sighted on a yacht in the Cayman Islands. And Ruby's wedding is in *OK* magazine.'

'All quiet at home, though?'

For a time 54 Mersey Road had been of interest to the police. Based on Charles Franklin's statements they had spent time trying to locate a George and Dorothy Valentine in connection with The Rialto Incident. They interviewed Laura and searched the house but found no clue as to her parents' whereabouts aside from a travel brochure highlighting a number of Middle Eastern destinations. The only trace of the couple was a single photograph of George on his police file taken when he had a full head of hair and a moustache. The police concluded the Valentines may or may not have been involved in The Rialto Incident, or events leading up to it, but if they were they'd made good their escape. If they turned up again the police might take an interest, otherwise they had their man – Charles Franklin – who would be convicted and sent down. Porter was the one they were still looking for and several officers were presently scouring the Caribbean on expenses as the result of recent leads. Hannah looked at her husband.

'You'll never guess what's happened to Alan Leo?' she said. There was an incredulous tone in her voice. 'They've only given him a chat show. In America.'

John Ward climbed from the lounger, took off his shirt and stretched in the sun. He walked to the edge of the pool where he kicked off his footwear. He grimaced as his feet touched the hot concrete and stepped smartly onto the diving board, which was cooler. He walked to the end and curled his toes over the edge.

'Who'd have thought it?' he said, as he considered the water beneath. He'd been proved right on that one. Leo had not disclosed his sources.

'I told Laura to come and visit,' said Hannah.

'That should be fine, provided we're careful.'

'She'll probably bring that scruffy beatnik.' Hannah took a sip of her drink to banish the thought of the irksome musician. 'Anyway, what have you been up to?'

John Ward shook his arms, making ready to break the calm of the water and feel its cold rush.

'I've finished it,' he said. 'Thirty-seven chapters, three hundred and something pages, a hundred and nineteen thousand words. The unvarnished truth: *George Valentine's Retirement Plan.*' He savoured the title.

'What are you going to do with it?' Hannah asked.

'Publish it.'

'Is that a good idea?'

'A man's got to have an occupation,' he said, raising himself onto the balls of his feet. 'Anyway, I've thought of that. I'll publish it under a pseudonym with an address and bank account in Zurich. It should be pretty easy to set up.'

'You are dreadful, George,' said his wife. 'Why do you take such risks?'

'I can't just sit here, doing nothing. It'll be fine. And it's John.'

'John?'

'John Ward. You called me George.'

'Did I?' said Hannah. 'I'm just too relaxed.' She looked out to sea. 'Isn't it beautiful?'

John Ward looked from the shimmering pool, down to the beach and along the coast.

'Sensational,' he said. He looked round at his wife, who had turned on the lounger and stretched languidly, presenting her back to him.

'I think you should change the ending,' she said over her shoulder.

'Oh, yes?' He sank back onto flat feet.

'I don't like it ending with Charles. It should end with us.'

Her husband bounced lightly on the board as he considered the point. 'You may be right,' he said. 'Fancy another drink?'

'That would be nice,' said Hannah, her eyes closed. John Ward retraced his steps along the board and slipped on his Crocs. He picked up his wife's glass and headed for the villa. The pool could wait, he decided. He'd fetch her drink then sit down with his laptop. It shouldn't take long. One last twist. Then he'd prepare a few snacks, make Hannah another drink, maybe put some music on the outside speakers and take it from there. After all, they had all the time in the world.

THE END

ABOUT THE AUTHOR

Laurence Cooper has been a lawyer, an actor, a puppeteer and a PR man. An expert in reputation management, he is fascinated by tales of hubris, corruption and skulduggery. *George Valentine's Retirement Plan* is his first novel.

ACKNOWLEDGEMENTS

I am indebted to many who have helped me on this journey. Sincere thanks to Alison Radevski for reading each chapter as it was produced and offering encouragement through the early days; to Vivien Ravdin for applying her prodigious editing skills, love of language and fine judgement which has greatly enhanced the book. Thanks also to Jean-Baptiste Bacquart for insight that set me straight. And to the following for reading drafts, offering advice and criticism but above all encouragement: Linda Bateman, Lizu Bergus, Richard and Max Templar, Giles Fraser and Silas Woolley; to Liz Templar for seeming to know what I need before I do, and to all at ARVON for a unique creative space; to Marion Gilbert for applying her eagle eyes to the text. Thanks to Zoe Shtorm for cover design, Dea Parkin and Fiction Feedback for copyediting and all at Matador. Thanks to Kevin Walsh, Mark Higgins, Mark Thorburn and Dave Robinson for creative and musical inspiration, and to James Hasler and Ian Ferguson for lessons that apparently stuck. Above all, my love and thanks to Priscilla, Elizabeth and Katie Laurence for their patience and support.